THE GIRLS IN PLEATED SKIRTS

THE GIRLS IN PLEATED SKIRTS

Stephen F Medici

Thea & Golf Publishing

For more information contact:
Stephen F. Medici at sfmedici@hotmil.com

Printed in the United States

The Girls in Pleated Skirts
Stephen F Medici
1. Title 2. Author 3. Fiction

ISBN 10: 057814980X
ISBN 13: 978-0-578-14980-6

DEDICATED TO:

The men and women who have served in the

United States Armed Forces since September 11, 2001.

ACKNOWLEDGEMENTS

I am once again privileged to acknowledge the contributions others have made to my work. First, a sincere thank-you to my wife, Colleen who is usually the first one to hear my stories. Her constructive critique of my original draft caused me to rethink some of the story-line and rearrange some of the events. I am confident her thoughtful suggestions improved the final product.

Special thanks to FDNY Captain Paul T. Holly, for his guidance on the protocols surrounding mass casualty incidents in New York City and terminology used by the FDNY. Also, many thanks to FDNY Lieutenant Michael Magerle for his insights about emergency response terminology and the explosive capabilities of various fuels.

Thanks also to Dino Werbeck for his guidance and to Bryan Amsterdam and Carissa Voegele for helping me edit the final proof.

And thank you again to my good friend, Jerry DiCola who waited patiently for me to complete the first draft so that he could offer his valuable feedback on character development. In this work, his input was invaluable.

JULY 1991

BROOKLYN, NEW YORK

CHAPTER 1

Freddie and Jorge were trapped. In their attempt to outrun the two uniformed cops, they'd turned into an ally with no way out. Hiding behind a green dumpster, they could hear the running footsteps of their pursuers slapping against the hot pavement of Third Avenue. Then the sounds stopped and a voice called out from the entrance to the ally.

"Give it up assholes. You're not getting out of this ally!"

Through a crack between the dumpster and a cardboard box Freddie could see there were two cops. Both looked young; probably only a few years older than he was. And one of the cops was a chick. The other cop was a big black guy; at least two-forty, he looked like a linebacker. Both had their guns drawn and leveled at chest height.

Freddie had a gun too. He could feel the hot metal tucked in his pants pressing against the small of his back. Neither he nor his cousin Jorge had ever fired the gun before today. They used it to intimidate their victims, and held in the shaking hand of a seventeen year old Puerto Rican crack addict, the heavy Smith & Wesson was intimidating.

The two police officers took positions at opposite sides of the ally entrance. They knew the young punks were either behind or inside the dumpster but they also knew they had a gun, so their approach was by the book. They knew about the gun because Cindy Chou, the thirteen year old kid who was raped by Freddie and Jorge earlier that afternoon told them so.

It seems Freddie Lopez and Jorge Inez had been on something of a spree the last few days. Emboldened by the newest crack to hit the streets of Brooklyn, the two had raped three young women and robbed a nearby bodega. During the robbery, they were reported to have put a gun in the shopkeeper's mouth and threatened to blow his head off if he didn't give them the night's receipts. During one of the rapes, they used the same gun to sodomize a twelve year-old girl, and then knock her unconscious with it before taking turns abusing her lifeless body.

Officers Eddie Mullen and Lucy Caffuto had graduated together from the academy less than two years ago. They were both assigned to street duty in the Bayridge section of Brooklyn and had been walking beats in the neighborhood for the last eighteen months. Eddie was married with a baby girl less than a month away. Lucy was engaged to her high school sweetheart and planning a September wedding. Neither had ever needed to draw their guns before today.

"Hey, punks! You got nowhere to go. Don't make me come back there and shoot your punk ass." Eddie was giving it his best street cop bravado, hoping to encourage their surrender. Usually it was Eddie who took charge. Born Edward Patton Mullen to a career army staff sergeant, and named after the WWII general, he was always expected to be a leader. His large frame and deep voice helped in situations like this. And Lucy was happy to have him as her partner.

Actually, it was Eddie's sizable presence that got the two of them out of a few uncomfortable situations before. He was great to have along when they got a call for a domestic dispute. Lucy could usually handle the wife while Eddie got in the husband's face and defused the tension. They were a good team and they both enjoyed the other's company.

Lucy's attention was now on the gun she held tight in her hands at eye level and pointed at the dumpster. She and Eddie had just run twelve blocks chasing the suspects. She was wearing a bulky bullet-stopping vest and it was one of those hazy, hot, and humid days New York is famous for in July. Her light blue shirt was soaked with perspiration and the beads of sweat running down her face were beginning to affect her vision. Yet she stayed totally focused on the dumpster.

"Eddie, how long we going to wait them out?" She whispered to her partner out the side of her mouth.

"Call for backup Lucy. I got them covered."

Although he might have felt otherwise, Eddie seemed confident and certain of himself. Lucy was just scared. This was the first time they'd confronted an armed assailant- someone who had used a gun just a few hours before. Although they'd practiced the protocols a hundred times at the academy, somehow this seemed totally different from everything they'd learned.

"Negative partner. I'm not holstering my weapon to reach for my radio." Lucy's voice was cracking. Then she shouted out, "Hey assholes! You've got to the count of five to throw out the gun. I want to see the fucking gun on the ground. Now!"

So far Freddie and Jorge hadn't said a word to each other since diving behind the dumpster. Freddie was facing the two cops and Jorge had his back against the dumpster. They were both crouched down low. The high they'd injected a few hours ago was all but gone, replaced only by fear. They were trapped. They saw only three ways this could end; either they would walk out in handcuffs, or run out over the dead bodies of two cops, or they would be carried out in body bags. There didn't seem to be any other options.

"What's it gonna be cuz?" Freddie looked at Jorge as he bit his lower lip.

But Jorge didn't respond. Instead he banged his head back against the green steel then shook it back and forth. He seemed to be mouthing words but no sound came from his trembling lips. Freddie had never seen this before from his young cousin. It appeared as if Jorge was slipping into some sort of trance.

Then Freddie heard what Jorge was whispering.

"....thy kingdom come, thy will be done, on earth as it is in heaven." Jorge was praying to himself. His eyes were fixed on the brick wall just behind them and, despite the heat, he was shivering.

"Hey bro, you need to pull it together. I ain't goin to jail. I need your help if we gonna get out of this."

But Jorge was frozen. Freddie shook his head in disgust for his useless cousin. Maybe it was the residual effect from the crack or maybe it was just the way he was brought up on the streets, but Freddie was determined to leave the ally on his terms. Giving up just wasn't an option he considered.

Without forming a plan, he rolled out from behind the safety of the dumpster. He could see the chick pointing her gun at him from less than twenty feet away. To her left, the black cop was even closer and moving toward him. His disdain for women in general is probably what drove his decision to ignore the figure on the right and fire at the big black target. From his position on the ground he pulled the trigger three times. The first two clicks released thunderous bangs made even louder by the echoes of the ally. The third was just a click.

The first bullet whizzed by Patrolman Eddie Mullen's right ear and slammed into the brick façade behind him. The second hit him a half inch left of his nose, directly under his right eye. As the projectile exited the back of his head, it sprayed blood and skull fragments through the air. His legs buckled and he fell forward. He was clinically dead before he hit the ground.

Lucy turned to the right and saw her partner and friend collapse. As she did, she heard four more hollow clicks as Freddie came to the realization there'd only been two shells in his gun and tried desperately to fire another. But she couldn't take her eyes off Eddie's lifeless body. For what seemed like an eternity, she was unable to move. All she could think about was Eddie's pregnant wife getting the visit from the NYPD chaplain.

Then she heard the sound of Freddie getting to his feet. He was running directly at her and hit her in the stomach before she could turn back toward him. The impact knocked her from her feet. She fell back with Freddie on top of her. He was beginning to punch

7

her face but couldn't land solid blows because his legs hadn't yet found solid footing.

Lucy's left arm was pinned underneath her but her right hand still held the gun. She swung her arm as hard as she could and caught Freddie on the side of the head with the handle of her gun. He collapsed to the left rolling on the ground and holding his head.

"You fucking bitch! I'll kill you." He screamed. Blood was flowing from his ear. The head trauma must have affected his balance because when he tried to stand, his left leg gave out and he toppled over still grasping his head.

This was Lucy's chance to stand and point the business end of her weapon at Freddie.

"Freeze," she screamed. She took two steps back from Freddie so he couldn't reach her without getting to his feet. Then she added, "Get on your stomach and spread your arms out wide on the ground."

For several moments, Freddie was motionless. Except for the rapid breathing, it would be difficult to tell he was alive. Lucy took two more steps away from him. Her gun was pointed directly at the center of his back. She was determined to fire if he tried to get up.

Finally, Freddie complied and rolled onto his stomach. But he was nearly unconscious. The blow to his head had cracked his skull. He had no interest in trying to escape. He knew he needed to get to a hospital. Standing was out of the question.

Lucy was reaching for her handcuffs when she saw Jorge emerge from behind the dumpster. He was on his knees and had his hands in the air.

"Don't shoot! Please don't shoot. I give up." He was crying so loudly, the words were lost in sobs.

She swung around and pointed her weapon at the boy. It occurred to her that he looked so young. And yet he and his cousin had brutally raped three girls in the past three days. The image and the facts seemed incongruous.

"On the ground!" She screamed. "Hands spread apart."

Jorge did as he was told. The two crack-heads were now lying face down directly next to each other. Jorge could see the blood flowing from Freddie's head and ear.

Keeping her weapon aimed directly at them, Lucy took two more steps backward, toward the body of her partner. She knew from the size of the exit wound on the back of Eddie's head that he was dead. There was nothing she could do for him and she felt a sudden urge to vomit. But adrenaline was surging through her and she resisted the nausea. Her mind was racing. She needed to make smart decisions fast. The thought of getting close enough to these animals to try to get cuffs on them terrified her.

Less than ninety seconds had passed since the first two shots killed her partner. Apparently no one was nearby the ally to hear the shots because so far, no one passing by had come to investigate. She needed help. She needed to call for back up but she was afraid to take her eyes off her two prisoners even for just a second. She could feel her heart pounding against her vest.

She glanced down at Eddie again. Just for an instant. *What would Eddie do?*

Again, the image of Eddie's pregnant wife flashed before her and she was repulsed by the damage these two creatures had done. Then she thought about the three girls they raped. One of them was only ten years old. The other two had been badly beaten and sodomized. Lucy had seen firsthand what they'd done to Cindy Chou and saw photos of the other two. It was these gruesome animals on the ally floor that did it all; that caused all this pain.

She took one more step away from their outstretched bodies. "Get on your feet. Both of you." Her voice was now steady and calm.

Jorge, still sobbing, stood with his hands on his head but Freddie was nearly unconscious from the blow. He staggered to his knees but was unable to stand. He was still holding his head.

"I need a fucking doctor. I need a hospital." His voice was still full of hate.

"No you don't." She said softly.

Lucy shot Freddie twice in the chest. A look of total shock covered his face as he fell back on his legs. Then she shot Jorge once in the head and once in the chest. His body flew back as if shot from a cannon.

Then she holstered her weapon and pulled her radio from her belt.

"Ten-thirteen. Officer down in the ally between twenty third and twenty fourth off Third Avenue. Repeat officer down, ten-thirteen."

CHAPTER 2

SPRING 1997

Carol McGovern sat near the door in the back of a large the-ater-like classroom. The night class was Deviant Behavior, a psych elective she needed to graduate in May. Her four years at Rutgers had flown by, and now she was about to face the real world in just a few months with a B.S. in Psychology and about sixty thousand dollars in student loans. She hoped to work with children in some way but didn't see herself teaching.

As the instructor droned on about varying levels of depression, Carol doodled on the edge of her notebook. She'd realized from the start that this prof took all his test questions from the glossy text he'd written years earlier, so lecture notes seemed foolish. In fact, coming to class at all seemed foolish except that a few weeks ago, Carol notice a guy sitting a few rows up that she wanted to meet but had yet to come up with an opening line.

But tonight the seat he usually occupied was empty so she day-dreamed about where he might be. She hoped he hadn't skipped class for a date. She'd been told by informed friends that he was un-attached; a fact she couldn't reconcile because he was so dammed cute. She loved the way his strawberry-blond hair hung over the back of his collar; the way he sat so upright while everyone around him was slouching at best; and the way he sprang to his feet the moment the bell rang, even if the prof was in mid-sentence. Without ever having spoken a word to him she knew he was boyishly rebel-lious- probably a lot of fun.

Then, just as she was finishing her ninth doodle, there he was, coming through the door right next to her. He was at least fifteen minutes late for class so he didn't dare walk down the center isle and struggle to find his usual seat. Instead, he slipped quietly into class and took the first seat he found- the empty one next to Carol.

"Did I miss anything monumental?" He asked as he settled into the seat. His voice was as soft as his green eyes.

Carol pointed to her doodling as an indication that he'd missed nothing significant and to indicate how bored she was. She whis-pered, "All his questions come from the text anyway."

For the next several minutes they sat silently, each pretending to lis-ten to the lecture, but actually both planning a snappy line that could be used at the class's conclusion to invite the other for a beer at the student union. It was Carol who broke the silence when she noticed he was eating cookies from a package he held on his lap under the desk-top. Judging by the brown wrapping paper and homemade nature of the cookies, Carol guessed he'd picked up his mail on the way to class and found a "care package", as food from home was called.

"Are you going to share any of those?" She thought that was a great opening line.

"Sure, have one", he whispered. "But I'm not sure my girlfriend would be happy with me sharing her chocolate chips with a beautiful blond." He gave her a sly smile and a wink.

Most young woman would have interpreted that sentence as an indication that the guy was spoken for; in this case, by a woman at home who made really great cookies. But for Carol, the term "beautiful blond" trumped everything that came before it. She saw the statement simply as a challenge- and she loved a challenge. And she was hungry.

Maybe if she hadn't been hungry; maybe if she'd taken a different seat that night; maybe if he hadn't come to class late; maybe if his girlfriend had not sent him the cookies; maybe she never would have met Billy Simon.

If she could do it over again, she would have skipped class that night.

⚊⊹⊹⊱

They sat up all that night finishing the cookies and talking on a bench outside the lecture hall. It was late February and the clear, cold sky was filled with glistening stars. He told her about his girl at home, Sue Zent, who'd sent the cookies; how he felt trapped by her plans to marry as soon as he got out of college and by her father's insistence that Billy work in the family business. He told Carol he just didn't know how to break it off from a distance. After all, Sue was at home in Kansas; baking and waiting patiently for him.

Carol was immediately taken by his sincerity and his reluctance to hurt another human being. He seemed so real; so honestly boyish. He was refreshingly genuine- especially after all the hormonal morons she'd dated the last three years. She wanted to know everything about him. But he was reluctant to talk about his family. Instead he focused on his high school and college athletics and why he wanted to join the marines when school ended.

As the sun began to light the early morning sky to the east, they left the wooden bench and walked back to his dorm where they sat in the lobby for another hour, talking about anything that came to mind. When Carol finally realized she had a class in a few hours, they agreed to meet at the local pizza shop for lunch. Carol told him she really liked meeting him and leaned in to offer a kiss, but Billy shifted his stance and kissed her on the right cheek.

⚊⚌⚊

For the next fourteen weeks, they were inseparable. When they weren't in class or working, they were together. They ate together, studied together, walked to classes together and began sleeping together after their second date. They fell deeply in love. Carol fell in love with Billy's boyish charm and how simple he seemed to make everything seem. Billy fell for Carol's radiant good looks and the way she treated him when others were around- always making him feel like the only person in the room. It was treatment to which he was unaccustomed and it felt wonderful.

They talked as if they'd known each other all their lives. They shared their dreams for life after Rutgers. Both were scheduled to graduate in May, but their plans, or the plans they had before meeting each other, would take them in very different directions. Billy had always planned to join the Marines after college. Though he wanted no part of the ROTC program, or being an officer, the Marines had always been his boyhood ambition. Ironically, he'd spoken to a recruiter the morning of the day he met Carol, and been promised a September enlistment date. Most likely, he'd be stationed in the Middle East somewhere. That was fine with Billy. He wanted to see the world.

Carol's dreams couldn't have been more different. She wanted to take a few months to travel around the United States looking for the right job and the right place to live. She was very focused on someday having a family, the dog, and the white picket fence. Her parents, long since divorced and moved away from the small up-state New Jersey town she was raised, leaving her no real home to return to after graduation.

The one post-graduation issue they had in common was debt. They'd both borrowed heavily to get through Rutgers and six months after graduating, Carol would need to start repaying the loans. Billy's debt would be further deferred while he was in the military.

They agreed that immediately after graduation, they'd pool the little savings they'd accumulated from part-time jobs that spring, and drive across the country. For Billy and Carol it was a way to postpone the reality of life-after-college and linger as children for just a few more months. They wanted to see as much of the country as possible and joked that they would try to have sex in every state before the summer was out.

So on May 16th, 1997, one day after graduation, they jumped in Carol's green '89 Toyota Camry and began their journey by heading straight down route 95. Between them, they had $3,225 in cash and two credit cards. But they had the wonderful gift of youthful exuberance. And they were madly in love.

Their adventure took them to Key West, then along the southern route to California. They camped outside Muir Woods for several days. Billy thought it was the most beautiful place in the world. They drove north to Washington State then crisscrossed through the west, hitting most national parks. And it was in Yosemite, while having lunch at a picnic table near El Capitan, that Billy told Carol he wanted to marry her. They agreed to be married as soon as Billy finished basic training; probably sometime in January. The wedding would be small; neither wanted a traditional ceremony or east-coast festival like so many of their friends were doing.

So after sixty-three days of driving and over 14,000 miles added to Carol's odometer, they made their way back to the east coast and rented a small apartment in Brooklyn. Carol took a job in a childcare facility called Children First, in the lobby of the Goldman Sachs building. It was exclusively for the children of Goldman Sachs employees and a state-of-the-art facility.

Billy only had a few weeks before he needed to report to Parris Island for basic training so he took a part-time job helping out at a bar in the neighborhood. He made some good money but needed to work nights so his time with Carol was limited to weekend days.

Though their time together was limited, their love continued to deepen. On the Saturday before Billy was to report for duty they spent the entire day walking the paths of Central Park. Carol packed a lunch of ham and cheese sandwiches on rye complete with the quintessential gingham tablecloth for picnicking on the Great Lawn. With the Manhattan skyscrapers on the horizon, they lay on the checkered cloth and pledged their eternal love.

"Since I won't see you for twelve weeks, what do you want to do tomorrow soldier boy?" She was staring straight up at the wispy September clouds.

"Is it really up to me? Seriously, whatever I want?" Billy sounded like a child with a five dollar bill about to enter a candy store.

"Completely up to you. Whatever your heart desires."

For a reason neither of them could remember, Billy had begun calling Carol "Beans" soon after they left on their cross-country trip. Now it was the only name that seemed to fit.

"Well Beans, my dream day would go something like this." He too was lying on his back looking up at the passing clouds. "Let's sleep late; you'll ravage me two or three times before we even get out of bed. Then let's go for blueberry pancakes at Sheppy's. Then let's rent bikes for the day and ride over the Bridge and down to Battery Park. We can have an early dinner in Little Italy, then head back here and get back into bed. If it's going to be my last night with you for months, I'll need to stare at you in your birthday suit for a long time. That image will keep me warm."

The thought of being apart from Billy for so long worried Carol. She relied on his centered view of the world; his chronically positive attitude. She'd spent so much of the last six months with him that she was frightened by the thought of being alone.

"What am I going to do without you?" She said as she gently ran her finger along the ridge of his jaw.

"You're going to be fine Beans. Besides, you said it yourself; you'll be really busy at work for the next few months." Then he added, "Just don't meet a tall, dark stranger and get swept off your feet."

CHAPTER 3

For some reason, Billy didn't find basic training on Parris Island as tough as he'd feared. The strict regimentation fit his disciplined personality to a tee. Other than the early morning runs, he almost enjoyed the experience. Sure it was physically demanding and the food could have been better but he had no problem with the drill sergeants or any of the seemingly arbitrary rules they imposed on the recruits. Military life suited him. He reveled in the structure.

Even so, as his time on Parris Island neared its close and graduation from what others thought to be the toughest basic training in the world approached, he felt an enormous sense of accomplishment. And he looked forward to the pomp and grandeur the U.S. Marine Corp produced for the recruits' graduation ceremony. Families were expected from all over the country for the weekend-long festivities.

Of course, Billy had no family to invite, but Carol would be there. She'd booked her flight from New York weeks ago and had a room at the Holiday Inn reserved for their reunion. He'd been dreaming about Carol the whole time he was away. He'd daydreamed about the moment; he in his dress blues with polished brass buttons and symbolic saber and she in the white sun dress she told him she'd bought just for the trip.

They planned to be married two days after graduation in Hilton Head and honeymoon for the rest of his three week leave. After which he was off to San Diego for ten weeks of combat training, and Carol was back to work in Manhattan. He begged her to move out to San Diego so they could be together, at least on his days off, but she was beginning to feel roots in New York and during several of their phone calls, she resisted.

On the day of Billy's graduation, as he and his brothers-in-blue marched on the parade grounds, he spotted Carol sitting in the grandstands reserved for family. He'd never been so proud. Proud- both of his accomplishment and proud of Carol. He couldn't wait to show her off to several of his new friends.

The January sky was crystal clear and crisp with just a hint of chill. Carol was wearing the white sun dress she'd told him about and a blue cardigan over her shoulders. She looked as beautiful as she'd been in his dreams.

As Billy took his standing position for the ceremony, he had a clear view of Carol. She was less than fifty yards away and he imagined he could smell her "Heaven Scent" perfume drifting down from the stands to tease him and make him desire her more than he already did- if that was possible.

But after twelve weeks of learning how to use his senses to survive, Billy sensed something different, even from a distance. Carol's face, although just as he remembered it, seemed more serious. Her expression lacked that playful joy he always found in her eyes. Her smile wasn't as broad.

As the speeches wore on and Billy struggled to maintain his rigid position, lest one white hat might seem askew in the long line of white, he convinced himself that it was more likely that he'd changed. After all, he'd been taught to look for anything that might pose a danger to him or his men. He'd been taught to be suspicious of subtle changes. He'd been trained to find threats before they found him. And he'd been taught, and taught well, how to kill. For the first time in his life, he felt as though his instincts were honed on a single focus: survival.

At the conclusion of the ceremony, when the marines were permitted to join their families on the parade field, Billy found Carol searching the sea of blue on her toes and opened with the line he'd practiced for weeks. "Mam..., I would be honored if you would escort me to the nearest Holiday Inn."

"What did you have in mind, sailor?" Her smile was radiant and she smelled as sweet as ever. They kissed and then held each other for almost a full minute.

The next twelve hours were a blur of sheets flying off the bed, champagne poured directly from the bottle, and lustful passion. They didn't emerge from their hotel room until eleven the next day. Billy later recalled to a fellow marine that he and Carol had made love, "at least eight times that I can remember. And I'm not sure everything we did in there was legal in the state of South Carolina."

They were both tired and hungry, so the following morning the nearest Denny's was the perfect place for breakfast. They grabbed a booth by the window. Their eating was as voracious as their sex. And for Billy, the meal was just a time-out before heading back to the hotel room. Then they had to find a chapel and a preacher that could marry them on Saturday.

But Carol had another plan. "Billy, let's not go back to the room just yet. Let's take a walk on the beach. It's so nice out compared to the weather back in New York. I'd just like to be outside for a while."

And then she added the phrase that would haunt Billy the rest of his life. "I loved last night and I'm so proud of you,... but there's something I have to talk to you about."

⇤⇥

Three hours later they finally arrived back in front of the Holiday Inn. They'd walked several miles along the unusually still ocean. Carol did most of the talking. She hated having to hurt him.

She explained that she'd met someone else; a guy from the building she worked in. His name was Alan Wallace. He was a bond trader at Goldman Sachs; formerly part of their associates program. They met one rainy day while Carol was taking some of the children from the day care center for a walk around the lobby. The first thing she noticed about him was that his shoes had tassels.

How could she say it without hurting Billy? Yes, Alan was a very successful and polished guy. He'd swept Carol off her feet with charm, and then followed up with impressive dinners at some of the best Manhattan restaurants- places to which most of the public had no access. He used limousines to get around town and would send one to Brooklyn to pick Carol up when he couldn't get there himself. They'd been to the opera at the Met, charitable galas at the Guggenheim, and sat in the lavish Goldman Sachs skybox at Madison Square Garden when the Bulls and Michael Jordan were in town to play the Knicks.

Alan had opened Carol's eyes to a whole new world; one she didn't think existed for anyone other than movie stars. Before Alan, she'd never tasted the soft bubbles of a $200 bottle of champagne, or felt the luxurious leather on a Mercedes front seat. And, although it shamed her to admit it, she loved it. She fit into his social circles with graceful ease. During a decadent Thanksgiving party, one of Alan's bosses mentioned to Carol that she just might be his greatest business asset.

During their walk on the beach, Carol only gave Billy the bare minimum of detail about her relationship with Alan. She didn't mention that they'd been seeing each other for almost the entire time Billy was on Parris Island, or that Alan had begun pressing Carol to break off her engagement to Billy after only two dates. She didn't mention that at twenty-eight, Alan was the youngest Managing Director at Goldman Sachs or that he was expecting another seven-figure bonus soon. And she didn't mention that they'd been sleeping together at least twice a week for the past five weeks.

What she did tell Billy was that she needed to talk to him in person; that she still loved him and wanted to be there for his graduation; that she was proud of him. She told him she was conflicted about her feelings; that she didn't think she could feel this way about two men. But in the end, she knew in her heart that wasn't entirely truthful. The truth was she was just trading up. She understood the harsh reality of becoming a marine's wife and being transferred all over the world for the next four years versus the life Alan could give her. She'd had a taste of the finer things and wanted to taste more. And she was painfully honest with Billy about that.

Billy was devastated. On one level he was devastated by the betrayal. All his plans for the future had just blown up. He had a wonderful life planned out for them and after a short walk on the beach, he had no plan at all; no idea of what he would do tomorrow, no less for the rest of his life. He felt as though he'd just taken a powerful blow to the body and had all the air in his chest pushed out. It felt as though there was nothing left inside himself.

On another level, and this is the one that really pained him, Carol was leaving him for money. She said she still loved him, but yet she was leaving him. In his linear mind, that didn't make any sense.

"Are you telling me this is all about his fucking shoes? You're leaving me because this guy wears expensive shoes and has a nice car and buys you things I can't? Because if that's the case, you know what that makes you? It makes you a whore!" He was screaming at her.

"What the fuck did you come down here for? Just to crush me in person? Is that it? You just had to see how much you'd be hurting me? Is that it Carol?"

Billy was now sitting on the sand facing the ocean. Carol had yet to sit. She wasn't sure if she should. But when he looked up at her with desperation on his face, her heart softened yet again and she knelt beside him.

"Oh, Billy. I do love you. And I didn't want to hurt you. I didn't go looking for this. It just happened. If I could undo the last four months I would, but I can't." Her hand was on his shoulder.

"Of course you can. You can do anything you want to do Carol. You can choose not to go back to New York." He said hopefully.

There was a long silence. They both starred out at the ocean for several minutes without saying a word. They both knew that their futures would be determined by whatever was said next, and neither wanted to be the first to speak.

Finally, it was Carol who spoke. "I do love you Billy. I love you so much. I'll probably love you forever. But I know that I'll always want more than we would have together. I've thought about this a lot. I don't want to wake up in five years and resent you for the rest of our lives because of something that's not your fault. I don't want to get up every morning and resent the house we live in and wonder what might have been. I want us both to be happy but I don't think that would happen if we're together. I think there's another life out there for me."

The more Carol spoke, the more she was sickened by her own words. She knew she was choosing a life of privilege over a life with Billy. There was just no other way to put it. There was no way to say it that made it better. Billy was right. In a way, she was a whore.

"You're right Billy. Right about a lot of things. I do have a choice. And I choose the other life." She said it as calmly as if she'd just chosen an entre from a menu.

"Then get out of my sight." And Billy Simon got up and walked away from the only person he'd ever loved.

Carol gazed out the window on her flight back to New York. The clouds below softly glided by as she reflected on her decision. Alan had already called her at the airport to find out how the conversation with Billy had gone. She gave him most of the details but didn't mention that before breaking up with Billy, they'd spent the previous twelve hours ravishing each other in the Holiday Inn.

She knew Alan intended to ask her to marry him sometime the following summer. He'd already talked about a July wedding up on the Cape at his parents' summer place. She assumed the formal engagement would occur as soon as she returned. Alan had hinted as much and asked her to select a setting for an engagement ring once while they were window shopping along Fifth Avenue.

Everything was happening so fast. This time last year she hadn't even met Billy, the boy she'd fallen so in love with. Now, she was planning to spend the rest of her life with Alan, someone completely different from anyone else she'd ever known. She wondered what her life would look like in another year.

But what kept haunting her thoughts during the ride back to New York was the painful word that Billy used- "Whore". Isn't that what people call someone who sells out for money? Isn't that what anyone would call you if you married a man for the material things he could give you rather than marrying the man you really love?

And it wasn't that Carol didn't love Alan as well. She did. She just wasn't sure how much her affection for Alan resulted from who he was versus what he had. When she tried to imagine a life with Alan but without the wealth, she was no longer as confident in her decision. He did have many wonderful qualities. He was generous and thoughtful and handsome and came from a good family. But would she have fallen for him if he was a school teacher? That was the question she kept asking herself.

And then there was the sex. Alan was fine; gentle and caring. But with Billy, Carol felt things she'd never felt with anyone else. Billy was a spectacular lover. It wasn't any one asset she could come up with. Billy just knew exactly how to bring Carol to the edge of ecstasy and hold her there. He made her moan and sigh and could take her breath away with one stroke of his fingers. Alan had never done that.

Billy knew how to touch Carol in ways that made her quiver. Sometimes it was a line he would gently draw on her back with his thumb. Sometimes, just a soft kiss would do it. But the move that made Billy such a wonderful lover for Carol was when he would rub the back of his fingers softly against her cheek, then slowly down her neck, then gently over her nipples and onto her belly. Still just the back of his hand touched her skin and ever so lightly, but it drove Carol wild. She would climax even before Billy's hand reached its eventual target. And then she would climax again.

So in choosing Alan over Billy, she was walking away from that sort of passion in favor of comfort. She struggled with whether that made her a gold-digger or just painfully practical. In the end, and before her flight landed at LaGuardia, she decided she could live without the passion.

CHAPTER 4
JUNE 1998

Carol hadn't seen Billy since they were on Hilton head five months ago. They hadn't spoken or written a single word. So when she got a phone call from him yesterday, she wasn't sure how to respond. Billy wanted to see Carol, "One last time before he left for Iraq", as he put it. He said his entire division was being deployed in southern Iraq for at least thirteen months, and that he had a twenty-four hour leave before they reported to a base in New Jersey. He sounded so sincere on the phone that Carol couldn't say no.

When she hung up the phone in her office, she knew a part of her still ached for Billy. Maybe it was the moth drawn to the light but Carol missed Billy's boyish charm and ravenous lovemaking. She hadn't felt that deep stimulation with Alan, who was becoming increasingly preoccupied with his access to the boardroom and less so with their time in the bedroom. She needed to see if just sitting across the dinner table from Billy was as warming as she remembered.

It also helped that Alan was in New Orleans with six of his buddies at his bachelor party and wouldn't be back until Friday. With their wedding only ten days away, the last thing Alan would want to hear about is Carol catching up with her old flame, Billy. No it would be better if he never found out about it; even though it was to be just an innocent dinner at the South Street Seaport.

The restaurant was just a few blocks from the apartment she and Alan now shared in lower Manhattan. She left work a little early to have time to go home, shower and change into a skirt and V-neck cotton sweater. She splashed on some Heaven Scent, and remembered it was Billy's favorite.

She was surprised to see him enter the restaurant in civilian clothes; a pair of well-pressed jeans and a yellow collared shirt. But he did look great; well-tanned and more fit than even the last time she saw him. Even as he approached her table from a distance she could see he walked with a confident swagger. He was no longer a boy. The Marines had turned him into a man.

She rose from the table and he offered a glancing kiss on the cheek. "You look fantastic Carol." Then he motioned for her to sit again and told her about his training over the last five months, the places he'd been stationed, and his mission in Iraq. "We'll be over there for at least a year, so I had to see you again."

Somewhere between their appetizers and the second bottle of Merlot, Carol realized that Billy had come to New York to be sure their flame was completely out. If there was any hope at all of getting her back; if Alan wasn't all she had expected, he wanted to know before leaving. Just that bit of hope would sustain him until he could come back and begin the process of winning her back. He hoped seeing him again might reignite some level of passion in

Carol. He had no idea that her relationship with Alan had moved so fast.

"Billy, I still have deep feelings for you. But I'm going to marry Alan." She emphasized the word "marry". "In fact, we're getting married in two weeks. I wanted to write and tell you but I had no idea where you were. And even if I did, I wasn't sure you'd want to hear about it."

She wasn't sure what to expect. She knew Billy had a temper that he sometimes couldn't control. She was afraid he'd make a scene in the otherwise quiet dining room. But he sat across from her in complete silence. He took another sip of his wine then held the glass in front of him on the table.

"Well, then I feel like a fool." He said so softly she barely heard him.

The restaurant was dark and it was difficult to be sure, but Carol thought she saw a tear fall from Billy's right eye. He bit his lower lip and just seemed to stare at his wine goblet. Then he leaned toward Carol across the table and ran the back of his hand softly along the contours of her face. "I hope you have a happy life Carol. I really do."

Maybe it was the alcohol, maybe it was pre-wedding blues, or maybe she just wanted to feel the warmth one last time; but the next words out of Carol's mouth surprised both people at the table. "Billy, we had so much for such a short time. We may never see each other again. I want to spend the night with you. I want to love you one more time." And then she added, "My apartment is just a few blocks from here. Please take me home."

⟞⟝ ⟞⟝

July 2005

Twenty miles from Jalalabad, Afghanistan

Billy rolled onto his stomach and reached out to find his cell phone. He'd been asleep for less than three hours but his unit was scheduled to accompany a caravan of Red Cross trucks from his camp to Kabul at 06:00 hours; less than an hour from now. The temperature in his tent was already over ninety degrees and the sun was just lifting over the parched horizon. It would get a lot hotter today.

He rolled again and lay on his back, gazing up at the flies circling the highest point in the tent. He'd been at Camp Tomatta, just outside Jalalabad, for nearly a year, but he still couldn't get use to the intense heat. Even lying on his cot, in nothing but a pair of military-issue boxers, he was beginning to sweat. The ride to Kabul, in full body-armor would be gruesome. But it would be foolish to dress any other way. Without full body-armor, a marine's life expectancy in Afghanistan was less than a month.

The reason was twofold. First, the IED's; the improvised explosive devices the locals liked to put along the road to kill as many American soldiers as possible. Second, the large caliber bullets the same people liked to shower onto the Americans as those, lucky enough not to be killed by the explosions, ran from the flaming trucks.

He'd been in Afghanistan less than four years and had already been in sixteen roadside bombings. Six of the guys he came over with were dead. Another six had been sent back to the states without the legs they arrived with. And thirteen of the original thirty men in his unit were either in the hospital or recuperating at a military hospital in Germany. That left only five men from his original unit that had not been killed or maimed by the IEDs.

He considered himself lucky. Lucky to be alive, but also lucky he hadn't been injured. That was his greatest fear; losing an arm or leg and having to lie around a military hospital until the overworked and understaffed medical staff could work their magic. Too many of his friends had gone through it. Too many had been sent home already to recuperate at a veteran's hospital.

Billy sat up on the edge of his cot. He wondered where the last few years had gone. He'd spent four years in or around Iraq, mostly in the south. At first he enjoyed the work; it had a clear purpose; something Billy needed. He understood his mission was to find and eliminate insurgent groups who were still trying to disrupt the new government and kill American soldiers. That mission was clear. But later, when he was assigned to a training unit, his purpose had far less clarity.

He couldn't understand why Americans were training Iraqi soldiers; people Billy was convinced he'd be asked to fight against someday. It seemed only like a matter of time before the Iraqis would use their new skills, equipment and training to once again rebel against the West. He could see it in their faces. They hated him. And he'd grown to hate them in return.

After a while, Billy realized his disdain for the people of Iraq was poisoning his soul. He needed to escape the desert and rededicate himself to a more noble mission; one that he could embrace. And so, when an opening came up in a munitions unit that was rumored to be on its way to Afghanistan, Billy asked for the transfer. It meant another three years in the marines but he had no other ambitions. The marines had become his family.

But, increasingly, he felt that his family had been cut off and forgotten by the country they were fighting for. He and his unit would gather in the rec hall after dinner and watch taped segments of the evening news shows from American television. They expected to see reports about the noble work they were doing. They expected to see stories about how they'd volunteered to defend their country while their families struggled at home. But there were surprisingly few reports about the American soldiers' efforts in Afghanistan. Instead, the evening news focused on the American economy, the Kardashians, reality TV, and the everyday lives of self-absorbed Americans.

Why didn't his country appreciate what they were doing? It was almost as if America was trying not to think about the war they were fighting on the other side of the planet. It was as if the American people were trying to distract themselves from the ugly reality that so many people hate them. If they could watch fat people glorified on TV for losing weight, maybe nothing else mattered.

It had been a mere four years since these animals used American airliners, filled with American citizens, to crash into the Pentagon and World Trade Center. How could the people of his country forget so quickly? Why did they want to forget so quickly? It seemed like the only time American television paid any attention to what was going on in Afghanistan was when Osama bin Laden suck his head out of a cave to piss in our face again and remind America that it had failed miserably in its attempt to find him.

America had lost sight of who its real enemy was. Billy's country had taken its eye off the ball because it was being told to do so. They were told that everything will be okay; just go out and start shopping again! As long as bin Laden hadn't destroyed the American economy, he hadn't destroyed America.

Billy began to think that the best thing that could happen to America would be if Osama tried again. If a few more landmarks disappeared into a cloud of dust on American television, maybe the American people would be reawakened. Maybe this time, they'd rise up like their parents had after Pearl Harbor, and focus on the true enemy. And stay focused until the job was done.

Billy glanced at his cell phone. The screen was cracked; the result of his drunken condition the night before. It had been a horrible day that turned into an equally horrible night. It had been his day off and he used the down time to watch a few movies in the rec hall, escaping the blistering heat for a few hours. It was his way of putting a million miles between himself and the third-world animals he lived among.

Yesterday, right after lunch, the movie was "City Slickers". He'd seen it several times before but the rec hall was cool and Billy Crystal never gets old so he settled onto a folding chair and got lost in America's southwest. But it was the second film, "The Notebook" that started Billy in the wrong direction, because once again he was reminded of Carol McGovern; someone he'd been trying to forget.

Somehow, the lead characters reminded him of himself and Carol. And that reopened the painful memories. Why couldn't Carol have been more like Rachel McAdams? Life could have been wonderful for them. Instead, his fists clenched every time the thought about Carol in the arms of her Wall Street husband. It infuriated him to be reminded of her betrayal and the way she tossed him aside after using him one last time.

For over five years he'd been trying to forget Carol McGovern, or whatever her name was now. For over five years he'd buried himself in his military life, trying to distance himself from the life he knew with Carol, in hopes of getting past it all. But recently he came to the realization that hers was a pain he could not outrun. That there was no distance he could put between them that would lessen the hurt. He came to understand that forgiving Carol was impossible and forgetting her was not going to erase the pain. And if forgiving and forgetting weren't going to work, maybe he needed to sever the memory in another way.

She'd hurt him in a spectacular way. She'd debased him and embarrassed him. And she used him. If he couldn't get past it, and the last five years told him he couldn't, he'd have to reconcile the relationship in another way. He'd have to hurt her back.

And that was the day Billy began to work on his plan.

CHAPTER 5

JUNE 2013

Nina Morales was working behind the bar at Finnegan's, a watering hole for the local Panama City crowd, when she first met Billy. He and two of his marine friends came in around one in the morning after attending some sort of going away party. The way she remembered it, a fresh batch of marines were about to ship out for Afghanistan and Billy had arranged a send-off in their honor. In any event, when he and his friends came in to Finnegan's they were already very drunk and louder than the usual crowd would have preferred.

It was the Tuesday after Memorial Day and already the temperatures on the Florida panhandle were in the nineties; and not much cooler at one A.M. Billy wasn't in uniform, he'd been out of the service several months, but his two friends wore the required attire and were sweating through their heavy brown shirts. The first thing she noticed about Billy as he stepped to the bar was his tattoo; a colorful rendition of a naked half-woman/half-panther crawling up his right forearm. What she should have remembered about him was his smooth opening line. Recognizing him as a manipulating con-artist might have saved her life.

"I don't usually say things like this to women I don't know but you have the sexiest shoulders I have ever seen. They're so smooth." His flawless diction did not betray his inebriation. And it wasn't too far from the truth. Nina's halter top revealed enough of her golden brown skin to make a man understand why her Cuban/Mexican parents kept her on a very short leash until she was seventeen and ran away from their doublewide forever.

"You sure it's my shoulders you're looking at?" she said before she even turned to face him.

Billy ordered a Miller and two for his friends, then motioned for them to get lost so he could pursue the saucy bartender. They complied by taking up positions at the far end of the bar and focusing their attention on the sixty-five inch TV with the Giant-Dodger game.

Nina remembered Billy told her he'd been in the marines for several years and spent most of the time in countries she'd only heard about on the evening news; places like Afghanistan, Iraq, and some provinces she couldn't pronounce ten seconds after he mentioned them. He revealed he'd been a munitions expert and it didn't take him long to talk about the many friends he lost to his Islamic counterparts. He came back from the Middle East to train new marines in his explosive craft at Camp LeMarc, just outside Panama City. That's where he'd been the last eight months of his service. He left the marines just before Christmas last year. Since then, he'd been working for a friend at a sheet metal factory nearby.

But what drew Nina in was that after just a few minutes he made the entire conversation about her. What did she like? What were her dreams? Where did she want to live? No one had ever done that with her before. As a bartender she was accustomed to listening to other peoples' stories. No one had ever asked her for hers before. Someone was taking an interest in her and it felt wonderful.

They hung on opposite sides of the bar long after closing time. Billy liked Nina from the start. She was real. Coming from Topeka, Kansas, he could relate to someone like Nina. They were both small-town kind of people and liked small-town sorts of things; high school football on Friday nights, hunting, fishing, and Walmart. He'd met a lot of women while in the Middle East, most of them were either junior officers who'd do anything to move up the military ladder, or the local whores who'd do anything for twenty-five American dollars. He cared for neither.

And he quickly learned that he and Nina shared a common distain for most minorities, especially those she called "A-rabs". Apparently, Nina's current employer, Sami, a recent immigrant from Turkey, had purchased Finnegan's shortly after arriving in Florida. Sami had been a successful exporter in Istanbul until the events of 9-11 soured America's taste for most things from his part of the world and he was forced to seek his fortune elsewhere. He'd been schooled in England and was a clever businessman. His plan was to purchase several low-end bars like Finnegan's, send his two daughters to the University of Florida, and live the good life Americans took for granted.

Nina hated him from the start. She couldn't put her finger on exactly why but it began when Sami insisted all shifts of bartenders pool their tips. She and Sami got into it over that one because she worked all the high-tip shifts and resented the fact that Sami's daughters, who worked behind the bar only when they felt the urge, benefited from her hard work and hustle. She also didn't like his heavy breath on her neck whenever he would look over her shoulder to watch her pour a drink.

So it didn't take long before Billy found himself sharing with Nina his concern that his country, the country he'd defended for fifteen years as a marine, had seemingly forgotten what a threat the "towel-headed lunatics" from the Middle East still posed. It had been less than a dozen short years "Since sixteen of those cocksucking religious fanatics took down the twin towers and Pentagon", and yet America seems to have forgiven and moved on. This outraged him. "How the fuck can anyone object to profiling? Isn't that exactly what we need? Find the assholes that are trying to kills us and kill them first. Isn't that what we're supposed to be doing?"

Nina listened from across the bar as an increasingly drunk Billy vented. He was genuinely concerned that America had let down its guard too soon. Just because a few years had gone by without a follow-up attack was no reason to believe one wasn't being planned. He'd seen what kind of people these were. He'd watched fifteen year old kids walk into a crowded market with C-4 strapped to their chest and blow up themselves and every innocent shopper around them. They didn't care about human life. What makes anyone believe they won't do exactly the same at the Mall of America the first chance they get? And what if they get their hands on a nuke?

"America needs a wake-up call." Billy was staring down into his beer. "Something's got to get us out of this malaise and remind everyone who our real enemies are."

Nina found his intensity arousing. To her, Billy was what men were supposed to be like. Men like that took charge; they didn't wait for some politician to say 'charge'. They did what had to be done. And she could sense from his intensity that Billy meant every word he said.

"You're probably right. But who wants to see another attack?" She was beginning to slur her words. It was nearly five in the morning. A garish light was streaming through the front windows and onto the mirror behind the bar. And Nina was really tired.

"Come on Sweetie. I've got to lock up. Then I'll take you home and make you some of my famous grits and honey." She put her hand softly on Billy's arm. He seemed not to notice.

"I do," he said almost to himself.

"What Sweetie?"

"I do."

"You do what?" She was confused.

"I want to see another attack."

CHAPTER 6

The nightmare started as it always did. Billy was sitting at the kitchen table with his younger sister. His mom was at the counter making his school lunch and folding over the top of the paper bag. The kitchen had a darkness to it that Billy thought odd for a school morning. The corn flakes he swirled in his bowl were growing soggy and began to sink to the bottom of the milk.

His mom looked tired. Life wasn't easy for a single mom in a small town. If it weren't for the help she got from Billy's grandparents who lived on the other side of the river, it would be a lot worse. His mom's parents stopped by every Sunday to take Billy and his sister to church services. On the way back from church they'd stop at the Food King and stock up on vegetables and cereals for the week.

The realization of footsteps on the front porch sent a chill down Billy's back. He straightened in his chair. His father didn't tolerate slouching. And although his visits were growing more and more infrequent, Andy Simon made sure his occasional presence received the proper respect from his children.

Billy's father lived in Kitzen, a small town about ten miles to the east. From conversations he overheard between his mom and grandmother, it sounded like Billy's father had another family there. He'd been the assistant sheriff for as long as Billy could remember but hadn't lived with Billy's mom since Billy started first grade, about five years ago. Billy's only memories of him were based on these unannounced visits. He had no recollection of happy times.

There was no sound in Billy's nightmare- just the oppressive, silent feeling of a hot, muggy morning and the smell of cigarettes. The terror revealed itself just as it had a dozen times before. Once his father was in the kitchen, his mother would untie her apron and fold it neatly over the back of the wooden chair directly across the table from where Billy sat. Then she would take Billy's little sister and put her in the kitchen sink.

Andy Simon pulled his ebony nightstick from its holster and tapped it on the table. Several chips and scrapes on its edges proved it was his favorite tool. He'd used it many times before.

When Billy looked up from his corn flakes his father was completely naked with an enormous erection in one hand and his nightstick in the other. The bizarre image was always the same. Billy looked back at the bowl of cereal. He had to look away from his father. But now the milk in the bowl had turned black and was circling as if it were water going down a drain.

Something forced Billy to look up again. He saw his father sodomizing his mother with the nightstick as she bent over the chair holding her folded apron. His mother's scarlet face was just inches from Billy's and her mouth gaped open as if she was singing or screaming but there was no sound. At one point Billy thought he could see the shape of the nightstick's evil head pounding in his mother's chest, as if it was trying to break through from the inside of her.

Then, instantly, everything in the room disappeared and Billy was left sitting face to face with his father. A Lucky Strike dangled from his lip as he began to hit Billy with the nightstick. The first blow caught him on the side of the face and Billy could smell his mother's blood and fecal matter on the stick as it crashed into his jaw. The second blow came down solidly on his right hand which was lying flat on the table. The pain was excruciating but there was no sound to be made.

Billy awoke, as he usually did after the nightmare, in a complete sweat. Both fists were tightly clenched. Hatred pounded in his chest.

CHAPTER 7
SEPTEMBER 2013
LT

What should I tell you about myself?

My name is LT Hadman and I'm a cop. People have called me LT for as long as I can remember, but it's certainly not because I look anything like Lawrence Taylor or Ladainian Tomlinson. In fact, guys at the eighth precinct say I'm about the whitest cop they know. But I think they're referring to my complexion, not my attitude toward other races. Anyway, although I'm still in pretty good shape for a 44 year old cop with an addiction to Sam Adams, believe me, I look nothing like those great football players.

I've been a New York City cop for almost twenty years now and a detective for the last eight. I come from a family of cops. My father was a cop. My twin brother Bill is a cop in Philadelphia where he lives with his wretched wife Sylvia. And my grandfather was a cop up in Boston. He's gone now but when the rest of us get together for holidays, we swap stories about police work all day long. It drives most of the wives crazy but what the hell- this is what we are. My loving ex had no tolerance for the cop talk at dinner either but that's just one of the many reasons Terry and I divorced after just two years. I love being a cop. Terry, an elementary school teacher, wanted to be married to an investment banker; someone who wore expensive clothes to work and brought home a fat paycheck. Last I heard, Terry's now married to a foreign exchange trader from Morgan Stanley and has four kids.

For the last three years I've been working with a joint task force that includes people from the NYPD, the FBI, and ATF. We're supposed to be dealing with scumbags that pose a threat to New York City. Everyone else calls them terrorists but we just call them scumbags. Most of the scumbags aren't trying to fly a plane into the Citibank building. The nut-jobs we deal with are mostly selling guns, drugs, and assorted goodies that could be used to make bombs. They want to sell them to other nut-jobs.

Today, my partner and I are watching a well-dressed Jordanian fellow window shop along Madison Avenue. Alec Al-Sidad is about twenty-seven years old, went to Brown University where he majored in chemical engineering, and is the son of a guy back home who could light his cigars with my paycheck. Alec's wearing a gray Brioni suit and easily blends in with the tourists and regular pedestrian traffic on the sidewalks outside some of New York's finest shops.

Ken Stallings, my partner from ATF, and I have been walking a hundred yards behind Mr. Al-Sidad and lingering outside store windows whenever he enters a store, for over three hours. There was a tip from Intel that he was planning to meet another outstanding middle-eastern fellow sometime this morning and exchange an envelope filled with cash for a flash drive. The smart guys at Intel suspect the flash drive contains a list of names we'd like to get our hands on.

We've been leap-frogging him since he crossed 72nd Street. Ken and I take turns getting ahead of Al-Sidad (no one ever looks for a tail ahead of them), just in case he makes the tail behind him. So far, he doesn't seem at all concerned with his surroundings and has actually stopped to ogle the occasional good looking woman. He seems partial to women in short dresses. I guess you don't get a lot of that over in Sandland.

Our instructions are not to apprehend or even interrupt Mr. Al-Sidad. We're to keep our distance and simply photograph anyone with whom he has contact on the street. The boys back at Penn Plaza will look at the pictures and sort out who Alec's been playing with. Our boss was very clear about not getting in his space. Apparently our task force has been watching Mr. Al-Sidad for a long time and doesn't want us to arouse any suspicion of their surveillance.

"What do you think those shoes cost?" Ken's attention was on the scumbag's Bruno Maglis.

"More than I'll ever pay for shoes," was the best I could come up with while trying not to lose our subject at the crosswalk.

At 53rd Street he turned right and walked to Fifth Ave, then turned south. It was almost noon and the bright September sun glistened against the walls of the glass canyon. Even with sunglasses it was difficult to pick him out of the crowded stream of people walking down Fifth. We needed to get a little closer.

"I'll cross over and get ahead," Ken said. He hurried across the street and continued his pursuit on the other side.

All the while we've been tailing this guy I'm thinking about why the brass doesn't want us to just apprehend Mr. Al-Sidad after he trades for the flash drive. If he's willing to pay for the information I'd assume we'd be interested in knowing exactly what's on it. Sometimes I don't understand our methods. If we're really trying to keep the bad guys from doing bad things, shouldn't we just put them in jail when we have the chance?

It's at times like this that I begin to question why I don't just get out at twenty and do private security work. I'd have a decent pension and could earn a lot more working security for one of the big banks or pharmaceutical companies. It would be safer and I probably...

My daydreams about the future were put on hold when Mr. Al-Sidad stopped in front of St. Patrick's Cathedral. Ken was directly across the street from him standing on the end of a bus line. I have to admit, he knows how to blend in. I continued to walk on the east side of Fifth, passing within ten feet of Al-Sidad, crossed the side street, and lingered in front of Saks Fifth Avenue like a dozen other window shoppers. I was less than fifty feet from our subject who now seemed content to stand on the cathedral steps. I assumed he was waiting for his friend with the flash drive.

Waiting is usually the toughest part of my job. I'd rather be walking in circles over hot coals than just standing around waiting for something to happen. I get bored quickly. But today, the wait wasn't too bad. It was a beautiful morning, much like the one a few years back when Mr. Al-Sidad's friends flew a couple of planes into the Twin Towers. I was working uptown that morning and can remember seeing the first tower disappear into a cloud of dust as I ran down Vesey Street.

Today I had Mr. Al-Sidad at a disadvantage. From where I stood, I could appear to be looking into the Saks window at a mannequin sporting some sort of expensive jeans, when actually I was watching Al-Sidad in the window's darkened reflection. It's nice to be able to observe someone with your back to them. Ken saw what I was doing and called me on my cell just to bust my chops.

"I see you checking out that mannequin's ass."

"You still waiting for the M-4 Mr. Stallings?"

"I am good buddy. Subject scumbag seems content to bask in the sunshine. How long before you want to switch positions?"

"Let's give it fifteen minutes."

"Okay, but I'll need to take a leak before we switch. I can duck into this building. They've got public restrooms in the lobby."

I could see Ken motioning to the Rockefeller Center building behind him. And he was right. There is a restroom in the lobby. A good street cop knows where they are and Ken spent fifteen years walking a beat for the NYPD before he moved to ATF. I'd bet he knows every public shitter in midtown Manhattan.

Just as I was sticking my cell back in my jacket pocket, I noticed a tall, very attractive woman approaching Mr. Al-Sidad from a cab parked in front of the cathedral. She was tucked tightly into a pair of jeans that looked something like the ones on my mannequin topped off with a gray Columbia University sweatshirt. She looked to be about twenty-five and of middle-eastern descent. As she approached our subject they exchanged a friendly kiss.

My phone rang, "I'm getting this but see if you can get a shot from the side view." Ken had already snapped several shots from across the street but he was right; my view would be better for a facial profile.

One of the nice things about working for the anti-scumbag task force is that the Feds have great toys. The newspaper that was folded under my left arm concealed a state-of-the-art camera that started clicking off three shots per second once I activated it with a remote in my right pocket. Between the two of us, we probably already had fifty shots of Mr. Al-Sidad and his girlfriend thanks to the generosity of the American taxpayer.

Just as our Intel people had predicted, Al-Sidad handed the woman a brown envelope he took from his suit jacket and she handed him a white envelope from her purse. Neither seemed concerned about secrecy. I mean they were standing on the front steps of St. Pat's at high noon with loads of people around.

Within thirty seconds of the exchange, Al-Sidad was walking back up town and the girl with the cash was back in her cab heading down Fifth Avenue. I got a few more good shots of her profile as the cab went by, but didn't get to bust any bad guys. It's frustrating but sometimes you've got to let the little ones get away so you can learn more about the big ones.

I'd call it a productive morning. Kind of routine but not exciting.

It was the last one of those I'd have for a long time.

CHAPTER 8

LT

I had just returned to the 20th floor when I noticed a yellow sticky on the handle of my desk phone. I share an office at Two Penn Plaza with my partner, Ken. Because Ken came from AFT, he had first dibs on a choice of desks and commandeered the larger one right from the start. Mine kind of looked like an afterthought crammed up against the wall to the side of Ken's. The office had no windows but three walls of glass so we both had pretty good views of the rest of the floor and the dozens of desks and cops circling us.

As I said, although I technically outranked Ken, both in seniority and rank, Ken had been assigned to the Joint Task Force (which everyone calls the JTTF) about two weeks before me. And for that reason he's decided he's the alpha dog in the pack and everyone else, including me, is some sort of rookie. It's odd because as I look around the huge expanse of the 20th floor, I see a lot of older guys. I'd guess most have at least twenty years on the job either with the NYPD like me, or with ATF, FBI, or some other nefarious federal agency you don't hear much about. There are even a few women and I for one, are happy to have them around. They're nicer to look at and help keep a lid on this otherwise bubbling cauldron of testosterone we call a unit.

Ken was sitting at his desk peeling an orange. "Who's Terry?"

"What?" I said.

"Somebody took a call for you from a Terry. There's a sticky for you on your phone with her phone number."

"What makes you so sure Terry is a woman? And why are you peaking at my messages asshole?" I really liked Ken Stallings but every so often I needed to bark back to keep his alpha dog thing in check.

"Actually, I don't give a fuck." He was on his feet and tossing the last of his orange peel into the trash can. "We need to see Jacobson down on sixteen as soon as you and your girlfriend catch up. He's putting together a detail for tomorrow and I volunteered the two of us, so meet me down there as soon as you're off the phone."

He was out the door before I could come up with a suitably vulgar response. And it was just as well. I hadn't spoken to Terry in almost ten years. Ken knew I'd been married but never really asked much about it and I never spoke about Terry to him. There just wasn't any point. It was all a long time ago. I was just a kid and Terry was just..., well, Terry was always just way too driven for me.

I wasn't even sure I wanted to return the call. Since the divorce, Terry had only called me twice, and any cop will tell you, when your ex calls, it's usually because they need money or they want to remind you that you ruined their life. I was lucky. Terry's second try at marriage was to a successful Wall Street type, so I should be looking for money from them. Not the other way around. Which meant the call was about something other than money.

I took a seat at my desk and tore the sticky note from my phone. It said, "Call Terry. Urgent. 516-721-8365." The area code made sense because I knew about the three kids and the house out in Lattingtown. I fingered the yellow piece of paper while deciding whether or not to make the call. I just couldn't see anything good coming from it.

But, being a cop, my curiosity got the better of me and I dialed the number and leaned back in my chair.

After the third ring a man answered. "Hello."

"May I speak with Terry, please?" I said. I didn't really care who the man was but he wanted to know who I was.

"Sure. Who's calling?"

"This is LT Hadman. I'm returning Terry's call." I should have added "*What the fuck do you care?*" But I didn't.

In the background I could hear a lot of people talking. It almost sounded like a party; lots of separate conversations, none of which I could make out over the phone. I pictured Terry in a big house with the children and the white picket fence I never wanted. Aside from my career as a cop, it was the argument we had most often; kids. Terry really wanted to have a family and I didn't.

A voice came on the phone. It was softer and more subdued then I remembered but I recognized Terry's voice right away and I could tell something was wrong.

"Thanks for calling back so soon. I wasn't sure if I should call you at all but I thought you'd want to know... my father died." Terry was holding back sobs. "Dad always liked you and I know you liked him, so I thought you should know."

I did like him. He was about the only person on Terry's side of the family that I liked. Jack had a nice way about him and we used to jab at each other about the Mets and Yankees. He was a die-hard Mets fan. I did some quick math in my head and tried to figure out about how old he was. I came up with about seventy.

"I'm sorry to hear that Terry." I heard myself saying. "How old was Jack?"

"He was almost seventy but the last few years he'd been fighting stomach cancer. The end came very fast once it spread from his stomach. Actually, until July, he was feeling pretty good. He'd been in the hospital the last few weeks." It was the voice of someone saddened by the loss of a father and I felt bad for Terry.

So I added, "So how are you doing?" That was a mistake.

As usually happened when we were married, Terry launched into a ten minute monolog about just about everything except the question I'd asked. I heard about the kids, the riding lessons for Brent who I assumed was one of the kids, the new pool house they built because the old one just wasn't big enough, the vacation in Spain they all just got back from, and of course, how well things were going on Wall Street. Terry had left teaching and was now completely devoted to parenthood. Big surprise.

"And how are you doing? Still a cop?"

I thought about saying I'd switched over to neurosurgery but we we're supposed to be talking about a dead father so levity seemed inappropriate. "Yep, still a cop. I'm working with the feds now on a task force that…" I never got to finish.

"Listen sweetie; I have to go but I wanted you to know about dad and to know we're having a funeral tomorrow morning at St. Agnes in Rockville Centre. It starts at 9:30. Just in case you wanted to come."

I was about to make up an excuse for my planned absence when Terry added, "I've got to run. Thanks for calling back. Bye."

And just like that; the person I was married to for a short time so many years ago was gone again.

As it turned out, I wouldn't have been able to go to the funeral anyway. We'd be really busy tomorrow.

CHAPTER 9

LT

After we met with our boss Danny Jacobson, Ken and I took the pictures we'd taken earlier that day up to the tech guys. Because I'd been less than fifty feet from Mr. Al-Sidad when I snapped the shots of him and his girlfriend, I expected the quality of the shots would be excellent. And I was right.

I don't understand the technology behind it, but those tiny cameras sure take great shots. So now the JTTF had several terrific shots of Alec Al-Sidad. Since we already knew all about Alec, it was the woman's face that was of most interest. Within minutes, the digital image readers had matched her picture to the name Sara Miller, a second year law student at NYU. It seems Ms. Miller had spent the last two summers working in sandland for some oil company and made a lot of friends with guys we would, but for the U.S. constitution, like to kill. Apparently, she'd become some sort of currier for the scumbags. I hate it when otherwise solid citizens start helping the scumbags. They do it for the money, of course.

Oh, they'll tell you they buy into the fundamentalist bullshit, but at the end of the day, it's about the money.

Chief Jacobson had briefed Ken and me along with a few other agents, about a demonstration that was planned for tomorrow at the UN. It was another opportunity for us to use our photography skills and try to get some shots of KA's. A KA is a "known associate" which means if you stand too close to one of the scumbags or say something to one of them, we want your picture. That's how you become a known associate and that's why we have thousands of potential bad guys here in New York. So when I came to the JTTF I had to unlearn a lot of what I'd learned while on the NYPD payroll. For example; in the real world, you're innocent until proven guilty, but in the post 9-11 world, just standing next to someone at a rally can get your name up on the wall. And about half the time, the boys and girls up on the wall do turn out to be scumbags.

Since we needed to be back on the job at seven A.M. for the demonstration detail, we knocked off a little early and grabbed a beer at our favorite watering hole, a place called Vinny's. It was too early for dinner, and Ken's wife had dinner waiting for him at home anyway, so we just ordered a couple of Stellas and a bowl of nuts. This was sort of a routine for Ken and me. He wouldn't agree, but I think sometimes we come to Vinney's because we need to unwind, but other times it's because Ken's in no hurry to get home and I'm in no hurry to get back to an empty apartment. He's always told me his marriage is solid, but that's not what his face tells me. His kids are grown and on their own and he and Sue spend a lot of time watching HGTV instead of dealing with the eight hundred pound gorilla in the room- the fact that they don't really like each other anymore.

"So who's Terry?" He wasn't in the booth thirty seconds before asking.

"If you must know, Terry's my ex. Until today, we hadn't spoken in about ten years."

"So why the sudden interest again? You miss an alimony payment?"

"No. Dead father. Can we talk about something else?" I really didn't want to get into my marriage with Ken. It was a long time ago. He didn't know me when I was married, so why go through it all?

"Oh, sorry." He seemed to be taken back by my comment. Or maybe it was my tone.

"It's okay. He was a nice guy. Big Mets fan. Died of cancer at seventy. Probably never regretted a day of his life." I hoped that was enough to satisfy my partner and end the conversation. I was wrong.

"You going to the funeral?"

"No. We drifted apart a long time ago. Shit, I've been divorced for almost twenty years now. Terry's got a whole different life now; married to some sort of banker, three kids, big house out on Long Island. It's not my place."

To my surprise, Ken didn't ask any follow-up questions. That was unusual. Like any good cop, he liked to poke and prod until he got what he was looking for. Tonight, he was sort of pensive. I used his silence to switch subjects.

"So I've got ten bucks that says we see that kid Sara Miller again in the next few months."

"I'd put twenty in the same direction. You know what they say. Once they get a taste of that middle-eastern cock, there's no going back to the local stuff." Ken was very philosophical. But he was probably right. If my twenty years on the job have taught me anything it's that the most dangerous criminal is not the one trying to steal your wallet. It's the idealist who wants you to see their point. Young kids like Sara Miller can be very dangerous precisely because of their passion. They honestly believe in their cause and they believe we all should too. That's usually when it gets messy.

Ken and I sat at the bar for nearly fifteen minutes in near silence. Actually, we were both listening to the Willy Nelson songs someone had paid the juke box to sing for us. Vinney's has one of those old fashion juke boxes with the glass dome and real vinyl records that are transported from the rack to the turntable by a mechanical arm. It's full of great music from the fifties and sixties. Classics from Elvis Presley, Ricky Nelson, Neil Diamond, and groups like the Beach Boys, Righteous Brothers, and even a few country-western groups. What it didn't have was anything I'd call hard rock or anything by an artist not born in the United States. Seems Vinney didn't care for the British invasion, which suited me fine.

I noticed my partner was more pensive than usual. Normally, he'd talk or shout over the music, the bar-room chatter, or even the TV that hung over the bar. Ken didn't let the noise of others keep him from making some of his own even when that led to a painful cacophony for the rest of us. But tonight he was just staring at his beer, turning the bottle slowly in his hands and looking straight through it to whatever was on his mind.

I figured I'd offer to let him unload; not because I had some prurient curiosity, but because it's what partners do. Sometimes your partner is the only guy you can turn to when there's something you can't talk about with anyone else. We're expected to be each other's confessors and often the barstool serves as the confessional. So I gave Ken a supportive and nurturing opening.

"So what's eating you, asshole?" I'm not a nurturer.

He fidgeted on his seat then swiveled towards me. Ken finished his beer with one long swig, put the bottle down on the bar, and put his right hand on my shoulder. "LT my friend, don't ever get married again. It's just too painful."

"I learned that after less than a year of marriage. It took you twenty-three to figure that out?" I didn't know what else to say.

"No. That's just it. I think we both figured it out a few years ago but we've been afraid to deal with it." He shook his head.

"Deal with what?"

Ken pointed at the bartender, a young kid from Galway, Ireland, and signaled for two more Stellas. He waited for them to arrive before continuing. "That's just it. I'm not sure what it is. It's like we're both bored to death. Now that Kelly's in college it seems like we have nothing to talk about. I mean we'll sit through an entire dinner and not say a word. And it's not like we're angry about something. We're just bored. Is that supposed to happen?" He looked at me with a sadness I hadn't seen in Ken before.

"I don't know buddy. I wasn't married long enough to get bored. With us it was..." I stopped in mid-sentence because I knew he didn't want to hear about my torture. He needed to do the talking, so I needed to either shut up or ask questions. My stories about my past weren't going to help Ken. So I asked a really stupid question. "You think she's fucking around?"

"No and neither am I. It's just that there's this numbness. We go through the motions. We peacefully coexist, but this can't go on for long."

"Have you talked about it? I mean with each other?"

"No. I think we're both afraid of where that conversation could go."

"What do you mean?" I honestly wanted to know.

"I mean, once we talk about it, we have to deal with it."

"Yeah. Isn't that a good thing?"

"Maybe. But it could also force us to recognize that maybe we shouldn't stay together. I don't know. I just wish things were the way they used to be."

"But at some point you've gotta talk to her about it. You gotta let her know how you feel. Otherwise, she's guessing. And for that matter, so are you." I pointed my beer bottle at his chest. "You gotta have the balls to ask the tough question."

"What question?"

"You need to ask her if she wants to try; if she wants things back the way they used to be too. If she doesn't, then you're fucked. But if she does, then you have something to work on."

That actually sounded like good advice and I was a little surprised it came from my mouth. Giving other people advice, especially advice about marriage, is something I steer clear of. But this time I came up with something Ken seemed to be rolling around in his head. Hey, everybody's lucky once in a while.

After a few thoughtful minutes Ken said, "You're probably right. I'm just scared to death that she says it's not worth saving. That'd really hurt. I've never thought about being single again."

"Hey. You're a long way from single again. You guys are going through what most couples go through at some point. You look over at that stranger laying next to you in bed and think about seeing only that stupid, drooling face the rest of your life. It's scary shit. But it's not unusual."

"Maybe. I hope to hell you're right." Ken finished his third beer, then said, "LT, I don't know what I'd do without Sue. I don't want to lose her."

I wanted to do or say something to make him see the world a little more clearly. I mean I haven't been partnered with Ken for very long but I've never seen him like this. He was nearly crying when he said he didn't want to lose her. I'd only met Sue a couple of times but on appearances, they seemed perfect together. She's a nice looking lady; about three years younger than Ken and probably wearing a few more pounds then when they married, but still classically pretty. She didn't look like the cheating type. But what the hell do I know?

The mood needed to be lightened so I decided to tell Ken about a woman I knew from my old precinct that would make Sue seem like an angel in comparison. She was a lawyer in the DA's office and married to a guy who owned a bunch of Burger Kings. The husband had lots of dough and didn't want Colleen (that was her name, Colleen McCoy) working. But she loved the work and sometime after their third kid, told the husband she was in it for the full twenty.

"So he tells her if she doesn't leave the job to stay home with the kids, he's leaving and taking the kids with him. This Colleen was a looker, a cute little Irish thing, but she wasn't going to let the husband, I forget his name... she wasn't going to let him push her around, even if he did control the dough."

Ken seemed to forget his domestic trouble for a moment, so I continued. "So things must get pretty chilly at home and after a while, Colleen finds out the husband's been banging his twenty year-old secretary for over a year. She throws him out and he gets some hotshot lawyer and before you know it he files for divorce and wants to take the kids. Like he'd ever get them."

Ken motioned for the kid from Galway to bring us two more, so I went on. "The divorce thing drags on and it looks like it's going to take forever and cost her more than she could afford because now he's giving her just enough to keep the kids fed. Meanwhile he moves onto his sixty foot Bertram with the secretary and is living the dream. The prick had a box at Shea and one at the Meadowlands and he's making her sweat."

"So one day, just before the divorce goes to trial, it's the oldest kid's birthday and they decide to bury the hatchet for one night and take the kids out for pizza; you know, as a family. Now I wouldn't believe the next part except that Colleen told me this herself. So she and the husband Brian- that's his name, Brian. So they're sitting having pizza with the three kids at some Pizza Hut out on Long Island celebrating junior's birthday and Colleen notices her soon-to-be-ex-husband is choking on a glob of cheese from the pizza. He's turning blue at the table and grabbing his throat. No one in the restaurant can see this because his back is to them but Colleen sees it and she just crosses her arms and looks at him. She's thinking she'd be a lot better off as a widow than as a divorcee. And the kids are right there watching their father choke to death but they're kids and they really don't know what's going on yet."

"She sits there for more than two minutes letting the poor schmuck choke until he passes out, face down into the pizza. All the while Colleen's doing a mental balance sheet to determine if there's any possible way she's better off with the guy alive. She told me. She said she actually realized that she had her hands positioned in front of her like a scale as she weighed the options. That was probably the last thing Brian saw before he blacked out."

"So she lets the guy die?" Ken said incredulously.

I waited a moment for effect, then said, "No. And here's where I need to use her words exactly. She says, and I quote, "*Some pain-in-the-ass good Samaritan comes along from the kitchen, sees the prick face down in the pizza, and gives him the Heimlich. A piece of mozzarella the size of a golf ball flies out of his stupid fucking mouth and hits me in the chest. What an asshole.*"

"Now that's one nasty bitch." Ken said putting emphasis on each of the last three words.

We had two more Stellas and two chasers before Ken went home to Sue and me to my lonely apartment. After the story of Colleen McCoy, both looked a lot better than they had an hour ago.

CHAPTER 10

O'Connell's Funeral Home is snuggled between a savings bank and a Korean deli on the main street in Valley Stream. The white stucco building has been run by members of the O'Connell family for over sixty years and has served the mostly middle-class community with a place to grieve. Jimmy O'Connell started the business right after he returned from fighting the Germans in Italy. His sons took over in the sixties when Jimmy's knees could no longer stand the long days required of a mortician. They still own the business but are seldom seen in the building anymore. The current proprietor, Jimmy's grandson Frank, runs the day-to-day and is usually the one to counsel the grieving families and help them arrange a proper sendoff for their loved ones.

Tonight Frank was overseeing the Saccenti viewing. Not that there was much to do while a wake was in session, but Frank always made his presence known to the guests by sitting at the large mahogany desk in the entrance foyer. From there he could greet everyone who came in the front door and offer a sober and respectful welcome.

The past few hours had been unpleasant, even for an undertaker. Judy Saccenti, the deceased, was a fourteen year old girl from the neighborhood who made the fatal mistake of stepping in front of a Pontiac driven by someone who'd just robbed a convenience store and was speeding down Judy's street. The impact of the collision threw the child forty feet into a stone wall surrounding a neighbor's property. She died from the head injuries on the way to the hospital. The driver never stopped.

In his many years in the business, Frank never got used to the reality of dead children. They caused so much pain to those left behind. In this case, the parents and sisters of the deceased were devastated. The girl's mother sobbed through the three hour wake to the point where Frank felt the need to bring her a glass of ice-water for fear of dehydration. And the father, only a few years younger than Frank himself, collapsed in front of his remaining daughters when he saw his precious Judy lying in a white casket.

Throughout the night, Frank had been needed to assist one person or another. Especially vulnerable to fainting episodes were the classmates; kids who, in many cases, had never been in a funeral home before and were unprepared for the spectacle. Tonight, the room was filled with high school kids. Many were openly crying, most just stood around in stunned silence until Father Corero came to say a few prayers.

After the priest left, the place was completely without sound for several minutes. Many took the quiet as their cue to begin filing out, everyone saying a farewell to Judy's parents and promising to see them in church the next morning for the funeral mass. By ten o'clock, only the immediate family remained and, as usual, Frank had to prod them toward the exit with comforting words. This was the second and final night of viewing and the parents lingered just a few extra moments to say one last good night to their daughter while Frank escorted Judy's sisters to the front door.

He glanced back to see the young mother weeping as she kissed her daughter's forehead. The father had to pull his wife away from the small casket. Frank thought about the pain they must feel and how he would feel if it was his daughter lying there. The image was too painful to conjure and he turned his attention back to the two young girls by the door.

"Please make sure you're all here at 9:15 in the morning. We'll have a short time to say our goodbyes to Judy before we need to leave for the church. The mass starts at ten."

The parents of the dead girl joined them at the doorway.

"Frank, you've been so wonderful," the mother said through her sobs.

Then he gave them his usual sendoff. "Try to get a good night's sleep. Tomorrow's going to be a long and difficult day. I'll be here early if you want to sit with Judy in the morning but make sure you're here by 9:15."

What was left of the Saccenti family slowly shuffled through the door and out to their car. Frank locked the front door from the inside then went into the viewing room to straighten up the chairs and inspect the carpeting. When there were large crowds, the carpets needed vacuuming between sessions. He wheeled the vacuum from a hall closet and began cleaning. As he did he glanced over at the lifeless body lying just a few feet away. Judy died from swelling within her skull but you'd never know it from the peaceful look on her face. Frank admired his craftsmanship. He'd done a good job, using just enough makeup to hide the bruises on her face and hands, but not too much. After all, she was only fourteen.

By eleven o'clock he was finished with the cleaning and some leftover paperwork. He needed to be back in the morning by eight, just in case the deceased needed any last minute touch up work. He was looking forward to getting home and hoped his wife had saved him some of the dessert he didn't have time for earlier. He switched off the lights and exited through the back door that led to the parking lot in the rear of the building.

Frank O'Connell drove home without noticing the white van parked in the rear of the lot. A few moments later, the van pulled up to the back door of his funeral home. Two men and a woman emerged from the van and stood in the darkness. They waited to be sure no one was around to witness their nefarious activities.

⟩⟨⟩

The next morning, Frank O'Connell arrived just before eight. The sun was already shining brightly and it looked to be an unusually warm day for mid-September. It was always better to have a sunny morning for a funeral. If the Saccenti family had to bury their daughter today, at least God could give them a break as they gathered around the grave. At least that's the way Frank saw it.

When he arrived at the rear door he could tell immediately that the door had been pried open. The wooden frame had been crushed by some sort of wedge and the door was ajar a few inches.

He quietly pushed the door open all the way and could see down the center hallway. If it hadn't been such a beautiful morning he might have been more concerned that the intruders were still inside. But emboldened by the bright daylight, Frank slowly entered his building.

He flicked on the main panel of lights. No sound.

An umbrella stand stood next to the door and Frank reached for an umbrella as a potential weapon. He walked down the center hall, listening for any sounds.

There were none.

Then he went to the right, into his office.

No one there. Nothing seemed out of place.

He checked the closets to be sure no one was hiding.

Nothing.

He stuck his head into the viewing room across the hall. No one there. Not a flower or chair out of position. Then he went down stairs, to where the embalming room and casket display room were. This is where he expected to find whatever vandalism had been done. Once before, about two years ago, someone had broken in and stolen some tools before trashing the casket room.

But everything seemed to be in order.

Convinced that nothing was missing, his attention turned to the upcoming funeral. He needed to be sure there was no damage anywhere upstairs that would be noticed by the Saccenti family. They had enough to deal with today.

Satisfied that nothing had been stolen or vandalized, Frank focused on some quick mending of the damaged door frame. The Saccenti family would be arriving soon and if he could prop the door open, as if to say "*welcome*", they'd probably never notice the splintered wood. They'd have other things on their mind today.

With the back door held open by the umbrella stand, Frank debated whether he should call the police to at least file a report of the break-in. He knew his insurance company would have to be notified but decided to wait until he returned from the cemetery to make those calls.

He needed to check on the deceased's makeup before her family arrived. If any touch-ups were necessary he'd have time to make them. It was just past eight A.M.

When he entered the viewing room and looked at the white casket across the room, the sight knocked the breath from him.

"Oh God! Oh no!" He raced to the casket.

The casket was empty. Judy Saccenti was gone.

CHAPTER 11

For the third time in as many days, Billy Simon sipped his coffee and waited. The outdoor tables in front of the Starbuck's on 83rd Street gave him a great vantage point from which to watch his future prey. The past two mornings had given him all the information he needed. Today was just to be sure he hadn't missed something.

From his seat at the round metal table, Billy could see across Second Avenue to the corner where three young girls waited for their school bus. They were dressed alike in white blouses and green-plaid pleated skirts, green knee-high socks and brown loafers. Billy guessed they were all about fourteen years old. He knew for certain that Mary Jane Wallace, the tallest of the three, turned fourteen a few weeks ago. They looked like any other three girls waiting for the bus to private junior high school on a Wednesday morning.

But there was nothing ordinary about these girls. They were among an elite group of privileged and talented children who attended the Freemen Academy on Long Island. Each day, small buses like the one that would soon be arriving for Mary Jane and her friends, would ferry some of Manhattan's most fortunate children to Oyster Bay where they would pass through the huge iron gates that hide the Freemen Academy from the outside world.

The academy, founded in 1842 by Marcus Freemen, a grandson of Nathan Hale, is set on forty acres of Oyster Bay's most sought-after property overlooking the Long Island Sound. Much of the land is rolling fields of grass used by its students specializing in equestrian interests; primarily show jumping and dressage. At the center of the property and perched on its highest point, sits a spectacular fieldstone building. Once the home of Marcus Freeman, the elegant estate fell into disrepair in the early twentieth century but was restored beyond its original glory by a philanthropic New York banker who then donated the building and most of the land to Nassau County with the provision it be used only for education. After a few years, the county realized it could not justify the cost of maintaining such an estate and sold it to the Freemen Academy.

Since then, the school has served as an oasis for young women who possess two rare qualities. First, the student must demonstrate unusual talent in music; either playing a classical instrument, writing new music or exceptional vocal skills. The second rare quality the student must possess is the good fortune to have been born into a family that can afford the $60,000 annual tuition.

Most of the school's two hundred students commute from Manhattan or Long Island's affluent suburbs. A few, from more distant origins, board in some of the main building's twenty bedrooms. Each morning, dozens of small school buses pass through the magnificent fronts gates delivering from one to ten young women. The buses are privately arranged by the students' parents.

This morning, Billy was interested in only one bus; the one Mary Jane was waiting for. He knew from his prior recon work, and confirmed earlier this week, that it was driven by a sixty-eight year old black man named Davis. He knew Davis would pick up the three girls on this corner sometime in the next few minutes, then proceed south and pick up one more girl on 55th Street before heading for the Queens-Midtown tunnel. He assumed the parents of the four lucky kids were splitting the cost of the private transportation, and he couldn't help but smile at the thought of his own trip to junior high, back in Topeka. He used to walk two miles to get to the road where the school bus would pick him up for the dusty, bumpy ninety-minute ride to East Topeka Middle School.

Billy leaned back on his chair and brought his digital camera to his face. He zoomed in to get a good look at Mary Jane, pleased to find she was wearing the same necklace as on previous mornings. It was a simple silver chain with a quarter-size medallion. Only because he'd snapped a picture of the locket yesterday, and enlarged the image on a computer at the library, did he know the inscription read "MJW". He thought about how much help a trinket like that would be to the police. At least they'd have something to help identify the body.

The short yellow bus pulled up to the curb next to the girls and Billy could tell that Davis had said something to them as the three boarded the steps and took their seats. Billy was too far to hear the words but it didn't matter. They each took the seats they'd taken the past two mornings. Mary Jane was in the first seat on the passenger side of the bus. The other nameless teens sat a row or two behind Davis.

"It was perfect," Billy almost said aloud.

He finished his coffee as the bus turned left and headed down Second Avenue. It was a pleasant morning. People were walking by briskly on their way to work. Traffic crawled along at its usual pace. There were even a few birds chirping in the small trees outside the coffee shop.

He thought about how different everything would be in twenty-five hours.

CHAPTER 12

Family and friends began arriving at 8:45 AM. The airy and bright Catholic Church was about half filled but even half full, between family and classmates, there were over three hundred people in the pews. In happier days the church of the Blessed Sacrament had been witness to Judy Saccenti's baptism, first communion and, just a few months ago, her confirmation. Today her relatives and friends were gathered to share in yet one last sacrament.

It was now after ten and the crowd had begun to buzz with conjecture about why the funeral procession was so late. Most assumed the family's final farewell at O'Connell's, just a few blocks away, had been painful. After all, she was just a child.

Earlier, as the church was filling, passing sirens were heard in the distance. Several of the mourners, mostly fathers of girls Judy's age and local volunteer firemen, checked their smart phones to see if the sirens represented an incident to which they needed to respond. Nothing appeared on the tiny screens but several minutes later, more sirens could be heard through the tall stained glass windows flanking Blessed Sacrament. Satisfied that the sirens represented a police action- and not a fire or recue event which would have required their prompt departure, most of the men returned their attention to the young priest and two female alter-servers patiently waiting at the front of the church.

But Bob Morrissey, a retired chief in the Valley Stream Fire Department, leaned over to his granddaughter, one of Judy's classmates, and whispered, "I'll be right back honey. I just need to see what this is." His granddaughter was accustomed to him racing from family dinners to answer calls. He'd even bolted from his niece's wedding last year when a call came that indicated an *"elderly man having chest pains"*.

But it was the address, not the signal that stirred Bob from his pew. After living in Valley Stream for most of his life, he recognized the address in the text message, 121 Central Avenue, as O'Connell's Funeral Home. As he walked toward the back of the church his assumption was that someone in the Saccenti family had collapsed at the funeral home, requiring an ambulance. He'd been on hundreds of similar calls during his forty years in the fire department; a grieving window, mother or sister is overcome with emotion and faints, causing quite a stir for everyone around. Usually, by the time the ambulance would arrive, the person was sitting in a chair and, purely as a precaution; the EMT's would transport them to the hospital for a quick evaluation and release.

Bob Morrissey stepped out of the church and into the bright September morning. It was going to be a beautiful day he thought; sunny and crisp but warm enough to remind you summer hadn't yet officially ended. He stood at the top of the steps looking out on the adjacent church property. There was a large convent, now used as some sort of group home. The nuns who once filled its sixteen bedrooms had long since fled. To the right was the elementary school- also recently shuttered due to lack of students, and a large rectory that used to house several parish priests. Now there was just one.

He reflected on his many years in the community. He and his neighbors had built all these buildings; not so much with their hands as with their pledges and fundraising efforts. They built them so their children would have a church and a school, never expecting that by the time his grandchildren were old enough to take their turn, the neighborhood would have changed so dramatically. What was once a growing, youthful community of teachers, cops and firemen moving from the city to the potato fields-turned-suburbs, was now yielding to the next generation of lower middle-class people migrating eastward, away from the city, in search of the American dream. As the predominantly Irish Catholic community grew old and moved away, Asian and Indian professionals took their places, and everything changed. The bakery now catered more to the tastes of the new residents and less to the "After Sunday morning Mass" crowd of years gone by. Even the barber shop and grocery stores were different.

Bob had always envisioned growing old in his life-long town; watching his grandchildren play on the rope-swing he'd strategically placed in his back yard, and someday leaving his modest home to his three daughters. But as his friends departed for Florida and others died off, he found himself increasingly alone in his hometown. His oldest daughters had followed the careers of their husbands to Washington and Chicago so his only grandchild left in Valley Stream was Amy, who he'd just left in church, sobbing over her best friend.

The thought of Judy Saccenti stirred him back to the present. The poor thing was just a kid, a freshman in high school. The bastard who drove his car into her tiny body didn't even stop and, so far, the police had few leads as to his identity. All they knew was that it was a white van of some sort. That was the only description a passer-by was able to offer. Things like this just didn't happen in Valley Stream. Not in the old days anyway.

From the top of the church steps, he checked his phone one more time to see if there had been any other signals in the last few minutes. Nothing. The last call had been a signal 10 which simply told him the police had been summoned to the scene. He considered treating himself to a cigarette and waiting out there until the funeral procession eventually showed up, but before he could light up, he spotted a police patrol car turn the corner and pull up in front of the church.

Bob recognized the officer even before the car came to a halt. It was Billy Wilbur, a senior- level guy who had no business driving a patrol car. Billy had over twenty-five years on the force and had been a gold-shield detective and in plain clothes for the last ten. In fact, Bob could see through the car window that Billy was in street clothes today. It didn't make sense that he'd be driving a patrol car.

When Billy stepped out of the car and saw Bob Morrissey on the church steps, his head dropped. The two men knew each other professionally- in his capacity as fire chief Bob had worked with Billy at many scenes, and personally- their daughters played soccer and softball on the same school teams. So it seemed odd to Bob that Billy would be shaking his head as he approached.

"I saw the call. What's going on at O'Connell's?" Bob asked as the two men shook hands.

Billy took off his sunglasses and looked directly at his friend. "There ain't going to be a funeral today Bob. They sent me over here to tell everyone to go home. The funeral's been postponed."

"Postponed? What the hell does that mean? You don't postpone a funeral."

"I'm afraid in this case you do." He seemed to be clearing something from inside his mouth, then continued, "Seems there was a break-in last night at O'Connell's. They took the body."

"What?" Bob muttered incredulously.

"You heard me. Someone stole that poor kid's body. Frank O'Connell came in this morning and discovered it missing. And it appears to be the only thing missing. He called us right away but by the time we got there, the Saccentis were already arriving. They got a big family you know. The kid's mother freaked out. We had to take her to the hospital. She was having trouble breathing- not that I blame her."

"Why the hell does anyone steal a body?"

"I have no idea." Then he added, "But there must be a reason."

CHAPTER 13

Christina and Andy Meinen had just walked out of the theater and into a crisp September-in-New York evening. The fresh air felt good after sitting in the crowded theater for three hours watching Phantom of the Opera. Christina couldn't get the haunting melodies out of her head.

"How about a nightcap? I know a great bar down in Chelsea that shouldn't be crowded on a weeknight." Andy offered.

"And just how do you know about this bar?" His wife of twenty-eight years wanted to know.

"It's where I take all my dates; especially the ones that seem easy." He joked.

In the cab on the way downtown Christina said, "Wasn't it nice of the kids to get us those tickets for our anniversary? They're so thoughtful."

Andy knew darn well that his three sons had little to do with the decision to get them play tickets. Their wives were obviously in charge of this gift. But he said, "Yep, they're good kids."

The taxi let them off in front of Vinny's and the Meinen's took a small table near the door. The bar was dark but Andy could see a few people were sitting at the far end of the bar, way in the back. He thought about suggesting they take a place at the bar, but changed his mind when he spotted one particular bar patron sitting with a very attractive blonde woman.

"Honey, guess who's sitting at the bar with a hot young number?"

Christina turned her chair to get a better look. "Oh my god, that's Ken Stallings. We should go say hello. We haven't seen them in years."

Christina and Andy had lived on the same street as Ken and Sue Stallings until a few years back when the Meinens moved to New Jersey. They'd been good friends; they used to play tennis together once a month and shared a lot of the same friends. But after the move, they drifted apart. Christina talked to Sue every few months but mostly the conversation focused on their children. The youngest Stallings daughter, Kelly, had once dated one of the Meinen boys.

"Let's go say hello." Christina was already on her feet when Andy grabbed her by the arm and maneuvered her back into her seat.

"That may not be a good idea. That's not Sue he's with." Andy said.

"Oh my god, you're right. You know, I heard they were having troubles. I wonder if they're still together."

"Well, apparently, Ken has moved on with or without Sue's knowledge. And by the looks of things, he's done pretty well."

They both eyed the woman sitting with Ken. Their bar stools were very close and her hand was on his arm as they spoke. She was considerably younger than Ken, very shapely with long blonde hair pulled back in a ponytail. She wore a navy blue pleated skirt and a pale blue blouse which, in Christina's view, had too many buttons opened.

"So this is what you bastards do when our backs are turned?" Christina joked.

"How do you know Sue's back is turned? They could be divorced for all we know."

"No way. I would have heard something."

"You said you heard they were having trouble. Maybe the trouble was that Ken was coming home with long blonde hair on his clothes."

Christina gave the blonde a closer look. "She looks slutty. And how could he go with someone so much younger? He's no Don Juan you know."

"How do you know she isn't just his accountant?"

"At eleven forty-five at night? With her hands all over him?"

"Chrissy, come on. You don't know anything."

"I know that I'm going to call Sue Stallings tomorrow and see how things are going.

"Don't you dare say anything about seeing Ken here tonight."

"You men are all alike."

CHAPTER 14

"This size is good." The man in the "I Love New York" tee shirt didn't seem to want to devote much time to his decision. He'd only been at the Ryder truck rental office for a few minutes and had already picked out the vehicle he needed.

The young woman behind the counter was already writing up the order. Jackie, as her name plate indicated, was happy to help. In fact, she thought her client was cute, in a rough sort of way. His short reddish hair and three-day beard made him resemble those guys in the outdoorsy magazines who just climbed down from a mountain or hauled their canoe from a rushing stream. He looked like the all-American boy next door; the ones that twenty-four year old all-American girls wanted to find out more about.

"So, I need you to fill this out for me," she said sliding the lengthy rental form across the counter.

Billy gave her a big smile and his puppy-dog eyes. "I'm sorry. I forgot my reading glasses at my apartment. Could you possibly fill it out for me if I give you the answers?" He smiled again. His smile said, "*Please*" in a flirtatious way.

There was no one else in the small office and Jackie was happy to engage the handsome guy in some flirting of her own so she turned the form back in her direction and leaned on the counter making sure the cleavage this created was evident to her customer.

"Okay. Let's start with first name of the renter."

Billy had no intention of giving any legitimate information and had the forged credentials to support his alias. "John." He said. Then added, "It's nice to meet you Jackie."

Jackie pretended not to notice his soft tone. "Last name?"

"Williams."

"Home address?"

"Here's my driver's license." He offered her the card from his wallet. "This should save you some time. Not that I don't like the sound of your voice." He made sure she noticed him looking at her. "And here's my credit card. We'll need both trucks the day after tomorrow for two days. We can have them back by five in the afternoon."

The truth was that neither truck would be coming back. Ever. Although he expected that in the days to come, Jackie would be getting a lot of attention from the FBI about the guy who rented the trucks. But it didn't matter. By then Billy would be twelve hundred miles away.

"Who will the other driver be? I'll need to have his license as well."

Billy had anticipated the request and was already pulling the photocopy of *Mark Hassberg's* license from his shirt pocket. "He's my partner. We need to get a shit load of flowers out to a wedding in Riverhead on Wednesday and both my usual trucks are in the shop.

"You're a florist?"

"I love flowers." It was probably the only truthful thing Billy said since walking into the tiny office.

"I do too." She said before a long silent pause made them both realize they were staring at each other.

"Um, which size did you need again?"

"The fourteen foot should be fine. If we have two we'll be fine."

"You know you could take a bigger truck and then maybe you'd only need one." Jackie was trying to be helpful. After all, her name plate said she was "*Jackie. Let me help.*"

Billy hadn't anticipated this question and, for a moment, was flustered. He didn't like to be flustered. He'd put too much careful planning into this. He didn't need a bimbo from Queens to throw a wrench into his schedule or his operation. He quickly recovered.

"No. We'll need to make separate pickups. We need two trucks." Again he smiled.

Jackie spent less than ten minutes filling out the form, then had to do it all over again for the second vehicle. When she was through she slid them across the counter and asked Billy to, "Sign here and here."

He did so, making sure to use his left hand and not to touch any part of the form or the counter. When Jackie reached for a stapler to secure the forms together, Billy pocketed the pen. The Feds would have to really get cleaver if they were going to find any of his fingerprints anywhere in this crumby little office. The only security camera was focused on the front door and Billy had made a point of entering from the rear as he would on Tuesday when they came for the trucks.

"Will you be working Tuesday morning when we pick up the trucks?" He asked.

Jackie rolled her eyes up to the ceiling trying to visualize her schedule for the week. "Yep, I'll be here."

Billy was about to leave when Jackie had one more question.

"Mr. Williams, do you want to prepay for the gas or return the vehicles with the tanks full?"

Billy thought for a moment and a wicked smile crossed his face.

"I'll make sure they're full Jackie. You can count on that."

CHAPTER 15

The pigeon pecked at the pavement near Billy's feet. A black woman who'd been sitting on the bench just before Billy arrived had thrown the last of her popcorn to the hungry birds before walking back to work. Billy sat at the base of Battery Park looking out at the Statue of Liberty in the distant harbor. It was a place he often came to think. The pigeons didn't seem to mind.

Since leaving Panama City, this was one of the few places that gave him inspiration. Maybe it was the majestic statue itself; maybe it was the throngs of New Yorkers going about their business as if nothing had happened just a few blocks from where he sat. Maybe it was the newly finished Freedom Tower, which cast its significant shadow on the ever-cascading twin memorials. Maybe it was just the combination of all the reminders. Something terrible had happened here and Americans seemed content to forgive and forget, to move on with their self-absorbed lives. It made him sick.

What really pissed him off was that since the events of September 11, 2001, it seemed to him, the only thing that had really changed in America was that Americans had lost the freedom they claimed to cherish. He was sitting about two hundred feet from the entrance to the ferry that shuttles people to and from Liberty Island, the National Park that is home to the statue. There were several hundred people waiting on line to board the next ferry. But before they could take a simple ten minute ferry ride, they were herded through the same security screening as had become the norm at America's airports. Elderly people forced to empty their pockets and take off their shoes and belts. Women with baby strollers asked to remove the child from the stroller so a National Parks Ranger could make his inspection. And groups of children, obviously on some sort of class trip to our symbol of liberty, having their bagged lunches x-rayed.

It occurred to Billy that the enemy had actually won. If what they really intended was to instill terror into the hearts of Americans, they were successful beyond their wildest dreams because the U.S. government was now constantly harassing its citizens. It wasn't any potential terrorist who was being inconvenienced by all the extra security at our airports, stadiums, and parks; they weren't the ones waiting passively on the lines to be humiliated. No, the people suffering through the dehumanizing treatment were the law-abiding Americans who were just trying to visit grandma, see a Yankee game or take a tour of the Capitol. This incensed him.

And what made him absolutely insane was when the TSA worker or security guy checking him over was of Middle Eastern descent. It was as if the insane were running the asylum in Billy's mind. America had just bent over and kissed the collective asses of those who'd fucked us- the people he was sent to Afghanistan to kill. In

Afghanistan they were the enemy, but here in America they were the guys telling you to empty your pockets and remove your laptop.

Billy gained resolve from his visits to this park and the constant reminder that America, his country, had gone astray. Seeing the lines of people waiting to board the ferry made him more certain that what he was about to do was noble. America needed to be reminded of the enemy. It had grown complacent and fat and sloppy. He was sure this would not have happened in any other generation. After the Pearl Harbor attack, America knew what to do with the Japanese living in our country. They were either imprisoned or kept under very close surveillance. No one used the words "racial profiling". We just did what had to be done. And within five years, we crushed that enemy. He was convinced what he was about to do would turn things around; put his country back on the right track.

And so he would come to this place to confirm his commitment. He'd done it many times. Today was a day for reflection; a day to review his mission one more time. He needed to be sure he'd thought of everything.

He reflected on the farmer in Vermont who'd sold him the chemicals. He thought about the drive up from Florida with the crates of ball bearings and metal shards he'd stolen from his last legitimate employer and the six boxes of C-4 Camp LaMarc would never know were missing. He thought about all the five-gallon cans of gasoline he and the boys had been accumulating the last two weeks; the cars and vans they'd rented using the bogus credit cards Nasi was able to easily obtain from his friends, the ones Billy was never allowed to meet; and about all the old, pre-GPS cell phones he'd had to buy with his fake ID. He thought about the pretty girl behind the counter at the Ryder Truck rental office and how she might feel in a few days when the police questioned her about him.

And he thought about Carol and her cock sucking, capitalist husband living in a penthouse on the Upper East Side, and how much they'd be hurt tomorrow. He wished there was some way he could see their faces when they hear about the tunnel explosion. He wished there could be a video camera at the morgue when they had to identify the charred corpse they'd assume was their daughter. He wanted to see their pain but felt solace knowing that their pain would get even worse.

He didn't want to merely hurt Carol for what she'd done to him. He wanted to destroy the plastic life she and Alan shared; the life they'd bought. Carol had abandoned Billy because she saw a shiny trinket dangling in front of her when Billy had none to offer. Instead of standing by her man, a man who was protecting his country and putting his life on the line every day, she chose the prick with the tasseled shoes; the guy who could make her life easy. Well, life isn't easy. Life is hard.

Billy was committed to his mission. If a few dozen bystanders had to die, it was minor collateral damage. There was a greater good that needed to happen and Billy was determined to be the instrument of America's reawakening. After tomorrow there would be no doubt about who America was at war with. After tomorrow, everyone would know that the remnants of Bin Landen's army were alive and well walking the streets and cities of America. He recalled how easy it had been to find them.

Billy glanced down at the pigeon that had now moved under the park bench to retrieve the last of the popcorn. A few small kernels had blown against his right foot and the hungry bird was debating the wisdom of approaching any closer. Billy reached down and retrieved the last few pieces. He ground them in his fist then gently held out his hand with the reconstituted feed so the bird would see it. The pigeon backed off at first but soon made a few movements toward the outstretched offering. Billy lowered his hand to the ground and held it there. And waited. And quietly waited.

After several minutes the pigeon moved even closer; now just a few inches from Billy's hand. Finally, it pecked a piece of the ground corn directly from his hand. Billy kept his hand completely still and the bird pecked again then backed off a few inches to enjoy the treat. When it returned for another peck, Billy snapped his fist closed around the pigeon's neck. His other hand covered the bird's head. He twisted his clenched fists in opposite directions and snapped the bird's neck, then dropped the lifeless limp body on the ground and walked away.

CHAPTER 16

"My friends, you have all done well. By this time tomorrow the godless infidels will be stricken with fear, and we will be back here watching our glorious endeavor replayed endlessly on CNN." Billy spoke to his soldiers like a general preparing for battle.

They were assembled for one last review of the coming day's schedule. Sitting comfortably in the spacious suite on the 16th floor of the Tarrytown Hilton, Nina, Rem, Nasi, Mo, Gabby and Suniel listened to each word from Billy as if from Mohammed himself. It was 8:45 PM and they had feasted on Domino's pizza and Dr. Peppers, both favorites of Nasi who'd been put in charge of food for the final meeting.

This sort of hotel get-together was not new to them. They'd been through this several times before; each time adding one more layer to the complex events to follow. Tonight was to be the final run-through of the schedule; to be sure the timing of each event was flawless but also properly coordinated with the other events.

Billy wanted to be sure the bridge explosion and tunnel massacre were virtually simultaneous. The train bomb would be a few minutes later. Since the train schedule was out of their control, and Billy wanted the bomb to detonate as the commuter train was entering Penn station, he would have to hope the MTA lived up to its reputation of predictable tardiness. If one explosion occurred too much before the others, it might alert the authorities to close down the tunnels and bridges just as they'd done in the moments after the second plane hit the towers twelve years earlier.

"I want us all to be sure. If anyone has any doubts or questions, we must deal with them now." The five men from the Middle East never understood Billy's obsession with thoroughness. To them, it seemed like they were going over the same points as if to go in circles. It wasn't part of their culture. They didn't get his concern about timing. They couldn't grasp his compulsion regarding the school bus or why it had to be that particular school bus. And none of them understood why their hostage had to be the girl in the first seat.

Billy had explained that she came from a wealthy family and, based on the research he and Nina had done, it was likely her father would pay a ransom without question. This, they understood would finance their next, and even greater jihad; one that would involve the following year's Super Bowl, and surely make them legends among their people.

"Nasi, what will you do if someone says you have forgotten your luggage on the train?"

Nasi sat up from his slouch on the sofa. "If it happens while I am still on the train, I will thank him and retrieve the luggage, then, when I am sure he has not followed me, I will board the next train bound for New York, leave the case on that train, and step off just as the doors are closing. If I am approached after I've left the train and it has already begun to depart, I will feign regret and ask where I go to claim a lost bag."

"Excellent." Billy turned to Mo. "Mo, what is the signal I will give when I want you to leave the bus?"

Mo responded as if bored by the repetition, "Two goes."

Billy glared at him. After fifteen years as a marine, Billy was accustomed to repetition and drilling until something seemed an extension of himself. He understood its importance, especially in the heat of battle. And he had little patience for those who were too lazy to do the repetitive exercises required to get it right 100 percent of the time.

Maybe that was part of the problem. After fifteen years in the Corp., eight of them spent in Iraq and the southern portion of Afghanistan, Billy had come to see the Afghani people as generally lazy. He recognized they could sometimes be tenacious fighters, willing to endure hardship for years if it resulted in a victory, but they were also easily distracted. He felt they lacked discipline and were generally dishonest. "Sneaky cocksuckers" was the term he most often used when referring to the locals.

He barked at Mo, "Be precise damn it! You may not give a shit about your life but I want to live to fight another day." The room was silent.

Finally, Billy said, "Now, once again Mo. What is the signal I will give when I want you to leave the bus?"

Mo decided this was not the time to challenge Billy's authority; not in front of his woman. He begrudgingly offered, "Go-Go."

To show his indifference to Mo's apparent contempt, Billy moved directly to his next question. "Gabby, you've just triggered the timing device on the bridge, what is the route you take to return here?"

Without hesitation, Gabby complied, "Exit the Bridge on to the FDR north. Take that all the way to the Major Deegan. Then exit onto the Cross Westchester, and then exit nine to the hotel."

"And Suniel, how are the two cars to be positioned on the bridge?"

"At the crest of the span we will stop. Gabby will raise his hood."

"Right, but don't forget to take the keys with you Gabby. We don't want some impatient asshole to try to move the car before the charge goes off."

Then Billy turned to Nina. "Nina, read us the list of calls you will make in the order you will make them."

Nina read from her script. "First call at 9:20 A.M. to 911: *There has been a huge explosion in the Holland Tunnel. Please send many ambulances.* Second call at 9:21 using second cell phone to 911: *There's been a huge explosion at Grand Central Station. We need help.* Third call at 9:22 to WINS radio: *I am stuck in traffic on route 3 in Jersey. There's been some sort of huge explosion in the tunnel. I see smoke coming out the Jersey side from here.*"

She read off eight more bogus reports of calamities throughout the city, each to a different news source. It was Nina's job to create the hysteria that would allow Billy and his men to escape notice at the sites of the three real events. It was also her job to point the finger at "Arab looking men fleeing the scenes". This part of her job she didn't mention. But Billy knew the script. After all, he'd written it word for word. When the media and communication frenzy began tomorrow, he wanted to make sure the rumors began as early as possible, thus giving them a chance to crescendo into full blown hyperbole by the time the police found the carefully planned clues Billy would leave, leading them to the bodies of Mo, Gabby, Suniel, Rem and Nasi.

Billy looked at his soldiers slouching in various positions around the room. He felt contempt for their culture and their ideals but, at some level, respect for their commitment. They were adequate soldiers. But make no mistake; he viewed them as the enemy.

Conjuring an image of General Patton addressing his troops, Billy paused for effect. "You all have your assignments. Tomorrow we must be precise. Everyone must be precise. There can be no mistakes. Tonight I want you to sleep well. We will meet back here tomorrow at precisely 10:45 A.M. Do not be late and if you are early, wait in your cars in the parking lot. Do not come up to my room until 10:45. We will only be here a short time before we will leave for Vermont where we will await our prize. I don't want any of the hotel staff to see us entering the building until just before 10:45. Does everyone understand?" It was a rhetorical question. He'd been over this point with them many times before."

"I think we are ready." He said pretending to appear proud. "Tomorrow will be a glorious day; for all of us. And although you understand we do not share the same set of beliefs and reasons for our actions, we are united in our mission. Americans must suffer. They have inflicted suffering on too many people for too long and must be punished. This will only be the start of their punishment."

CHAPTER 17

Carol Wallace stopped brushing her hair to admire herself in the bathroom mirror. Fresh from the shower and still sporting a healthy tan from seven weeks in Bridgehampton last summer, she liked what she saw. She took a step back to take it all in. The steam had dissipated and the oversized bathroom was bright with morning sun. Her skin had always been tight and now at thirty-six it seemed the ravages of age had not yet begun to work their evil on her.

Carol was, by everyone's view, a beautiful woman. Always had been. From the day she married Alan, she hadn't changed. Not on the outside anyway. Her youthful blonde hair was still soft and begged to be touched. Her light brown eyes still had the twinkle of a teenager. Her lips, which had never been full, still held their sexy shape and her face was wrinkle free.

She let the towel fall to the marble floor and stood in silent admiration of the statuesque frame reflected in the full length mirror.

The bathroom door was closed and Alan was already downstairs in the kitchen preparing Mary Jane's breakfast, so she could enjoy her moment of self-indulgence. Her gaze worked its way down from her face to her shoulders- still smooth, round and firm. Then to her breasts- also still smooth, round and firm; and most importantly- still pretty much where they were at her senior prom.

Most women her age with children would kill for her flat and well-toned abs. Two hundred sits up a day had their rewards she thought. Her personal trainer insisted on them every day and always with a five pound weight held behind her head.

Carol turned slightly to view her ass and although her view in the mirror was incomplete, she was pleased. Not much sag at all. She knew the treadmill helped. Thank God Alan made a fortune and could afford all her youth-perpetuating indulgences. But she wondered how much longer she could fend off the barbarians at the gates of time.

She put on red satin panties, a pair of True Religion jeans and a yellow Brooks Brothers V-neck cashmere sweater. No bra. She seldom wore a bra, except for when she was working out. It was her way of telling the world, "I'm still young and sexy." And she liked the way the soft fabric felt against her skin.

Today was going to be a big day. Her daughter had her first solo performance at school later that afternoon. Even taking into account a mother's pride, Mary Jane was a gifted violinist. She'd been playing and taking serious lessons for ten of her fourteen years. It was her unusual talent that opened the doors to the Freeman Academy. This wasn't a place wealthy families could buy their way into. Freeman was well endowed and took a harsh view of parents who offered to make significant grants to grease the path for their children. They were, of course, happy to accept generous gifts but only after a student had been accepted on the legitimate merits of their academics and musical talent.

Carol had a long list of errands to run before heading out to Oyster Bay for the recital. That was one of the things she really loved about living in Manhattan- she could walk to just about everything. From their apartment on East 82nd Street she was within minutes of their dry cleaner, butcher, hair salon, dentist, and most everything else she needed on a daily basis. She could go weeks without taking the car from the garage buried deep under their apartment building. And when she did need the car, all she had to do was call down to the garage and some pleasant young man, eager for a tip would bring it around to the front of the building.

She slipped on a pair of sneakers, threw her hair into a ponytail, and hurried down the stairs to the kitchen where Alan was reading the Times and sipping coffee at the counter. Mary Jane was just finishing a bowl of Cheerios.

"So, what's the story Alan? Are you going to be able to come to the recital today?" She already knew the answer but wanted her husband to explain his likely absence in front of their daughter. Carol had grown tired of making excuses for Alan. They both loved their daughter beyond measure but Alan saw his role as provider and Carol's as nurturer. He seldom attended any of Mary Jane's school events.

"Sweetie, I don't think I can today. I've got meetings downtown all afternoon." He was looking at his daughter and had his left hand on her shoulder but kept one eye on his wife's face, searching for approval. He found none.

"It's okay dad. Most of the other fathers don't come to these. But make sure you can come to the one in November. Bridget and I have a duet in the concerto in D minor. It's going to be huge. We'll be the only two on stage for over ten minutes. You've got to come to that one, Okay?" Her voice was filled with hope.

"Second Friday in November. I've already got it on my calendar. I'll be there." This time all his attention was on Carol's reaction.

She poured herself a mug of coffee and leaned back against the counter. Her skepticism was obvious to Alan but her words, as usual, were supportive. "Your dad's got so much going on right now honey. And anyway, at that time of the day, it would take forever to get from dad's office out to Freeman. I'll be there for both of us."

Most of that was truthful. Alan Wallace did have a lot going on at work. He and two of his partners had been vying for the senior spot at their boutique investment bank for the past six months, in a footrace arranged by the outside board. The current CEO was retiring at the end of the year and the board wanted his replacement to come from within the prestigious firm. This translated into an all-out sprint for the three heirs-apparent. He'd been putting in more hours than usual, taking on more clients and more overseas trips than he wanted and more dinners with senior traders, all in an effort to gain traction against his two younger opponents. The pace was frantic and he knew he couldn't keep this up forever, but the finish line was in sight. He wanted this badly.

Outwardly, Carol supported her husband's ambition. She dutifully attended as many business/social functions as she could, always putting her best face forward. And she was the perfect corporate wife; attractive to distraction, intelligent and engaging. "Your greatest corporate asset" was the way one associate once described Carol to Alan. But inwardly she hoped Alan would be passed over. She didn't like what the pressure was doing to him or to their marriage. She didn't see how Alan could be a better husband sequestered away in the CEO's office. And they didn't need the money. They already had more than they'd ever need thanks to his career and an inheritance from his father. She wanted things to be the way they used to be; before he started climbing the corporate ladder.

Carol glanced at her daughter as she lifted the cereal bowl to her mouth stretching for the last few drops of milk and Cheerios. She'd just begun to blossom into a woman. Always intellectually ahead of her age, Mary Jane had been a late bloomer physically. At fourteen, she was just beginning to fill out her school uniform the way her peers had a year ago. For the first time since sixth grade, Mary Jane wasn't self-conscious about her juvenile appearance. She was becoming a woman.

And a beautiful woman. Carol couldn't help thinking about how classically pretty Mary Jane was becoming. Each morning she seemed to be more mature than the night before. She was already as tall as Carol and starting to resemble one of the movie stars from the forties- Lombard or Lamar. She wore her wavy dark hair cut short. The only jewelry she ever wore was a locket her grandmother gave her for her tenth birthday. She wore it every day.

"Come on squirt. I'll walk you down to the corner." Alan said as he put his coffee cup in the sink. "You've got a big day and you don't want to miss the bus."

Mary Jane kissed her mother on the cheek, flung her backpack over her shoulder and ran for the door. "Well then. Let's get moving." She said.

On that particular day, she would have done well to miss the ill-fated bus.

CHAPTER 18

The alarm on Billy's phone rang at 3:30 A.M. He glanced around the dark hotel room and noticed light coming from under the bathroom door. Nina was already up and showering. He walked from his room, across the suite's common room, and banged on the door of the second bedroom. Rem and Mo were also already up, dressed and lying on their beds watching CNN. "Today's the day, boys. Today we make the world listen." Billy seemed to be in excellent spirits.

He returned to his side of the large suite and knocked on the bathroom door. The shower sounds had ceased. "Can I come in?"

The door swung open. Nina stood in the steamy fog completely naked and combing out her wet hair. On any other morning this might have aroused Billy, but today was not any other morning. "Can you finish out here, I really need to pee?"

Nina grabbed one of the hotel's oversized towels, wrapped it around herself and gave him a peck on the cheek as she walked pass. "I wanted to let you sleep. You were talking in your sleep last night again."

"What did I say?"

"Nothing I could understand but it sounded like you were yelling at someone."

Billy's nightmares were occurring more frequently as the mission day approached. He had the dark dream twice already this week and when he awoke, it was usually hard to fall back asleep. As a result, he hadn't had a good night's sleep in quite a while. He hoped tonight would be different.

Fifteen minutes later, Billy, Mo and Rem were in the van driving over the Tappan Zee Bridge towards New Jersey. Nina stayed behind at the Hilton to prepare for their return. Her work wouldn't take long but she couldn't begin until after the men had left.

On the ride west and then south, Rem drove while Billy and Mo sat silently. Their destination was a small warehouse Billy had rented just a few minutes from the George Washington Bridge. It in, waited their Ryder trucks, all their supplies, and the body of Judy Saccenti. There was still much to do before the mission could begin.

"Tell me again about the farm." Rem asked more to break the uncomfortable silence than out of real curiosity. They'd been over this many times before. "Will we have horses to ride during the days?"

The plan, as Billy had explained it, was for them all to retreat to a large farm in northern Vermont; a place none of them had ever been. Essentially, to distance themselves from all the investigations that would occur following their successful mission. Billy said the farm was abandoned for several years until Nina leased it a few months ago. He'd described it as a large farmhouse with a barn which would serve as the holding tank for their captive until the ransom was paid. The main house had several bedrooms and even room for a pool table and ping pong table that would help pass the many hours of waiting they anticipated ahead. He described it as the perfect place to hide out.

"But no horses, Rem. There's no one there to care for horses. The closest neighbor is four miles away. It will just be the seven of us. But Nina and I stocked the place with all the foods you asked for and we probably don't have to go to town for anything for at least two weeks. She even had the cable and internet connection turned on." Billy said, "Believe me, you're gonna love it. And from the safety of northern Vermont we can watch the world scramble to understand what has happened and how much more is coming."

To make his story about the imaginary farm more real, he'd shown them pictures of a farm he'd taken from the internet. The five young men from Yemen envisioned the lush greenery and rolling hills as near nirvana. And, in some ways it was like Nirvana because, like Nirvana, they would never get there. Billy had other plans for his soldiers post mission.

But, for now, the destination was the warehouse, a place that really did exist. As they approached the commercial district of West Patterson in the early morning darkness, it was clear to all why Billy had chosen this place. The surrounding area consisted of nothing but drab and rundown warehouses. Fifty years ago the area was vibrant with import/export businesses that needed to sort and store their goods before taking them to market on the streets of Manhattan. But today fewer than half the buildings still operated; many were boarded up with generations of fading graffiti gracing their walls and doors.

They turned onto Tenth Street and stopped in front of one of the smaller buildings. Billy jumped out of the van, unlocked the garage door, and lifted the heavy barricade. Rem eased the van into the dark cavern and waited for Billy to find the light switch before turning off his engine and headlights. Billy closed the garage door behind them.

The warehouse was empty except for the two Ryder trucks, the equipment they would soon load onto them, and the dark blue body bag lying next to the first truck. The three men knew what had to be done but Billy insisted on directing every phase of the loading. Each truck was to be packed in precisely the same manner. The order of the load would determine its ultimate fire power. First the C-4 and timing devices set at thirty seconds, had to be installed at the forward ends of the six-by-twelve cargo areas. Then the plastic bags filled with ball bearings and metal fragments would be packed in and fit tightly against the walls of the truck much like shot would be packed into an eighteenth century musket to maximize its exit speed. Then the gasoline-filled water bottles at the rear of each truck.

With the rear doors swung open the explosion triggered by the C-4 would propel the ball-bearings and fragments through the plastic containers, focusing the combustion, metal, and flaming liquid on everything behind the trucks. The walls of the twenty-foot wide tunnel would further focus the fireball backwards. Billy estimated the first ten cars behind the trucks would be unrecognizable; perhaps as many as another twenty would catch fire from the flames and heat.

And the bearings and metal fragments would rocket from the back of the trucks as if they'd been shot from a cannon, which, effectively they had been. The quarter inch bearings would mutilate metal and human flesh back at least four car lengths leaving the bodies of the five souls on the bus riddled with holes; holes that would be indistinguishable from bullet holes. Then the gasoline and flames would devour whatever was left of them.

It was Billy's hope that the carnage in the center of the tunnel tube would be so severe and burn so long, that it might be days before anyone would be able to reach his ground zero. He was counting on the back-up of traffic to provide an endless supply of fuel for the fires. After all, each waiting car carried up to twenty more gallons of gasoline and there was nowhere for them to run. He only wished he could somehow watch such a fantastic chain reaction.

Then there was the body of Judy Saccenti which, because it was beginning to stiffen, had been stored in a sitting position within the body bag and needed to be put in the back of the van. Billy instructed Rem to open the bag. She'd been dead less than a week but rigor mortis had already taken hold of Judy's fragile frame and lying on her side she appeared to be sitting on an imaginary chair. "We need to get her into these," Billy said to Rem as he threw a bag of cloths in his direction.

"What difference does it make what she's wearing? It's all going to be ashes in a few hours." Mo knew he shouldn't question Billy but he was genuinely curious.

Rem opened the bag and revealed a plaid pleated skirt, a bra, and a white blouse. He knew the skirt and blouse were similar to those the girls on the bus would be wearing.

"A hundred percent certainty, Mo. That's what I want." Then he said, "Rem, you're probably going to have to cut her out of the cloths she's got on."

As Mo and Rem removed the cloths from the body, Billy realized he'd overlooked an important point. The naked body of Judy Saccenti revealed a large scar running from her neck to her pelvis. The stitches were only days old and Billy assumed it was from either an autopsy or from organ donations. Still, he hadn't anticipated this and it angered him to acknowledge his mistake in front of his two soldiers, who looked to him with questioning faces.

"Don't worry about it. The fireball will take care of it for us." But he was worried about it. He was worried that even if the flames made the surface of one girl indistinguishable from the other, an autopsy would reveal the difference. "By the time anyone sorts this out, we'll be in Vermont."

They dressed the body in the new cloths and Billy poured almost a full gallon of gasoline on the newly clothed corpse, allowing time for the fabric to absorb the fuel. Then they lifted the "seated" corpse into the back of the van.

⊶⊷

Back at the hotel in Westchester, Nina had finished her work. She looked around the suite one last time before closing the door and stepping into the hall. She put a "Do Not Disturb" sign on the doorknob.

CHAPTER 19

Nasi stepped out of his second floor room at the Gateway Motor Inn and breathed in the crisp clear morning air. He loved this time of year in the United States. The mornings were often like this one; fresh and alive with cool dry breezes. Not at all like Yemen, where a September morning could bring winds off the desert that carried dust at 105 degrees.

He'd settled his motel bill the previous night so there was no need to stop at the office on the first floor. He carefully wheeled his oversized piece of luggage down the stairs and walked across the highway to the train station directly across the busy street. The Long Island Railroad ran parallel to the highway along most of the south shore of Long Island before heading into Manhattan. The train station at Merrick, like most others, was elevated and he was glad to find the escalator to the platform was working this morning. On previous occasions, when he'd done test runs, it was not. That had concerned him because, although it had wheels, the brown Samsonite luggage concealed seventy pounds of metal and plastic explosive material; more than Nasi wanted to carry up a long flight of stairs.

But this beautiful morning Allah was with him. He purchased a round-trip ticket with the credit card Billy had supplied, then waited for the train to arrive. During his three test runs the previous week, the train arrived at the station nearly filled with commuters. Apparently, at this time of the morning, no one who got on at Merrick could expect a seat. The best they could hope for was enough room to stand and read their newspapers. Because this particular train was scheduled to stop at Jamaica, Queens before entering the tunnel into Manhattan, riders could transfer at Jamaica to the airport shuttle-train. This accounted for the several passengers who carried luggage. Just as Billy had promised, Nasi and his large brown suitcase would fit right in.

As he waited on the platform, Nasi caught a glimpse of his reflection in the darkened glass window of the waiting room. He was pleased with the image looking back. He wore a tight fitting powder blue Tommy Hilfiger T-shirt that showcased the biceps he'd been working so hard to develop. His hair was a little longer than he usually wore it, but Billy had insisted on the look. Actually, he kind of liked the way his dark brown hair looked pulled back behind his ears. What he couldn't get used to was the clean shaven face- another one of Billy's mandates. It made him look too young; almost like a teenage boy.

Nasi glanced around the crowd waiting on the platform. He noticed they represented a fair cross section of suburban America; an equal mix of men and women, about half the men wore ties, about half the women wore slacks. They were mostly white but the crowd had enough blacks, Asians, and Middle Eastern types to justify the term "ethnically diverse".

There was no magic to the choice of Merrick as a starting point. It just happened to be about thirty miles outside the city, which was Billy's criterion for the operation. This far from Manhattan there would be no bomb sniffing dogs on train platforms, no heavily armed national guardsmen patrolling the station, and no significant police presence. In fact, Nasi didn't see any police at all. From a suburban town like Merrick, someone could board a train anonymously, carrying a significant payload, ride the train as far as he wished, get off wherever he wished, leave his payload behind and have the Long Island Railroad deliver it to its intended destination- Pennsylvania Station in the heart of Manhattan. For a device with a timer, all one had to know was when the train was expected to arrive at its terminal and the Railroad was kind enough to provide on-line schedules that listed arrival times to the minute. Nasi couldn't believe it could be this easy to get a seventy pound payload into Penn Station; a terminal that sits directly below Madison Square Garden. It was a Jihadist's dream.

The train Nasi expected to board was due to arrive in a few minutes and due to conclude its journey at Penn Station at 8:58 A.M. On his three previous trial runs, the train was on time once, late one minute and late three minutes. In all cases, once all passengers had disembarked, it sat in the station for at least another ten minutes while the crews changed and new passengers loaded on for the return trip. For this reason, the timing device in Nasi's luggage was set to work its magic at 9:01 A.M. By that time, Nasi would be safely on his way to the Westchester hotel.

A young woman wearing a white blouse was standing next to him and talking on a cell phone. He assumed she was speaking to her baby sitter, giving instructions about who needed to be shuttled to soccer practice after school but only if his sore throat was better and who had a piano lesson at four. It seems the written instructions she'd left behind just a few minutes earlier weren't clear and he could sense the woman's anxiety at having to juggle a career in Manhattan with raising a family. For some reason, he liked her. She seemed to be struggling and Nasi could identify with that. He hoped, for her sake, she was getting off somewhere before Penn Station.

The train appeared in the distance and the crowd, standing on the platform, positioned themselves for where the doors were expected to open. He'd marveled at this behavior last week. The people would assemble in beehive-like clusters hoping the train would stop in just the precise spot to position a door directly in front of their hive. And it seemed to work. Today the huge silver doors opened directly where the crowd expected and they filed on with minimal shoving.

The few empty seats were quickly taken by the first on board and everyone else filled the vestibule and jockeyed for favorable standing positions. Nasi rolled his Samsonite onto the train and leaned it against a bulkhead. He took out a paperback book like he was told to do and pretended to read. When the doors closed and the train began to move, he glanced around to see if anyone was looking at him with any suspicion. Assured they were not, he crossed his right leg over the luggage so it was between his legs and leaned against the bulkhead.

The train made one more stop where even more commuters climbed aboard and struggled to find comfortable standing room. Nasi held his position straddling his luggage. He smiled to himself at the thought of several pounds of grade B C-4 explosive resting between his legs. He wished his boyhood friends could see him now. How jealous they would be of his Jihad.

As the train rolled west, the morning sun filled the vestibule through heavily soiled windows. It was a beautiful morning and as he pretended to read his paperback, Nazi thought about his brother, Suneil. By this time Suneil would be close to his destination on the Brooklyn Bridge. How glorious would be this day. How proud of his sons their father would have been. Not just that they'd both finished college in America but that they were taking a stand against the imperial monster that had been contaminating their culture for decades.

He spotted the young woman in the white blouse seated in the center of the train. She seemed to be asleep. She looked so peaceful. Nasi hoped that if she didn't get off the train in Jamaica, she would remain asleep and not feel the death that awaited her moments later in Manhattan. His years in American had hardened his hatred of its political system and its government but softened his view of its people. He had many friends here. Five years at NYU studying electrical engineering had introduced him to many American students. Many were friends; young people like himself who wanted to make their mark on the world in some way.

A few minutes later there was an announcement on the train's PA system. *"Next stop will be Jamaica. Change here for the train to Brooklyn. Change here for the rain to Woodside on track two. Change here for the Air-train to JFK and all other stops. This train makes Jamaica and Penn Station stops only."*

Some of the commuters surrounding Nasi began to shuffle closer to the doors as the train slowed and eventually came to a stop. The doors slid open and a rush of people shoved their way out onto the platform in search of their connecting trains. Others scurried for the now empty seats left behind. Nasi stood his ground. His practice runs had taught him the train wouldn't leave again until more passengers boarded from a train across the platform that was just coming to a halt. Its doors opened and several men moved quickly across the platform and began boarding Nasi's train. No one paid him or his luggage any attention.

When the last of the new passengers had boarded Nasi quietly stepped through the doors and off the train. The doors slid shut and the train began to creep out of the station. Nasi watched for a moment to see if anyone seemed to notice the luggage left behind without an owner. No one did. Their heads were already buried in newspapers.

As the train slid by he could see through its window the girl in the white blouse still seated and sleeping peacefully.

"Sleep well pretty lady." He heard himself whisper. "It will be over soon."

CHAPTER 20

"Mr. Wallace. There's a call for you on line two." A young girl yelled across the crowded room.

Alan Wallace's usual secretary, Claire was on vacation and the summer intern filling in from NYU still didn't know how to properly screen his calls. He was walking back to his office from the trading floor. When he was close enough to be heard without yelling he said, "Do you know who it is, Rita?"

"No. But it's a woman."

Because Claire would be back from Block Island on Monday, he chose not to bother correcting Rita. She wasn't worth the investment of his time and would be gone soon anyway. Instead, he said, "Put it through to my office and ask Jimmy and Sal to meet me at Vittorio's for lunch with the guys from Citibank."

Alan's office was a fishbowl. It sat in the middle of the trading floor and consisted of four walls of clear glass. He usually kept the door open so he could hear the tone of the action going on around him; the action being the trades his salesmen were executing at their terminals and the cacophony of CNN, MSNBC, and whatever other news shows his people had streaming at their desks.

He picked up his phone. "Wallace."

"Hey you." The soft female voice was barely audible over the din from outside his office. He knew who it was immediately.

"Hold on. Let me close my door." He quickly ran around his desk and closed his office door. Then he checked the faces of those nearest his office to see if anyone on the floor was looking his way. No one seemed to notice so he returned to his desk and picked up the receiver.

"Hi Jess. What's up?" He tried to sound relaxed. He wasn't.

"Ben's in London and I'm expecting trouble with my electricity again tonight." Her voice was smooth and sexy. "Do you think you could come over and make sure it's okay? Maybe around nine?"

Jessica Kitman lived three floors above Alan and Carol Wallace in a four thousand square foot penthouse overlooking the East River. She and Carol had become friends soon after she moved into the building and began taking a pilates class together. Her live-in boyfriend, Ben, worked for the department of defense and was almost constantly traveling the world in search of high tech gadgetry. This left Jessica, whose trust fund repressed her occasional and lackluster urges to work, available to accompany Carol on day-long shopping sprees up and down Fifth Avenue. It also gave her a feeling of entitlement, even when that extended to the husbands of friends.

Jessica's reference to "electricity trouble" caused Alan to drift back to his own surrender just a few days ago. It had been an exceptionally hot day for early September and the archaic system of wires under Second Avenue couldn't keep up with the demand for electricity. Just after dinner the entire city block was blacked out- something Con Ed called temporary power disruptions, but the residents knew as planned outages to give the utility the ability to send power to where it was most needed- the high-rent side of First Avenue.

By eight-thirty, everyone in the affected area was perspiring, lighting candles and sitting on their balconies to catch what little breeze there was. Alan's balcony faced the river so he, Carol, and Mary Jane were making the best of a hot situation and listening to music from Mary Jane's iPad. What little local news they could get indicated the power would likely be off until morning.

At one point Carol went inside to refresh her diet Dr. Pepper. When she returned to the balcony she told Alan that her friend Jessica had just called her cell and asked if one of them could come up to her apartment to help her get something down from a high shelf in her closet. Carol knew the oversized closet she was referring to and volunteered Alan for the job. "I'd go myself honey", Carol said, "but I just took an Ambien and I don't think I could reach that high shelf anyway. Besides, you know how I hate the fire stairs." Then she turned to Mary Jane and said, "Why don't we both take a couple of cool showers and go to bed? Hopefully, when we wake up in the morning, the power will be back on."

So Alan grabbed a flashlight, kissed his two favorite women good night and walked up the three flights of fire stairs to the 32nd floor penthouse. He was wearing a pair of linen kaki shorts and a black tee shirt, but by the time he got to Jessica's door he could already feel the perspiration beads running down his back.

The door to Jessica's apartment was the only one on the 32nd floor. It reflected her style completely; a rich amber-colored wood that Allen assumed required the desecration of some portion of the South American rainforest. Before he could knock, the door swung open and Jessica Kitman stood in the threshold holding a small pillar candle. "Oh, thanks so much for coming up Alan. I'm so sorry to bother you but my good flashlight is on the top shelve of our closet and I can't reach it." Her voice was soft and sincere.

"No problem, Jess. Where's Ben off to this time?"

She ignored the mention of her boyfriend and closed the door behind them as she led Alan down the long hallway and into the magnificent living area. On any other night, the glistening lights of lower Manhattan would have filled the fourteen foot windows that ran the length of the room. Tonight, he could see that although most of the city still had power the immediate neighborhood was completely black. Yet, the distant buildings still provided just enough light to allow him to see his way around the apartment even without Jessica's candle.

"Boy, even on a night like this, you get a lot of light from those windows." He couldn't help stopping to admire the view. He also couldn't resist admiring Jessica. In the dim shadows, her petite figure seemed even more so. She was wearing a loose-fitting white tee shirt with a deep V-neck and a pair of pink sweatpants that hung on her shapely hips. They looked so soft and thin that he couldn't imagine they were ever really used for sweating.

As she stopped next to him to look out the window, he also noticed the contours of her breasts beneath the white cotton and concluded she was not wearing a bra. Her auburn brown hair was pulled back in a ponytail. This wasn't the first time Alan had taken notice of Jessica. He'd thought about her often.

They stood at the window for several moments, both looking out at the city below. They were standing less than a foot apart and Alan could notice the smell of some sort of alcohol emanating from Jessica. He knew from his wife, that she liked to drink but he'd never seen her drunk at any of the social functions they attended together. She was a classy drinker; always sipping something exotic, never wine and certainly never beer.

He became aware of the awkward silence that lingered between them. Aware that they were alone.

He stumbled over the words, "So where's that high shelf you need help with?" Jessica could tell he was uncomfortable and answered, "It's my closet in the bedroom. But let's enjoy the quiet for a moment more. Don't you love it when the city is quiet and dark, Alan?" She was practically whispering.

Before he could respond, she added, "Let's sit here for a minute and soak in the darkness." She motioned toward the round ottoman about three feet from the window. "How about I get you something cool to drink before all my ice melts? I'm having Amaretto on the rocks. How's that?"

Being a red-blooded American male, Alan liked being flirted with. He even liked the notion that someone as hot as Jessica Kitman would flirt with him. He was flattered by it. After all, she was at least ten years younger. She was rich and gorgeous and sexy. But this was his wife's friend. And he recalled the advice of a crusty old bond trader at Solomon Brothers from years ago; "You don't shit where you eat, kid." That advice had served him well. So far.

But for some reason, he said, "Sure. Amaretto on ice sounds great."

Jessica wandered into the kitchen with her candle leaving Alan sitting on the ottoman in the silent darkness. He wasn't entirely sure what her intentions were, but he was enjoying the game so far. And what's wrong with a little harmless flirting if that what makes her happy? He was just being a good neighbor. He was just being a man.

His mental rationalizations were interrupted when Jessica returned with two stemless wine glasses filled with ice and Amaretto. She sat next to him on the ottoman. Right next to him. Then whispered, "Here's to drinking in the dark," as she raised her glass in a one-sided toast. Alan clinked his goblet-size globe against hers and took a full drink. The smooth sweet liquor warmed him immediately and even though it was probably close to 85 in the penthouse, the inner warmth felt wonderful. He took another mouthful and rolled it around in his mouth a few seconds before swallowing.

"I'd forgotten how nice Amaretto can be," he said quietly. "I'm usually a red wine guy, but this is nice."

Jessica pulled her legs up under her on the ottoman and leaned back against him so that he was supporting her. She took a long sip and purred, "It's my favorite on a hot night. Makes me sleepy."

They held that position, she leaning back against his back, for nearly twenty minutes while they emptied the glasses then crunched the ice with their teeth. The fact that they were facing away from each other made the situation seem a little less inappropriate. With only the light from the candle and the dim glow from distant skyscrapers, they began to talk quietly. Jessica had something to say about just about everyone she knew in the building starting with the doorman and ending with Mrs. Pfiefer from 28H whom she believed had once dated Mike Bloomberg. And Alan enjoyed listening, and in some cases, learning about his neighbors.

When she got up to refill their glasses, Alan didn't object. And upon her return, they both sat on the floor, leaning against the ottoman so they were now face to face. The conversation turned to her previous marriage and all that was wrong with it, then on to Ben, who Jessica said was "safely in Milan for a few more days". Neither of them noticed when the candle burned out, possibly because by then their eyes had adjusted to the darkness, or possibly because of the alcohol.

After almost an hour, it was Alan who rose to his feet and said, "Hey, we better get to that shelf while I can still see straight."

Jessica arched her neck back against the ottoman and rolled it from side to side. "Oh, I was just getting comfortable." But she too got to her feet and, realizing now that the candle was out, began searching for a match. She found a book of matches in the kitchen, relit the small candle, and offered Alan her hand to guide him to the closet.

The closet, which was at the far end of her bedroom, was about the size of a two-car garage. All four walls were filled with shelves and hanging clothing. The room had twelve foot ceilings and was decorated in deep mahogany woodwork. In the center was a free-standing island of mahogany drawers topped with white granite. Alan studied the island and estimated it alone contained more storage space than he and Carol had in their entire walk-in closet. He placed the candle on the granite and asked, "Where's the famous flashlight we're here to find?" His words were slightly slurred.

Jessica, who was also obviously impaired by the Amaretto, leaned against the center island and pointed to a shelf about ten feet high. From where he stood, Alan could see the edges of some shoe boxes sticking out on the shelf but, because of the height, anything more than a few inches from the shelf's edge was hidden. He thought it an odd place to store a flashlight.

"I'm pretty sure it's up there," she said in an exaggerated whisper.

Even if he brought a chair into the closet on which to stand, Alan realized he wouldn't be able to reach the lofty shelf. If he stood on top of the center island he'd be high enough but, being in the center of the room, it was too far from the walls to allow him the reach the shelf. And with the mellow buzz he had going, he didn't want to risk climbing on anything anyway.

"Jess, it's too high."

"Oh, come on. Give me a boost. I can get it." She motioned for him to boost her up so that she could stand on the shelving itself and, as long as someone was holding her legs, she could reach up to the top shelf without falling backwards. She cleared a shelf of some cashmere sweaters, placing them on the island, then motioned for him to give her a boost up to the vacant perch. He cupped his hands and let her step up and onto the shelf. She reached up over her head and held on to the shelf where she hoped to find the flashlight. "Don't let go of my legs or I'll fall back."

Alan was now supporting her by reaching up and holding the back of her thighs while she struggled to grope for the flashlight. He was right; the pink sweatpants were very soft.

"Shit! I don't see it." And with that, the search for the light was over.

"I'm coming down. Don't let go."

"Try using the shelves as steps to come down. I'll hold on to you." He coaxed her.

She did as he suggested, stepping gingerly from shelf to shelf until she was just three feet off the ground. He continued to hold the base of her back for support. But then her foot slipped and she fell the last three feet. As she did, Alan tried to keep her from falling backward by maintaining contact with her lower back but as she fell, his hands slid under her shirt and by the time she landed his hands were around her torso and, for lack of a better term, caressing her breasts. He was simultaneously embarrassed and aroused. Embarrassed by his clumsiness and aroused by the firmness of Jessica's ample and bare breasts.

He expected her to recoil. She didn't. Instead she slowly arched her head backwards and extended her arms over her head and around the back of Alan's neck. She pulled herself even closer to him. There was no mistaking her body language: she wanted him to keep his hands right where they were.

There was a moment of intense silence in the dark closet. Her silky white blouse, which had been pushed up by her fall and Alan's hands, now surrendered to gravity and began to softly cascade into place. The situation could no longer be considered an accident. Alan's hands remained tightly under her blouse and cupping her breasts. Jessica gave a whispered sigh.

This was a moment of decision for Alan. Either he quickly removed his hands from under her blouse and offer a perfunctory apology for his clumsy attempt to catch her, or he was committed to succumb to Jessica's enticing body. He froze in place for what seemed like days.

Then Jessica sighed again and, still arching back into him, pushed her cheek against the side of his face.

"That feels wonderful", she whispered.

There was a dim flickering glow on the ceiling, reflecting the candle sitting atop the center island. The closet seemed like a cavern and Alan became aware of the isolation they enjoyed. He also became aware of the increasing firmness he felt. His hands were now moving; ever so slowly- almost unnoticeably- but moving gently over Jessica's breasts. His fingers softly glided over her hard nipples then back down again to cup each breast fully in his palms, while her fingers began to scratch the back of his head.

He wanted to speak but there were no words. And so he surrendered to his desires. His hands drifted away from her breasts and onto the soft skin of her underarms. With one fluid move he lifted her blouse over her head and began to kiss the back of her neck.

"Ooooh", she whispered. Her hands were still entwined behind his head.

Alan moved his hands around to Jessica's front, slowly rubbing her belly as he continued to kiss her neck; first on the left, then the right. Her skin was as soft and smooth as he'd imagined.

"I need this," she purred. "I need you, Alan." Then her hands dropped from behind his neck and she began caressing her own breasts while his fingers continued to explore her lower torso.

Time seemed to stand still. Total silence filled the shadowy chamber.

Alan began to kiss her shoulders, then the center of her back, and then her lower back. He could taste the salty sweat on her skin. His tongue lapped at the center of her back and followed the bumps along her spine all the way down to her waist. His hands moved to her hips and he began to slide his tongue along the rim of her sweatpants. He was completely aroused.

"Oooh, Alan. Please don't stop." She cooed. Her hands were still massaging her own breasts.

Alan felt the plush carpeting on his knees. He slid his hands down the sides of her hips and gently pulled at her pink sweatpants. They fell softly to the carpet. He kept his lips in contact with her skin by kissing her butt cheeks; first the left, then the right, then he crouched lower and kissed and licked the back of her sweaty thigh.

Jessica turned around, leaving Alan's face right where she wanted it. She put her hands on the back of his head and pulled him in close.

Forty-five minutes later, Alan went back to his apartment. Carol and Mary Jane were sleeping soundly. He brought his flashlight into the bathroom placed it face up on the sink vanity and showered to get the strong scent of Jessica and infidelity off his face.

⚔ ⚔

Back in his office, on the phone with Jessica Kitman, Alan surprised himself.

"Nine's good. I'll bring my flashlight."

CHAPTER 21

At the same time Nasi was getting off his train in Jamaica, his brother Suniel turned onto the entrance ramp of the Brooklyn Bridge. He'd been parked and waiting for five minutes in his rented Ford Focus. Gabby, who had rented an identical Ford Focus had been delayed in traffic on the Brooklyn-Queens Expressway, but was now in position: directly in front of Suniel.

The two cars inched their way onto the entrance ramp and slowly made their way into the morning Manhattan-bound traffic on the ancient bridge. They'd practiced this three times before; always with the usual sluggish morning traffic. Today was no different. It would take them nearly ten minutes of excruciatingly slow movement to creep their way to the center of the bridge.

Today, the sun shined brightly on the stone towers supporting the roadway. Suniel thought it was the most impressive of all the bridges connecting Manhattan to its surroundings. He'd lived on the Brooklyn side for almost two years and would often walk over the bridge in the morning instead of taking the subway to his job at the NYU bookstore.

When he was given his assignment by Billy, Suniel began studying the history of the giant structure. He learned it was built by John Roebling and opened in 1883. It was, at the time, the longest suspension bridge in the world and the first to use steel cables to support the roadway. He read about how it arched and how many men died during its construction; most from falls into the swift currents of the East River. He also read archived copies of the Daily News which chronicled the previous acts of terror his people had unleashed on the bridge. He knew about Rashid Baz who, in 1994, opened fire on a van crossing the bridge carrying a bunch of Chabad-Labavitch Orthodox Jews, killing one and injuring several in retaliation for the Hebron massacre. And most recently, Lyman Faris, another Al-Qaeda youth with whom Suniel once shared an apartment in Paris, who in 2003 tried to bring down the mighty bridge by cutting several of its cables.

He thought about how meaningless those events would seem after today. He tried to imagine the headlines in the newspapers tomorrow. Would they have pictures of his destruction? More important- would they have a picture of him leaving the bridge. He knew there were cameras everywhere. He even knew where all the surveillance cameras were on the west side of the bridge that might capture his image. Not that anyone would be able to recognize him under the baseball cap and sunglasses Billy insisted they wear. How glorious this would all be!

As he, and Gabby in the car in front of him, crept up the span, he could smell gasoline fumes. He wondered if any of the other drivers behind him could also smell the 65 gallons of gas he'd concealed in five-gallon plastic water bottles in the trunk and rear seat of the Focus. They were covered only by a bed sheet and he laughed when he thought about the so-called increased security New York's mayor boasted about in a post 9-11 world. Perhaps he should have written something profound on the sheet as a final insult to the infidels that mock his people and their religion.

He wondered how much damage the explosives and gasoline would actually do. It didn't bother him in the least that he would probably incinerate dozens of people on their way to work. They lived in a godless country and deserved none of Allah's mercy. What bothered him is that his mission might damage the bridge itself more than he'd intended. He couldn't imagine that a mere eight pounds of C-4 plastic explosives along with the gasoline could create enough force to take down the bridge. But would it take out some of the critical cables that supported the roadway? He hoped not. It was not his intention to destroy a beautiful work of engineering, especially after his study of its history revealed the radical politics of its creator, Roebling.

As he reached the apex of the structure's long arch, he followed Gabby's car into the center lane. Gabby slowed to a crawl, then came to a complete stop precisely at the roadway's highest point. The long-running construction on the right lane provided another blocking point. Suniel pulled his Focus directly behind Gabby's and turned off the engine. He glanced down at the timing apparatus in the passenger seat. He didn't understand the electronics involved but Billy assured him he and Gabby would have 45 seconds to drive off the bridge once he set the timer.

Traffic was already starting to back up behind him and the cacophony of horns had begun. He stepped out of the car and walked to the front where he opened the engine hood feigning interest in the motor long enough to make it all seem like just another breakdown. Then he returned to the front seat and, leaning over the console, he pushed the green lever Billy had constructed to set things in motion. The unexpectedly loud click startled him and for a second he heard nothing. Then the unmistakable sound of a timer ticking off its count filled the cabin.

Suniel emerged from the car and looked back at the long line of cars his unfortunate breakdown had created. The fools were making it all worse by trying to get around him which only created even more of a bottle neck on the one passable side. Despite the beautiful morning, tempers were already beginning to boil. Commuters were screaming at each other. The black fellow in the BMW directly behind the Focus shouted something in Suniel's direction that sounded like, "What the fuck are you doing asshole?"

Suniel stepped away from his car so he could get a better look at the fellow.

The young black man followed up with, "Yeah, you asshole. Get that piece of shit over to the right."

Suniel, mindful of the ticking sounds coming from his vehicle, smiled broadly at the man and whispered, "Sleep well my friend."

Then he walked quickly to the passenger side of Gabby's car, jumped in, and the two men sped away on the virtually empty roadway. They were on the Manhattan-bound exit ramp leading to the FDR Drive when the last of the 45 clicks ticked off.

CHAPTER 22

B illy waited in the grey minivan on the corner of 38th Street and Second Avenue. The cool September breeze felt refreshing as it rolled through the open window and across his face. It reminded him of the morning breezes down on Parris Island when he and his platoon would walk four miles before breakfast, just to *"Get the creaks out"*, as his drill sergeant would say. It all seemed so long ago and so far away; a time when he and the men around him were doing noble deeds.

Today his mission was no less noble, although others would initially see it differently. Today, because of his bold mission, America would be reawakened to the constant threat from Islamic fundamentalists; a threat most people walking by the minivan, less than five miles from the World Trade Center, had all but forgotten in the twelve years since 9-11. But after today, America would have a hard time forgetting again. This time, they would understand that everyone was at risk. And at least for a while again, they would focus on America's true enemy.

He didn't see the NYPD Crown Victoria until it was passing to his left and rolled through the intersection. Obviously, its occupant hadn't noticed the pieces of white duct tape used to alter the numerals on the minivan's license plate. With all the street cameras around New York, he knew by the end of the day, the police would have several images of his vehicle emerging from the tunnel. But that wouldn't help them find him. No, Billy had this well thought out. In about five hours, no one would be able to find Billy Simon because he would cease to exist.

He checked his watch. The bus should be coming down Second Avenue in less than two minutes. He dialed a number on his cell phone. Rem picked up immediately but, as they rehearsed, said nothing. Instead, they both sat in their respective vehicles in complete silence until Billy eyed the bus approaching in his side view mirror.

"Okay, we're a go." Billy's voice seemed calm and reassuring to Rem.

"Roger the go." Rem replied, and then placed his phone next to him on the front seat.

Billy allowed the bus to pass him then pulled out and followed directly behind the yellow target. Two blocks further south he could see Rem and Mo positioning the twin Ryder trucks onto Second Avenue. At the next traffic light they took up their positions in front of the school bus and turned left into the entrance to the Queens-Midtown tunnel. Traffic was moving well in the eastbound tube. He thought about the surveillance video at the tunnel entrance and considered offering a single-finger salute to the millions who'd be watching this play out tonight on the evening news, but decided against it. Why bother?

As soon as the two Ryder's were in the tube, followed by the school bus, Billy made his move; accelerating into the left lane and overtaking all three vehicles. As soon as Billy went by, Rem, in the lead truck moved to the left lane and fell back, directly abreast of Mo's truck. Rem gave the phone signal to Billy, "Both in position".

Billy and the two Ryders reduced their speed to 40 MPH and, as the tube descended, allowed gravity to pull them deep beneath the East River for the next sixty seconds. About half way through the tunnel, the roadway leveled off, having reached its maximum depth. It was here that Billy slowed his minivan even more; 25 MPH, then 20, then 10. Just as the tube began its upward climb, Billy and the Two Ryder trucks came to a complete stop, effectively putting a cork in the eastbound tunnel and stopping all traffic behind them. Since delays in the tunnel were a common, almost routine occurrence, none of the cars behind them suspected anything more than typical rush hour traffic.

Billy gave his final phone command, "We're a go".

Rem and Mo were out of their trucks and flanking the minivan in less than five seconds, just as they'd practiced. They retrieved the cold body of Judy Saccenti from the rear of the minivan and carried it along the right side of the truck in the right lane, towards the bus. Meanwhile, Billy had jumped from his seat and swiftly walked back toward the bus. As he approached the bus door he could see Mary Jane Wallace sitting, as usual, in the first seat. He tapped on the glass door and motioned to the driver as if he had something to tell him about the traffic.

Davis, the driver, hesitated for a moment. He didn't see Rem and Mo approaching. He didn't see the gasoline pouring from the back of one of the trucks and he didn't see the Glock in Billy's right hand. So he pressed the button to open the folding door.

Billy waited until Davis was looking directly at him. He needed to make sure the trajectory of the bullet would align with the trajectory of the other projectiles that would soon be filling the tunnel. Then, just as Davis turned enough in his seat to face Billy, Billy raised his right hand and fired once, hitting the driver directly in the heart. There was no time for any of the girls to react or to scream. Billy stepped up into the bus and fired once at each of the three girls in the back of the bus, hitting each either in the chest or the head. Blood exploded onto their white blouses. By the time Billy fired the fourth round, Rem had also climbed into the bus and had a rag in Mary Jane's mouth. He pushed her head down into her lap. Billy holstered his Glock and reached over to unclasp Mary Jane's locket. It opened easily.

"Go", he shouted at Rem who had no trouble dragging the young girl from her seat, out the bus door past Mo and the corpse and toward the waiting minivan. As soon as he went by, Mo lifted the lifeless Saccenti child up to Billy and the two of them positioned her in the seat that Mary Jane just left. Billy put the locket around her pale neck and secured the clasp. Only forty seconds had elapsed since he got out of the car.

"Go, go", he barked at Mo.

At the same time Mo and Billy were exiting the bus, Rem was loading Mary Jane into the back of the minivan. She offered no resistance at all; something Billy had predicted assuming she would be in shock. He put her face-down on a large green blanket, then pulling her arms behind her, secured plastic handcuffs on her wrists. He covered her with the blanket and said, "Stay very still little girl. If you move or make any sound, he will kill you". Then he slammed the rear door and ran around to sit in the front seat, next to Mo. Billy had opened the rear doors on both Ryder trucks to allow the percussive force of the coming blast to project backwards-directly at the school bus and its five dead passengers. As soon as Mo climbed in the minivan and had his door closed, he gave the third signal; "Go three". Mo put the minivan into drive and pulled away from the damage they'd done and were about to do.

They exited the tunnel into Queens less than eight minutes after entering on the Manhattan side. The toll plaza was just a few hundred feet from the tunnel exit and completely empty. Every car that had preceded Billy's into the tunnel had already emerged, paid their toll, and were safely on their way into Queens. They knew nothing of the atrocity that occurred in the darkness behind them. Mo used the stolen E-Z Pass without incident and was one hundred feet beyond the toll plaza when Billy gave the final signal, "Go for it!"

Rem touched four keys on his cell phone and pressed "*send*".

CHAPTER 23

D an Donovan needed to catch the eleven o'clock shuttle to Boston. As was his custom on business travel, he left his office on Madison Avenue with plenty of time to spare. Dan didn't mind arriving at LaGuardia an hour early. He had plenty of work he could do while waiting. What he couldn't do was miss his flight. He was to be the featured speaker at a conference of like-minded asset managers from all over New England and his firm stood to gain a lot of good will from his presentation. That's why he'd asked his secretary to get him a cab so early. This was a flight he couldn't miss.

And so, as his taxi turned off Second Avenue and into the Queens-Midtown Tunnel, he settled back in his seat and unfolded the morning's Journal. Traffic seemed to be moving well even as the four lanes of eastbound cars and trucks converged into the two large holes that ran under the East River to Queens. His driver flipped his sunglasses to the top of his head as they entered the tunnel and darkness filled the cab. The yellowish lights on the tunnel's walls provided just enough illumination for the Journal's headlines but not enough to read the stories.

Usually, with no traffic, the four and a half mile ride through the tunnel took just a few minutes. Dan had taken this trip to the airport a hundred times and never ceased to marvel at the engineering behind the cavernous roadway that connected Manhattan Island to Long Island. The trip always reminded him of his dad and his first trip through the tunnel at age six. Back then, as they entered the tunnel from the Long Island side, his father joked that he'd better roll up the windows because they were about to go under the river.

Millions of the small white ceramic tiles that covered the tunnel's walls and ceiling whizzed by as Dan gazed out the cab's window. With traffic so light he'd have plenty of time at the airport to go over his speech one more time and return a few calls. It looked like it was going to be a very good day.

But then he noticed the pattern of tiles flying past his window was slowing and so too was the sound of the taxi's tires. As they reached the bottom of the decent under the river, the point at which the road begins to turn upwards again, traffic slowed considerably. A moment later it came to a complete halt; not unusual and not yet a threat to his connection at LaGuardia but enough to annoy his driver, a young fellow from Sri Lanka named Rev.

What was unusual was that even after a few moments, the cars weren't moving at all. This usually meant the problem wasn't volume but some sort of accident. In the event of an accident or breakdown in the tunnel, emergency vehicles needed to enter from the other side to clear it. Dan and his frustrated driver knew that could take a long time, and Dan was discouraged when Rev turned off his engine to save gas.

"This might take a while sir. I am sorry." Rev's English was excellent but heavily accented.

"It's okay. I left myself plenty of extra time." Dan said as he leaned to the left to see if he could spot the trouble up ahead.

But all he could see was a green Mercedes directly in front of them, another taxi to his left, a yellow school bus in front of him and two panel trucks ahead of that. What he didn't notice was the clear liquid flowing from one of the trucks and running down the pavement under them and all the other cars backed up behind them. He didn't notice the mini-van in front of the trucks or the men who got out of the trucks. He didn't notice that one of the men from the trucks had opened the back of the min-van and was carrying something large towards the bus. Nor had he noticed that the other man from the trucks had gone into the school bus.

But he did hear something. Something loud. It was four sharp popping sounds and they sounded like they came from somewhere in front of them, though it was hard to tell because of the tunnel's echoing effect. Rev, a bit more street-wise than his passenger, recognized the sounds immediately.

"Oh my goodness! That sounds like guns," he said.

But the four loud noises were followed by complete silence. With the tunnel jammed with immoveable cars and shrouded in the eerie yellow light, the silence seemed to hang in the air. Nothing happened for several minutes; just the stillness of frustrated drivers stuck in traffic. Then Dan heard a car door slam; then another, and another. People from behind his cab were beginning to get out of their cars and trucks to see what was holding up traffic. Some craned their necks from their windows others began to walk forward. As the first curiosity seeker passed Dan's cab, Dan rolled down his window to ask him a question.

But just then, it appeared that traffic would begin moving again. Dan could see the mini-van in front of the two trucks begin to move forward. That sound sent everyone scurrying back to their cars in preparation for the stalled caravan's eventual movement. Yes, there was no doubt about it. He could see the mini-van's taillights disappear around the next bend in the tunnel. He'd be on his way soon. Rev had already restarted his engine.

But the trucks that now seemed to be blocking everything didn't move. Like two large corks, they had everyone behind them bottled up tightly and until they moved, nobody moved.

Ten seconds passed; then twenty, then thirty. Impatient drivers began to sound their horns.

"These guys must be asleep," Rev said. "I don't know why they're..."

It was the last sound Dan Donovan heard. There was a blistering flash of light in front of the cab followed immediately by a moment of excruciating pain. Then there was nothing.

CHAPTER 24

Sarah Smith sat across from two men in business suits, both reading the Wall Street Journal. Normally she would have already been at work by this time, but today her ex hadn't shown up so she needed to drop her eleven year old son at school before running for a later train. She felt lucky to get a seat at all so she didn't mind the cramped conditions on the 8:22.

She glanced at her digital watch; 8:59, she could still make the marketing meeting scheduled for later that morning, but would have to rearrange a few things before that. Realizing that the morning wasn't a total disaster, she relaxed a bit for the first time since stepping out of the shower. She could see that the train had entered the long dark tunnel which always preceded its arrival at Penn Station. Flashes of red and green lights whisked by in the darkness as some passengers began to fold their papers and head for the vestibules to be the first ones to detrain.

Sarah was sitting in the center of the eighth car of a ten-car train. The conductor had just walked by, checking everyone's tickets, when she felt the train's cadence begin to slow. "Great," she murmured to herself. The train was pulling into the station just about on time. If she hurried, she could be at her office in less than ten minutes. Maybe she wouldn't need to cancel her 9:30 conference call with the west coast.

Since she was near the back of the train, her passenger compartment entered the station just before coming to a complete stop. Light from the station platform now filled the sooty windows and Sarah stood to begin the slow cattle-drive-like process of disembarking. She had her pocketbook in her right hand as the familiar "ding-dong" sound chimed which always preceded the opening of the doors. From the corner of her right eye she saw a bright flash of white light.

The fireball created by Nasi's suitcase lifted the sixth and seventh train cars off the ground, crushing them against the porcelain tiles on the station ceiling. Everyone in the seventh car, the one with the suitcase, was incinerated almost instantly. The first five cars were propelled forward, away from the blast. Those inside were tossed about like ragdolls but spared the agony of a fiery death.

The last thing Sarah Smith saw was a wall of shattered glass and twisted metal flying towards her from the forward car. She and everyone standing near her were pulverized by the shrapnel then mercifully incinerated by the heat and flames following close behind. The ninth and tenth cars were shot back into the tunnel from which they had just emerged. They were the least damaged.

More than four hundred people were standing on the train platform when the blast occurred, having just disembarked from a train on the opposite side of the platform. Many were killed instantly by the tremendous percussive power. Some caught fire from the heat and ran screaming up the escalator steps with their cloths on fire. Some were cut in two by the flying metal debris. Still others were blown completely off the platform onto the adjacent tracks and into the path of an oncoming train.

Within thirty seconds of the blast, over two hundred humans were dead, six hundred more severely injured. The thunderous sound was heard by people on the street, one hundred-twenty feet above and nine blocks away. The explosion had severed critical power lines running along the tunnel ceiling, casting Penn Station in total darkness. Thick black smoke began to billow up and out the entrance to the ill-fated platform, filling the crowded cavernous chamber of shops two stories above. Those who were close enough to the exit stairs could see enough daylight to make their way toward the fresh air waiting above. Most were trapped in the dense black fog of sulfur dioxide and collapsed gasping for breath just a few feet from safety.

CHAPTER 25

Wayne Wasserman had just taken his seat in the large conference room on the 32nd floor. He and his partners at Barnes, Wasserman and Noble, one of New York's up-and-coming personal injury practices, liked to have their morning coffee in the spacious room overlooking the East River and Brooklyn Bridge. This morning, they had another reason to gather. They were participating in their monthly nine A.M. video conference call with their partners in their Chicago office. The lawyers based in New York enjoyed these calls because they pissed off the mid-west guys who had to arrive at the office earlier than normal to attend.

The call had just begun and Wayne twirled in his soft leather arm chair to face the large flat-screen and camera. The subject of the monthly get-togethers was always revenues; how much the business expected to take in during the coming month based on expected settlements and jury awards. Basically, the calls amounted to each lawyer estimating the revenues from his unit and patting themselves on the backs for being such successful rainmakers.

Usually, the guys in Chicago went first with the New York contingent pressing for more details as to how the estimates were derived.

This month Wayne wasn't looking forward to his turn. His department of six lawyers, all specializing in pediatric medical malpractice, had warned him that none of the cases they were currently working were expected to conclude in the following thirty days nor were any expected to settle in that period. Such a report wasn't that unusual, but it came on the heels of a similar report the previous month. In short, Wayne's unit was way behind last year's numbers and had nothing good to report about the last quarter that would keep this year from being his worst ever.

He twisted his chair to the right and rested his feet on the window ledge. As he listened to each lawyer in Chicago drone on about their results, he couldn't resist the spectacular scenery. He could see helicopters taking off from the helipad thirty-two floors below on the bank of the river, just past the South Street Seaport. He could see boats struggling to move northward in the turbulent waters and traffic snarled on the bridge. It was a beautiful, clear morning and the river glistened as it moved past the piers that jutted from Manhattan into its path.

From his vantage point, high atop the classic skyscraper known as 55 Water Street, Wayne could also watch the busy docks on the Brooklyn side of the river where giant cargo ships were loading and unloading their products. Beyond the docks, the Brooklyn-Queens Expressway snaking its way along the shoreline, seemed unusually crowded. Traffic going north was completely stopped for as far as Wayne could see. When his gaze followed the snarled road northward, the traffic led all the way to the Brooklyn Bridge and to the crest of the bridge where it seemed to abruptly end. He leaned forward in his chair to get a better look at what was causing the jam.

At that moment, the center of the bridge flashed. Flames and debris shot from the source and outward in all directions. Something was being propelled off the south side of the span and falling into the river. He had no idea it was pieces of automobiles and their occupants. The pieces were too small.

"Holy shit!" He gasped. "Something just blew up on the bridge!"

Everyone at the table turned their attention from the video screen and toward the window. They could see smoke billowing from the center of the bridge and cars, lined up to the right of the center span, exploding in what looked like some sort of planned chain reaction. Because of the distance and thick plate glass windows, there was no sound; just the eerie silence that accompanies things seen from afar.

CHAPTER 26

The explosion triggered by Rem's cellphone call could be heard on both sides of the East River. Just as he'd intended, Billy's strategic placement of the vans, the C-4, the gasoline and shrapnel, produced a fireball of death and total destruction extending almost one hundred yards behind the vans.

By leaving the back doors open and using the narrow tunnel much like a cannon barrel, the percussive power of the blast was amplified tenfold and directed primarily westward onto the long line of idling traffic. The two hundred gallons of gasoline that had been intentionally leaked from the vans and flowed back down the tunnel towards and under the waiting cars was instantly a river of fire.

Directly behind the vans was the school bus. As planned, the bus and its dead occupants took the bulk of the ball bearings and other shrapnel which flew from the vans like bullets a millisecond ahead of a wall of fire. What was left of the driver and three students after the barrage was quickly consumed by the flames.

Dan Donovan's cab and all the cars within one hundred feet of it were also instantly incinerated by the heat and percussive blast but spared most of the shrapnel. Another thirty cars behind that became engulfed in flames and began to explode as their gas tanks ruptured. Some people were able to get out of their cars only to find themselves standing in the fiery river flowing down the tunnel floor. With nowhere to go, they were consumed within moments.

Most of the porcelain tiles lining the sides and ceiling of the tunnel anywhere near the blast broke free and were now turned into shards of razor sharp glass. Traveling at the speed of the explosion, they penetrated metal and flesh far beyond the reach of the shrapnel and were later found stuck in tires a quarter mile back in the long line of cars.

Three hundred feet from the vans, a few people were able to scramble from their cars and run back towards Manhattan before the chain reaction of exploding vehicles reached them. But many were overcome by the thick black smoke and fell to their deaths just a few feet from their cars, and thereby blocking the path for others.

Thirty seconds after the initial blast, cars were still exploding from the fireball pushing at them from the cars in front, which had themselves, just exploded. This chain reaction of exploding vehicles continued two hundred feet from the vans and might have gone all the way to the tunnel entrance had it not been for two fortuitously placed empty UPS trucks. The twin eighteen-wheelers were positioned side by side, and although their cabs did explode, killing the drivers, their hollow thirty-foot cargo areas acted as a fire-break for the rest of the tunnel occupants. The explosions stopped with them.

Unfortunately, many of the drivers and passengers trapped behind the UPS trucks also perished in their cars from the dense and toxic smoke. In all, 317 people were dead. Another 225 were seriously burned or overcome by fumes. Only sixteen people, occupants of the last twelve cars to enter the tunnel, escaped injury.

CHAPTER 27

N ina sat in her car at the far end of the Hilton parking lot. She'd finished her work in the hotel room and was waiting for the clock on her car radio to read exactly 9:20. She had her AM dial tuned to 1010 WINS, New York's primary all-news station. Spread out on the seat next to her were three cell phones. Each would be discarded after today.

At precisely 9:20 A.M. Nina dialed the first number on her list and began reading from her script. The first call was to 911: "*There has been a huge explosion in the Holland Tunnel. Please send many ambulances.*" She tried to sound hysterical and got off the line quickly.

Second call at 9:21 A.M. also to 911, using the second cell phone and her best Latino accent: "*There's been a huge explosion at Grand Central Station. We need help.*" Again, quickly off the line.

Third call immediately after the second to WINS radio: *"I am stuck in traffic on route 3 in Jersey. There's been some sort of huge explosion in the tunnel. I see smoke coming out the Jersey side from here."*

Forth call, also to WINS, using a different cell phone: "My son just called me to tell me he's on the 59th Street Bridge and a car has exploded on the Queens side of the bridge."

Fifth call to WINS and back to the Latino accent: "Hey. These four Arabs just came running out of the tunnel. They jumped in a red Mustang and drove on to the BQE. I'm at the toll booths. There's smoke coming out of the tunnel."

In all, she made nine calls; three to WINS radio, three to 911, and three to the control room at TV-1, a local all-news cable TV channel. She mentioned the "Arab-looking" men in three of the calls. Billy's script was designed to focus the authorities attention on a red Mustang going south on the BQE; nowhere near where Billy or the others actually were.

The calls took less than seven minutes and sent the New York media into a frenzy of unconfirmed reports about the three authentic explosions and several other bogus events.

CHAPTER 28

LT

Ken Stallings crashed through the door to the office we shared like a bull who'd already been worked over by the picadors. "Get your head out of your ass Hadman. Don't you ever look at your screen?"

Ken was referring to one of the monitors we have on our desks. Usually one has a real-time feed from CNN, the other, from WINS radio. I'd only been in the office a few minutes and was preparing for our demonstration surveillance so I'd yet to even turn the screen on, but I could tell by his tone that I'd missed something big.

"Bombs set off on the Brooklyn Bridge and in the Midtown Tunnel. Both at the same time." He was still huffing from his run up the two flights of stairs to our office. The JTTF had six floors in the building called 2 Penn Plaza, just above Madison Square Garden and Penn Station, but our office was temporary so we were two floors away from the rest of our unit. The climb was always tough on Ken but the elevators were just too slow.

"Tell me more," I said in a calm voice just to piss him off.

"Turn on CNN. They seem to be up to speed."

I complied and within seconds my monitor was filled with the image of black smoke billowing out the tunnel entrance. An attractive woman in glasses was on the right side of the split screen telling us about the bombings. What we quickly learned was that there were unconfirmed reports of bombs going off all over the city, but so far, CNN was only confirming the two incidents.

Then, a few moments later, the image on the left changed and a very familiar scene appeared on my monitor. It was the entrance to Penn Station, just sixteen floors below where we stood at the moment. What was disturbing was that people and smoke were flowing from the main entrance to the station. The anchorwoman put her finger to her ear and said, "I'm being told there are now confirmed reports of another explosion in Penn Station, which is the terminus for the Long Island Railroad and New Jersey Transit. I'm told that at approximately nine this morning, about twenty minutes ago, a train exploded just after arriving in the station. We don't know where the train was from."

"I'll tell you where it was from. It was from sandland." Ken seemed to be ahead of CNN.

Just then, my cell phone rang. It was Danny Jacobson, our boss. Our presence was requested at a meeting in his office two floors below us. Our entire unit was called to the meeting. Maybe they didn't hear the basement of our building had just blown up.

CHAPTER 29

A few minutes after Alan Wallace got off the phone with Jessica Kitman, he found himself sitting at his desk starring out onto the immense trading floor. The thought of another night with Jessica had produced a bulge in his Brioni slacks and he had to uncross his legs to get comfortable. He looked forward to the evening but needed to come up with a plausible excuse to leave the apartment tonight; one that his wife would expect. Or perhaps, he should just not go home after work. He could say he had to entertain some goons from one of the many banks he did business with. That would buy him several hours; maybe even until midnight. After all, it wasn't unusual for him to get home from business functions quite late, especially when he was entertaining people from out of town. The only risk is that he might be spotted coming into the building around nine, then not show up at his apartment for a few hours more. Unlikely, but difficult to explain.

He was shaken from his nefarious daydream by the sound of someone from the trading floor banging on is glass wall. Alan motioned for the young associate, a shapely brunette from Stamford, to open the door and come in.

"Alan, turn on your TV. It's 9-11 all over again!" She was frantic.

Alan glanced out the door at the hundreds of men and women on the floor. Most were huddled around the screens on their desks; some in groups of seven or eight. And it was unusually quiet on the trading floor. That, Alan found unnerving. It's never quiet on the floor. It can't be- there's too much high-stakes business being done.

"What's going on?" He said in a very controlled tone.

Natalie, the brunette, took a deep breath. "There are explosions all over the city. CNN is reporting at least six; Penn Station, Grand Central, the tunnel, and three of the bridges. It seems like they're trying to blow up all the ways off Manhattan. And it's definitely terrorists again. Someone saw Arab-looking guys running from the tunnel right after the explosion." She took another breath. "My boyfriend called and said he can see smoke coming from the Brooklyn Bridge. Bloomberg has a live feed from outside Penn Station. It's a shit storm over there. No one can get in or out. I don't see how..."

"What's the market doing, Natalie?" Again, he was oddly composed.

It took her a moment to comprehend the question. "The market?"

"Yes, Natalie. The bond market; the place we all make a living. What's it doing?"

"I...I don't know," The first year associate was embarrassed to admit.

Alan pushed the on button on the remote control to bring his flat screen to life. The TV, which was always tuned to CNBC, crackled then showed a split screen. On one side, Carl Quintanilla was saying something about the President. On the other, smoke billowed from the mouth of the Queens-Midtown Tunnel. And beneath them both ran the ever-present ticker indicating a huge selloff in stocks in Europe and Asia. New York markets didn't open for another ten minutes but Dow futures were down two hundred points.

He turned up the volume. Quintanilla was reporting the President had been briefed on the events unfolding in New York while on his way to a fundraising event in California. Air Force One was scrambled and it was unclear just where the President would land. "Generally, in situations like this, Air Force One will stay in the air until it is determined safe to land. It has the ability to remain in....."

Alan screamed a request to the temp sitting outside his office door. "Get Jimmy, Margot, and Arjun in here right away." He was determined to take advantage of whatever panicked market inefficiencies resulted from whatever was going on. He needed his top three lieutenants to get that done. A panicked market could provide a significant buying opportunity for investors who kept their heads. Margot McConnell and Arjun Patel covered the Europe and Asian desks and would have a strong sense of which way to bet this. Jim Garrity would have his finger on the pulse of most New York bankers.

When Alan Wallace looked up from the TV he realized Natalie, someone he didn't need, was still standing in his office. "Okay, Natalie. Let's see if we can go out there and make some money today. Okay?"

She took the cue and squeezed past Margot as she was entering the doorway. "Patel's at a meeting uptown but I already spoke to him. He thinks we wait until we know more. Is this shit going on anywhere else? Do we know if Al Qaeda's behind it? Is it over or is it part of some grander plan? Shit like that." Margot knew Allen would want a briefing before she even sat down.

Their eyes were glued to the TV screen as they spoke. "That's what I expected. What about Europe? They're open another four hours. Any opportunities there?"

The phone on Alan's desk rang. "No calls." He shouted towards his door but at no one in particular.

"Huge risk until we know more. I agree with Arjun. Let's give it another thirty minutes and see where we are then. Bonds may follow stocks into the can but they'll bounce more quickly. We need to have a buying strategy for repos and hi-yield ready to go. There may be big opportunities until Europe closes if this isn't any bigger." She was referring to the next few hours until the European bond exchanges closed.

The temporary assistant, whose name Alan couldn't seem to remember at the moment, was standing in the doorway. "Mr. Wallace. Your wife is on the phone. She says it's urgent."

It was only then that Alan Wallace realized he hadn't yet thought about his family. He assumed Carol was safe at home and that his daughter was at school on Long Island; also safely away from whatever craziness was happening on Manhattan. So for a moment he considered telling his assistant to put Carol on hold. But as he rolled his eyes toward the ceiling, he caught Margot giving him a look that said "Take the call asshole."

"Give me a second, Margot." He motioned for her to take a seat on the sofa while he went around behind his desk to take the call.

"Hey Carol. Are you Okay?" He was still watching the TV.

"Alan. Have you seen the TV? There was an explosion in the tunnel." She sounded scarred. She was crying.

"Yeah, honey. Actually there seem to be several explosions. I've got the news on here in my office. I don't think you need..."

"Alan, Mary Jane's bus goes through that tunnel every morning."

CHAPTER 30

As the explosions roared on the bridge, train, and in the tunnel, the mastermind and his five soldiers began their escape. Suniel and Gabby were already on the FDR Drive heading north when they heard the blast just behind them on the bridge. Without even looking back, they followed the FDR north to the Third Avenue Bridge then onto the New York State Thruway. They exited the Thruway just after crossing into Westchester County and parked in the Hilton's parking lot. The trip had taken just over an hour and they were fifteen minutes early, so, as instructed, they waited in the car.

Nasi had disembarked the ill-fated Long Island Railroad train in Jamaica and taken a cab five miles to LaGuardia airport. He walked through one terminal and into the next, then hailed another cab and said, "How much to go to Tarrytown in Westchester? And don't try to fuck me. My brother drives a taxi." The driver, also a young man of Middle Eastern heritage, agreed to run the meter. Nasi was pleased by the man's honesty. He knew from his practice runs it was about a sixty dollar fare. "Take your time. I'm not in a hurry." Then he settled into the back seat and watched his phone for the first reports of their mischief.

The van with Rem, Mo, Billy, and Mary Jane Wallace was just clear of the toll booths when the tunnel behind them erupted into a fiery cacophony. Theirs would be the most challenging journey. Anticipating the bridges and tunnels around New York would be closed as soon as word got out about their morning's handy-work, they needed to be over the Whitestone Bridge as quickly as possible. If not, they'd be trapped on Long Island. Ordinarily, the drive to the bridge connecting Queens to the Bronx could take forty minutes, but because they'd bottled up the traffic that would have flowed through the Midtown Tunnel and onto the Long Island Expressway, traffic was unusually light and they were on the bridge in less than twenty minutes; ten minutes before the Port Authority closed it to all but official vehicles.

It wasn't until they were over the bridge and had paid the toll that Billy relaxed a bit. If anyone had reported the grey minivan leaving the tunnel he might have been stopped at the bridge's toll plaza. There would have been no escape. Now that they were driving north and away from New York, the muscles in his face began to loosen. He even turned on the radio and tuned in WINS, New York's local all-news station. They were already reporting the tunnel and bridge explosions but nothing yet about the train in Penn Station. Billy wondered if something had gone wrong or if Nasi had to abort his mission for some reason.

Then the minivan erupted into cheers when the report came over the radio, "*And now there is an unconfirmed report of some sort of explosion in Penn Station. We're not sure if this is related to the other reports of explosions but here is what we do know at this point.*" A somber voice continued, *"We have had confirmed reports of a major accident of some kind in the eastbound tube of the Midtown Tunnel. Possibly a bombing. We have eye witness reports of a car explosion on the westbound side of the Brooklyn Bridge. Both of these seem to have occurred within minutes of each other; probably around 9:05 A.M. And we have unconfirmed reports of explosions at Grand Central Station, the Holland Tunnel, Penn Station, and at the entrance ramp to the 59th Street Bridge."*

The radio crackled as the minivan passed between two tall buildings. *"This is John Montone at the 32nd Street entrance to the Queens-Midtown Tunnel. Thick black smoke is billowing out of the eastbound tube. There are several fire engines and emergency response vehicles on the scene but there is no way they can enter the mouth of the tunnel. The smoke is just too thick. I can see people running from the tunnel through the smoke. One of them was smoldering as he fell into the arms of EMS workers waiting outside the tunnel. I think his coat was actually on fire because the EMTs immediately threw a blanket of some sort over him. I can't see much beyond the first..."* There was silence for several seconds. Apparently the signal from the street reporter was lost because the next thing Billy heard was, *"We seem to have lost our connection to John Montone. Repeating what John said; there has been some sort of....."* Billy asked Mo to turn off the radio.

"My friends; we have done well today." He didn't like using the word 'friends' but today his soldiers had done their job admirably. That, he had to admit.

The rest of the drive to the Tarrytown Hilton was relatively quiet. Rem spoke briefly about how he looked forward to watching CNN later that afternoon, after they arrived at the farm. And Mo, who was quiet to start with, mentioned that he was grateful there would be no checkpoints as they would need to travel from one state to another. In Yemen, checkpoints were frequent inconveniences as one moved from province to province.

And Billy thought about the two men riding with him; men who had accompanied him in battle; men who trusted him. While they couldn't begin to understand the mind of a former U.S. Marine, they probably had a code of their own that involved some sort of loyalty to each other. And Billy knew he was about to betray them; to betray his men. It created a cognitive dissonance for Billy that troubled him.

But then he remembered the mission. If his mission was to be successful on both fronts, Mo and Rem and the other Islamic nut-jobs waiting for them at the Hilton, had to die. It was the only way. For America to reignite its passionate fight against the evil serpent from the Middle East, America had to understand the atrocities they'd just committed had been the work of Islamic fundamental-ists; people bent on the destruction of our western way of life. Just as they did in the weeks and months after September 11th, after today, Americans would clearly see their enemy. They would be repulsed by anything Middle Eastern and support just about any legislation that empowered our government to protect its people.

After today, the American people would once again be united in a cause; something other than just making money; something noble. But Billy knew that whatever feeling of nationalism he cre-ated today would not last long. Americans were too forgiving. They were too focused on their soft lives even while a fraction of one percent of America was fighting in places most hadn't even heard of, to preserve their soft way of life. Americans were just too materi-alistic. They'd forgotten how close we came to losing our freedoms a generation ago. And they'd forgotten that to preserve those free-doms, so many soldiers had to die.

Billy could feel his grip tightening as he thought about these things. His country's obsession with comfort and wealth made him crazy. He'd seen too many of his fellow marines die defending those misguided obsessions. And what bothered him most was that most of the guys who died were just like him; men who didn't come from privilege; men who didn't go to college just to get rich on Wall Street. These were the salt of America; the people who really made America work; poor kids from farms and cities who just wanted to do the right thing and loved their flag.

So…, yes. Rem and Mo and the others had to die today so that America would be reawakened. And maybe America would come to appreciate the sacrifices made by such a small number of its youth. Maybe Hollywood would stop making movies that glorified the decadence of America and once again, as it did during World War II, make movies that made heroes of its soldiers. Was that too much to ask? Why couldn't…

Billy was torn from his idealistic daydream by a sound coming from the rear of the minivan. It was the muffled sound of screaming. Mary Jane was trying to scream through the rag in her mouth. For a few minutes, he'd forgotten she was lying on the floor behind the rear seat. Her hands and feet were bound with plastic ties but the gag was coming loose and she could now make noise.

"Shut the fuck up!" Billy barked at Mary Jane from the back seat. "Or I'll shove that fucking rag down your throat so you get the message."

Mary Jane heard the command and immediately went silent.

The rest of the trip to Tarrytown was uneventful. Mo pulled the minivan into the parking lot in the rear of the hotel and parked next to Gabby and Suniel's green Focus. Nasi, who'd arrived by cab a few minutes earlier, was leaning up against the car talking to Suniel. Billy glanced at his watch. It was 10:25 A.M. Perfect.

"Did everyone have a nice morning?" He said in a devilish tone.

"Mission accomplished," was the response from Nasi. "I listened to reports of the fire in Penn Station all the way from LaGuardia. My Lebanese taxi driver was almost in tears."

Gabby offered a similar reply. "I think the Brooklyn Bridge will be out of service for some time to come. And, according to my iphone, CNN is reporting there were also bombs in the Holland Tunnel and 59th Street Bridge. It appears, Nina is very convincing."

"Excellent. Alright, let's get our bags from the hotel room. I'll wait for Nina to arrive. Then I will join you in the room. Nina will stay down here and keep an eye on our young prize." Billy motioned with a tilt of his head toward the rear of the van. "Don't forget. Enter the lobby one or two at a time. We don't want to start spooking the American people just yet. And wait for me up there before you open the champagne."

Rem, Mo, Gabby, Suniel, and Nasi walked from the parking lot and through the hotel lobby, leaving about fifteen seconds between each of them as they did. As soon as she saw the last of them go through the lobby and into the elevator, Nina, who'd been secretly waiting in her car just a few isles behind them, joined Billy. She was carrying two large duffle bags; their clothes for the next few weeks and some clothes for Mary Jane. She flung the bags onto the rear seat of the van and gave Billy a passionate kiss through the driver's open window.

"Hop in. We've got some work to do."

⋙⋘

The clock on the cable-TV box said 10:43. Rem and Mo were watching the reports on CNN. Gabby and Nasi were in the other bedroom watching channel 4, a local station that had preempted all its morning shows to cover the tragedies. Both newscasts implied the bombings may not yet be over and that reports were still coming in from all over the city about possible acts of terror. Suniel was standing at the hotel room window looking out over the expansive golf course surrounding the Hilton.

The telephone on the nightstand next to Suniel rang. He wasn't sure if he should answer it so he looked to Rem and Mo for guidance. Rem nodded his head. "It might be the front desk. You'd better answer."

"Hello."

"Suniel, it's me, Billy. Nina just called my cell to say she'll be a few more minutes. Is everyone there?"

"Yes. We're all here. Do you want us to bring the bags down?"

"No. What phone are you on?" Billy knew the suite had several phones, all on the same number.

"I am in my room, on the phone by the bed."

"Please pick up the phone in the living room and have everyone gather round. Put me on the speaker. I have wonderful news."

Suniel shouted in the direction of Rem to pick up the phone and put it on speaker. Then he shouted into the other bedroom for Gabby and his brother to join them. "Billy wants to talk to us."

When the five men were gathered around the phone on the cocktail table Suniel said, "Billy, we're all here."

"Excellent," Came the response from the speaker. "Can you all hear me?"

"Yes."

"Enjoy your virgins."

The men looked at each other with puzzled faces. A few seconds passed. Then Gabby figured out the meaning of Billy's taunt. But it was too late.

The cable-TV box clicked to 10:45.

The explosion that originated from the suitcase next to the cocktail table incinerated the five men and the entire suite. Very little would be left for the police to find.

Billy and Nina watched from the minivan as the sixteenth floor of the hotel disappeared into a cloud of smoke and flames. They sat motionless for several seconds. Then Billy put the van in gear and drove east. They had a ferry to catch.

CHAPTER 31

B illy and Nina were filled with adrenaline on the drive from the
Tarrytown Hilton to Bridgeport, Connecticut. They reveled in
the radio news which was still reporting about the bogus explosions
as well as the three real ones. Emboldened by their wildly successful morning, the co-conspirators slapped high-fives every time the
radio announcer mentioned a report of, "Several *Middle Eastern-
looking men leaving the scene.*"

"It's a little frightening how easily a news station will spread a
rumor for you." Billy said as he drove.

Mary Jane Wallace was securely tied and lying on the floor in
the back of the van. Nina thought she heard her crying at one
point but wasn't concerned. There would be plenty to cry about
later- after the ransom was paid. Billy would see to that.

When they were less than thirty miles from the Hilton, just
barely over the Connecticut border, WINS radio interrupted a

commercial message for more breaking news: *"We have confirmed reports from two sources at the scene of a major explosion at the Tarrytown Hilton Hotel. The hotel is just a short distance from the Tappan Zee Bridge, which has not been targeted but which is another major artery into New York. Our 1010 reporter John LaPalma is on the phone with us. John, what have you seen so far?"* There was a short pause and some static, then, *"Susan, this is John LaPalma. I was driving from my home and had just crossed the bridge when I heard the explosion. I was still a quarter mile from the hotel but I could see smoke rising over Route 287 to the east. By the time I arrived at the hotel there were dozens of people in the parking lot and many more fleeing the burning hotel. It appears the explosion occurred on the sixteenth floor and the fire has now consumed the two floors above it. I'm standing at my car because access to the hotel has been restricted to the first responder equipment which has been arriving from Greenburg, Yonkers, and Tarrytown. There are at least twenty pieces of fire equipment here already and ambulances are just now beginning to make their way through the parking lot towards the hotel entrance. This hotel is only a few hundred yards from...."*

Billy snapped off the radio. "It will be interesting to see how long before they tie the hotel to our Manhattan projects." He laughed out loud at the unintended use of the term "Manhattan Project"; the code name for the first atomic bomb.

When he turned the radio back on, the focus had shifted to the events in the city. He and Nina listened in silent amusement as they traveled east on Route 95. They had another forty miles to Bridgeport where a ferry would take them across the Long Island Sound back to Long Island. Billy made the assumption that the only safe way to circle back to Long Island would be by ferry. He expected the bridges would all be closed for several hours, which they were. But the Bridgeport-to-Port Jefferson ferry was far enough from Manhattan so as not to be considered a terrorist target.

Nina had rented a modest house in Commack, a suburb of New York about fifty miles from the city. She and Billy had spent many nights there preparing the rental for their needs. The main floor of the ranch style house would be their home for the next few weeks. She rented the house furnished but added a few personal touches Billy had insisted upon. A new flat screen TV replaced the owners' conventional model. That one went to the basement. And Billy wanted blackout curtains for all the windows so that when drawn, no one could see inside.

The basement was almost perfect and the main reason Nina chose the house from the several she surveyed. The small cellar windows had been previously bricked up by the owner. There was only one way to enter the basement from inside the house and no access from the outside. There was a full bathroom, refrigerator, microwave oven and a small cooktop with one burner. The basement had been used as a sub-rental by the previous owner who seemed to like the color grey. He'd painted the concrete walls grey, which, by itself, wouldn't have been so bad. But he'd also put down grey carpeting throughout the one large room. The ceiling was a full ten feet from the floor and covered with gypsum board. Billy figured this would provide some soundproofing. In the center of the wall farthest from the staircase was a full size bed with headboard made of chrome bars. The only other furniture was a wooden chair and a lamp.

Billy had run a cable line to the basement and connected the old TV. He intended Mary Jane to spend the next few weeks down there and he didn't want to hear from her. He figured if a fourteen year old kid had some entertainment she'd be quiet. He also installed a heavy door at the top of the stairs with metal backing on one side. It was the sort of fireproof door usually reserved for the entrance from a garage and would be virtually impossible to break through without the right tools.

The house itself sat on an acre of wooded property and was barely visible from the street. It was unlikely anyone passing by would give it a second thought. From the outside, the well maintained home resembled all the others on the street. An occasional deer might wander by the back yard but it was the perfect place for a man, woman, and their captive to disappear for a few weeks.

Billy intended to keep Mary Jane Wallace securely housed in his basement. He didn't want her screaming for help or trying to escape so he made both impossible. He hadn't yet shared the complete details of his nefarious plan with Nina. He'd told her they would contact Mary Jane's parents and demand a ransom. He told her Mary Jane's parents were rich and lived on the upper east side of Manhattan. And he told Nina that when it was over, they'd live the rest of their wealthy lives in Canada, enjoying the Wallace's ill-spent ransom.

What he hadn't told her was that he'd once been in love with Mary Jane's mother. He hadn't told her this was completely about revenge.

CHAPTER 32

She hadn't taken her eyes off the television in over an hour. Carol Wallace was glued to the local NBC news broadcast that had preempted the Today Show just after the first report of explosions on the Brooklyn Bridge. She'd surfed all the networks and CNN. NBC seemed to have the most reporters on the ground and were providing a live feed from the Manhattan entrance to the Queens-Midtown Tunnel; the only place Carol was really concerned about. She knew her daughter's school bus took the tunnel on its way to the Freeman Academy on Long Island and her eyes were fixed on every human walking or staggering out of the tunnel entrance. Many were covered with dark soot.

Carol had called the academy fifteen minutes after she first heard about the explosions but the switchboard operator could only confirm that the bus had not yet arrived. That, in itself, wasn't unusual. The bus generally didn't arrive at Freeman until close to ten o'clock. Mary Jane's first class, Latin, didn't begin until 10:15 A.M. But with each passing moment of silence, Carol's anxiety crept upward. She asked the operator to have Ms. Bryant, the Dean of Women, call her as soon as the bus arrived.

She's also called the mothers of the other three girls Mary Jane shared the bus with to see if anyone had heard from their daughters. But because Freeman prohibited students from bringing cell phones to campus, none of the parents had any more information than did Carol. One of them hadn't even heard about the explosions yet and none could realistically expect to hear from the girls until they arrived at school. Carol silently cursed the stupid rule about cell phones.

She pictured her only daughter sitting on the bus, jammed in traffic not far from the tunnel's entrance, curious about the hold-up. She told herself the bus driver would likely keep the young girls on the bus rather than having them walk back out the tunnel. But what about all the people coming out covered in soot? Something terrible must have happened. She hoped her daughter was far from the trouble.

It was now 10:25 A.M. The anchorwoman on NBC was confirming that several bombings had been reported around the city in an apparent attempt to isolate Manhattan Island. A former CIA anti-terrorist specialist was being interviewed by the anchor on one side of the screen with the smoky image of the tunnel's entrance on the other. When pressed about why terrorists might want to block all entrances to the city, the CIA guy responded, "It may not be that they want to keep people out. It may be they want to keep people in. Why they might do that is anyone's guess but one possible answer is that they plan some other level of terrorism from which people would want to flee the city but were now trapped; a dirty-bomb perhaps." He went on to say, "I'm concerned about the next few hours. Once the methods of egress from the city are blocked, we could see another round of activity. Or, worse yet, maybe we won't see it at all. Maybe they intend to use some form of bacterial…"

The phone in Carol's left hand rang. She prayed she'd hear Mary Jane's voice.

"Hello."

"Mrs. Wallace, please. This is Virginia Bryant at the Freeman Academy."

"This is Carol Wallace. Has our bus arrived yet?" She raced through her question.

"No. The bus hasn't arrived yet and we haven't heard from the driver who always carries a cell phone. But it may be that if they are somewhere in the tunnel, he has no cell reception. They may just be stuck in a horrendous traffic jam deep in the tunnel." Ms. Bryant was trying to infuse optimism into her otherwise bad news. "They may also be stuck in traffic outside the tunnel on the Manhattan side, but I would have thought he would have called us if that were the case." She regretted the words the moment they left her lips.

"Have you heard from any other students who use the tunnel?" Carol didn't know what else to ask.

"Yes. We only have two other buses that come from Manhattan. One arrived on time and knew nothing of the trouble this morning. The other arrived about an hour late. It crossed the 59th Street Bridge, apparently before the explosions there, and was stuck in traffic on the Queens side. But they made it here safely." Again, she regretted her choice of words.

Carol heard the clicking in her ear that told her another call was waiting. She leapt with hope.

"Virginia, I have another call. Maybe this is Mary Jane. I have to go. I'll call you back."

"Hello?" Again, she prayed for a young girl's voice. And again she was disappointed.

"Carol. It's me." Her husband sounded hurried. "Have you heard from MJ yet?"

She took a deep breath. "No. I was just on the phone with Freeman. They haven't heard from the driver. They think he's just stuck in traffic in the tunnel. You know…no cell service." She surprised herself with her reassuring voice. Then she added, "Alan, I think you should come home."

There were several seconds of painful silence on the line. For a moment Carol thought the line had gone dead. Then the words that stung like a hot sword jammed into her gut.

"Carol, I've got a lot going on here. The markets are going nuts. Call me when you hear from MJ. I've got to go."

Carol Wallace bit her upper lip as she always did when she was thinking. She pressed 'END' on her phone and dropped it on the sofa. From her apartment window there was no evidence anything horrible was going on today. The tree tops in Central Park held on to their summer green even though they'd already endured a few cool September nights. Second Avenue traffic was a little heavier than usual for a weekday morning. If she looked east she could see the western edge of the 59ᵗʰ Street Bridge. No vehicles were moving in either direction. It looked a bit eerie but she remembered hearing on the TV that all traffic on all bridges and tunnels had been suspended by the police.

It all looked so calm. And the silence, provided by the thick glass and distance from the ground, added to the almost peaceful scene. "How could anything so horrible be going on?" She thought. "It's such a pleasant morning. Just like that morning... in September, 2001."

CHAPTER 33

For Ted Holly, the morning had begun like so many others. Whenever he worked a twenty-four hour shift, his morning routine as a probationary firefighter, was pretty much the same. Beyond arriving at least an hour before his shift began, Ted was expected to make sure there was a fresh pot of coffee and make breakfast for the nine other firefighters with whom he shared the 32nd Street firehouse. After cooking three pounds of bacon and scrambling two dozen eggs, he and Bobby Iannuzzi, the other probie, were expected to serve the more senior firefighters and clean the dishes afterwards. He didn't mind the job because he liked to cook and because he understood probies were expected to do such tasks. Then he and Bobby would do an equipment check of the rigs, making sure all the saws, nozzles, and hand tools were in their proper locations. In a couple of months, there would be a new kid coming from the academy and he'd take over the menial jobs. And Ted would have earned his place among the guys he'd already grown to respect so much. He'd be one of them; the most important feeling in the world to a firefighter.

It had been a quiet night; only one alarm- a small kitchen fire in the back of a bodega on 34th Street. They had the fire out, the hose packed, and were back in the station in less than an hour. Ted got to be the nozzle man which meant he was beginning to earn the trust of the seasoned guys. It was only the second time in his eight week career he was given the nozzle. It felt great.

From his young perspective, life was great. He was doing the job he always wanted to do. He was stationed in a great house, with great guys- guys he could really learn from. The pay was good and because his two years as an EMT counted toward his seniority, at twenty three years old, he was only eighteen years from pension eligibility. He didn't think life could get any better for a kid from Brooklyn with a two-year degree from John Jay.

Ted leaned back on the metal folding chair on the truck room floor of the ninety year old firehouse. It was a beautiful September morning. A few of the senior guys were standing outside the building, leaning on the brick façade and watching the well-dressed young girls walk by on their way to their office jobs. It was a warm day and the more senior guys had on shorts and FDNY tee shirts, but Ted was still required to wear his probie garb; Navy blue work pants, black belt, black shoes and navy blue FDNY shirt.

He didn't often get to sit and he was enjoying the brief break when the tranquility was shattered by the station's alarm. He rocked forward on his chair and stowed it inside the door. He was only a few feet from his gear so there was no need to run. Ted stepped into his boots and pulled up his fire-resistant pants. After slipping each arm through the blue suspender straps he clasped the giant carabineer that secured his bail-out gear around his waist. It was unlikely he'd ever need the bulky harness that became mandatory after Black Sunday; the day three firemen fell to their deaths for lack of a piece of rope. But if he ever found himself at a smoky window, it was nice to know he had the gear to safely bail out and repel down the wall.

"What have we got, Lieutenant?" His question was directed at the tall Irishman from Staten Island everyone called JR, except when it mattered. When it mattered it was Lieutenant Mullen. And when there was a call, it mattered.

"Car fire in the tunnel."

Ted threw his bunker gear over his shoulders and his helmet on his head as the huge doors grinded upward. In the front of the truck were the chauffeur and the Lieutenant. Ted shared the cab with Bobby Iannuzzi, Jimmy Beans, and Mark Brando, a crusty veteran who couldn't string together eight words without one of them being fuck. But Brando knew his stuff and Ted felt good about working with him.

The station was only ten blocks from the tunnel entrance and the sirens roared as the first pumper rolled out onto 32nd Street. Ordinarily, the guys in Ted's station wouldn't wear the heavy cylinders filled with breathable air for a car fire, but this car fire was in the tunnel where visibility and air quality can go south fast. "Turtle up boys and girls. The fuckin air in the tunnel's bad enough but add some smoke to that and you can't fuckin breathe for long." Mark was advising his young students to darn the special breathing apparatus called SCBA packs which were attached to the back of each seat in the cab. By "turtle up" he meant for them to do it by the book, which meant each man would wear a mask, connected to the breathable air, a Kevlar hood, a helmet and gloves. Even though it was a warm morning, they would also secure the Velcro clasp around their neck to fully protect themselves from potential burns.

"Don't mask up until I tell you to. We may have to walk into the fuckin tunnel." Then Mark shouted toward JR in the front seat. "Lieutenant, how far into the fuckin tunnel we have to go?"

JR Held up one finger as if to say, "Hold on. I'm getting info on the radio now." He was listening to the dispatcher on the department radio mounted in the truck and trying to listen for meaning in the static. The men in the back seat couldn't hear the message their Lieutenant was getting from the dispatcher but they could tell from JR's face he didn't like what he was hearing. JR Mullen had seen his share of action during his twenty-two years in the FDNY. He didn't scare easily. He loved firefighting and loved leading his men into battle against the flaming enemy.

So the men in the cab were surprised when their seasoned Lieutenant leaned over the front seat and said, "Holy shit. We've got ourselves some work. Seems like there was some kind of explosion in the tunnel with multiple vehicles involved. PD is guessing it's about midway into the eastbound tube. It's already been declared an MCI."

Ted looked to Mark for an explanation. He responded without even looking away from his Lieutenant, "Mass Causality Incident. In other words, a cluster-fuck."

Once reminded of the acronym's meaning, Ted recalled learning about MCI's at the academy and during his EMT training. He'd never been to one, but he knew Mark's colorful description was about right. Mass Causality meant there would be at least ten injured victims. That meant at least four ambulances on the scene and God-knows how much fire apparatus. The coordination of even a small MCI fell to the senior fire officer first on the scene, probably a Captain or Battalion Chief who arrived with one of the engines, and is referred to as the Incident Command. This official would establish a command post from which he would coordinate the effort until relieved either by someone of higher rank or by someone with a technical expertise required by the incident.

As their engine raced toward the tunnel on 32nd Street, Lt. Mullen began giving assignments from the front seat. "Mark, you take the two probies, a radio, and a can. We're not going to be able to drive into the tunnel because it's probably going to be full of backed up traffic. You guys are going to have to walk in and be my eyes. Priority is evacuation of victims but I'm going to need intel on what's going on in there." He held up his finger again because another static-filled message was coming over his radio. He listened for 45 seconds then continued his instructions to his crew.

"Okay, PD says we have cars backed up all the way to the tunnel's entrance on this side. So we can't get a truck in there. The good news is there's not much smoke on our side. There's a shit-load of apparatus responding on the Queens side but that's where all the smoke's coming out so they can't make a push in the east-bound side yet. So you three go on air and get in from this side. I need to know what we've got in the middle of the tube. The rest of the cavalry coming from Manhattan will lay hose and connect to a hydrant at the mouth of the tube. I'm guessing the engines will use the standpipes in the west-bound tube, then cut through at the crossovers. Any questions?"

Ted asked, "What's a crossover?"

Mullen shot Mark a look that said, "You take this", and got back to his radio. Mark explained, "A crossover is a little fuckin tunnel that connects the east-bound tube with the west-bound tube.

There's about five of them in the tunnel. It's the best way to fight a fire in there."

The truck came to a stop a few seconds later on the corner of First Avenue and 32nd Street, just outside the tunnel entrance. Lieutenant Mullen jumped out first to check in with the Incident Command post, already under the command of a Battalion Chief from lower Manhattan who was first on the scene. The rest of the crew remained in the cab while the chauffer positioned the rig to the side of the street so that ambulances could get by when needed. When Ted stepped out he realized Mark's "Cluster-fuck" was already in progress.

Although the police had already removed all the cars backed up outside the tunnel, Ted could see taillights stuck about twenty feet inside the tunnel. Victims of the smoke were sitting everywhere there was a place to lean. Most were coughing and covered with soot. Many had vomited as they gasped for clean air leaning against the stone walls usually channeling vehicles into the tube. Four ambulances were on scene but their crews were overwhelmed by the number of injured. People, police and EMS workers were running in all directions.

Ted followed Mark and Bobby who had already begun walking to the tunnel's entrance. When Mark gave the signal, he reached around behind his back and turned on his air supply. The deep, Darth Vader-like sound of breathing began to fill his mask. He felt Mark tapping him on his shoulder. He was pointing toward the north tunnel exit and the three FDNY pumpers driving into the gapping tube.

"How 'bout that shit? Those guys are going in the wrong fuckin hole." But Ted and Mark both knew what was happening. The engines, each carrying 500 gallons of water, would travel in the parallel tunnel until they were approximately halfway through; then their crews would lay hose through the short crossovers that connected the two tubes at various points. It would give them good position to attack the fire without having to fight the smoke pouring out the Queens side. They might have the fire under control by the time he, Mark and Bobby walked all the way in.

But he also understood their mission was search and rescue; search for fire and rescue victims. Once they found the fire, they would radio back to Lt. Mullen using the handie-talkie clipped to his lapel. Although he was entering a smoky, dark tunnel with little more than a flashlight and ax in his hands, Ted felt he was going to be okay. He was with two of his brothers; one who had a lot of experience on the job. And he felt good about all the training he went through at the academy. Because of that training, he was never in better physical shape. The half mile walk wearing seventy pounds of gear shouldn't be a problem for him and Bobby. He wasn't as sure about Mark.

The tunnel had two lanes of traffic, both currently at a stand-still. As they approached the first cars, it was clear their occupants had already gotten out and may have been some of the people puking on 32nd Street. Ted shined his light into the next row of cars. Still no occupants. The same was the case for the next seventeen rows of cars. Everyone had obviously exited the tunnel on foot before FDNY arrived. As they checked each empty car Mark reached in and turned on the vehicles headlights. The extra illumination helped a little, but each car's headlights could only shine as far as the back of the next car; usually just a few feet ahead. Still, it was some help and helped to make the blackness in the tunnel seem less eerie.

The three firemen could now see thick, black smoke rolling along the roof of the tunnel. It was menacing in appearance but still several feet above their heads and no need for immediate concern. Ted shined his light into the open window of the next car, a white Mercedes. Again, no one home. But as he turned to head toward the next car his foot caught on something soft. It was the head of a woman lying face down on the pavement. "Mark! I have a victim here." He shouted through his mask.

Ted knelt down to evaluate the woman as Bobby held his flashlight directly on her head. He checked for a pulse on her neck. There was none. Her skin was cold. He heard Mark calling from between the next two cars, "Got a pulse?"

"Nothing."

Mark radioed his Lieutenant, "Search one to IC."

JR's voice came over the crackling radio, "This is IC. Go ahead search one."

"We have a victim about 400 feet into the tube. Not breathing and no pulse."

"Confirmed. One victim 400 feet in without breath or pulse. North or south side of tube?"

At first Mark didn't understand the relevance of the question but then responded, "North side. I'll leave a light next to the victim and continue our search." He knew that no bodies would be removed until all viable victims had been removed. He, Ted, and Bobby needed to trudge on if they had any chance of reaching the incident before running low on air.

He signaled with his hands that Ted and Bobby were to follow him and continue the search. After another fifty feet, they came upon another victim, still clutching his car keys but also quite dead. Mark rolled him over and shined a light on his lifeless face. He was only about twenty-five and his face was covered with soot. Mark suspected his lungs were full of the same soot.

Mark radioed his report, then continued into the darkness. They came upon another body a few cars up, then two more as the tunnel began to curve around a bend. This time Mark used his experience to plan ahead. They'd been in the tunnel less than five minutes but had a long way to go. "Search one to IC."

"Go ahead search one."

"Two more bodies 600 feet in, north side. Both dead." Mark was using the number of cars they'd walked past to estimate the distance they'd traveled. He added, "IC, have we got apparatus in the west-bound tunnel? We may need fresh masks for the return trip." Mark was referring to the Specially Contained Breathing Apparatus (SCBA) they were each carrying on their backs and the knowledge that even an experienced firefighter could exhaust an air cylinder in under fifteen minutes.

"Confirmed search one. Plenty of extra air waiting for you."

Mark looked at his probies. "You guys okay?"

Both indicated a thumbs up.

"Don't even think about taking those fuckin masks off. Whatever killed these poor bastards is still in the air down here."

Both men nodded their understanding and continued walking forward. Bobby walked on the south side of the tube and Ted took the middle, between the two rows of cars. They continued to find bodies. Ted assumed all the victims were trying to run from the tunnel because they were all found head-first. All had the soot on their faces; especially under their lifeless noses. They'd walked the equivalent of five football fields and discovered thirty-two bodies.

Suddenly Mark stopped and indicated they were to get down on their knees. He waved his arms up and down and led by example. Ted crawled between two cars to get close to Mark; the place he wanted to be if something was going wrong. When his mask was inches from Mark's, he asked, "What's up?"

Mark pointed at the tiled ceiling of the tunnel. The black smoke had turned to a light gray and was becoming less dense. But it was now moving much faster than before. Then Ted heard what Mark heard a few seconds earlier. The sound was coming from a long way off but it was the unmistakable sound of glass breaking and water.

Mark shouted through his mask, "The engines must have come through the crossover. They're putting water on the fire. Stay down."

Ted understood. The engines in the other tunnel had made their way through the crossover and had at least one good hose on the fire. That's why the black smoke was turning gray. It always did when the good-guys were winning. Gray smoke told the firefighters they were making progress against the enemy. And the sound of glass breaking was the sound of car windows being shattered by the force of the water screaming out a hose line.

And Mark was right about them staying low. As the other firefighters cooled and smothered the fire with water, they were also pushing the fire and its heat and smoke directly toward Mark and his men. Since he wasn't sure how far they were from the hose line, it was probably a good idea to stay on the ground a few minutes and let whatever was coming their way pass overhead.

Ted lay on his belly listening to the distant victory. But mostly he just heard the deep sound of his own breathing. He propped himself up on his elbows and waited. After a few minutes Bobby Iannuzzi crawled over to be next to Ted and Mark. They could now hear the unmistakable sound of steam forming. They assumed firemen pushing from the other tunnel must be getting close because the smoke above their heads was now turning from gray to white; another sign that the fire was succumbing to the volumes of cooling water and producing superheated steam. Also, another good reason to stay low.

Mark shouted through his mask, "Turn your lights on and aim them at the ceiling in front of us. I want these fuckin guys to know we're here." Then he shouted into his handie-talkie, "Search one to IC."

"Go ahead Search one." Mullen's voice was unmistakeable.

"Tell the fuckin guys from the engine company that we're in here and they're pushing the shit onto us!"

Condensing water droplets began to rain down from the white porcelain tiles lining the tunnel ceiling. Mark exposed a small area of his wrist by pulling his glove back an inch. He was checking to see how hot the droplets were. This meant nothing to Ted and Bobby but, to a veteran like Mark, it was important information. "Okay boys. The fuckin cavalry is getting close."

Just as he said it, the three men felt a heavy deluge coming from above. Water from the hoses was ricocheting off the walls and ceiling and soaking them. "Wave your fuckin lights!" Mark cried. The moving beams of light had the desired effect. Within seconds, the deluge stopped and Ted could hear firemen calling to them from further in the tunnel.

"Any fire behind you?" Came from somewhere ahead.

"No. Shut down the fuckin water!" Mark responded. For a moment there was silence. The steam had rolled by and the air was beginning to clear although it was still pitch dark without the flashlights. Mark got to his feet and his probies followed. It was only then that Ted realized his heart was pounding.

A light appeared in front of them. It was coming toward them. "Hey. What the hell are you guys supposed to be?" The question came from a stocky Captain from the 288th in Queens. He and his team had entered the westbound tube, met up with the three engines from Manhattan and had pushed three lines on the fire from the crossover.

"We're the search team from the 116th. Mark responded.

"You guys okay?"

Mark ignored the question and was on the radio with Lt. Mullen. "Search one to IC."

"A series of crackles preceded, "Go ahead search one."

"Lieutenant, the boys from the north tube seem to have knocked down the fire. We'll continue forward, change our bottles at their trucks, help them pack hose, then ride back to you with them."

"Acknowledged search one. Try to play nice, Mark." Lt. Mullen's tone was noticeably less formal now that he knew his men were out of harm's way.

"I'm Nick DiGiorno," the stocky Captain offered his gloved hand. "Just the three of you?"

Mark became the spokesman for the men from Manhattan. "Yeah, just the three of us. We were the first truck on the scene at the mouth of the tunnel. We were sent in to see what the fucks up. Found multiple DOAs from here all the way back to the entrance. All of them seemed to be smoke victims. What have you got up ahead?"

"We pushed through a crosswalk about a hundred yards back. By the time we came through, most of the big fire had burned itself out. We've been putting water on the cars for about ten minutes. Looks to me like a couple of vans stopped in the tunnel, backed up traffic, then blew their wad. I'm guessing there was a lot of gasoline involved. The vans and the first six rows behind them are fucked. Behind that, it was probably the smoke that killed the drivers; many of them are still in their cars." He motioned for Mark and his men to follow him. "Come on. Take a look. It's not pretty."

Captain DiGiorno barked some orders at the firemen who were still putting water on a smoldering red BMW. They shut down their nozzle and began to retreat back into the tunnel. As Mark and his probies followed the Captain they began to pass cars that had sustained fire damage. Then they saw the first of many bodies that were slumped over their steering wheels; the victims of smoke. The further they walked the more severe the damage got.

After twenty yards, all the cars had fire damage. After fifty yards the cars became burned out shells, some with charred bodies now drenched from the fire hoses. A bit further, Ted looked in the window of a burned out minivan and saw what he guessed was an entire family. In the front seats were the remains of two adults, burned beyond any recognition. In the back seat: two small bodies, one still in the charred remains of a car seat.

There was death everywhere Ted looked. In his short time in the department, he'd only seen one burned body before; and that was from a distance. This was like a macabre nightmare. If he'd come across these incinerated corpses in any other setting he might not have recognized them as human remains. There was just nothing left that humanized them. They resembled blackened mannequins; no clothing, no hair, no facial features, nothing that made them human except the fact that they were sitting in burned out cars.

The three men walked in total silence, following Nick DiGiorno deeper into the tunnel toward the source of all the destruction. They shined their lights into every car as they passed, each producing increasingly gruesome results. Ted didn't know it but Mark was counting victims. He was sent in to provide intel to his IC and that's what he intended to do.

Ted could now see light coming from the crosswalk on the left side of the tunnel. The firemen were withdrawing their hose lines into the crosswalk. There was no more fire in the tunnel. All that remained were the drenched cars and bodies and massive puddles of water. The smell of burning rubber lingered from the melted tires.

The captain turned toward the men as he approached the crosswalk. "Why don't you guys give us a hand and we'll get you back to your IC?"

"In a minute Cap. I need to go all the way up." Mark intended to give his Lieutenant as accurate a body count as he could and to do that he needed to walk another twenty yards. "I need to give my IC a body count."

"Okay. Captain DiGiorno said. Then he pointed to the left. "Those two vans up there; that's where the shit started. There's no one in the vans but the big black thing behind it was a school bus; one of those short ones. It had a driver and four passengers."

CHAPTER 34

It was nearly dark when the van turned into the narrow driveway. The ferry crossing had gone without incident and the drive to Commack from Port Jefferson took less than an hour. Nina had duct-taped Mary Jane's mouth and eyes and made sure she was completely covered by a tarp in the back of the van. Billy and Nina stayed in their car for the crossing just in case anyone became curious about the van's contents. They weren't sure just how jumpy people would be after the morning's bombings.

But by this time the media was reporting that several "Arab-looking" males had been seen near the tunnel and also fleeing the Brooklyn Bridge area. Billy thought that if the rumors kept working off themselves, by this time tomorrow someone would report seeing the same Arabs leaving Penn Station just as the bomb went off and carrying pictures of Osama Bin Laden.

As they drove up the driveway the van's headlights illuminated the small brick ranch and the Blue Ford Focus Nina had rented for their future travels. As soon as the police studied the surveillance cameras at the tunnel exit, they'd be looking for the van. It was no longer safe to use it.

The lights Billy had set on timers inside the house cast an eerie glow through the blackout curtains. He was satisfied that no one could see in at night even if they got close enough, which they had no reason to do.

"Home sweet home my dear." Billy said as he turned off the engine. "At least for the next few weeks."

Billy grabbed the two large duffle bags. "You get Goldielocks. Make sure you keep the tape on her eyes until we're inside. I'll get the door."

The house had no garage so the van was left in front, unseen from the street because of the trees and brush, but still visible. Billy would have preferred a garage.

Once inside, he threw one duffle on the living room floor. The other, the one containing clothes and supplies for Mary Jane, he flung over his shoulder. Nina had taken the initiative to buy a few pair of sweatpants, panties, socks and tee shirts at a thrift shop as well as toilet paper, soap and tampons. She carefully guided the blindfolded teen into the house, prompting her to take small steps.

"Let's take her downstairs." Billy said.

"Okay kid. We're going down a set of stairs. Hold the banister on your left. There're about fifteen steps. I'll tell you when you're at the bottom." Nina was using the nurturing voice she and Billy had agreed on. She would be the one the kid felt she could trust and Billy would be the one she had to fear. It would help them manipulate her when they needed to later.

Up to now, the frightened teen had said almost nothing. So Billy and Nina were surprised when her first words were, "I really need to pee."

Billy snuck up next to her and shouted in her right ear, "Shut the fuck up and get down the stairs before I throw you down. Would you like me to throw you down?" He put his hand on her back.

"No!"

"I said shut the fuck up!"

Nina put her arm around her and used her soft voice to tell Mary Jane to inch toward the stairs, guiding her along the way. They descended the wooden stairs slowly. Nina kept a hand on the teen's shoulder as she worked her way down the darkness. When they reached the bottom Mary Jane could feel the cool carpet with her bare feet. She was sweating and shivering even though the basement was warmed by a working oil burner in the far corner. She could hear it rumble.

Nina guided her toward a chair Billy had positioned in the middle of the room near the foot of the bed. "Sit back on this chair. Stay right here for a few minutes. We'll be right back."

Mary Jane could hear the sound of two people going up the stairs. She sat and waited in the darkness. She thought about her bus and her friends. What had happened? It all happened so fast? A few moments later, she heard two people coming down the stairs.

"Okay. Take the tape off her face." It was the man's voice.

As the world came into focus, Mary Jane could see she was in someone's basement. The concrete walls were painted with a shiny grey paint, the kind she'd seen on the hull of a Navy ship she visited on a class trip. The floor was also grey but most was carpeted. Directly in front of her was a bed with no sheets or blankets. Her first lucid thought was that she had been kidnapped to be in some sort of pornography. She'd heard about such things and had recently seen the movie "Taken".

Then the man and woman she knew up to now only by voice, came around from behind her and sat on the edge of the mattress. Both were wearing black ski masks. They were a frightening image. The man was holding a baseball bat. He spoke first.

"Listen to me carefully because I'm only going to say this once. If you do exactly as we say, we will not hurt you. Do you understand?"

Still afraid to make any sound, Mary Jane nodded.

"Good. Now, we've gone through a lot of trouble to get you here. Make sure you do what we say. I really don't want to hurt you." He didn't sound as mean as before.

"So, here's what's going to happen. You're going to stay here for a few weeks. We will be in touch with your parents to let them know you're okay. You will stay in our basement. We'll make sure you have plenty to eat. There's a fridge over there." He pointed toward the small kitchenette. "There's even a TV. You can watch TV all day if you want. If you want some books, we'll get them for you. If you need something, you tell us and we'll get it."

Even though the masked characters frightened her, Mary Jane tried to look Billy in the eyes. Somehow they seemed familiar but she didn't recognize the voice.

"Then, in a while, your parents are going to pay us a lot of money to return you to them. If they pay, we will. It's kind of as simple as that. You just need to stay quiet. If you scream, I will kill you. If you try to escape, I will kill you. If you don't do exactly as I say, I will kill you."

Then he pointed to the bathroom. "There's a bathroom over there. There's some cereal in the fridge. We'll get more food in the morning. Have you got any questions?"

Mary Jane nodded, but stayed silent. She was too afraid to speak.

"Well..., what's the question?" The man said impatiently.

Mary Jane mustered all the courage a fourteen year old can muster and whispered, "What happed to my friends on the bus?"

Billy thought for a moment about what he should say. He conjured the image of earlier that day- of the three other girls on the bus in the tunnel and their terrified faces as he fired his gun at them. He hesitated, not out of concern for the young girl, but because he wanted to make sure his answer would ensure her compliance. Then, in a very calm voice he said, "They're all dead, Mary Jane. Consider yourself the lucky one."

The masked man and woman stood. They went up the stairs and closed the large door behind them. Mary Jane could hear it lock.

She looked around and saw a duffle bag on the bed. There was a small lamp on the floor; the only source of light in the grey box that was to be her home.

CHAPTER 35

Carol Wallace hadn't moved from her kitchen table in three hours. Her attention was glued to the CNN reporter on the TV who, by now, had confirmed mass fatalities resulting from the Midtown Tunnel bombing.

She'd called the Freeman Academy several times but always with the same result. The bus carrying her daughter and three other students had not arrived and had not been heard from. They promised to contact her the moment they heard anything. Carol was beginning to fear the worst.

Never a spiritual person, she found herself talking to God; trying to strike some sort of deal if only her daughter would walk through the front door. She used standardized prayers she hadn't bumbled in twenty years: words that until today had no meaning to her.

Her husband had not called back since their conversation in the morning. She wanted desperately for the phone to ring with Alan on the other end saying he'd just heard from Mary Jane. She wanted nothing more than for this to be a normal day. But her motherly instincts told her it wasn't going to be a normal day. Something was terribly wrong. She could feel it.

She thought about her daughter and the way she would rush around the kitchen in the morning before leaving for school. She thought about how she took such everyday things for granted and promised God she would never take Mary Jane for granted again. She remembered looking down at the very kitchen table her daughter had eaten Cheerios at that very morning.

And that was the last thing she remembered.

>=<+ +>=<

Carol saw a white light shining at her and heard someone calling her name. She tried to focus but her head ached terribly and she felt a little nauseous. She could tell she was lying on her back, probably on something hard. She closed her eyes to avoid the garish light trying to intrude. Something was pinching her left arm; something very cold.

"Who's there?" Was all she could say without pain.

"Carol, it's me, Alan. I'm here."

"Alan? Where am I?

"You're in the ER at St. Luke's. You passed out at home."

She tried to open one eye and found that she could focus if she looked only through one eye. Her husband's face began to come into focus. She could see other people standing behind him. One of them was dressed in white. The others were too far away to see. Her headache was unbearable.

"Why am I here?"

"You fainted and hit your head on the kitchen counter. I called 911 and an ambulance took us both to the hospital. You've been here almost an hour. I'm so glad to hear your voice. Oh God. I thought I'd lost you too."

"I feel like I might vomit, Alan."

"It's okay. I'm here. I've got a pail here on your left. Just lean this way if you feel sick. The doctor said you might wake up feeling sick."

Carol leaned to her left and wretched without producing much vomit. She did it again and then a third time before wiping her mouth with her free hand. Then she looked up at her husband.

"Too? Oh God, no."

CHAPTER 36

LT

W e'd spent the last three hours in Jacobson's conference room watching CNN and getting occasional briefings from NYPD. Since the whole idea of the JTTF was to share information and have the FBI, CIA, NSA, and the NYPD all work in harmony, it was a little frustrating that the Joint Task Force on Terrorism was locked up on the sixteenth floor of a building whose basement was one of the bombing targets.

By noon, here's what we knew. We knew that much of the hyperbole and hysteria was bullshit. Despite the reports to the contrary, the 59th Street Bridge was not targeted. Nor were the Holland or Lincoln tunnels, or the George Washington Bridge. Grand Central Terminal and the other sources of egress from Manhattan were also unharmed. NYPD had bomb squads going over them all with a fine toothed comb but nobody expected them to find anything.

Someone at CNN or one of the other networks must have started the rumor that the purpose of the attacks was to cut off Manhattan from the rest of the world. That just didn't seem to be the case. So, three hours into the investigation, we could confirm only the following:

- A sizable bomb had been placed on a train originating on Long island and detonated as the train entered Penn Station at approximately nine A.M.
- A car bomb had been detonated remotely on the center span of the Brooklyn Bridge at approximately nine A.M. The bridge itself did not seem to suffer structural damage but engineers will have to determine that for certain. In the meantime, the bridge is closed.
- Also, at about nine A.M. two panel trucks, rented from Ryder, and carrying considerable explosives, shrapnel and gasoline, exploded in the center of the south tube of the Midtown Tunnel.

And that's about all we knew for sure. It was far too early for accurate casualty numbers but it looked bad; certainly several hundred in the tunnel and Penn Station alone. About an hour ago we got a report of a major explosion at the Hilton Hotel in Tarrytown, which is an hour north of the city. CNN made a big deal about it and had a reporter and camera crew on the scene but it was hard to see how it could be related.

All the fires associated with the explosions had been brought under control by eleven A.M. It seems the FDNY has its shit together in ways the JTTF can only dream about. The mayor was scheduled to hold a press conference in fifteen minutes but his information came from this building so we didn't expect to hear anything we didn't already know.

Basically, we were sitting around being fed data and speculating as to who, why, and how. Actually, I think I already know the why- they hate us. Not much has changed in the twelve years since 9-11 except that now we've got a lot more people pissed at us because now we have massive armies occupying their countries.

While we waited for data to trickle in, we speculated about why those three sites. Nobody had much to offer. Ken said he thought the scumbags were trying to make a point; that even though we've clamped down hard on air traffic since 9-11, all other forms of transportation are painfully exposed. He said, "If you really want to terrorize a country, make it believe none of its transportation systems are safe. Make people think twice about going anywhere."

I think he's giving the bad guys too much credit. When you're angry enough to explode shrapnel and gasoline into innocent people on their way to work, you're not concerned about the long-term plan. You just want to strike a blow now and make people fear you today.

It was one in the afternoon and the Chief was about to dole out assignments. Although we all agreed the three incidents were the work of a single planner, we expected the investigations would all be separate. The JTTF has dozens of really smart people who do nothing all day but use their computers to find common threads. So if one agent picks up even the most innocuous piece of information, through the miracle of twenty-first century computers, its available to all of us the next morning. Separate investigations would be the best use of our resources.

"Alright ladies and gentlemen, here's what I want by noon tomorrow." Chief Jacobson liked to throw out ridiculous deadlines. "Matthews, you and your team will take Penn Station. I want to know about every camera that covers any entrance. I want to know about any camera at every stop that train made before it pulled into

Penn. Let's put some faces with the crime. We have access to the NYPD lab guys so use them to gather fragments. We don't have enough people for that shit. And have victim lists for me."

He looked at Dean Matthews for several seconds without saying anything else. Then he added, "Well, what the hell are you waiting for? Get to it boys and girls."

Dean and his three lieutenants scrambled to their feet and left the room. Within an hour he'd have the two hundred people that worked for him combing New York and Long Island for cameras. I had no doubt he'd come up with a face.

Next Jacobson turned to Ken, who had a much smaller staff. "Stallings, I want you and Hadman and your people to cover the tunnel. The Ryder trucks were positioned next to each other in the tunnel so let's see if you can use the 800,000 cameras around New York to see where they came from. Work backwards from the tunnel entrance. We can't assume these scumbags were smart enough to use fake IDs to rent the trucks. Remember our friend from Jersey." The chief was referring to one of the clowns who blew up the garage at the World Trade Center in 1995 with a truck he rented in New Jersey with his own credit card. It didn't take long to find him.

Ken and I didn't need to be told twice so we were both on our feet before Jacobson could bust our chops. We needed to get our people together quickly and have them work with their liaisons in PD to find those cameras. There were hundreds of other things that needed to happen in an investigation like this but we all knew the psychological power of being able to put a face with the crime. If we could get the photos of these guys on the front page of the Times, good things would start to happen. It worked in Boston.

By three-thirty we'd met with the twenty-two people that work for us and sent them scurrying. Everyone knew they weren't going home tonight. They needed to make calls to wives and babysitters and dog walkers. Their lives were going to be shit until we had mug shots on the wall.

Ken called his wife then turned to me and said, "Let's take a ride down to the tunnel. I want to see this before PD fucks up the crime scene."

I had no one to call so I was ready to go.

CHAPTER 37

LT

When we arrived at the mouth of the tunnel there was still a
lot going on. The last ambulance was just rolling out, but
the command center was in full swing. FDNY had set up their incident command post about fifty yards outside the tunnel entrance.
It now consisted of a truck designed specifically for just such an
event, an adjacent tent, where the firemen could rehab- basically,
sit for a moment and drink some Gatorade, and another large tent
which was intended to be a temporary morgue. If there had been
any sort of hazardous material involved, they would have had a third
tent just for decontamination. Fortunately, I didn't see a third tent.

Technically, the JTTF has no jurisdiction in a situation such
as this. The FDNY controls the scene because there was a fire.
At some point, their chief would likely hand over the Incident
Command Post to a very senior NYPD who would be responsible
for the crime scene investigation. We don't get involved until it's
determined that terrorism was involved. At that point, the JTTF
trumps everyone.

But Ken had phoned ahead to one of his old buddies on the job and the cops were actually happy to see us. They all knew what everyone knew- this wasn't just a crime scene. And so they knew they'd eventually be assisting the JTTF in the investigation. They also knew we had access to virtually limitless resources. After all; we worked for the folks who can't run out of money- when they run low, they just print more. And so the cops tended to kiss up to us because they knew Ken could authorize a shitload of overtime for them.

The ass-kissing began in earnest as soon as we pulled up. We were greeted by a detective named Bob McEnerney who Ken used to work with when he was working homicide. They exchanged professional pleasantries then Ken introduced me to Bob. "Bob, LT Hadman. Doesn't look like much of a cop but LT spent time with PD before moving to FBI and eventually JTTF." Then he added, "Good people." That was Ken's way of saying I knew my shit. I was glad he gave me his seal of approval.

"So, you guys want to see what the scumbags did?" I was glad Bob referred to our criminal associates the same way we do. It will make it easier to work together if we don't have to tiptoe around politically correct terminology.

As we walked into the tunnel Bob briefed us on what he knew-which was pretty much what we already knew. But our eyes told us the story. All the cars that could be driven and still had the keys in them had already been removed. Further into the tube, NYPD tow trucks were hooking up the cars and trucks that were not so lucky. We passed by increasing degrees of destruction as we moved deeper into the tunnel.

Because the entire tunnel was considered a crime scene, the coroner had just begun to remove the bodies. But it didn't matter.

There isn't much we're going to learn from looking at the positions of people who were in the wrong place at the wrong time. Maybe autopsies and toxicology reports would help us figure out the type of explosive, but that could wait. For now, the dead needed to be taken from their cars.

The first few bodies we came across were slumped over their steering wheels or lying on the ground- victims of the smoke. Then we walked past a couple of burned out cars with equally burned out people still inside. The charred remains still looked like humans and I had to turn away when we passed a minivan with dead kids in the back seat. I hope they were dead from the smoke before the flames got them.

We'd walked about five hundred yards when the destruction became hard to describe. What we assume used to be cars now resembled hollow charcoal briquettes; only these briquettes had equally charred bodies inside them. Ken's a tough bastard and he just walked by. But I couldn't help think about the last few moments of these people's lives.

I heard Bob tell Ken we were getting close to ground zero- the place where the bombs went off. I could see a few more burned out shells of cars and trucks up ahead. Again, the bodies were right where they were when the explosion occurred. No one had a chance to duck or run.

"Just beyond the bus are the two trucks. Looks like they opened their back doors and shot their wads. My guess is Symtec and a lot of gasoline and shrapnel. Cocksuckers." Bob didn't like the sort of people who would do such a thing. Neither did I.

Ken asked, "Why do you think shrapnel?"

"Look at the fuckin ceiling and walls. The porcelain tiles are beat to shit. They have perforations twenty yards away. These pricks didn't just want to cause a traffic jam; they wanted to kill a lot of people."

We stopped walking when we got to what used to be two trucks, parked side by side. This is where all the police work needed to be done. An army of forensic guys will be pouring over this spot for days. They will bag the tiniest fragments in hopes of something leading to the guys who did this. Maybe a piece of shrapnel imbedded in a melted tire will turn out to be from a particular place in Jersey that makes who-knows-what, and the boss there will remember that a certain towelhead used to work there. Sometimes that's how we get our best breaks.

Bob explained, "I figure they had the doors open because the front of the truck isn't as fucked up as the bus."

I'm not sure what he was referring to on the truck. Like I said, it didn't even look like a truck to me. But when I turned back to look at the bus I could see what he meant. The blast pattern was clearly directed backwards, towards the bus. I could see the blackened metal of the bus frame had been perforated by thousands of tiny pellets. But it was only when I walked around to the front of the bus that I realized it was a school bus.

"Holy shit! This is a school bus. One of those short ones." It made me furious.

"Hey your partner doesn't miss a trick." Bob offered sarcastically to Ken. "There was a driver and four kids. We don't even have enough tissue left to tell what sex they were. Although the driver was pretty big; probably a guy."

I walked around to where a door would normally be on a school bus. The front of the bus had so many pea-size wholes from the shrapnel, it was almost like looking through a dirty screen. I shined my flashlight into the bus but didn't want to look. Before my eyes could focus, I heard Ken mutter, "Jesus!"

That should have been my cue to look away but I'm a cop and a cop needs to do some horrible stuff. This was the most horrible I'd ever seen. The driver was little more than blackened bones. All his flesh and internal organs had burned away. Even his bones had been massacred by the shrapnel. His frail, black, skeletal remains were slumped over a melted steering wheel.

But the truly horrific image was in the back of the bus. Four blackened corpses sat on the metal frames and springs that had been seats. Steam was still coming from their bones. I could tell from the size of the remains that they were just kids; maybe young teens. I assumed the corpse in the first seat was female because it looked like a necklace of some sort still dangled from her charred neck bones.

CHAPTER 38
LT

Two days after the explosions, a day that had become known as the TBD for "Three Bombs Day", the head of the New York JTTF called a meeting of all available agents. Close to two hundred of us were jammed into a theatre-style meeting room meant for no more than one hundred eighty according to the fire safety sign on the wall. The meeting was intended to bring everyone up to date on our latest intel and give us an opportunity to share ideas.

I expected it to be a complete waste of everyone's time because we all get instant updates of intel on our computers and smart phones, but, as usual, no one asked my opinion. It also struck me as a waste of important human assets at a time we should all be out tracking down the few leads we already had. Again, oddly, I wasn't consulted.

Frank Scala, our regional head and my boss's boss, addressed the group from the podium. Behind him was a twenty foot screen with images of the TBD events. The enormous screen made Frank look small even though we all knew he was over six feet tall. He's also a total prick who clawed his way up to his current position by stepping on a lot of people at the FBI along the way. Nobody likes Frank but he's a "take no prisoners" kind of guy so, as a cop, we respect him. Hey, I'd rather work for a prick than a pussy.

So Scala fills us in on all the stuff we already knew about TBD. Two hundred pairs of eyes begin to roll. Then he goes into what had been reported by the media that we've since learned was bogus; things like the bombs on the 59th Street Bridge- pure bullshit. What we didn't know was that the smart boys and girls down on the fourth floor had figured out all the bogus info came from the same person in a series of calls made on several different cell phones, but all within eight minutes of each other. Some were made directly to news networks and some to radio stations. "We suspect the calls were made by a woman in her late twenties or early thirties who spent time in the southeast; probably the Florida panhandle or Alabama, Mississippi, or Louisiana. She's probably white and unless she's a pro at disguising her voice, probably didn't go past high school."

Okay, I was impressed. The guys on the fourth floor know their shit when it comes to voice recognition. They spend a lot of time listening to recordings and using their zillion dollar computer to analyze voices, most of which have a distinct Middle Eastern accent.

"NYPD forensics tells us all three explosions originated with military grade C-4, a form of Symtex that's not easy to get outside the military."

Now everybody started taking notes.

"The bomb in the tunnel also consisted of shrapnel, lots of it. Looks like it came from some sort of manufacturing by-product.

Chief Masterson's units will find the source of the shrapnel. And when we know the source, we'll know who had access to it. Also, the tunnel bomb was detonated remotely using a micro, probably from a cell phone. The other two bombs, the bridge and Penn Station, were on timers."

Scala had everyone's attention now. Even I was impressed that we could figure that out from the miniscule pieces pulled from melted car tires, auto parts, and human remains. From what I saw in my short time in the tunnel, this was pretty amazing police work in a very short time. It's good to be on the side of the guys with the most expensive toys.

"So, as we all assumed, there was a well-coordinated effort to have the devices all blow at the same time. I'm asking you to all think about why that would be important."

"Also, we now have surveillance photos." He turned and clicked his hand-held device to bring up new images on the gigantic screen. This is what we were waiting for. "First, we have a shot of a gentleman getting on to a LIRR train at 8:21 A.M. at the Merrick station." We all knew that when an agent used the word "gentleman" what he really meant to say was "scumbag with Middle-Eastern facial features". But that would be racial profiling so we just say "gentleman" so as not to upset the politically correct. Frank continued...

"Notice, even though the picture is grainy, he's wheeling a large suitcase onto the train." He clicked to the next shot. "This was taken at 8:49 A.M. at the Jamaica station. Looks like our guy walking along the platform without the suitcase. Since this was the train that blew a hole in Penn Station eleven minutes later, we assume he left the suitcase on the train when he detrained in Jamaica. The LIRR did the rest of the work and delivered his package for him.

You'll have enlarged images of this gentleman's face on your computers by the time you get back to your desks."

Another click. "And this is the last shot we have of him descending the east staircase at Jamaica. I want to know where he went from there. Bus, cab, awaiting car… I want to know."

Everyone in the room knew that when Frank said, "I want to know", it meant that we were to find the answer and report back. Each of his seven unit chiefs, my boss being one of them, would dole out assignments as soon as we got back to our offices. A few guys would now get the unenviable assignment of walking the streets of Jamaica handing out fliers with the "gentleman's" face on them and asking every cab driver, bus driver and pedestrian if they'd seen the guy two days earlier. That's the bread and butter of good police work.

"I turn your attention to the Brooklyn Bridge surveillance tapes." Another click and the screen filled with an image of traffic. "The bridge has sixteen cameras placed at various points. Five of the cameras picked up images of our friends." By the way, "friends" is another way to say "scumbags with Middle-Eastern facial features". But back to Frank. He explained, "Here we see a green Ford Focus entering the bridge on the Brooklyn side. And here, you can see another green Focus entering from the BQE ramp. In the next shot you can see they came together, one directly behind the other until they stopped at the crest of the bridge."

The images from the bridge were remarkably clear and each had a digital clock in the upper right corner. The one we were now looking at said 9:01 A.M.

"Here, the driver of the second stopped car gets out of his car and into the one in front." Frank then zoomed in on the "friend's" face just as the man was getting into the forward car. We could all see that despite a poor attempt at a disguise, he was indeed a "friend". There was no doubt about it. He then flicked through several more shots of the green Focus exiting the bridge, one of the car getting on to the FDR drive, and another on the FDR at 168th Street. "That's the last camera image we have so far. But we know where they wound up."

"Finally, we have only two good shots of our friends from the Midtown Tunnel." Another click and the screen refreshed. Here you can see two Ryder trucks entering the tunnel on the Manhattan side. These guys were ground zero in the tunnel." He clicked to the next shot. "Here you can see a grey minivan, just in front of one of the trucks." Frank now began to speculate. "We think the minivan stayed in front of the trucks until they got to the bottom of the tunnel, then all three came to a stop. Since the Ryders were side by side, they completely blocked the traffic behind them. The drivers of the Ryders get out of their trucks and jump into the mini-van and drive off."

Frank returned to the direct evidence on the screen. "This one's from the toll booth camera on the Queens side of the tunnel. You can see our friends exiting the tunnel in a grey minivan. Looks like a Town & Country to me. You can also see there are two men in the front seat and what looks like the hand of a third man sitting in the back." Frank used a laser pointer to show us the details he was referring too. "We even got a clean shot of the license plate from the toll booth camera. These guys weren't very smart."

I thought to myself that they may not be smart but they got a lot done. And now they have the resources of the entire JTTF, hundreds of NYPD, and dozens of FBI people devoted to their antics. They may not be smart but how smart do you really have to be to blow something up? And for the first time in twelve years, our country had been awakened. Maybe that's all they really wanted anyway.

"We're still waiting for data from cameras on the LIE and other bridges to see where they went. Again, we think we know where they went."

Although most of us hadn't seen the photos until right now, we knew they were being gathered and analyzed since the morning of TBD. There were no big surprises yet. But few of us expected what Frank Scala said next.

He clicked his magic button and the screen filled again; this time, with the passport photos of five Middle-Eastern men. Under each photo was the man's name and country of birth. All five were from Yemen.

"Ladies and gentlemen, these are five of our perps." He went through them one by one. "Nasi Saman; twenty-four years old and until last May, a student at NYU. This was the guy on the LIRR. No priors or significant history." He moved to the next picture.

"Suniel Saman, Nasi's younger brother. Also a student at NYU. Also, no priors."

Next picture. "Gabriel Maclov; twenty-six years old. He was on the bridge with Suniel. Him we have some Interpol data for: a couple of arrests in France for minor shit and an eighteen month gap in his credentials. We think it was during this time he was back in Yemen for training with Al Qaeda."

"Two of the three guys in the tunnel were Mohamad Ben-Dor and Rem Hasan; both here on student visas. Mohamad is the youngest of the group at nineteen and Rem is the oldest at thirty-one. Neither have any known priors, although we have a huge gap in intel for Rem between 2004 and 2007. The third guy in the van, the guy in the back seat, we have nothing on. It may be the woman who made the bogus calls and it may not. All we can see is a hand."

He waited for the full effect of his revelations to sink in. In less than seventy-two hours, we had positive IDs on five of the scumbags! By any measure, that was pretty impressive police work. But Frank saved the best for last.

The next slide on the screen was a shot of the Tarrytown Hilton. Smoke was billowing from the south side of the building. It looked like the shot was taken while the fire department was putting water on it from aerial ladders in the parking lot. I could see one of the ladders in the background.

"So it seems that our friends from the bridge, tunnel and Penn Station all rendezvoused at the Tarrytown Hilton at about ten-thirty A.M. We found the green Focus in the parking lot and have surveillance photos of the minivan entering the parking lot. Someone, maybe the third passenger, drove it out of the lot a few minutes after they got there. We have one good shot of the rear but no shot of the driver. Same New Jersey license plate."

Frank cleared his throat with a sip of water from a Poland Springs bottle, then continued. "Cameras in the lobby of the hotel captured all five perps entering the hotel between 10:30 and 10:40. For some reason they didn't go in together. Then we've got them in the elevators." Frank showed shots of the friends in the elevators. "They all got off on the sixteenth floor and went into room 1605, a suite registered to a stolen credit card- Mary Harkins. So that confirms there's a woman involved, probably the same one who made the bogus calls. In fact, she was making the calls at just about the same time our friends were in the elevator."

"Then something goes wrong. At 10:45 A.M. a shit load of C-4 explodes in their suite. It was on some sort of timer so I'm guessing there might have been a fourth target and the device malfunctioned. Anyway, the five perps are killed in the explosion. Two people and a maid in other rooms on the same floor were also killed. The C-4 was the same stuff as was used in our three bombs. And it appeared the boys were on their way back to sandland because they all had packed suitcases in the suite. Everything was burned to shit but we got positive IDs on the five bodies."

Frank spent another fifteen minutes doling out assignments. One unit was responsible for the Hilton. We needed to find the woman who checked into the room three days earlier. One unit got the Penn Station detail. One group of unlucky lads was on their way to Yemen to look into the backgrounds of our friends.

Our unit still had the tunnel, which, to me, seemed like a dead end, but I'm a good soldier and always do what I'm told. Ken and I and a handful of other agents needed to find out who'd rented the cars and trucks. I would have bet it was the chick with the stolen credit card.

I would have been wrong.

CHAPTER 39

LT

The first time Ken and I visited the Ryder Truck office in Astoria, we were able to get the original rental agreements for the trucks used in the tunnel, but Jackie, the woman who'd waited on our friends, was off on Saturdays, so we went back on Monday. In the meantime the boys and girls back at 2 Penn had analyzed the forms for prints. We didn't expect the perps used their real names but had to check them out just the same. The names Hassberg and Williams came back with nothing. And the lab said the forms were clean. The only prints belonged to Jackie, the Ryder sales clerk.

We'd also struck out on their surveillance camera but we confiscated all the pens in the office in hopes of someday matching a print with one of our perps. The five losers who blew themselves up in Tarrytown were kind enough to hang on to a finger or two so we had print samples for five of the perps. We assumed, since the people who rented the trucks were males, that two of our friends already in the morgue were the guys we'd match up to the rentals.

But on Monday, Jackie, a cute little thing with more boobs than brains, said that there was only one guy. "Yeah, he said he and his partner needed to make a big flower delivery out on Long Island. That's why they needed two trucks." She said. "I still can't believe that cute guy had anything to do with the bombings. He seemed so sweet."

"Can you give us a description of this sweet guy who killed three hundred people?" My sarcasm was lost on Jackie.

"He was about your height and probably about your weight. He had light hair; maybe you'd call it strawberry blonde. It was cut very short and he had a little stubble on his face; you know- sort of a three day beard. Other than that he was just sort of cute; sort of regular looking but in a handsome way."

Ken and I both looked at each other and knew what the other was thinking. This didn't sound like one of our friends from sand land. This sounded like Opie Taylor from Mayberry.

"And you're saying this is the fellow who called himself John Williams? Is that right?" Ken pushed a little.

"Yeah, that was his name. He had a driver's license and credit card. He seemed so nice. There has to be some mistake."

"Jackie, why did he fill out the forms for both trucks? Don't you need to have a driver for each truck rented?" Ken knew the answer but wanted to hear it from her. He hadn't yet ruled out the possibility that Jackie had some involvement.

"Well, he said his partner would be driving the other truck and he had a driver's license for him too." She hesitated for a moment, and then continued. "But actually, I filled out the forms for him. He said he didn't have his reading glasses with him and couldn't see the small print so he asked me to write down his answers. I did it for both forms."

Well, that explained the lack of prints on the forms. We asked Jackie to show us exactly where the perp stood when she filled out the forms and if she had forged his signature.

"No. No no. He signed both forms himself. I would never sign for a customer."

"Did he use one of your pens or did he have is own pen?"

She hesitated as if in thought. "I honestly don't remember. Usually we have a bunch of pens here for customers to use. For some reason they're not here today."

I was about to explain that we already had all the pens but thought it might overload an already fragile mind. But I was still curious about why the surveillance cameras hadn't picked up an image. Anyone walking through the front door would be seen on the video monitor. So, if he hadn't come through the front door, he came in the back door; the one that led through the office and into the parking lot.

I asked if we could see the back entrance and Jackie was happy to show us the way. As I exited the building through the back door, it occurred to me that there were only two cars in the lot. "Why so few cars in your lot today?" I inquired.

At first, the young clerk didn't seem to understand my question. Then, as if a light had suddenly turned on, she said, "No. This isn't the lot for our rentals. This is just where Bob and I park when we're working. This is just for employees. Our rentals are all around front."

I said to Ken, "If you came here for the first time, do you think you'd realize there was an entrance in the rear?"

Ken didn't answer. He knew what I was getting at and asked Jackie, "Do you know how long the video from your surveillance cameras is kept?" He immediately realized he'd asked the wrong person, so he added, "Maybe Bob knows. Let's go see him."

Thankfully, Bob, the manager, was in his office and able to confirm that their security company assured him, if he ever needed to, he could go back three months on the video. We told Bob we'd need to take that hard drive with us and borrow Jackie for a few hours as well. We needed her to watch video of all the customers who came through the front door as far back as we could go in hopes of identifying the perp. He must have come in at some point to scout the building. That's the only way he would have known about the back door. Maybe it was the day before TBD or maybe it was a month before, but I was pretty sure, if we put Jackie, the only person who saw his face, in front of a monitor long enough, she'd see him again.

Bob explained that it may not take that long to go through the video. The device only activated when the door opened. "So maybe there are twenty to thirty people a day that come in. That means you'll only have twenty to thirty clicks a day. A click is each time the video comes on. Then it stays on a few seconds until either the door opens again or until someone's motion is detected. That would start it again."

We thanked Bob for his doing his patriotic duty and offered our condolences on his two trucks. Confident that the tech gurus at 2 Penn could access the images for us, we took the hard drive and offered Jackie a ride back to Manhattan with us. She asked if she could drive herself in after lunch which worked out fine because we needed to find the tech guys anyway before there was anything for her to look at.

On the way back to Manhattan Ken said, "I'd like to get her voice analyzed against the female voice on the bogus calls. It's probably a one in ten shot but, what the hell. She'll be in the office anyway." He was right on both counts. It was unlikely our perky sales clerk had the intelligence to be part of this but we needed to be sure.

We went back to the office, dropped the hard drive off with the techies and grabbed a couple of corn beef sandwiches McCoy's on 31st Street. Almost everyone from the JTTF eats at McCoy's. The food is great and its one of those dark, old-fashion bars with a long bar and booths along the opposite wall. On any day, between noon and three, at least ten of the patrons are JTTF agents. I hope someday some asshole tries to rob the place. He'd have ten Glocks pointed at him before he could finish the sentence, "This is a stick up."

CHAPTER 40

The chilly air bit against Alan Wallace's face. His wife clung to his arm. She'd been hanging there all morning. But without her husband to hold her up, Carol could not have stood at her daughter's funeral.

Standing on the grass just a few feet away from the shiny white casket, Alan, his wife, and a few dozen friends and relatives were saying their last good byes to the young girl. Several young classmates attended, chaperoned by one of Mary Jane's teachers. The cemetery was only a few miles from the school.

A white-haired funeral director led the group in a few prayers but Alan's thoughts were a million miles away. He was already trying to envision a life without their precious Mary Jane. Since she was born, she'd been the center of their universe, often the only thing holding the family together. Now that she was gone, he questioned the strength of his relationship with Carol. He didn't think they could survive this.

Carol sobbed uncontrollably as the participants were invited to toss a rose onto the casket as they said their individual good byes to Mary Jane. One by one, she watched their friends and family walk to the edge of the casket and shake their heads as they gently placed their roses on top. Carol's mother, Mary Jane's grandmother, needed to be carried away from the casket by her two sons. The last person to walk by with a flower was Jessica Kitman, Carol's good friend from upstairs.

Now the funeral director was indicating it was time for Carol and Alan to walk by and leave their daughter forever. They each held a pink rose. Alan used one hand to support his wife. With the other he softly placed his rose at the head of the casket. Tears rolled freely down his face. "Sleep well my baby." He could say no more.

Carol Wallace refused to leave her daughter's side. She wasn't even aware she was holding a rose until being prodded by Alan. She knelt by the coffin's side and threw her arms around its polished lid. "Nooo!," she screamed. "I won't leave her here. She's too young." She sobbed violently.

Alan tried first to coax her away, then pry her off the coffin, but Carol held tight. The funeral director was obviously experienced in such matters and came to his assistance. "Mary Jane is with God now Carol. He's welcomed her with open arms. He's embracing her as we speak. You have to let him have her. She belongs in heaven with the angels." All words that had worked for him in the past.

Then he added the clincher, "You have to be strong for Mary Jane. She needs you to be strong. So does your husband." Still, Carol had to be lifted off the ground and helped to her feet. Eventually, she released her clasp on the rose and let it fall to the ground next to the casket. "Sleep well my baby." The whispered words were the hardest she'd ever said.

Carol's mother had arranged a luncheon back in the city for close friends and family. Carol, her parents, and her husband sat in the back of a stretch limo for the forty minute ride back to Manhattan. No one spoke. Alan reflected on the last few days; the darkest days of his life.

First there was the call from the police about the bus. Alan got that one at his office. Then he had to break the news that their daughter was dead to her mother who fainted dead away when told and spent the next several hours at the hospital hoping this wasn't going to kill his wife.

Mercifully, they were spared the ordeal of identifying Mary Jane's remains; basically because there were so few remains to identify. Alan was told even identification by dental records would be impossible since the young girl's skull had been so badly damaged by the shrapnel and burned by the resulting fire. Two police officers came to their apartment the next morning with the only positive identification available; Mary Jane's locket which they said was found on her "person", their euphemism for skeleton.

Carol couldn't bring herself to further destroy her daughter's youthful body, so they quickly ruled out a cremation and decided to bury what was left of Mary Jane in a beautiful white coffin. Through a process of 'mind over reality', Carol refused to picture the charred corpse within the white box. Instead, all she could envision was her angelic daughter, lying peacefully with her hands clasped on her chest. Alan knew that what they actually had left back at the cemetery was a bag of blackened bones, held together only by the bag itself. He wondered if he could ever rid his dreams of that image.

They held a one-night wake. Carol couldn't have done more. Hundreds of people came. Most were from Alan's office and the Freeman Academy. Carol's brothers and a few cousins came in from California and dozens of neighbors from their building paid their respects even though most were just elevator acquaintances. Jessica Kitman never left Carol's side. As he stared out the limo window watching the world go by, Alan felt shame at the thought of Jessica.

CHAPTER 41

LT

The first thing we had Jackie do when she got to 2 Penn is give us a voice sample. She was happy to do so and we were happy when the results came back negative. She seemed like a nice kid even if she was a bit simple. Hey, not everyone gets to go to the Mensa picnic.

By 2:30, the techies had us set up in a room that looked a little like a corporate boardroom but probably had the computer power of an F-15 cockpit. There was a large flat screen on one wall. Jackie, Ken and I sat on one side of the wooden table; the technician from the thirteenth floor, a junior agent named Phil, was on the other side making the magic happen.

Phil said, "We can't go in reverse order but I can reverse order the days. In other words, we'll start with one day before TBD, look at all the events of that day in order, and then go back one day, and so on." Even Jackie seemed to understand.

"Okay, we'll start with the morning of September 17th." Phil produced the first image on the screen.

Just to be sure Jackie understood what we wanted her to do, I said, "Jackie, just tell us if you see the guy who called himself John Williams the day you rented him the trucks. Okay?"

She seemed to get the idea and we all settled back in our chairs and watched the images roll by on the screen. One by one we watched customers come through the door. Phil would freeze the frame so Jackie could take a good look. In the interest of time, he didn't freeze for female customers or for black or Asian customers. After a while Jackie got good at this and immediately said, "No" if the image wasn't our guy. Phil could forward to the next customer which took a few seconds to do, but saved time.

After an hour we'd gone back eighteen days and I was beginning to think we were wasting our time. Phil had just started on a new day and the first person through the door got a rise out of Jackie. "Wait," she said. "That might be him!" She stood up to get a better look. Phil let the video roll to see if we had a better shot when the subject was leaving the building. We didn't. He rolled back to the best image we had and froze it. It was a male, about thirty to thirty five, with a fair complexion and average height and weight. The problem was; he was wearing a Yankee baseball cap and sunglasses. Only the lower portion of his face was clearly visible.

"I think that's him. Doesn't he look like a sweet guy?"

⟞⟔ ⟓⟝

After Jackie identified our sixth perp, who we were now calling Opie, we had her look through another ten days of video, just to be sure and to be sure he hadn't also entered the store on another occasion. When we were satisfied we'd squeezed all that was useful from Jackie's pretty head, I gave her my card and thanked her for her service to her country.

The image she had identified as John Williams was grainy and incomplete but valuable for two reasons. First; it confirmed that there was at least one other male suspect involved in the events of TBD who hadn't been killed at the hotel in Tarrytown. Second; it gave us a time and date the suspect was in the area of the Ryder Truck office. We knew from the video, that he entered the Ryder office at 9:06 A.M. on August 27th. That was an important starting point.

That afternoon we told Danny Jacobson what we had, and asked for several agents to assist with a door-to-door the next morning. Jacobson was impressed with our work so far and gave us four junior agents for the day. Our plan was to check with all the shops around the Ryder office to see if their surveillance cameras had picked up a better image of Opie as he approached the Ryder office. It wouldn't be hard since we knew exactly when to be looking- around nine in the morning on August 27th. With the cost of a good camera coming down by the day, almost every retail store, gas station, bank and supermarket has at least one keeping an eye on their customers. Many also have them outside their shops, watching the sidewalks and streets. They've become an invaluable asset to the police. Just ask the Boston police about all the cameras that got a glimpse of the two assholes that blew up their marathon.

So the next morning, Ken and I hold a quick meeting with the agents assigned to us for the day, distribute copies of Opie's picture, exchange cell phone numbers with everyone, and we were on our way back to Astoria, Queens. Ken and I drove in his car. The other agents, two men and two women, piled into a standard issue fed-mobile; a black Crown Victoria. It was a beautiful morning so I didn't mind doing a little legwork.

I had a Google map of the neighborhood and divided up the work by geography. Each agent got four blocks to cover. Ken and I took the eight blocks closest to the Ryder office. This wasn't lost on our junior associates but rank has its privilege. And we all knew, the further from the Ryder office, the less likely of getting lucky.

As it turns out, one of the juniors got lucky within an hour. I got a call on my cell from agent Moss, one of the few younger females in our unit. "LT, this is Moss. I think we got lucky. I'm at the Sunoco station on the corner of 114th and Brewster. Come on over and take a look."

I called Ken as I walked the six blocks to the Sunoco station. "Hey buddy. This may be our lucky day." I gave him the address and he arrived just as I was turning the corner myself. Peggy Moss was waiting for us by the gas pumps. She's a cute little thing and reminded me of my niece, my twin brother's oldest daughter. After law school, Peggy Moss spent six years with the FBI before transferring to the JTTF eight months ago. She was probably about thirty but looked no more than twenty-five. She was noticeably attractive and bright. I wouldn't mind working with her more.

As we approached, she pointed towards a camera above the gas pumps, well hidden in all the Halon fire extinguishers up there. "I think this is the one that got him. He's walking up the street from that direction." Agent Moss pointed in the direction from which I'd just come. "It's a great shot because the sun was behind the camera, just as it would be now, and shining right on his face."

She led us inside the station's office, introduced us to the manager, a fellow who could someday be one of our "friends", and asked him to show us what he'd shown her. Sure enough, there's an image of a clean cut guy walking toward the gas station. As Peggy had promised, it was a great shot of his face. And the best was yet to come; because as he approaches the camera he looks up, seems to squint from the sunlight, then puts on a pair of sunglasses and a New York Yankee cap.

CHAPTER 42

LT

Sometimes I wonder why criminals think they have a chance of getting away with the shit they pull. I mean, if the bad guys understood anything at all about the technology we have going for us, they'd probably chose a different line of work. Maybe we should hold classes for them to show off all our cool crime-fighting toys. That could save us all a lot of trouble.

I mention this because even I was astounded at how fast we had a name to go with the face from the gas station picture. The JTTF probably has the most sophisticated facial recognition equipment in the world. Our rocket scientists back at 2 Penn were able to take the grainy image from the gas station's camera, somehow enhance it, and run it against our database of DFI's, which stands for Documented Facial Images. Only the JTTF and the FBI have access to the DFI database which consists of every passport photo, driver's license photo, mug shot, military ID, Federal employee ID, and many more I probably don't know about. Basically, if your picture was taken in the last five years and your name was attached to that picture, we've got it. Even tagged photos from Facebook are making their way into the DFI, but we'd probably deny that if asked.

So, by 4:30 P.M. we had a name to go with the face, and by 6:10 P.M. we had a complete file assembled on our new friend, William S. Simon. Ken and I sat in Jacobson's office as he looked through our suspect's half-inch thick file. Ken assured Danny that only four people from our unit knew the name William S. Simon and they'd all been told to share that information with absolutely no one. It was too soon to let this out. First, we needed a strategy.

Within the folder our boss was holding was Simon's entire life: high school transcripts, prior addresses, military commendations, credit reports, employment history, finger prints, medical records, DMV info from his home state and every state he's lived in, bank accounts, credit cards, and a detailed list of every item he'd purchased with a credit card at Lowes and Home Depot in the last twelve months. We had his high school yearbook picture, his Florida DMV picture and his official U.S. Marine Corp photo.

"This guy is a decorated marine for Christ's sake!" I guess Jacobson was hoping for more of a scumbag. Actually, we were too.

"Yeah, Iraq and Afghanistan. He did five tours. It doesn't make sense."

I added, "I agree. He really does seem like Opie Taylor on paper, but he also worked with munitions for four years while in Afghanistan. So we've got a guy that knows how to put a bomb together."

"Bullshit. From what I've seen so far, there was nothing all that sophisticated about any of the devices from TBD. It was basic stuff. The kind of stuff anyone can pull off the internet." Ken was skeptical.

Jacobson asked, "What's the degree of certainty on the facial recognition? Before we do anything, we need to be sure this is our guy."

"They said it's a match. They didn't hedge at all." I wanted to believe our guys knew what they were doing.

Ken had a good point though. "Yeah, but the woman at the Ryder office may have been wrong in the first place. Maybe this is the guy in the video who walked into the Ryder office on August 27th. But maybe she's wrong about him being the same guy who rented the two trucks two weeks later. We might have a good X-Y match but are we a hundred percent sure it's really X we're after?"

"Ken's right. We can't put this guy's face out to the media until we're sure. We'd look like assholes going after a decorated Marine." Jacobson was always doing what the bosses should be doing- covering our asses.

"Okay. So the five of us keep this to ourselves for now. What we need to do is find Mr. Simon and see what he was doing at the Ryder Truck office on the 27th, and where he was on the morning of TBD. This is one time I really hope this isn't our guy. But we need to move fast on this. We need to find this guy fast. I want one of you clowns on a plane tonight to Panama City, Florida. That's his last known address and I'm not handing this off to the locals. This is too important. One of you has got to go see Mr. Simon and either cross him off our list or arrest him. But I want to know by noon tomorrow." Jacobson sounded like a boss who was getting pressure from his boss.

⊷⊶

Well, as it turns out, I drew the short straw and was headed for Panama City. The trouble is- there are no evening flights to Panama City from New York. In fact, you can't fly directly from New York to Panama City at any time. You need to go through Atlanta and there are only three flights a day anyway. So I made a reservation on a 6:08 A.M. flight from JFK to Atlanta with a transfer to Panama City. If all goes well, and allowing for the one hour time difference, I'll be in sunny Florida by noon tomorrow.

I called Jacobson just to let him know about the delay. He'd already gone home so I left a voicemail and headed for Vinney's. I needed a drink. I hate flying.

CHAPTER 43

For four days, Mary Jane Wallace watched television. She focused on whatever station had coverage of what had become known as the "Three Bombs Day" or TBD. The more she watched, the more she cried. CNN showed scenes of what was left of her bus being towed out of the tunnel. The thought of her three friends burning to death sent a chill down her spine. For some reason, she had no recollection of Billy shooting the girls long before the flames devoured them. Perhaps it was just too horrible to remember. It was just as well.

Nina assured Mary Jane several times that her parents had been contacted and that they knew she was alive and well. In a few days, they would pay the ransom Billy had demanded, and Mary Jane would be set free. Of course, this was a lie. Carol and Alan Wallace were standing at their daughter's gravesite this very moment. Billy had not yet made contact with them nor would he for several more days.

Mary Jane was trying to make the best of her situation. The belief that she would soon be reunited with her parents gave her hope and with hope, she was able to endure. The pain of her friends' deaths hurt her deeply. She'd never known death before. But beyond that, she felt she could endure; as long as she would soon be back at home.

She spent her days dressed in a pair of green sweatpants, white gym socks and an M.I.T. sweatshirt that Nina had given her the day she arrived. She'd been given a duffle bag with some other cloths and some toiletries but these were the most comfortable. Her period wasn't due for another two weeks so she wasn't worried. "I'll be home by then," She told herself.

Nina kept the small refrigerator modestly supplied. There was water, apple juice, a bag of Fig Newtons, a box of Cheerios, and some packets of applesauce. Each day she would bring Mary Jane whatever fast-food she and Billy were dining on so dinner and lunch consisted of Big Macs, Kentucky Fried Chicken, or something from Taco Bell. Mary Jane looked forward to the meals partly because they interrupted the boredom and partly because these were delicacies she did not often get at home.

Even though she wore a mask, a paper bag with two holes cut out for eyes, when Nina came to the basement, she had told Mary Jane to call her Nina. Billy seldom came down but he too wore a mask when he did. She knew his name was Billy only because she overheard Nina call him that once on the second day. And she was happy he didn't come to the basement often. The few times he was there, Mary Jane could feel Billy staring at her through his mask. It was an uncomfortable stare; almost as if his eyes were thinking about eating her for dinner. She didn't yet understand lust.

Aside from the deep sorrow she felt for her friends, Mary Jane's spirit had not been broken. She was a remarkably resilient child and tried to make the best of each monotonous day. Because there were no windows, her only way of knowing day from night was the digital clock on the cable box beneath the TV. If she awoke and the clock said it was after seven A.M., she'd turn on the only light in the room and force herself to believe it was a sunny day. She tried to keep to the same schedule she had at home, except for school. She'd start each morning with a shower and a bowl of Cheerios while watching the Today Show. For the rest of the morning, she'd surf the channels, stopping to watch whatever game shows she came across.

Her solitude did not frighten her. Perhaps because she wanted so much to believe Nina, she was confident she'd be released at some point. The basement was certainly livable. It was warm, dry and partially carpeted. Her mattress smelled musty but was where she spent most of her day. She was given no pillow, sheets or blankets. It didn't matter; the room was warm enough even when she slept. The duffle bag and unused clothing made an acceptable pillow so she could sit up and watch TV.

Whenever the door at the top of the stairs would open, Mary Jane held hope she'd see one of her parents standing there; that this would be the day she was rescued.

CHAPTER 44

LT

U sually when I fly, I drink. It helps me deal with the reality that I'm six miles up in the air. But my flight to Atlanta was so early I would have been embarrassed to ask for a drink so I tried to avoid thinking about Pan Am 103, Air France 447, American 11, Avianca 52, or any of the other flights that we not supposed to crash but did, by focusing on the file of William Simon. Fortunately, the seat next to mine was empty so I could spread the folder out on my fold-down tray and look for any sort of clue we might have missed yesterday.

But everything in the file supported the notion that this guy was a boy scout. He was a decorated marine that volunteered for some dangerous campaigns and four extra tours. Since leaving the marines, he's worked for Zimmel Metal, a small sheet metal fabrication shop in Panama City, Florida; a long way from New York. He has no arrest record, no DUI's, and hasn't had a traffic violation since he was eighteen. He has only one credit card, a MasterCard that had not been used in the New York area during the previous twelve months.

Nothing about this guy validated the need for me to be going to Florida except the photo from the Ryder camera, and I was becoming increasingly convinced young Jackie had made a mistake in selecting William Simon as the guy who rented the two trucks from her. Nothing in his file connected him to any of the scumbags who blew themselves up at the Hilton. Nothing implied he had any reason to be anywhere near New York.

I transferred planes in Atlanta and found myself on a twelve passenger puddle-jumper that, thanks to the time zone difference, arrived in Panama City three minutes before it left Atlanta. I rented a yellow Mustang convertible and headed for Zimmel Metal which was only twenty minutes from the airport. As I approached the enormous building I could see from the parking lot that their primary product was windows. There were aluminum windows of all sizes and shapes stacked everywhere.

"Can I help you, darling?" A woman in neatly pressed khakis and a blue button-down shirt bearing the Zimmel logo asked as I got out of the Mustang. I wondered about the "darling" but then remembered I'm in the south.

"I'm here to see the manager." I said.

"You found her sweetie. I'm Anita Zimmel. But we don't have a retail showroom here."

I produced my credentials and explained that I'd like to inquire about one of her employees. Anita, who appeared to be about fifty, said, "Sure darling; come on in to my office. I just got back from the bank. Would you like something to drink? Some water or pop?"

She led me around the back of the building, through a door and up two flights of stairs to her office which overlooked the entire operation. From there I could see Anita had a pretty nice business. There must have been fifty people working on all sorts of machinery that was either bending or shaping aluminum into windows. No one working down on the plant floor could see me because Anita's office was behind a wall of glass to keep out the noise.

"So, Agent Hadman, what can I do for you?"

"I'd like to ask you a few questions about one of your employees, William Simon. And then I'd like to talk to him if he's here today."

"Billy Simon? He quit back in June. Nice kid. Ex-marine. Very disciplined; very punctual. Had a little temper as I recall but never caused any trouble. I was sorry to lose him."

From her answers, I got the impression Anita thought I was doing some sort of background investigation into Mr. Simon; maybe for a job with the government.

"Do you remember exactly when he left and why?"

Anita spun around and pulled up the suspect's personnel file on her computer. "Yeah, that's what I thought. He left at the beginning of the summer; June 11th was his last day. Said he was moving north for another job but I don't remember ever getting an employment verification from anyone."

I made some notes and asked, "Anything else you can tell me about Billy?"

"Well, I know for sure that he moved out of the place he was living. I know that because Manny, one of our new guys, took over Billy's apartment over on Clinton Street as soon as Billy left."

"And you have no forwarding address?" I made a note to check that out with the post office as well.

Anita scanned her computer screen. "Nope. He and his girl-friend came in to pick up his last check at the end of that week and I haven't heard of him since."

"Girlfriend?"

"Yeah; a little cutie he met over at Finnegan's."

"What's Finnegan's?" I had to ask although I thought I already knew the answer.

"Local watering hole about a mile out on Route 98, near the beach. I haven't been there in years but it's a big place now with the kids. You know; spring break kids."

"And by any chance would you know the name of his girlfriend?"

I guess Anita couldn't figure how that could be relevant to an employment background investigation so she shot me a disapprov-ing look. I produced my credentials again and said, "Anita, I'm just doing some legwork on a criminal investigation. Any information you can give me might be helpful."

"Oh. I think her name was Nina. I don't remember her last name but it was something Hispanic; Perez or Gomez or something like that."

After Anita gave me directions to Finnegan's she asked me if I wanted a quick tour of her facility. I got the impression she was very proud of her business so I said, "Sure, but I only have a few minutes."

We went down to the factory floor and I quickly realized why everyone was wearing headsets. The noise was excruciating; not so much because of its volume but because the metal-cutting machines gave off a high-pitched screech as the aluminum was scored then bent around the forms. I would imagine a few hours of this would be like listening to fingernails on a blackboard. But Anita seemed to revel in the cacophony and gave me a tour of the process by which her business took extruded aluminum and created dozens of different shapes of windows, minus the glass.

"The glass we add later at our other shop." She proudly pointed out. "My brother Jimmy runs that place; just down the road a piece."

I must admit, it was interesting but I wanted to get over to Finnegan's and hopefully back on a plane by the end of the day, so I was grateful when Anita opened a door that led to the parking lot. As we exited the building I noticed two large barrels, each filled about three-quarters of the way with some sort of small metal shavings. I inquired, more out of curiosity than anything else, "What are those?"

"Just a lot of aluminum scraps from the cutters. When the machine cuts the metal to form a corner, those little wedges are left over and fall to the floor. We sweep them up every few hours and sell them back to the manufacturer by the pound. It's hardly worth the effort but we have to sweep them up anyway. Can't leave them lying around. They're too sharp."

Maybe I've been a cop too long but I couldn't ignore the aluminum scraps. When Ken and I walked through the Mid-town Tunnel and saw the devastation caused by the shrapnel, I tried to imagine what sort of flying metal could cause so much damage. So, being a cop, I asked, "Do you mind if I take a few of these?"

"Help yourself but be careful reaching in there. Those babies are really sharp."

I carefully grabbed about ten pieces of the jagged metal and dropped them into an evidence bag I had in my briefcase. I didn't expect anything to come of it, but you never know. Like I said; I've been a cop too long.

Anita wasn't kidding. Finnegan's Bar was only a mile down the road. Good old Google helped me find a phone number and I tried to call as I drove over. My call went to voicemail; a pleasant young female voice with a serious southern accent told me the place opened every day at four. By the time I listened to the message, I was pulling into their parking lot. It was a seedy looking place from the outside and the inside confirmed my initial impression. At two in the afternoon, I didn't expect to find Nina working but I thought I'd take a chance.

The owner, a guy named Sami, was sweeping behind the bar and was startled by my presence. I introduced myself, flashed my credentials, and got straight to the point. I knew there was a 4:32 Delta flight back to Atlanta with a connection to JFK, and I wanted to be on it.

"Yes, Nina worked here about a year. She left over the summer; just as our busy season was starting. Is she in trouble?" Sami seemed sincere enough.

"No, no; I'm just doing some background work on her boyfriend and I didn't have a last name for Nina."

"Morales. Her name was Nina Morales. And if you mean her boyfriend Billy, he's the reason she left. She was moving up north to be with him."

"Is there anything you can tell me about Billy?"

"Nothing really." Sami spoke with a heavy Middle Eastern accent which seemed out of place here on the Redneck Riviera. "Seemed like a nice enough kid. I think he was a marine. Came in here a lot with other marines from the camp."

"Did you ever hear him say anything that was..., I don't know..., political?" I was fishing.

"Nah. He was like all the other rednecks around here. America, rah, rah, rah. You know. If it wasn't for my cute bartenders, these guys would never buy their beer from a Turkish immigrant like me. I know this. You know how I know this? Because when my daughters tend bar here, the tips go way down. I see it all the time. When my daughters are behind the bar, the tip pool is about half of what it is when two local girls are bartending. The locals just don't like foreigners, especially if the foreigner is from the Middle East." Sami was getting louder.

I let Sami vent a few more minutes then got him back on subject. "Do you have a last known address for Nina?"

"Yes, I have a copy of her driver's license. But I told you. She moved up north somewhere."

Sami made me another copy of Nina Morales' Florida driver's license and I was on my way back to the airport. As I maneuvered the Mustang along Route 98, I thought about the results of my trip. Everything in his file told me that William (Billy) Simon was a boy scout; a decorated marine who had already done more for his country than ninety-nine percent of Americans. He had a clean military career, a clean employment history and no known political affiliations.

What bothered me a little was that a few months ago he headed north. What bothered me was that in the military, he worked with explosives. What bothered me was that barrel of metal shards. And what bothered me was that less than a week ago, somebody used explosives and shrapnel to kill over six hundred people in New York.

But, like I said, maybe I've been a cop too long. I guess I just didn't want to admit my trip had probably been a complete waste of time and taxpayer money.

While waiting for my transfer in Atlanta, I decided to text Ken Stallings, just to let him know I'd be in the office in the morning. A few minutes later, my cell phone rang. It was Ken.

"What are you rushing back for? I thought you'd be lying on the beach and milking this for a few days. Nothing much going on this end. I interviewed two of the families from the kids on the bus today. That was awful. Tomorrow I'll do the widow of the bus driver. You can deal with the other two families when you get back."

There didn't seem to be any good reason to interview the families of the victims. These were people chosen randomly to be in the wrong place at the wrong time. Still, this was a murder investigation and we had to go through the motions if, for no other reason, to assure the local authorities, the NYPD, that we had jurisdiction. It sucked but had to be done this way.

"Anything else?" I asked as I heard my flight being called.

"Nothing much. We got back some reports on the foreign substances found in the tunnel. Turns out the explosive was C-4, as we thought. Military grade. And most of the shrapnel was aluminum."

"Aluminum?" Maybe my trip wasn't such a waste after all.

CHAPTER 45
LT

My flight from Atlanta didn't get into JFK until after ten so, by the time I got back to Manhattan it was too late to catch anyone at 2 Penn. But at seven-thirty the next morning, I was waiting with my bag of metal shards from Florida for the lab guys to show up. My boy scout had lost a few merit badges in my book when I heard Ken say the word aluminum on the phone yesterday. Now we needed to see if the shrapnel from the tunnel matched the stuff I had in the bag. If it did, our boy scout Billy becomes public enemy number one.

Ken got in a half hour after me and we walked down to the lab together so I could tell him what little else I learned in the Sunshine State. Neither of us was convinced we had more than a ten percent chance of matching the shrapnel to my aluminum shavings, but we were hopeful. Which is odd because forty-eight hours ago we were both hoping Simon was not our guy. Funny what a little soft evidence will do.

"So the meetings with the families of the two kids was rough, huh?" I said.

"Oh yeah. They were still a mess. With the Oakley girl, it was their only kid. They put her on the bus one morning and the next day the coroner gives them back a bowl of burnt bones. Can you imagine? The mother didn't stop crying the whole time we were there."

"We? Who's we? Who'd you take with you?"

"I wasn't doing these by myself. I wanted a woman with me to deal with the mothers so I took Jenny Henley. It was good experience for her. I was glad to have her there."

"What about the other family?"

"Almost as bad. And it's not like we can do them any good. That's the worst part. Their kid's not coming back. At least the other couple had a few kids; you know, something to live for. But this kid was their youngest and the father had donated one of his kidneys to her when she was five because she got some sort of kidney disease as a kid. Their box of bones was a little bigger because she was in the last row of the bus. But I don't think he's getting his kidney back."

"You're an asshole." Was about all I could say. Sometimes Ken's morbid sense of humor pisses me off but I know it's just because he really does get upset by these things. It's his way of distancing himself from the shit we have to work with.

"So have you scheduled my two families yet?"

"No. I didn't think you'd be back so soon. You got the Wallace kid and the Palmeri's. Both live in the same building on Second Avenue; nice place." Ken checked his notepad. "The Palmeri's have four other kids but Mary Jane Wallace was an only child. Good luck. I'd suggest you take Jenny along but she's with me today. I have to do the widow of the driver at eleven."

When we got to the lab, the technician, a new kid I didn't know, took my bag and wanted to know, "Where'd you get this?"

I didn't want to bias his analysis. Sometimes, if the techs know where a sample came from they start drawing conclusions they shouldn't. It's better if we keep them in the dark until after the analysis is complete, so I said, "None of your fucking business!" Like I said, he was new. You gotta keep these kids in line.

We went back down to our office. I made appointments with both mothers for later that day. I really dreaded this part of the job, especially when kids are involved. And in this case, the usual questions just don't make any sense. This was an act of terrorism that killed their daughters. *"Did your daughter ever talk about someone from school who she may have had an argument with?"* just didn't make sense here. But it had to be done.

"So we have the bus covered. Who's covering the other victims?" I was curious.

"All the other fatalities are being covered by Lewis and his crew. They did a lot yesterday I think. The non-fatal injuries Peterson and Meyers' group will take next week. They're still working the trucks for clues. So far nothing."

"Is the tunnel still closed?"

"Shit yeah. The ceiling was falling down. They had to build these big scaffolds so our guys could work in there. Meyers said the fire was so hot, the cement in the ceiling started to pop. That thing will be closed for months."

"Any news on the bridge?"

"No structural damage at all. Wasn't much C-4 on the bridge. Just enough to get everyone's attention and tie up traffic for a few hours. Same with the train at Penn. It could have been a lot worse."

"Yeah. I'll be sure to tell that to the mothers of the two kids today."

"Right. But it sure seems like these assholes put most of their effort into the tunnel. Doesn't it? I mean, think about it. They use two trucks, not one. They don't just blow them up. In addition to a shit load of C-4, they fill them with gasoline and shrapnel. That's what I don't get. It couldn't be that they hoped to wreck the tunnel. The gas and shrapnel was there to hurt people not the tunnel itself. So why was their MO different in the tunnel? Makes no sense to me."

CHAPTER 46

LT

Because the lab results on the aluminum shards wouldn't be ready until five P.M., I called both families and tried to schedule my interviews for later that day. This was going to be unpleasant and I wanted to get it over with. When both mothers agreed to meet me in the afternoon, I was surprised when one of them suggested we do both interviews together. Apparently, Mrs. Wallace and Mrs. Palmeri knew each other well and felt better about doing it together. That was fine with me. I figured they'd each have a familiar shoulder to cry on.

I was glad Jenny was helping Ken today. I didn't want anyone tagging along with me anyway and Ken needed the female support more than I did. When I need to, I can turn on the soft and nurturing side along with the best of them.

The mothers had agreed to meet me at the Wallace apartment on the 29th floor at two P.M. and I arrived on time. Carol Wallace, a noticeably attractive and youthful woman greeted me at the door. Her eyes were red from a week of tears but still beautiful.

"Mrs. Wallace, I'm special agent Hadman, mam. Most people call me LT."

"Most people call me Carol." She showed me into the spacious apartment.

I remember thinking that their apartment was larger than the entire piece of property on which I grew up. It was at least 3,500 square feet of modern decorating and floor to ceiling windows with views of both the river and the park. By New York standards, it was spectacular.

Carol Wallace showed me in to the main living area where Stella Palmeri, also acceptably attractive, was sitting on a Queen Anne chair near the window bouncing a baby on her knee. She apologized for bringing her youngest child along but there was no one around to watch him. I assured her it was fine.

I gave each of the ladies two of my JTTF cards and offered my condolences for their losses. I began by explaining the necessity of my visit: that because a crime had been committed, we must first treat the investigation as a murder investigation and then as an act of terror. I decided that the most sensitive way to handle this would be to start by asking each mother to tell me something about their daughters.

As it turned out, having the two grieving mothers in the same room worked well. As they related stories about their children they would look to each other for acknowledgement and validation that they weren't exaggerating when they said their daughters were exceptional. I learned that Mary Jane Wallace and Lucy Palmeri had been classmates since the first grade. They were both within a few months of fourteen and because of their keen interest in music, both attended the Freeman Academy in Oyster Bay, Long Island.

"LT, do you have any children of your own?" Stella asked.

"No. I was married once for a short time, but no children of my own. Just a few nieces and nephews in the Philly area. My twin brother has four kids and I get to see them a lot." I thought I needed to add, "So I can only imagine the pain you're going through as parents."

I tried to picture these poor women standing at the morgue to identify their teenage daughters' bodies, lying on a gurney. What a horror. Then I remembered what Ken said about the remains amounting to little more than a bag of charred bones. No parent should ever have to go through that.

Both mothers confided that positive identification of their daughters was made solely on the basis of where they sat on the bus and the jewelry they wore that fateful morning. I was going to ask if the police had asked for DNA samples, but decided against lingering on such a troubling area. Besides, I assumed the morgue was taking a lot of shortcuts last week with so many bodies from the three explosions.

Actually, I asked very few questions. This suited the mothers just fine since both were willing to talk about their daughters with very little prompting from me. And besides, what questions could I possibly ask that would do my investigation any good? Well, in retrospect, there was one and I missed it.

After nearly an hour the baby on Stella's lap began to get restless. That was my queue to wrap things up. Because I felt so sincerely sorry for these two tragic characters, I told them to call me if they needed any other information and that we'd keep them informed about our investigation. That was completely untrue but it allowed me a comfortable exit and I breathed deeply when I got out of the building and back on the street. After all, I'm a street cop at heart.

Ken had the Crown Vic today so I was hoofing it around Manhattan. It was a pleasant September afternoon so I decided to walk back to the office. As I approached 2 Penn, I noticed the police ropes were still around the Seventh Avenue entrance to Penn Station, which, as I've mentioned, is just below our building. So I flashed my credentials to the two patrolmen positioned at the top of the steps and asked if I could take a look at the damage myself. But before I could descend the stairs, my phone rang. It was Ken.

"LT, where are you?"

"Actually, I'm right below you."

"What?"

"I was just on my way down to take a look at the damage in the station. I finished up with my interviews a little early and was looking to kill some time until the lab results come down."

"Well my friend, the lab got done early. The results are on your desk."

"And...?"

"Just get up here."

CHAPTER 47
LT

"L T, you may not be much to look at, but you are one hell of a cop." His feet were crossed on top of his desk and he held a single sheet of paper in his right hand.

And, just for the record, Ken kids me all the time about my appearance. He knows I'm still pretty hot for a twenty year vet, but he likes to bust my chops because he's losing his hair and growing a gut. So I said, "Fuck you fatty; what's in the report?"

"*Conclusive match of foreign substance*; is the way they put it. Miller told me he knew it was a match as soon as he saw your shavings, or whatever you call them. He said they were the same as the shit they pulled out of the tires and victims in the tunnel. Same triangular shape." Ken was happy for me. Happy for us.

"Well I guess our boy scout just lost a few more merit badges. But just because he worked at one of the thousands of places that manufacture aluminum windows doesn't mean he's our guy."

"LT, you're not listening. Miller says they're the same. Not just that they look the same. He says the chemical analysis or whatever the fuck they do up there, shows, and I repeat…, a *conclusive match of foreign substance.* According to him, that means your shavings and the ones from the tunnel came from the same place. He quoted some sort of metallurgical mumbo-jumbo that proves they came from the same extrusion process. I think it's like the same way they can prove a particular bullet was fired from a particular gun. It's got something to do with the scratches on the metal itself." Ken threw up his hands. "Hey, I don't know but the geeks seem to be sure about it."

"Wow. Home run, huh?" I wasn't ready for such good news. "So what's next?"

"Well, from what little you told me yesterday, our boy hasn't been seen in the Panama City area since June and took off for points north, according to his former employer, with his girlfriend. If he came to New York and spent the last three months here planning these attacks, he had to leave some sort of trail. You know; hotels, rental cars, restaurants, gas stations. If he was part of the ring that blew themselves up in Tarrytown, they had to leave a footprint some-where. They had to interact with a lot of people in three months."

Ken was right and we needed to come up with a strategy to track Mr. Simon down. But first things first. We needed to talk to our boss and let him know the good news. Then we needed to decide who else we let know about Billy Simon.

I suggested we talk to Jacobson as soon as possible so Ken called is cell. He was on his way back to the office from a meeting with the mayor and would see us in ten minutes. Next, we needed to know what we wanted to suggest to Jacobson. I knew from working with him in the past, that he'd want to hear our plan before telling us what he thought. It would also be a good idea to bring ourselves up to speed on all the intel gathered so far about the five scumbags who may have been working with Billy Boy. But we only had ten minutes so our priority was a plan.

"I say we name him as a person of interest, get his name and picture out to the media, and wait for a response. We don't tell the media about the aluminum, in fact, we don't even say why he's a person of interest. We just throw it out there. The American people are not going to want to hear that a decorated marine was working with the towel-heads but if the media does its homework maybe they'll come up with something from his background that'll help us figure out why he'd be a part of this."

Ken liked the approach but added, "We need to be careful here. For all we know, his total involvement may have been to sell the scumbags a couple of buckets of the aluminum. Simon may have played a very minor role."

"Agreed. But remember, we still have one more perp in the back seat of the minivan who's not in the morgue. My bet is it's this guy. And that's a lot more than just selling them aluminum."

So after a few more minutes of discussion, we agreed to approach Jacobson with the recommendation that William T. Simon be named as a person of interest; a guy we'd like to have a chat with. That's about as far as we got before the boss walked in.

Ken briefed him on my quick trip to Panama City, the aluminum shards, and the lab results. In the six months I've been working for Danny Jacobson, I don't think I ever saw the fat Irishman smile. Until now that is.

"Well done boys and girls. Well done." He said as he scanned the lab report.

"On paper, this guy still looks like a boy scout. But we know he had access to the aluminum, we know he was headed north three months ago, and we know his specialty in the service was munitions with training in IEDs. We also have his picture walking into the Ryder Truck office and a positive ID from the clerk." I wanted him to see the whole picture.

"Sounds like this is our sixth guy. How do we find him?" Jacobson got right to the point.

Ken and I glanced at each other to see who would walk the boss through our strategy. Ken took the lead and did a good job. He also threw in, "LT did some pretty good police work here."

The good thing about Danny Jacobson was that he could see two moves ahead. I'd bet he was a mean chess player. "You know once you give his picture to the media, there's going to be a shit storm from the Defense Department. I'm wondering if we should give them twenty-four hours to cover their asses if it turns out we have a rogue marine on our hands. Maybe they can even find the guy before the media circus begins. The American people can celebrate five camel jockeys blowing themselves to Allah. Shit, they'll dance in the streets over that the way they did when we got Bin Laden. But they don't want to hear that one of our own soldiers had anything to do with it. Maybe Defense needs time to spin this."

A savvy political animal, Danny Jacobson was already thinking about how to make this work to his advantage. He didn't want to turn this over to Defense any more than I did. If they found Simon, we'd be completely shut out and this was our home run. There would be plenty of kudos for the team that broke this case. Danny didn't want to miss out on his trip to the White House.

But if we plaster Simon's face all over the internet and it turns out he's living with his mother and doing volunteer work at the Veteran's Hospital, we're fucked. Yes, we had his face at the Ryder Truck store and yes, he worked at the Zimmel factory where the aluminum might have come from, but it just didn't make sense that a decorated Marine would be part of this.

We needed a third data point; one more thing that would tie Simon to the tunnel or any of the other explosions. We needed a bit more of a smoking gun. But all we had was a grainy image of a hand in the back seat of the minivan from the tunnel. Even with the Star Wars stuff our guys use to enhance digital images, we'd never be able to make Simon for that picture.

I could see Jacobson was running through the same analysis in his head. The three of us sat there for several minutes in silence. We were each working the problem in our own way; weighing the pluses and minuses of each approach. Finally Jacobson asked, "What about the girlfriend?"

"What about her?" Ken said.

"You said you have her driver's license, right? Let's use her as our person of interest; bait. If we find her, there's a good chance we'll find him, or at least maybe she points us in the right direction to find him. This way, we don't go public with any information about our marine until we're sure one way or the other. We don't mention him at all. We just want to talk to her."

I could see Jacobson liked this idea. His enthusiasm increased with each word.

"And what excuse do we use for wanting to talk to her?" Ken asked skeptically.

Jacobson paused for a moment, but quickly came up with an idea. "We can say we have reason to believe she may be responsible for the prank calls to the media on the morning of TBD. The media made a big deal about it being the voice of a woman. Didn't they?"

Ken said, "That's true. But if Simon is our boy and he sees that we're looking for..." He hesitated and looked at me.

"Nina Morales." I said.

"So if he sees we're looking for Nina Morales, we're going to drive him further underground. That is, assuming he's still in the U.S. at all."

I added, "Don't you think claiming she's the woman who made the calls, without any evidence, is a little weak? It's a lot weaker than the evidence we have to support bringing Simon in for a chat." I was also concerned about driving Simon further into hiding but I didn't want it to seem like Ken and I were shitting on our boss's idea.

"But she's not a marine, LT. It would make a huge difference to the public." Ken said.

"I like your idea boss; I'm just concerned about probable cause. I wish we knew a little more about Morales. I should have spent more time with the guy she worked for." I thought back to my interview with Sami and my haste to make my flight. I should have gotten more info on the girlfriend while I was there.

"You interviewed her boss? You didn't mention that." Jacobson said, then took a seat on our couch.

"Yeah. That's how I got her driver's license. She worked at this bar near the beach. Her boss, this Turkish guy, said she quit in June to follow her boyfriend north. That's about all he could tell me." That wasn't entirely true. In my haste to get back to New York, I neglected to ask him for more background on Morales. Now I was feeling a bit guilty about that so I offered to call Sami again and poke a little deeper. Maybe he knew of a relative or a place she might stay in New York. It was worth a try before we started a full blown manhunt for the woman.

"Good idea. See what else you can learn and be in my office in an hour. We'll make a decision then." Jacobson was on his feet. "Have we even done a background on her?"

Again, I felt stupid for not thinking of that. Then again, until a half hour ago, I had little reason to believe her boyfriend had done anything wrong.

Ken cast me a disapproving eye and said, "We'll get it done and see you in an hour."

Ken worked on the background of Nina Morales, using her driver's license number and date of birth. With that little bit of information it's possible to reassemble a person's entire life. Schools, prior employment, credit cards, past addresses, bank accounts, arrest history, and, if you're the JTTF, even medical records. Unfortunately, nothing about Nina Morales' past was at all interesting. She finished high school then held a string of entry-level jobs; mostly bars and restaurants in the Panama City area. She had only one moving violation but that was probably because she didn't own a car until she began working for Sami. She had her appendix out at seventeen and a tubal ligation at twenty. The only thing we were waiting for was credit card usage, which might take a few hours. That was it.

I, on the other hand, had one of my occasional flashes of brilliance.

When I tried to call Sami at Finnegans' my call went to voicemail again. At first I was pissed. Then it occurred to me that the voice on the recording was a female with a southern accent. I remember Sami telling me that his two daughters worked at the bar but I assume, since they emigrated from Turkey, they did not have southern accents. So there was a chance that the voice on the answering machine was that of Nina Morales.

I took the elevator down to sixteen and grabbed Andy Mercer, our senior audio guy just as he was leaving for the day.

"Andy. I need you to stick around for a few minutes and run an audio check for me. It's really important."

Andy's divorced and he and I went out for a few drinks a while back. It's a long story, but let me just say, Andy owed me a favor so he agreed to walk back to his lab with me.

"What have you got LT?"

"Maybe nothing or maybe something big. I need you to queue up the voices from the bogus 911 and radio calls from TBD."

"I told you, that was all one person. It was in my report."

"Yeah; I remember. But I've got another voice I want you to compare to those and tell me if we have a match. Can you take the audio over a cell phone?"

"Sure." Andy was unlocking his lab as he asked, "Do you think this is her?"

"Maybe. It's a hunch."

We sat down in front of a set of monitors that resembled a NASA control room. "Give me a minute to bring up the 911 call." He fiddled with his mouse and a few moments later, the six screens directly in front of us all turned blue with a horizontal white line running across the center of each.

"Okay, I've loaded one of the 911 calls. Say something into this mic." He handed me a small microphone that looked more like a Cross pen.

"I took the mic and said, "Testing, one, two, three." As I spoke, the horizontal white lines began to jump all over the screens. It looked sort of like a seismograph when an earthquake hits. When I stopped speaking the white line became flat and still again.

"Alright; so when we add the new voice, the same thing will happen if it's not the same person as the one on the 911 calls. This machine detects very subtle differences in tone, pitch, etc. If it's not a very close match, the lines will jump around like that indicating varying degrees of differentiation."

"So I just dial the number and hold the phone to the mic?"

"Simple as that. Ready?"

I dialed Finnegan's again, hoping that no one would answer this time. Sure enough, the machine came on with the greeting about the bar's hours. The message was only about ten seconds long so when it was over I glanced at Andy for some reaction. It seemed as though his machines hadn't been working.

"Well?"

"Did you see any movement on the lines?"

"No."

"That's because it's a perfect match. Not even an attempt at disguise."

"Really?"

"Yep. Can I go home now?"

—◄‡ ‡►—

Our next meeting with Danny Jacobson didn't last long. As soon as he heard about our success in the audio lab, he wanted to fill in the chief who would then fill in the head of Homeland Security. It took only an hour for the information to go up the ladder and back down to us. We got the go-ahead to hold a news conference at nine

P.M. to make our announcement to the media complete with glossy photos of Billy Simon and Nina Morales, America's newly ordained most wanted criminals.

In two hours, every police agency in America would be looking for Billy and Nina.

CHAPTER 48

Everyone had lied to her. Just about everyone had told Carol Wallace that time would help make the pain go away. But nine days since the death of her daughter and the pain was only getting worse each morning. She couldn't yet imagine a day when she wouldn't expect to see Mary Jane sitting at the kitchen table doing her homework, or watching TV in her favorite curled-up position on the blue sofa. Time wasn't helping.

In fact, that morning, just before awakening, Carol had a dream that Mary Jane was graduating from Freeman Academy. The tragedy and all the pain had been some sort of dream and Mary Jane had grown up to be a beautiful young lady. But when Carol awoke and realized the reality in which she had to live another day, she cried. She cried so hard, Alan considered not going to work that morning and taking his wife to the doctor.

Carol refused and refused the tranquilizers her doctor had offered several days ago. She didn't want to be numb. She wanted to feel the pain because, in a way, the pain connected her to her daughter.

Alan, on the other hand, dealt with his grief by further burying himself in his work. Carol didn't want him to stay home and there was nothing he could do to make her agony any less real, so he returned to work two days after they buried their only daughter. He promised they would go away for a week at Thanksgiving. Neither he nor Carol could bear the thought of their first holiday at home without Mary Jane. Maybe it would be better if they went someplace the two of them could reconnect. He had his secretary working on it.

It was 4:15 in the afternoon. Alan would be home in less than an hour. Her devoted friend Jessica, had spent the afternoon with her. At first they reminisced about Mary Jane. Later, Jessica convinced Carol to get out of the apartment and accompany her on a short shopping trip down Second Avenue. The fresh air had done Carol some good. She measured her success by how long it had been since she last cried. In this case; about ninety minutes.

Jessica had just left and Carol put a tea kettle on the stove. Even the simple act of making tea caused her to cry because afternoon tea was something she often shared with Mary Jane upon her return from school. So when she first heard her phone ringing, she was tempted not to answer. She just didn't want to deal with one more old friend who'd heard the news and felt obligated to offer condolences. But she knew they meant well, and for a few minutes she'd be distracted from her agony, so she picked it up on the forth ring.

"Hello", she said as she cleared her throat and wiped her eyes.

The voice on the other end was oddly familiar. "Carol Wallace?"

"Yes; who's calling please?"

Billy made no attempt to disguise his voice. He had no reason to. "This is Billy. Billy Simon."

A flood of emotions washed over Carol. She hadn't heard from Billy in nearly fifteen years. How sweet of him to think of her in her hour of grief? Maybe he'd forgiven her after all these years. Maybe he'd married and had a house full of kids of his own. It was sure nice to know he thought of her.

"Billy. It's so nice to hear from you."

"I'm glad to hear you say that." Billy spoke slowly and softly.

Carol wanted to tell him all about Mary Jane. She wanted him to know what a talented and beautiful girl she was. She wanted him to know everything about her. But now wasn't the time. So, she offered, "How are you, Billy?"

"Oh..., I'm just fine, Carol." And then, almost as if it were an afterthought, he added, "Hey, there's someone here I'd like you to talk to."

"There's someone you want me to talk to?" Carol said, not understanding if she'd heard correctly. Then she heard....

"Mom. Mom. Mommy, it's me. They told me you knew I'm okay." Billy pulled the cell phone away from Mary Jane and listened for her mother's reaction.

If Carol hadn't already been seated she would have fallen to the floor. Her legs gave out beneath her and her hands trembled. She was as close to fainting as is possible but resisted because she felt a mother's instinct to be there for her child. Her heart was pounding and her breathing was rapid and shallow. But she knew her daughter's voice.

"What? What?" Was all she could say. Then the familiar voice came on again.

"Carol. I want you to listen to me very carefully." Billy was again speaking slowly. "Your daughter is safe. She's with me in Florida. She didn't die. She's alive and here with me. Do you understand me?" He mentioned Florida just in case Carol went to the police. He might as well have them barking up the wrong state.

Carol was breathing too fast to put together more than one word answers. "Yes." She wanted to believe against all odds that somehow this wasn't a dream.

"Good. Now, I want you to breathe deeply and slowly, or you're going to pass out and that won't do any of us any good. I know you Carol. You can do this. You have to do this for Mary Jane."

"Okay. I'm breathing."

"Good, now I want…"

"Let me talk to her again!" She screamed.

Billy thought for a moment. He had this entire conversation scripted in his mind but didn't see the harm in letting Carol speak to his captive. He handed Mary Jane the phone.

"Mommy! Please pay them. I want to come home."

"MJ, is that really you?"

"Yes, it's me. I'm here."

"But how...?"

"They took me off the bus after it stopped in the tunnel. I'm okay. They told me you knew I was okay."

"But, how did you...?" Carol was unable to complete her questions. Perhaps it was because she knew the answers to her questions were impossible and didn't want to face that reality.

"Mommy, please pay them the money. I want to come home. They'll let me go as soon as dad pays them. They promised."

Billy decided he'd listened to enough and again pulled the phone from Mary Jane.

"Carol? Are you there?" He said devilishly.

Carol's mind was still trying to reconcile the impossible. She'd buried her daughter six days ago and yet her voice was on the phone. Was she hallucinating? Was she going mad from the grief? How could this be? And yet, she wanted it to be. With every fiber of her being, she wanted the impossible to be real.

"Carol?

"I'm here."

"Good. Now listen closely. I need you to..." Once again she interrupted him.

"I need to ask her a question! I need to know it's her. Let me talk to her again!" She screamed.

Again, Billy saw no harm in departing from his script if it would help make this more credible for Carol.

"Okay, Carol. I'll let you talk to her again. But first I want you to calm down. Take some deep breaths. And while you're breathing, think of a question you can ask your daughter that only she would know the answer to."

"I'm calm!" She screamed. "Let me talk to my daughter!"

He handed the phone back to Mary Jane.

"Mommy, it's me."

"Okay, sweetie. I want you to tell me what you keep in the bottom drawer of the white dresser in your room." Carol closed her eyes and prayed to the god she'd abandoned years before that that the voice on the phone would say the word 'PROGRAMS'.

"That's where I keep my old diaries and the concert programs from Freeman."

"Oh, my baby. My beautiful baby." Carol was sobbing. "Tell me where we went on vacation last summer."

"London."

"Oh, sweetie. I love you so much."

Billy's voice was back on the line. "All right? Satisfied? Your precious Mary Jane is fine. Now you have to listen to me or you're never going to see her again."

Those words stung Carol. Lose her again? An unbearable thought.

"Okay. I want my daughter back. What do you want?" Carol was convinced that somehow it really was her daughter on the phone, but she wasn't yet sure it was really Billy Simon. It was beginning to occur to her that this was a kidnapping and that she may get MJ back again. But what would Billy have to do with that? Still, it did sound like him.

"Good. Now we're getting somewhere productive."

"How do I know you're who you say you are?"

"It doesn't matter who I am." Billy wasn't prepared for that one.

"It does to me. When was the last time I saw you?"

Billy thought for a moment. Not because he didn't immediately know the answer, but because he weighed the benefit of Carol thinking he was an impostor. Perhaps anonymity might be better.

"Manhattan, 1999. Just before I left for Iraq." He wanted her to know.

"Oh, Billy. What are you doing? How can you do this?"

"Listen Carol and listen carefully. I will only say this once. You are going to wire me four million dollars. I'll give you a day to come up with the money but you better be ready when I contact you with the wire instructions on Thursday. Five minutes after I receive confirmation of the wire, I will call you and tell you where to find Mary Jane. If you tell anyone about this other than your husband, you'll never find her and this time, it will be too late for me to save her. Do you understand?"

"Four million dollars ready to be wired on Thursday." She confirmed.

"See that wasn't so hard. But remember, if you go to the police, your daughter will die and it will be by your hand."

"Billy..., why?"

"We'll talk on Thursday." The line went dead.

The tea kettle was whistling.

CHAPTER 49

LT

Jacobson ran the press conference with Ken and I standing behind him and to his left. Pretty much everyone else from the unit had gone home for the night. But the media didn't care. Seven crews showed up to cover it, largely because our friends at Homeland Security are well connected with the press and told them this would be big. Our public information people had prepared press kits including 8x10 photos of Simon and Morales, bios for both and flash drives loaded with the same documents for the press to take with them.

Danny did a good job of explaining what we knew so far and that we believed Simon and Morales were still in the country, although he based this on the fact that no one with those names had crossed the borders since TBD. What he didn't mention was that Simon, and probably his girlfriend, had fake driver's licenses which we knew were used to rent the Ryder Trucks and the room at the Hilton. We also knew that Suniel Saman and Gabriel Maclov had also used fake driver's licenses to rent the cars used on the bridge.

So personally, I put the odds of Simon and Morales still being in the country at 50-50.

Danny took questions for ten minutes, thanked everyone for coming, then turned them loose to do their thing. We were hoping the story would make the eleven o'clock news and the morning papers. It would surely be on the internet by the time we got back to our offices.

I was pretty tired but Ken insisted we stop for a celebratory drink at Vinny's before heading home. Probably because he knew he'd have to pick up the tab, Jacobson decided not to join us, although we did offer a half-hearted invitation.

Ken and I took our usual seats at the bar but none of the usual bartenders were working that night. In their place was a very attractive African American woman named Shelia. Don't ask me where they get these names. Anyway, Shelia was giving me the eye and at one point actually put her hand on mine to make a point of whatever she was talking about. She was definitely putting the moves on me. Even Ken picked up on it. But Shelia quickly figured out I don't go 'that way' and Ken and I were left to ourselves.

Turns out Ken wanted to chat about his rapidly deteriorating marriage once again, so, because he's my partner, and for no other reason, I listened dutifully. I honestly feel for the guy. The word he used repeatedly to describe the situation at home was "numb". They're not fighting or even arguing more than any other couple; they're just numb. I guess that means they both stopped caring at some point. It's sad.

So we had a couple of beers and, after an acceptable amount of time, I tried to steer the conversation back to our case. "What I can't figure out is what the hell this guy and his redneck girlfriend have to do with the towelheads."

"Everybody has their reasons." Was Ken's philosophical spin on the question.

I responded, "What the fuck does that mean?" I tend to be less philosophical than Ken.

"I mean, everyone does things for a reason that suits them. That's all I'm saying."

"Yeah, but they took out hundreds of innocent people. You don't do that unless you've got some sort of political agenda."

"LT, people kill for all sorts of non-political reason; hatred, revenge, greed, just to name a few. You don't know what was in this kid's head. Maybe he got fucked over in Iraq somehow and was looking to settle the score."

"Yeah, but then he would have gone after the military. These were civilians; innocent bystanders."

"I know. It doesn't make sense yet."

"It would probably be easier to find the prick if we understood his motive though."

"Agreed. But hopefully, someone will pick up the newspaper tomorrow morning, see his picture and say, "Hey, I know that guy!""".

It was a little after eleven, so I was surprised when my cell phone started vibrating on the bar. I glanced at Ken and said, "This can't be good news."

Well, I was wrong. It was one of the conscientious guys back at the office who were still digging into Nina Morale' credit card records. Turns out, she hadn't used her card since the middle of June except on two occasions: once on Interstate 95 in Virginia on June 22nd, and once to pay for the Port Jefferson Ferry for a ride from Bridgeport to Port Jefferson on the afternoon of TBD.

"Now isn't that interesting?"

CHAPTER 50

Billy Simon was in a strange mood. His conversation with Carol had been every bit as satisfying as he'd hoped. After all these years, he was hurting her in so many ways. First, she thinks her daughter is killed in an act of mindless terrorism. She has to bury what she thinks is her only daughter. She has to say good bye to her child. What could be worse for a parent?

Then, two weeks after she buries her daughter, she learns that she's not really dead; instead, her child's fate rests in the hands of the lover she once turned her back on. And now she has to give up something else she holds scared- money. She has to buy back her daughter's life. Billy wasn't sure just how much pain four million dollars would cause the Wallace family, but he assumed it would put a significant dent in their opulent life. It didn't really matter. By the end of the week, they'd be out four million dollars and their daughter would be dead anyway. This time, really dead.

And though he'd never even met Alan Wallace, he hated him with a septic passion. He hated everything Alan Wallace stood for; the undeserved wealth, his feeling of entitlement, and of course, for seducing Carol away from Billy with his sparkling baubles. Billy wanted this to hurt Alan just as much as it would hurt Carol. He planned to send Alan pictures of the body with a note that said, "Thanks for the money. This was all your fault."

He was sitting on top of the bed when Nina came into the room from the bathroom. She'd just showered and was wearing only a long tee shirt that read, "Panama City Beach Spring Break 2010". The neckline had long-since been cut away so the shirt hung on her golden shoulders.

"We're almost there baby." He said. "A few more days and we start our new lives in a new land."

"Do you think I'll like Canada, Billy? Do they have all the same stuff we have?"

"You'll love it. And we won't be there very long anyway. After a few weeks, we'll fly to Rome and spend the whole winter traveling around Europe. Canada's too fucking cold in the winter anyway."

She climbed up on the bed and straddled Billy. "Are you sure I'm going to like it?" She said in a teasingly seductive voice as she grinded against Billy's boxers.

He became immediately aroused and Nina could feel his enthusiasm beneath her. She lifted herself off him and, with her weight balanced on her knees, slid his shorts down his legs. Then she lowered herself onto him and continued the slow grind.

"Hey. I just thought of something." Billy said. "This might be the last time we ever fuck in the United States."

Nina continued her unduluating motion. "Well then, let's make it a good one."

Billy reached up and put his hands around Nina's throat. He squeezed just hard enough to lessen the flow of oxygen-rich blood to her brain but not hard enough to impede her breathing. This is what she loved. With slightly less oxygen reaching her head, Nina began to feel a euphoric light-headedness. She knew, from their prior experiences, if Billy tightened his grip or held her neck too long, she would pass out. But the high she achieved if he did it just right was nearly orgasmic. She reached down and guided his rock-hard penis into her. She changed the cadence of her motion. Now, instead of grinding in a forward and backward motion, she was moving up and down to increase the penetration with each slow but intense thrust.

Billy kept his pelvis flat against the bed. This was a game in which Nina did all the work. His forefinger and thumb from each hand met at the front and back of Nina's neck. He squeezed a bit more as she moaned. Her thrusts were coming faster now and he knew they'd both come in a few moments. He closed his eyes and imagined it was Carol riding him. Harder and faster, until just as he climaxed, he fantasized he was strangling her to death.

CHAPTER 51

Nina looked forward to any time she could spend away from the house, so her daily drives to the shopping center next to the Expressway were a welcomed respite. Even though their sex had been satisfying, Billy had been growing increasingly short tempered the last few days. Ever since he made the call to the Wallaces the previous day, he had been on edge. Being cooped up with him in the three room house was beginning to strain the strength of their short relationship. And since Billy was reluctant to leave the safety of the house, it was up to her to run whatever errands were required. She hoped things would be different in a few weeks when they had the money and were strolling around Montreal.

Nina drove the rented Ford Focus about eight miles to a strip mall just outside Commack. There, she had access to an assortment of fast food chains, a bagel shop, a supermarket, a gas station, a liquor store, and several other shops she had no use for. Across the street was a 7-Eleven and two banks. This morning's mission was bagels and a newspaper.

She bought three newspapers at the 7-Eleven, then, with the papers under her arm, walked across to the bagel store. Billy had insisted she wear a baseball cap and oversized sunglasses whenever she went out. But this morning was cloudy and threatening to rain so she left the sunglasses in the car.

As soon as she had the six salt bagels, Billy's favorite, she got back in the blue car and drove directly home. Billy had been clear about that. He wanted no unnecessary traveling. Still, her time in the car was her daily taste of freedom, even if just for twenty minutes. It felt wonderful.

When she returned to the house Billy was just waking up. He was sitting at the table in the small kitchen and had just started a pot of water for his instant coffee. He was still scratching the sleep from his eyes and had yet to turn on the television, something he usually did even before his morning pee.

"Hey. We still have some cream cheese from yesterday so I just got the bagels. They're still hot. I'll say one thing for these Yankees; they know how to make a bagel. The shit we get in Florida tastes nothing like these." Morning conversation was usually Nina's responsibility if made at all.

From the kitchen table, Billy stretched and rotated his neck. He had a bit too much beer the previous evening and was paying for it this morning. But yesterday was a celebration and required some celebratory drinking. After nearly fifteen years, he'd settled the score with Carol. He'd waited a long time for that conversation and had played it over in his mind a hundred times before yesterday. His only regret was that he couldn't see the look on her face.

Still, it was sweet revenge. Whoever coined the phrase about revenge being a dish best served cold; was absolutely right. And it was his third well-planned victory in as many weeks. The explosions accomplished exactly what they were intended to do. Americans were frantic to point three hundred million fingers directly at the Islamic world. The country was once again united in its belief that it had an enemy it could see and touch.

And the five assholes who fell for Billy's ploy and had been incinerated at the Hilton, took the entire blame for the bombings. Perfect. Americans once again feared and hated the Middle East. Billy already considered himself wildly successful. And the best was yet to come. In the coming days he would inflict even more pain on Carol and her spineless husband and walk away with four million dollars of their money.

Billy, in his own somber way, was reveling in his successful mission. And he was looking forward to the next few days- days that would make him finally content. Aside from a minor hangover, Billy was feeling good. That is, until he glanced at the headline on the front page of the Daily News Nina had just flopped onto the table.

It read, "Manhunt for two more killers". Below the bold headline were pictures of Nina and himself. His picture was taken from his official U.S. Marine photo.

"Holy fucking Christ! How the fuck did they connect us to this?" He was incredulous. He was incensed. "I guess you didn't even look at the paper; you fucking moron."

Nina was like a deer in the headlights of an oncoming eighteen-wheeler. He'd never spoken to her like this before and she'd never seen him this enraged. She backed up against the kitchen counter and remained silent as Billy read the story supporting the headline.

For several minutes he said nothing; his eyes darting back and forth across the page absorbing each intolerable word. When he finished, he moved on to the New York Times, which gave the story its coveted right column and a full page two. Again the same two photos. He read the story and flung the paper against the wall. Then he moved on to the third paper, Newsday, which also gave he and Nina the entire front page followed by roughly the same story as the Daily News.

Billy buried his head in his hands. He was trying to think. He knew that in battle, he could not let surprise adversity distract him. He needed to focus. He remembered that from his basic training fifteen years ago. Stay focused on the mission and calculate an alternative solution.

After several minutes of reflection he came to the preliminary conclusion that the only problems this presented to his mission were: first, they needed to now stay off the street and hope no one who'd already seen them would remember their faces. Because they'd always worn baseball caps and sunglasses, he felt good about their continued anonymity. Second, crossing the border into Canada was now going to be harder. Harder, but still not impossible. They already had forged passports. They'd just have to work on their appearances. It could be done. All was certainly not lost.

He knew he'd have to spend a lot more time thinking about this to make sure he hadn't missed something, but, based on the information from the newspapers, their whereabouts were still a complete mystery to the authorities. In fact, the Times article quoted someone from the JTTF as saying, "We're not even sure they're still in the United States".

When Billy finally looked up, he noticed Nina had not moved. Then he remembered barking at her.

"Hey. Don't worry about it. I'm sorry I went off on you. This will be okay. They don't have a fucking clue where to look for us. We'll be fine."

But all Nina could think about was walking into the bagel store a half hour ago without her sunglasses.

CHAPTER 52

LT

I had a dentist appointment Tuesday morning so by the time I got to the office, a lot had happened. The prior evening's news and morning papers had already produced twenty-six calls from people who knew either Billy or Nina and had recognized their pictures. Unfortunately, all of the calls were from people in Florida who hadn't seen either for several months. The field guys, who took the calls, would eventually do follow-up interviews with each by phone to see if there was anything to be learned about our fugitives' background, but for now, we were focused on leads about their current whereabouts.

Even before I got to our office, I could see Ken Stallings jumping up and down while he spoke to someone on the phone. As I entered the room I heard the end of the conversation.

"Okay, okay. We'll be there in about an hour. I've got it: 540 Deer Park Avenue. Right. Great. Thank you Captain. I'll see you in about an hour." Ken was very excited about something.

"Good news?" I teased.

"Better than good. That was a Suffolk County police captain. He called in to tell us that someone on Long Island spotted Nina Morales in a bagel store this morning. Less than forty minutes ago. It's in Commack, Exit 54. Let's go. I told him we could be there in an hour." Ken was already reaching for his raincoat.

We commandeered one of the agency's Crown Vics and were on our way to Long Island before I could even grab a coffee. Ken drove. The Midtown Tunnel had reopened yesterday so he headed down Second Avenue.

"What exactly are you hoping to accomplish in person that you couldn't do over the phone?" I wanted to know.

As Ken turned into the tunnel entrance he said, "I want to talk directly to the store clerk from the bagel store. The Suffolk cop didn't get much from him and what little he did get was third hand; though their dispatcher. Also, if this turns into something, we may need their help. No harm in putting a face with a name; especially if we need Suffolk PD to do some tedious legwork for us later."

As usual, Ken made a good point.

As we approached the point in the tunnel where the explosion occurred, traffic slowed. Apparently, everyone, including Ken and I, wanted to get a look at the repair work as they cruised by. It was remarkable. Ten days after a major explosion, the only evidence of the destruction was the cleanliness of the affected area. Where the rest of the tunnel was covered in years of exhaust soot, the newly installed replacement tiles in the center of the tunnel were gleaming white. The asphalt roadway also became suddenly smoother as we rolled over ground zero. The three foot crater I'd seen ten days ago had been well repaired. I wish the entire tunnel was this smooth a ride.

"Seems like they should put a plaque on the wall or something." Ken said. "I mean, a lot of people got killed here. Are we just going to forget it happened?"

"Do we really want people trying to read a plaque as they fly by at sixty miles an hour?" I thought it was a fair, if not mostly rhetorical question. But again, Ken was right. The tunnel repairs somehow made me feel as though everyone was trying to forget TBD ever happened. Have we become this numb to terrorism in our own backyards? I hope not. I'd be out of a job.

As we paid the toll on the Queens side of the tunnel, we began to chat about the morning of TBD. Specifically, we speculated about where the minivan went after it left the tunnel. We knew that two of its occupants are dead; killed in the explosion at the Tarrytown Hilton. So they must have driven directly to Tarrytown because the hotel explosion occurred at 10:45 A.M.; less than two hours after the tunnel explosion. We wondered how they drove there.

We knew that the minivan was photographed entering and leaving the hotel's parking lot, so someone, most likely the person in the back seat, drove it somewhere else. And we knew that, about three hours later, Nina Morales used her credit card to charge a one-way trip on the ferry from Bridgeport, Connecticut to Port Jefferson, Long Island. What we didn't know was whether Billy Simon was with her. We also didn't know where Nina went after she got off the ferry in Port Jefferson; although we now have confirmation that she was seen in Commack, about ten miles from the ferry terminus.

It seems like we didn't know more than we did know, so we began to speculate.

"I'd like to know why the minivan was at the Hilton in the first place and why the third person in the minivan drove off after dropping off Hasan and Ben-Dor." I said.

"You're assuming it was the third person in the van who drove it from the hotel parking lot. You're probably right, but that's an assumption. It could have been anyone else and our mystery third person might have driven off in another vehicle that was waiting there. Or maybe he or she checked into another room and never left."

The latter was unlikely since the Tarrytown Hilton was forced to close because the explosion on the sixteenth floor had done so much structural damage to the building. But it pointed out that we had been making assumptions, and making assumptions can lead you off on a lot of wild goose chases.

Ken pointed out, "For example; we've been assuming Simon is a key player here and may have been the third guy in the van. But maybe his only roll was to rent the trucks. Maybe he was home watching cartoons on the morning of TBD. Maybe Nina was the third person in the van. Maybe she had something to do in the van before going up to the sixteenth floor. Maybe it took a little longer than planned and before she left the van to join her friends, the scumbags fucked something up while setting up their next bomb and she sees the explosion from the parking lot. She panics. She drives away; all the way to Bridgeport where she gets on the ferry."

"She could have been making the bogus calls from the van." I said.

"No, the times don't line up. The calls were made earlier. But nice try."

So for the rest of the drive out to Commack we tried a bunch of off-the-wall theories on each other. We do this a lot. It sometimes helps us see the possibilities we overlooked. But this time, so far, it just pointed out how little we really knew about motive.

We arrived at the Suffolk PD headquarters, parked the Crown Vic in a spot reserved for "PD ONLY", and found Captain McIntire and another uniformed cop waiting for us in McIntire's office. Ken did the introductions, as he usually does, and the Captain explained that the fourth cop was officer Brune, the guy who took the call from the Bagel store.

"As soon as officer Brune reported the call to me, I got on the phone with you guys. I figured you'd want to talk directly to the store clerk so we held off. I did call Leimgruber's, that's the name of the bagel store, to tell them we were coming around noon."

The captain seemed like a straight shooter, and not what I expected in a Suffolk County cop. He was about my age, maybe even a little younger; in excellent physical condition, and seemed genuinely proud to wear his crisply starched white shirt and grey uniform. He was classically handsome; sort of the Gary Cooper type. I liked him right from the start. I suggested we head over to the bagel store and, while we're at it, have lunch there, but Gary Cooper had other plans and wanted us to take officer Brune with us.

Leimgruber's Bagels is the kind of place you'd drive by a hundred times and never notice. Nestled in the middle of a small strip mall, there's nothing remarkable about it. Nothing except the remarkable smell drifting from its front door and enticing you in even before you get out of your car. It was just past noon and they were already nearly sold out of bagels; something Brune explained happened almost every day. Apparently Len Leimgruber, the owner, liked to close up by two so he could get in nine holes of golf as often as possible.

Len came out from behind the near empty counter to greet us. He was exactly what you'd expect a baker to look like; a bit overweight, about sixty-five and covered in flour up to his elbows. Before we could even introduce ourselves, he said, "Let's make this short. I've been here since 3:30 A.M. and I've got a four o'clock tee time at Bethpage."

There was no place to sit in the store. Apparently Len didn't encourage his customers to hang around. He just wanted to satisfy the people who lined up every morning to get their bagels and maybe a coffee and send them on their way. So Ken got right to the point, "I'm Ken Stallings and this is LT Hadman. We're from the Joint Task Force on Terrorism and this is officer Brune from Suffolk PD. We'd like to talk to whoever it was that called this morning."

"I'm the one who called. Who the hell else would it be? Do you see anyone else here? So what do you want to know?"

It's a good thing Len's bagels smelled so outrageous because he wasn't likely to attract customers with his charm.

Ken showed Len one of the 8x10's of Nina Morales. "Are you certain this is the woman you say was in your shop this morning?"

"Yep, and yesterday too."

"You're sure?"

"Hey, I said it was her. It was her. I saw her face on the news this morning not ten minutes before she walked in. It was her."

"What did she buy?" I asked.

"Half dozen salt bagels. Same as yesterday."

Anything else you can tell us about her that might be helpful?"

"Not much. I didn't get outside fast enough to get a look at her license plate. But she was driving a dark blue sedan. Don't know what it was but it was a regular car, not an SUV or pickup. By the time I got around the counter and outside she was driving away." He pointed to the north.

"So she went up Commack Road?" Officer Brune asked.

"Yep. And she made the right at the light up on Benice Avenue. That's when I lost sight of her car."

You say she was here yesterday as well. Did you see where she went yesterday?" I asked.

"Nope. Yesterday, her face wasn't all over the papers. Yesterday I had no reason to notice her; now did I?" He gave me a look that said, "Hell, you're not much of a cop."

Ken asked if Len had a surveillance camera, which he did not. So after a few more questions we thanked him for his time. I bought three plain bagels and we were on our way back to the precinct house to drop off Brune. But as we began to pull out of the parking lot, the young officer said, "Drive up the street and make the right on Benice. I want to show you something."

What the astute patrolman wanted to show us was that by making the right on Benice, we had entered a development of homes. He pointed out that there were only two ways into or out of the development; Benice or Gilford Road which was at the other end of the development; about two miles to the east. "There are about a thousand homes in here." He said as we rolled past a few of the wooded one-acre lots. "And it's unlikely Morales would drive in here just to get to Gilford Road at the far end. There are more direct ways to get to Gilford. No. If she came in here, I'll bet this is where she's living."

Unfortunately, many of the homes were hidden from the roads by thick brush or curving driveways, so driving around looking for a blue car didn't seem like a productive use of our time. But Ken had an idea.

"You say there are about a thousand homes in here, huh? I suggest we do three things. First, we check with other merchants in Leimgruber's strip mall to see if anyone has a surveillance camera that might have picked up Morale's license plate. Second, we have an unmarked unit at Leimgruber's tomorrow morning and every morning until we find Ms. Morales. Third, we get as many agents as Jacobson will give us, dress them up as utility workers and start going door to door here tomorrow morning. We can tell people someone smelled gas or something."

Brune added, "Better yet; you can tell them you need to read the meter one last time before PSE&G takes over. They're supposed to take over for LIPA at the end of the year. There's been a lot of news about it in the local papers so people are probably expecting something to happen as one electric company takes over for another. Everyone hates LIPA anyway."

"Great idea. So that gets us in the house to see if Morales is there. How do we get a peek in the garage for that blue sedan?" I wanted to know. We'd have to work on that one.

Then Brune added, "And I can probably get you three or four Suffolk PD. Everyone's looking for OT right now. I bet McIntire would okay it."

Ken told him to get in touch with LIPA. We'd need fifteen to twenty LIPA shirts and phony credentials by nine o'clock the next morning. He said we'd all meet at his precinct at 8:30 A.M. to assign each cop/LIPA worker streets to cover so we weren't tripping over each other and asked Brune to come up with a street map for us. Then we dropped officer Brune off and headed back to Manhattan. Ken called Jacobson on the way and asked for fifteen agents. He got ten; mostly junior people who were expendable for the rest of the week. With Ken and I and a couple of McIntire's guys, we could cover the entire development in two days.

Or maybe we'd just get lucky and Nina Morales would need more bagels tomorrow.

CHAPTER 53

LT

Ken and I and the ten junior agents met in Jacobson's conference room at six A.M. to go over tactics. Ken had worked with a few of them before; I'd never even met any of them. Four were strapping young guys who easily could pass for LIPA workers. They had that blue-collar look about them. The other six were women of assorted shapes and sizes. A few could pass as LIPA people; a little portly and in need of some makeup. Two were real knockouts and looked more like models than meter maids, but that's the hand we were dealt.

Ken explained the goals of the two day assignment. They'd all been told to bring an overnight bag rather than running back into the city. They were all told to wear their guns on their belts and leave the LIPA shirts (to be passed out in Commack) outside their pants to conceal the weapons. Two were assigned the unenviable job of staking out the bagel store once we got there. The Suffolk PD had it covered from midnight until we arrive.

"Your job is purely recon," Ken explained to those who'd be canvassing the neighborhood. "I want you to observe and report. That's it. If you are lucky enough to come across Nina Morales or the blue sedan, you are to phone it in to incident command. That would be me. You are not to question nor are you to apprehend the suspect. For today and tomorrow, you are LIPA workers. Everybody got that?"

"When we get out to Commack, their chief will review the maps and assignments with us. You are to check in with IC every hour and under no circumstances are you to deviate from the assignments you are given. Is everyone clear?" Ken was using his bossy voice.

There were no questions in New York so we all drove out to Commack in seven of the department's finest Crown Vics. Ken and I drove out together. The plan was for me to take the car on my assigned route while Ken stayed back at the Suffolk PD precinct, which was to be our incident command post for the next two days.

"So what do think the odds are we come up with something?" Ken liked to get me to commit before he offered his sage wisdom. He was driving so I humored him.

"If the kid is right about that neighborhood only having one other way out, maybe we get lucky. I mean, why else would she drive in there? He said you don't go in there to get anywhere else, right?"

"If, and that's a big if, he really spotted Nina Morales. You know how these things go. John Q. Citizen sees a perp on the news and the next guy that walks in the store is him. Happens all the time. I say we have a five percent chance of success."

The exits on the L.I.E flew by. After all, it was only 6:45 A.M. and we were driving against the rush hour traffic. The poor slobs going west were sitting in the usual gridlock that extended sometimes for thirty miles. The fact that the cars and trucks heading west were virtually sitting still, made our travel seem all the more speedy. It reminded me of being on a moving sidewalk at the airport.

When we were just a few miles from Commack, my cell phone rang.

"Hadman here." My usual greeting.

"Agent Hadman, this is Carol Wallace. You were at my home a few days ago."

"Yes, Mrs. Wallace. Of course I remember."

"You left me your card and told me to call if I needed to." She sounded very distressed.

"Absolutely. What can I do for you?" I said as I covered the phone and whispered to Ken sarcastically, "One of the mothers of the kids on the bus. Thanks a lot."

"I don't know how to explain this." There was a pause, then, "I got a call Tuesday from Billy Simon."

It's a good thing I wasn't driving. "What?"

"This was before I saw his name on the TV yesterday so..."

"Wait. Did you say you got a phone call from Billy Simon?" As I said the words I hoped Ken wasn't going to drive off the road.

"Yes. And it's the same Billy Simon everyone is looking for. Years ago, many years ago, we were engaged and it ended badly. We haven't spoken in fifteen years."

"What did he want?"

Carol Wallace recounted her conversation with America's most wanted criminal. She explained his demand for four million dollars and the fact that she had spoken to her daughter and was sure it was her. She told me about the question she asked about the dresser contents and that no one but Mary Jane could have known that. She was convinced her daughter was alive and that Billy Simon was holding her captive, possibly somewhere in Florida. Unfortunately, to a skeptical cop like me, this smelled like a scam; someone playing on the emotions of a distraught parent. A good con man could easily manipulate the fragile state of someone who lost a child; someone who wanted to believe so badly that their child wasn't gone.

She went on for several minutes telling me why it had to be her daughter and why her ex-boyfriend would want revenge. I have to admit, it was an interesting story. But, based on what Carol Wallace told me, even if it really was Billy Simon who called, this was a ransom demand and that means a federal crime and that means I had to report it to the FBI. By itself, it certainly didn't come under the jurisdiction of the JTTF. So I reluctantly explained, "Mrs. Wallace; if what you've told me is all true, then this is a matter for the FBI. They investigate kidnappings and ransom demands. I will get someone from the FBI to contact you within the hour. I'm sure they'll have a lot of questions for you."

"It sounds like you don't believe me." Her voice was soft and sad.

"That's not for me to decide. I would...."

"That's what my husband says. He thinks I'm crazy. He says there's no way we should pay the ransom. He says it's a con artist. He wanted to report it to the police right away but I insisted we wait until I spoke to you. That's why I called you so early."

What I wanted to say was, "Your husband's probably right." But instead, I offered, "The FBI deals with these things all the time. I'm sure they'll be a lot of help in sorting this out."

"All right. Please have them call me at this number as soon as possible. Billy said he would contact us again today to discuss the ransom payment." She sounded totally dejected.

"If that's the case, the FBI will certainly want to talk to you before he makes contact again. I'll get in touch with them as soon as we get off the phone."

"Okay, thank you. Good bye."

"Un-fucking-believable." Was Ken's summary of my conversation as I began to dial the only number I knew by heart at the Manhattan office of the FBI. We were just pulling into the parking lot at the Suffolk County Police station in Commack when Hank Waldron, a guy Ken used to work with years ago, picked up my call. Hank was a career Bureau guy and usually dealt with international money laundering and counterfeit crimes, but, like I said, his was the only number I had in my phone. I motioned to Ken to go into the briefing without me and that I'd join him as soon as I could. Then I spent the next ten minutes bringing Hank up to date on Carol Wallace's situation.

Hank assured me he'd have someone on the phone with Mrs. Wallace within minutes. Hank was good people. Although I never met him, he once set me up on a blind date with his cousin, a high school English teacher with a lisp. We had dinner once. It didn't work; probably because I find lisps hysterical.

So by the time I got inside, the strategy session was breaking up and the ten eager beavers from the JTTF, and the three cops Suffolk County was willing to lend us for the day, all dressed like LIPA people, were on their way to their appointed rounds. I checked in with Ken, filled him in on my brief conversation with Hank Waldron, and was handed two pages of streets I was to cover that day.

The day, which started very early, was going to be a long one.

CHAPTER 54

Hank Waldron didn't waste any time getting two agents over to the Wallace apartment. When LT mentioned they were expecting another contact later that day from the man claiming to be Billy Simon, he understood there was little time to waste. Even if it did turn out to be just a con man shaking the Wallaces down, the Bureau would want to have their phones tapped prior to any more calls. On the other hand, if it really did turn out to be Billy Simon, Waldron would be happy to have even a small part in his capture.

Agents Frank Sciarra and Jayne Eriksen arrived at the Wallace home promptly at eleven A.M., just as they'd promised on the phone fifty minutes earlier. That gave Alan Wallace time to get home from work, something he wasn't pleased about but the agents had insisted upon when speaking to Carol.

Frank Sciarra was a Bureau veteran; twenty-two years on the job with a full head of grey hair to show for it. He looked the part of the stereotypical G-man, right down to the black trench coat. He and

Jayne could not have been more different. She'd spent four years as an assistant district attorney somewhere in the Midwest before joining the FBI eight years ago. She was a stylish dresser and not afraid to accent her feminine side even on the job. She had short sassy red hair and appeared younger than her thirty-seven years.

Sciarra and Eriksen sat on a sofa directly across from Alan and Carol Wallace who also shared a sofa but noticeably apart. It was clear to both agents that the Wallaces did not agree on the course of action to be taken. Their body language was unmistakable.

After Carol filled them in on her conversation with Billy, they asked permission to put wire taps on their phones. This would allow the FBI to legally tape the conversations and, if they could keep the, "Alleged kidnapper on the line long enough, possibly trace the call." Frank Sciarra could not hide the skepticism in his voice.

"You don't sound like you believe this was really Billy Simon, Agent Sciarra." Carol said.

"Please, call me Frank." He offered politely. "And I'm sorry if I sound skeptical, but it is very unlikely this man is who he says he is"

"Thank you. Maybe you can convince my wife. I wasn't able to." Alan offered with his arms folded across his chest.

"But why do you say that? I heard my daughter. It was Mary Jane. No one but Mary Jane could possibly know the contents of her dresser." Carol pleaded.

Jayne Eriksen interjected, "Mrs. Wallace. It is possible that this man is who he says he is. But it's also possible that he's just a confidence man trying to shake you down. It's not uncommon for these guys to prey on people like yourselves; people who have suffered a terrible loss and are in vulnerable states. They gather a few pieces of information that is readily available through public records, do a little homework, maybe go through your trash for a few days, then offer you the one thing you want more than anything in the world; another chance with your daughter. They know you want desperately to believe Mary Jane might be alive and that's their secret weapon. They know you'll latch on to any hope she's alive. And they're hoping you'll pay to find out."

Carol sat up on the sofa. "Jayne, are you a parent?"

"No mam. I'm not."

"Well then, I can understand why you'd have trouble understanding that a mother knows her child's voice. A mother knows and I know that was Mary Jane. I could hear the fright in her voice."

Agent Sciarra got up and excused himself. "I need to make a call to get those wire taps going. I'll be right back." He left the room and used his cell to make the call.

Alan Wallace turned to his wife. "Carol, I think Jayne is right. You want to believe it's MJ so bad, you convince yourself it's her. Don't you think the…"

Carol cut him off. "Alan. I know my daughter. I know her like she was my own flesh. I nursed her, I spent countless hours cradling her in my arms when she was sick, I'm the one who talks to her when she gets home from school, I'm the one who tucks her in at night. Don't try to tell me I'm imagining this!"

To diffuse the growing tension, Agent Eriksen offered, "Okay, let's first work on the premise that the caller really is Billy Simon and that he has your daughter. That would mean the person you buried two weeks ago wasn't Mary Jane. Did you have to identify the body at the coroner's office?"

Alan replied, "No. The remains were so badly burned there was no way to identify our daughter. The police asked us for DNA samples but my wife was so upset at the time, we never did that. I think they used her necklace as a way to know it was Mary Jane." He looked to his wife to see that this line of discussion was upsetting her again.

"We could have the body exhumed to do DNA testing. It can be done..."

Carol interrupted. "Absolutely not! Once my daughter is back in my arms you can do whatever you want but not until then."

Jayne Eriksen rubbed the bridge of her nose. She felt for Carol and Alan. Losing a child had to be bad enough but to never get closure must make it even harder. Burying a sack of burnt bones just doesn't do it. She could almost understand Carol's conviction that her daughter was still alive.

Frank Sciarra walked back into the room. "Okay. The com guys will be here in less than an hour. Let's hope our boy doesn't call before they get their wires in place." Then he turned to Carol. "Mrs. Wallace; you said earlier that the suspect said he'd have wire instructions for you today. We need to talk about how you're going to handle that next call. We also need to deal with the likelihood your apartment is being watched. It may even be bugged already; but that's unlikely. Anyway, our guys will do a sweep when they get here to be sure. But we'll have to assume, the suspect will be aware of our involvement either because he's listening right now or because he's somehow watching. Either way, there's no point in lying to him when he calls. We need to build trust. He has to be able to trust us, even if we don't trust him."

"He said he'd kill her if I went to the police." She began to sob.

"Of course he said that. He wants to scare you. But if he somehow really does have your daughter, he's not going to hurt her yet. He needs to be able to assure you she's okay at least until the ransom is paid." Sciarra was kneeling beside Carol.

"Wait a minute. We're not paying any ransom. Carol, this is bullshit. I've seen enough movies to know that even if she's alive now, once we pay ransom, he has no reason to keep her alive. Hell, if this guy is who he says he is, he's already killed hundreds of people including three of Mary Jane's best friends. Why would we think he wouldn't kill her too?" Alan was on his feet.

Before Carol could erupt, Frank Sciarra said, "Mr. Wallace; can I talk to you out in the hallway for a moment." Then he added, "Just in case the room is bugged."

When he and Alan were in the hall, Frank asked, "How would this guy, whoever he is, have any idea if you have that kind of money?"

"I have no idea."

"What I'm getting at is; could this be someone you know professionally? Maybe someone you pissed off in business or a jealous husband?" Sciarra watched Alan's face carefully for a reaction.

"Look Agent Sciarra, I work for a boutique investment bank. You don't have to be Einstein to figure out we have some money. And I'm in complete agreement with you that this is a shakedown. My wife hasn't been herself since our daughter died. She's taking a few too many sedatives if you ask me. Her judgment is in the crapper. And, as to the question you have yet to ask, the answer is yes- we have the money."

When they returned to the apartment, Carol had begun making coffee. It was likely to be a long afternoon.

By two o'clock, the communication guys had done a sweep of the apartment for bugs and hidden cameras. They found nothing. They set up their equipment for recording and hopefully, tracing the next call, on the cocktail table in the center of the living room. Only now was it safe to talk strategy with the Wallaces.

It was determined, very much to Carol's dismay, that before they would take the caller's threats seriously, they needed another validation that Mary Jane was the female voice on the other end of the call. To do that, it was agreed that Alan would take the call and demand to talk to his daughter. It was also agreed that Alan would demand an explanation of how Mary Jane was still alive and who they'd buried in her place. Frank was hopeful that this line of discussion with the suspect would keep the call going long enough to triangulate a trace.

The skillful veteran anticipated Alan would be able to distinguish the voice on the line from his daughter's and at that point the investigation would switch from a kidnapping to a second-rate confidence scheme. But they had little chance of apprehending the person behind the scheme if they couldn't get a trace on the line. The other choice was; once they were convinced the kidnapping was a fraud, that Alan would play along, as if convinced he had spoken to his daughter, and try to trap the suspect during the delivery of the ransom.

So it was agreed that only Alan would speak to the caller and that either way, he would postpone the ransom delivery. Frank, Jayne, and the rest of the FBI communications team would all be there for support and advice. The FBI team practiced role plays with Alan for the next two hours.

Then they waited.

CHAPTER 55

Nina was making lunch for herself and Billy; peanut butter on salt bagels. Since yesterday morning, when their faces became the subject of so much attention, Billy insisted they stay in the house and make the food they had on hand last a few days longer. Even with the sunglasses and baseball caps, they couldn't take the chance of being spotted in the King Kullen. They were too close to their prize to blow it now.

Besides, by tomorrow morning they'd be able to confirm the wire transfer, graciously made in the amount of four million dollars by the Wallaces, and they had enough food to last well into next week if they decided to wait that long to emerge. Billy promised they'd be in Montreal by Sunday. So, a few more days didn't really matter to Nina.

Billy, on the other hand, was increasingly concerned about the next few days. With their identities out in the open, crossing the border into Canada was going to be a lot more difficult than he'd planned. At first he thought about contacting Victor, his friend in Panama City Beach who'd done such a great job on the phony passports, to see about getting new ones made. But that idea had two significant problems. The first was that, unless he had a way to alter his actual appearance, there was no point in altering the passport photo. The other problem was that he could no longer trust his friend in Florida. Now that he, and the rest of America, knew that Billy had something to do with the explosions in New York, his former friend might have a very different opinion of Billy. When Billy originally approached Victor about getting bogus passports, something Victor had a knack for, he'd asked no questions about the need. Usually, it had something to do with smuggling drugs into or out of the country, and he didn't want to know any more than he had to. But this was different. This was an attack on America.

So it occurred to Billy that Victor might decide to become a patriot and go to the police about the passports he'd already produced. If there was a reward attached, Victor might just do it. Billy wondered if Victor remembered the names he asked to have on the bogus documents; the names of two of Billy's bunkmates in Iraq. He sure hoped not. But that possibility gave Billy more reason to fret the border crossing.

But for now, he was safe. There was no reason to think anyone knew where he was. He knew enough about cellular triangulation to know the call he made to Carol Wallace could not be traced, not even to a general geographic area. Besides, she'd been told he was in Florida. If she had gone to the police, they'd be tearing apart his old apartment and any of his frequent hangouts in Panama City. Good luck with that.

Nina dropped his lunch in front of him. "Want something to drink with that? We have plenty of Gatorade."

"Yeah. That'd be great." Billy said, although his thoughts were miles away; hundreds of miles to the north.

"You know, baby, maybe we should just wait here a while longer. We could dye our hair, get glasses, you could get a phony mustache or something." Nina was trying to help.

"And how are we going to get hair dye or anything else as long as everyone out there is looking for us?"

Nina hadn't thought about that. "Well, we could ..."

There was a knock at the front door. Billy froze. He whispered to Nina, "Don't answer it. They'll go away, whoever it is."

The two of them sat in silence for thirty seconds. Then the knock repeated.

Billy went to the front of the house to get a look through the heavy drapes. He had a clear view of the front porch. An attractive woman in a uniform of some sort was standing on the porch with a clipboard under her arm. She appeared to be about forty with blonde hair pulled back in a ponytail.

"It's some sort of meter maid." He whispered back to Nina who'd joined him in the living room.

"She'll go away."

But after the third knock went unanswered, instead of going away, the meter maid walked from the front porch around the side of the house, apparently in search of a rear door.

"Shit!" Billy whispered. "What the fuck does she want?"

"We'd better find out before she..."

Another knock; this time on the back door. Billy motioned for Nina to come close to him.

"You go to the door and let her in. We need to get her in the house. I'll take care of her." Billy said.

Nina nodded and headed through the kitchen toward the rear door. Billy grabbed the baseball bat he'd left in the kitchen and positioned himself behind the door so that when it opened, the door would hide him from the visitor's view.

Nina stood in front of the door for a moment to compose herself. Her heart was racing. She wasn't sure she could do this.

The door swung open.

"Good afternoon mam. My name is Beverly Burns. I'm from LIPA and here to take a reading of your electric meter," The woman said in a monotone voice indicating she'd said the same words many times before.

Nina eyed the woman with suspicion. She was wearing a drab grey shirt that definitely said LIPA in bold red letters and had an

ID card hanging around her neck which she offered as documentation of her identity. But something was wrong. She didn't seem to act like someone who went from house to house reading meters. She seemed more polished than Nina expected from someone with such a monotonous job. And her eyes seemed to be taking in everything they could; glancing around the kitchen while never leaving Nina's face.

Before Nina could say anything, the woman continued, "With the switchover to PSE&G next month, we need to get one last reading before the billing cycles switch. It's so you don't get charged twice."

Nina still had one hand on the door knob and could see Billy in the corner of her eye waiting behind the door. "Well, we just rent here but I think the meter's in the basement. Come on in."

As the woman walked through the door Billy swung the bat hitting her in the back of her head. Her knees buckled and she hit the floor hard. The clipboard she'd been carrying flew across the room.

"Why did you have to do that?" Nina screamed. "She's just a meter reader or something!"

But Billy had no interest in Nina's objections. He was on the ground feeling his way around the woman's ass in search of a wallet. The LIPA shirt hadn't been tucked into her pants and when he pushed it up to get to her back pockets, he found a holstered Glock tucked into her belt.

"Holy shit! What the fuck?" He removed the gun and dug for a wallet. He flipped open the wallet. "Shit! She's a cop. She's a fucking cop!"

"A cop! What the hell is a cop doing here?" Nina screamed. But then she remembered walking into the bagel store yesterday without her sunglasses. She turned white.

"How the fuck do I know?" Billy screamed back.

"Is she dead?" Nina whispered.

Billy leaned around from behind his victim and could feel a pulse on the woman's neck. "No, not yet."

"What the hell are we going to do now? What are we going to do with her?" Nina asked.

"Shut the fuck and let me think for a minute." Billy barked as he put his right hand to his forehead. He was still straddling the woman on the kitchen floor and held that position for several minutes as he gathered his thoughts. Once again, he fell back on his training at Parris Island. "Think the problem through. Look for opportunities that didn't exist before the problem arose. Be creative." He thought to himself. "Why is this cop here? Is there a SWAT team just outside the door? Was she alone?" It didn't make sense.

After several minutes, Billy rose from the floor and announced, "Assuming she came alone, the first thing we need to do is get her in the basement, tied up tight. When she comes to, we may be able to get some of this cluster-fuck sorted out."

So, with Nina's help, he dragged their victim, down the wooden stairs and secured her hands behind her back using two plastic cable ties. He then used another two cable ties to secure those to a cast iron sewer pipe running horizontally along the far wall, about two feet off the floor. They positioned her in a sitting position with her legs extending straight out on the floor. All the while, Mary Jane looked on in amazement without saying a word. When he felt his unconscious prisoner was secure, he turned to Mary Jane and said, "This is what happens to people who piss me off."

Blood was running down the side of her face but Mary Jane could see the unconscious woman was attractive. She looked to be about the same age as her mom, maybe a little older. When Billy and Nina ascended the stairs and locked the door, Mary Jane slowly went over to the woman. At first, she wasn't sure if she was alive but as she got closer she could see her blouse rising and falling with each breath.

"Are you Okay?"

No response.

Mary Jane went to her bathroom and dampened one of the two towels she'd been provided. She put it behind the woman's head, on the place the blood appeared to be coming from. Still no response, but the bleeding seemed to be under control. At least it wasn't getting any worse. So she left the towel propped behind the blood-matted blonde hair and returned to her bed to await whatever was going to happen next.

CHAPTER 56

Alan, Carol and the five FBI people were beginning to think there would be no call. It was 5:30 P.M. and the only call came from one of Alan's brothers who was looking for the address of some distant relative. The group decided to order Chinese food. Alan said he'd buy. The FBI people said they'd stay until midnight.

Carol passed the time talking to Jayne about Mary Jane. Alan spent most of the afternoon on his cell phone working on a deal with a mortgage-backed trader at Morgan Stanley. He had nothing to say to the FBI. After all, he believed his daughter was dead and that this was a waste of everyone's time, especially his own.

Frank Sciarra and the communications people watched the end of a Yankee game on the sixty inch flat screen in Alan's office. Everyone was ready to jump if the phone rang.

As seven o'clock was approaching and the last of the leftover Chinese food was tossed in the trash, Carol asked Jayne to join her on the patio. She closed the sliding glass doors behind them.

Carol began, "I think it's important you understand why I believe it was really Billy Simon who called me."

"Okay. Let's hear it. I've got nowhere to go."

"But before I tell you, you have to promise this stays between us. I don't want anyone else to know; especially not my husband. He was always jealous of the affection I held onto for Billy. Can you promise me that?"

"Carol I can't promise that. This is a federal investigation. Anything you tell me could become evidence in any..."

Carol cut her off. "I understand. I just wanted to give you the history."

"Well, why don't you tell me whatever you're comfortable sharing. Unless there's some criminal act involved, there's no reason for me to divulge what you tell me to your husband. How's that?"

So Carol began to explain how and when she met Billy and their passionate romance. She told her how they'd planned to be married when he finished basic training. She was quite candid about their passion and their plans for the future, all of which she extinguished that day on the beach when she told Billy about Alan. "Basically I had to choose between a life with the man I loved, moving from one military base to another, or a life of considerable privilege with a man I knew I could love. I'm not ashamed of my decision but at the time I was."

"So you left your boyfriend for someone who seemed better. Happens all the time. Why would that make him hate you?"

"I think it's because Billy understood I was leaving him for the easy life. I couldn't bring myself to say I loved Alan at the time and that made it even harder on Billy. He called me a whore, and he was right."

"You're being too hard on yourself."

"Am I? Two weeks before I was to be married to Alan, Billy shows up. He was about to leave for a year in Iraq and asked to have dinner with me. Alan was out of town so I met him at a restaurant downtown." Carol looked down at the street below. "This is what I feel worst about. After dinner and way too much wine, I asked him back to my apartment for one last roll in the hay. I used him one last time and in the morning I told him to leave. That's why I feel so cheap. And I think, that's why he grew to hate me. I think I made him feel like all the words were a lie; that all I cared about was my own sexual gratification. I really did feel like a whore."

Jayne took a step toward Carol. "Hey. We all make mistakes. That's no reason for..."

The sound of a ringing phone pierced the glass doors. By the time they returned to the living room, Alan was standing over the phone and the FBI communications people were all in place. Frank gave him the signal to answer the call.

"Alan Wallace." He said with almost indignant authority.

The caller's voice was amplified on a speaker and filled the room. "Well, I might as well talk to you. You're the guy with the money." Carol was sure it was Billy's voice.

Alan read from the script that had been prepared. "Who am I speaking to?"

Feigning an apologetic tone, Billy responded, "Oh, I'm sorry. Did I forget to introduce myself? This is Billy Simon; the guy who has your daughter; the guy who's waiting for his money and the guy who used to fuck your wife. That's who you're speaking to!"

Alan kept to the script. "I want to speak to my daughter."

"Sorry, she must have stepped out. But I'll tell her you were asking for her." His tone was maniacal.

"If I can't speak to my daughter, I have no reason to continue this conversation."

"Good. You just shut the fuck up and listen. I'll do the talking. But you may need a pad to jot down a few notes."

"I want to speak to my daughter."

"Hey jerk off. You're not a very good listener. Get a piece of paper. I'm going to give you wire instructions and I'm only going to say them once. You need to..."

"I have no reason to believe you have my daughter. Put her on the line and I will talk to you. Otherwise I'm going to hang up."

"So you don't believe your wife, huh? I don't blame you. She's lied to you before. Okay. Wait one second."

The line went silent and Frank gave Alan a thumbs up sign. Nobody moved. Then the line crackled with static and the room filled with the voice of Mary Jane Wallace.

"Daddy? Daddy, it's me. Daddy please do what they want. They say they'll let me go."

Alan Wallace turned white. He'd just heard a voice he thought he buried two weeks ago. He looked at Carol who offered pleading eyes. Then he caught a glimpse of Frank Sciarra waving his arms and pointing at the script in Alan's hand. But Alan couldn't talk. His world had just been turned over.

Finally, after several uncomfortable moments, he said, "I need to ask her one question."

"Make it quick," Came the devilish response.

He glanced down at the paper. "MJ, what do you do every year on my birthday?" His voice cracked with the last word.

"I make you cupcakes with blue icing."

"Oh, Jesus. It's her." Alan was talking to the FBI agents. Carol was in tears.

"I want my daughter back." He screamed into the phone.

"Good, because unless you do exactly as I say, you just heard her voice for the last time."

"What do you want?"

"I've already told your wife what I want. Now I'm going to tell you how to give it to me. Ready to write this down?"

Alan looked to the agents for guidance. Frank motioned with a nod of his head.

"Yes. I'm ready."

"Good. First, give me your cell phone number."

Alan looked to the agents who shrugged then nodded.

"646-809-8876."

"Okay. Bank of Quebec, routing number 0021121143, account number 99337548. You are to wire six million U.S. dollars into that account at 9:00 A.M. tomorrow morning. Fifteen minutes after I have confirmation of the wire, I'll call your cell and tell you where you can pick up your daughter."

"Wait. You said four million."

"No. I said six million."

"But you told my wife four million."

"And you didn't bat an eye so the figure is now six million."

"Listen. You can't…"

"Hey, asshole. This isn't some Wall Street deal you can negotiate."

Alan responded with the only words he could think of. "Fuck you." He screamed.

"Fuck me? I don't think so. How about I go fuck your daughter?"

"Noooooo," Carol screamed as she ran toward the phone.

But the line went dead.

CHAPTER 57

B illy was furious. He flung the cell phone against the basement wall shattering it into pieces, some of which fell on the JTTF agent tied to the pipe and just beginning to regain consciousness. That left him only three of the original ten phones Nasi had bought with his fake ID. The others had been disposed of after their usefulness in more conventional ways.

"I can't fucking believe these people!" He screamed. "They think they're going to negotiate with me? He thinks he can tell me to fuck off? I don't think so."

He turned to Nina. "Get me some of those cable ties from upstairs. I'm going to teach these fucking people a lesson. Their Wall Street money's not going to help them now."

Nina complied and returned to the basement with four plastic ties. "What are you going to do?" She asked, afraid that she already knew the answer.

Billy looked at Mary Jane who had retreated to the edge of her bed. Until that moment, the fourteen year old really believed what she'd been told; that she would be unharmed and set free at the conclusion of this ordeal. Now, for the first time, she saw hatred in her captor's eyes. Until now, his eyes had only made her uncomfortable. Now she was terrified at what would happen next. His face had the look of a hungry wolf who was about to pounce upon its prey.

Without taking his frightening stare off Mary Jane, he said, "Nina, go upstairs for a while. I need to teach these assholes a lesson. When they get what I'm going to send them, they'll beg me to take their precious money."

Nina was far too frightened to argue with Billy. Although she'd seen his temper before, she'd never seen the look on his face like this. It was demonic and she dared not do anything but comply. She climbed the stairs wondering what sort of carnage was about to occur. In many ways, she was glad she wouldn't be a part of it.

"And close the door." He shouted up to her as she reached the top steps.

Billy removed his sleeveless tee shirt and rolled it on itself. He motioned for Mary Jane to stand and come toward him. When she complied out of pure terror, he told her to turn around and open her mouth. He used the rolled tee shirt as a gag and tied it securely at the back of her head.

Then he secured one cable tie around each of her wrists and told her to sit on the bed. When she did so, he pushed her down to a lying position and connected the cable ties to a column on the headboard using a third tie. As he did this, Mary Jane started to panic. She'd never been bound before and realized the sensation terrified her. She attempted to scream but the gag muffled the sound significantly.

Even so, the scream had an effect. The female agent who was bound to the sewer pipe just a few feet away began to stir. She moved her head for the first time and groaned. The bleeding from the head wound had ceased but there was blood caked to her hair. Her world began to take focus and the first image that came into near focus was a man taking his shorts off and standing over a teenage girl who was somehow shackled to a bed. The man had a firm erection.

"What the hell happened to me?" She said although she was already starting to piece together the scenario. She recalled seeing a figure to her right as she walked into the kitchen but was unable to turn toward it before the lights went out. She'd been cold-cocked before but never on the back of the head. She reached for her throbbing skull but realized her hands were bound behind her.

When Mary Jane heard the stranger's voice, she turned toward her and tried to scream, "Please help me!" But the gag turned the plea into muffled gibberish and Billy slapped her across the face for her insolence.

Because the JTTF agent was secured to the pipe only a few feet off the floor, she was unable to stand when she tried. From her seated position she could now see that the guy with the erection was public enemy number one- Billy Simon. She'd immediately recognized Nina Morales at the kitchen door although she had no idea how long ago that had been.

"How long have I been here?" She asked even though speaking made her head throb even more.

But Billy paid her no attention. He was already on the bed, straddling Mary Jane's legs and beginning to pull down her sweat pants. The young girl attempted to kick but the weight of his body on her legs rendered her harmless. Billy had the pants off and was now pulling at her underwear.

"Hey asshole! I'm a federal agent and there are twenty more combing the area looking for me right now." With each word she began to feel a little more alive again.

Billy turned his head toward her and said, "Right now, you're just a spectator. Shut the fuck up or I'm going to come over there and stick this in your mouth." The reference was to his engorged penis.

Although the agent was frightened, she decided the only way to divert his attention from the girl was to become a target. "I've had bigger toothpicks in my mouth." Then she decided to play all her cards, "I know who you are Billy. And so do all the federal agents and cops outside. There's no place for you to run."

Billy swung his legs over Mary Jane and faced the agent while sitting on the edge of the bed. "Do I look like I'm running?"

"No, you look like you're jerking off. Why don't you grow a pair and untie me. We'll see how much of a man you…"

Billy cut her off with a hard right-hand punch across the side of her head. The blow sent her back to a semi-conscious state. She was silenced for now but Mary Jane was screaming again through the gag. He turned his attention back to her and whispered in her ear, "We can do this two ways. If you shut up, I won't hurt you. You may even enjoy it. But I promise you, if you scream, I will make it hurt a lot. It's your choice."

Though her eyes relayed the terror she felt, Mary Jane stopped screaming.

"Smart choice." He said with the demonic voice again. "Are you going to behave?"

She nodded her head.

Billy glanced at his other captive, now also silenced. It occurred to him that he'd never punched a woman before. It was oddly stimulating.

Then he turned his attention back to Mary Jane. Once again he straddled her legs. Mary Jane could feel him pulling on her underwear. She felt enormous shame lying there with no pants; shame that was only made worse when he lifted her sweatshirt over her breasts and onto her arms. Because her arms were secured to the headboard, there was no place for the shirt to go. She could feel it resting on the top of her head.

She closed her eyes. She'd seen enough TV to understand what he was about to do and she thought it would only be worse if she had to see him doing it. Perhaps, without a visual image, she could someday try to wipe what was about to happen from her memory.

In her darkness she could feel his hot breath against her cheek; his tongue in her ear. Then she felt him licking her face, first her forehead, then her lips, which she kept tightly closed around the gag. He licked her neck then sucked on each diminutive breast for what seemed like an eternity. She thought she might vomit. She was sobbing silently and the pain on her breasts was intense.

Then, while he was still sucking on her left nipple, she felt his hand between her legs pushing them apart. Afraid to resist, and hoping it would soon be over, she complied and spread her legs. He immediately slid down and began kissing and licking her. She sobbed even harder but realized her body was reacting in a way she hadn't expected. Although she was repulsed, she began to feel a wetness where he was licking. Oh, the shame.

Then, suddenly, he stopped licking her and without opening her eyes, she could tell he'd backed off and was kneeling between her legs. Having no experience in such matters, Mary Jane hoped the attack might be over. But then she felt his hands on her butt, lifting her legs until her knees were bent over his shoulders.

It was only then that she understood what a rape really is. His penis found its way into her and began to pound at her; slowly at first, then faster and faster. He held her legs high in the air. The thrusts continued and the entire bed shook violently. Again and again.

Then it stopped. He pulled out of her. Oh, thank God. All she could hear was his heavy breathing but she dared not open her eyes. She felt him get off the bed and she could hear the sounds of him putting his pants back on. The fourteen year old was sobbing uncontrollably.

She summoned the courage to open her eyes. He was standing at the foot of the bed and holding something to his face. Her eyes hadn't focused yet so she couldn't see the cell phone. Then there was the unmistakable flash.

CHAPTER 58

To Mary Jane Wallace, the thirty minutes she lay naked and shackled on the bed, seemed like days. But finally, the basement door opened and, to her relief, Nina came down the wooden stairs. May Jane was still crying and shivering when Nina approached her holding a kitchen knife.

"Okay, sweetie. You're going to be okay now." She put a sheet over the shaking girl and used the knife to cut the cable ties. Mary Jane immediately ripped her attacker's tee shirt from her mouth. She grabbed her clothes from the floor and ran into the bathroom.

A moment later, Nina heard Billy's heavy footsteps on the stairs. He was carrying a pot from the kitchen stove and the baseball bat he'd used hours earlier. Nina shuttered at the thought of what he might be up to. But she was relieved when he walked to the JTTF agent, still unconscious on the floor, and threw the pot of water in her face.

"Wake up! I didn't hit you that hard." He said sarcastically. Then he turned to Nina. "Get her something to drink. Maybe some Gatorade."

The woman on the floor didn't move. Her head still rested limply on her chest. She appeared to be near dead. But in reality, she'd regained consciousness after just a few moments and had witnesses the rape of Mary Jane while feigning unconsciousness. When she realized there was nothing she could do to distract Billy from his violence, she decided to fake unconsciousness while plotting her escape. It was pure torture for her to listen to the whimpered sobs of Mary Jane and not be able to help her. A few times, she cracked an eyelid to see Billy inflicting himself on the defenseless young girl. The sight made her crazy with anger and she wanted to crush his skull with her bare hands but they were clasped behind her back.

After Billy had left the room, she realized the pipe she was bound to, was a cast iron sewer drain. It had a fair amount of rust on it which meant it could be used as an abrasive. So she began to rub her wrists back and forth along the pipe hoping that eventually, the thick plastic ties would succumb to the jagged rust. Because she couldn't move her hands more than an inch in either direction, the effort would take time; something she wasn't sure she had a lot of.

Still, the muffled screams from the young girl and the monstrous actions of the madman who'd done so much damage on TBD, gave her the resolve to survive. She was determined to see her foot on the throat of this serpent called Billy Simon. And so, she pretended to respond to the water.

"What happened?" She moaned.

"You mouthed off to me. The same thing will happen again if I don't get your full cooperation." Billy slapped the bat against his left hand. "Do you understand?"

She faked a groggy, "Yes. Don't hit me again, please."

Nina returned with a bottle of red Gatorade and handed it to Billy. He offered it to his prisoner then remembered her hands were bound behind her, so he opened the bottle and held it to her lips. She drank about half the bottle, and then began to choke when it ran down her throat too quickly.

"Okay. Here's the story. The only chance you have of living to see Sunday is if you help me live to see Sunday. I want you to understand this. It's very important. If anything happens to me; if I even see a cop; the first thing I do is put a bullet in your head. The second thing I do is put a bullet in her head." He motioned toward to bathroom door. "They may get me, but I'll get you two first. Understood?"

The agent nodded.

"Good. Now, you tell me what's going on out there. And re-member, your life depends on it." Billy waved the bat to indicate "out there" meant the rest of the world.

"I need to pee." The agent said.

"Go ahead. You're not going anywhere."

No, I need to pee now."

"Hey. There's no way you're getting off that pipe, so go ahead a pee."

Understanding the resolve of her captor, the agent tried another approach. "So, what exactly do you want to know?"

"I want to know who's looking for me, and why they're looking for me, and why they're looking here in beautiful Commack, New York."

She wasn't about to give this lunatic any useful information but she needed to give him enough information to get her out of this house and give her a fighting chance. If he thought he needed her to escape, he'd keep her alive long enough to use her. If he thought she was useless, she knew he'd kill her, and most likely, the girl too.

She thought carefully.

"I don't know how they made you for the bombings. That's way above my pay grade. But I know how they know you're here." She continued to think and make it up as she went along. "Someone spotted your car at a strip mall yesterday. Apparently, your girlfriend likes bagels."

Billy shot Nina a look.

"Someone saw your car turn into this development, which has only two ways in or out. There are about fifty cops and federal agents doing a door-to-door in the neighborhood. They've got the exits blocked." She looked at Billy and asked, "How long have I been down here?"

"I'm asking the questions." Billy replied.

"Well, if you want my help, I need to know how long I've been here."

"About six hours. Why?"

She thought back to the instructions Ken Stallings had given them that everyone was supposed to check in with him every hour. Why hadn't anyone come looking for her? She tried to think quickly. How could she use this to her advantage? If a rescue team was coming, she certainly didn't want to tip off Billy Simon. On the other hand, if things go south for Billy, he might make good on his promise to put one in her head on his way out.

She decided to stall. "I was supposed to call in at six, but I guess they knocked off for the night."

Billy eyed her skeptically.

"So, my suggestion for getting you out of here is we all drive out together, tomorrow." This was a stalling tactic to allow the rescue team, if there was to be one, time to kick in the door and take out Billy Simon before he could do any more damage. If there was no recuse coming, she needed to come up with a reason for Billy to untie her. Rubbing the plastic ties along the pipe might take days.

"My car, a Crown Victoria with an enormous trunk, is parked two blocks away. I suggest, once it's good and dark out there, that you go get it and bring it here. I assume you have my keys. Then tomorrow, I drive the Crown Vic, with the three of you in the trunk, right out the front gate. I'll flash my credentials at the gatekeeper, and we're off."

Billy thought about it for a moment, and then added his own twists to the plan. "I'll have a gun in the kid's mouth the whole time we're in the trunk. I'll also crack the upholstery on the back seat so I can see you, hear you, and have a clean shot at the back of your head. Anything goes wrong; you get it first, then the kid. Yeah, this could work."

"I hope so. It sounds like the only chance I have of getting out of here alive." She said, although she knew, even if it worked, Billy would kill her as soon as she outlived her usefulness. The trick was to stay useful until the cavalry arrived.

They refined the plan and the timing over the next thirty minutes. All the while, Mary Jane stayed sequestered in the bathroom. As long as she heard Billy's voice in the basement, she wasn't coming out.

When Billy was satisfied, he rose from the edge of the bed and said to Nina, "Come on. We have another call to make."

"Hey. How about something to eat?"

"Nina, make her one of your famous P&J's on a bagel." Then he went up the stairs and closed the door behind him.

When the room was silent, she said, "You can come out now. They went upstairs."

The bathroom door cracked open and Mary Jane peeked out. She walked over to the agent and knelt beside her. "Please don't let them hurt me. I heard what you said about getting in a trunk."

"He won't hurt you anymore. I promise." She said it softly but with conviction.

The two women sat on the floor in silence for several seconds. Then the younger one said, "My name is Mary Jane Wallace. They took me from my school bus in the tunnel."

"I know Mary Jane. I know all about it. I'm a special agent. I've met your mom."

Then she said, "My name is Lucy. But all my friends call me LT."

CHAPTER 59

Although her head was still throbbing from the two blows, LT was hungry, so the peanut butter covered bagel and Gatorade helped. She'd hoped the meal would arrive on a plate which she could break and have Mary Jane use the sharp edges to cut through the cable ties, and tried not to show disappointment when Nina brought them down on paper towels.

She and Mary Jane sat on the floor eating and talking. LT had a little experience with rape counseling from her days with the NYPD so she understood how important it was for the teen to talk about it. Otherwise, girls her age often assume the rape was somehow their fault and never get over the shame.

Still, in this case, with the victim so young and inexperienced in life's harshness, the conversation was difficult. LT tried to reassure her that what happened had nothing to do with love, or passion, or even lust. It was pure violence. It was an attack. She told her she had nothing to feel guilty about.

But LT knew that words weren't going to make this nightmare go away. This innocent young thing, confused and mired in the limbo between childhood and woman, would never get past this day. She just hoped the kid would have a chance to go home and be hugged by her mother. That's what she really needed right now. And that depended on LT and the cavalry.

What LT had no way of knowing was that the cavalry wasn't coming. Yes, she was supposed to check in with the incident commander every hour, and her absence should have been noticed. But Ken Stallings had been called back to New York in the early afternoon and left a text message for LT telling her he'd be back first thing in the morning. The text message was on LT's phone which, of course was now in the hands of Billy Simon. One of the senior Suffolk County PD had taken over the incident command, but because LT had been on the phone with Hank Waldron at the FBI that morning and missed the briefing, the officer had no idea LT was even in the field. As a result, no one knew she was missing.

Because she had no knowledge of any of this, LT expected there would be an assault on the house at some point during the night. She explained to Mary Jane, "They're going to come looking for me. If you hear anything at all during the night, get under the bed as quickly as you can and stay there until I tell you to come out. The SWAT team doesn't know you're here. They'll only expect me, so you'll be safe if you stay out of sight until I can tell them you're there."

"Do you really think they'll come tonight? Like on TV?"

"There's no way my partner will leave me here. Ken and I have worked together long enough to have a sixth sense about when one of us is in trouble. Don't worry, they'll be here." LT knew she was exaggerating a bit but the kid needed hope.

To take the young girl's mind off their predicament, she asked her, "Do you have anything in the bathroom to try to wash some of this blood out of my hair? I'd hate for the handsome young guys on the SWAT team to find me looking like this." She offered her first smile. "Some of them are real hunks."

So Mary Jane dampened her towel and did the best she could to clean LT's face and hair. While she worked, she asked, "So, why do they call you LT?"

"My name's Lucy Theresa Hadman. That's my married name. My maiden name was Caffuto. My dad was a cop and thought Lucy Theresa sounded a little too girlie; especially when my brother and I became cops. My first badge said LT Hadman, so LT sort of stuck. It made my dad happy because Lawrence Taylor was one of his favorite players."

"Who's that?" The fourteen year old asked.

"Sorry. He was a really good football player who played for the Giants, my dad's favorite team. Everyone called him LT."

"So, what's your husband like? What's his name? Do you have any kids?"

"Well, his name was Terry but we've been divorced a long time. He was a teacher. He's married now and has a couple of kids but he and I never had children." LT was glad to see the teen was distracted from her own misery.

Mary Jane worked on LT's hair as they spoke. LT asked about her mother and father. What was her favorite type of music, TV shows, movies? She stayed away from questions about friends because she didn't want to bring up the bus explosion. She stayed away from any questions that would lead them back to the present.

They sat there on the floor, talking for almost an hour. The blood was gone from LT's hair and her swollen face was responding to the cooling effect of the Gatorade bottle. Maybe because she'd met her mother, or maybe because she felt so sorry for her, but LT genuinely liked the little girl at her side. They each derived some level of comfort from the other's presence. In many ways, Mary Jane reminded LT of her childhood self. And she knew what they had in common was a loss of innocence; innocence that had been ripped from them too early in life.

CHAPTER 60

The digital clock on the desk in Alan's office said 8:37 P.M. It had been over two hours since Billy hung up on him. Carol was a nervous wreck and pacing the floor. The FBI agents were still watching the Yankee game and seemed confident they'd hear from the kidnapper again tonight. But the more time went by, the jumpier Carol got.

Just then a phone rang. But it wasn't the Wallace's house phone and it wasn't Alan's cell phone. It was Frank Sciarra's cell. He took the call and walked out into the hallway. A few moments later he came back into the den and asked Jayne Eriksen to join him in the hall.

"Wait till you hear this." He was amped up. "After Wallace took that last call and it became obvious he too recognized his daughter's voice, I got to thinking about how the kid could be alive if they buried her two weeks ago. So obviously, they buried the wrong kid. But everyone on the bus was accounted for so it's not a case of the coroner giving them the wrong body."

Jayne looked at him with a puzzled look.

Frank continued. "So I call Izzy at 2 Fed and ask him if there have been any missing persons lately. You know; kids about this age who disappeared. Nothing matched up but listen to this. He told me about a corpse that was stolen from a funeral parlor in Valley Stream a few days before the bombings. It was a girl named Judy Saccenti who was about fifteen years old. Body just walked off the night before her funeral."

"So you think maybe our creep lifted the body and somehow made the switch?" Jayne was skeptical.

"I have no idea how, but I think we need to get an order for an exhumation and run DNA tests on whoever's in that coffin."

"Jesus."

"I know. This is a first for me too. What kind of deranged son of a bitch does something like that?"

Jayne was shaking her head when Carol emerged through the doorway and asked, "I'm making coffee. Anybody want some?"

Frank could tell the sedatives Carol took right after the last phone call were beginning to take hold. Her speech was a bit slurred and she was unsteady on her feet.

"Mrs. Wallace, are you Okay?" He asked.

"No, agent Sciarra. I'm not Okay. A madman has my daughter and we may not get another chance to get her back."

"Believe me. He'll call again. He wants the money. It's all about the money."

Carol looked down at the threshold and murmured, "I'm not so sure."

Neither agent had anything to add so they moved back into the spacious apartment and Carol went to work on the coffee. The Yankees were clinging to a one run lead in the top of the ninth with Mariano Rivera working to get the save. Alan and the other FBI people didn't even notice them enter the room.

Then Alan's phone chimed. Everyone froze and looked at him.

"It's a text message." He said as he reached for his cell phone.

"Can we get anything on this?" Frank barked at his tech people.

"No. Not a text." Came the reply.

Alan accessed the message with a flip of his thumb, glanced down at the phone and closed his eyes.

"Oh my God." He said.

Frank, who was standing closest, took the phone from him just as Carol was entering the room. There was no text message; just a picture. It was a young girl, lying naked on a bed with her hands bound over her head and some sort of gag in her mouth. Carol leaned in to get a look.

"Noooo!" She screamed. "No, he didn't. Oh God, no. No, no, no..." She was hysterical. Jayne ran to her side fearing she was about to collapse.

Frank turned to Alan and said, "I'm afraid I know the answer, but I have to ask; ... is that your daughter?"

Alan nodded his head. Then he said, "Does this mean he killed her?"

Frank glanced at the gruesome photo. "Her eyes are open. There's no reason to think she's dead. Remember, he wants his money. Unless she's alive, he's got nothing to offer."

Carol was sobbing uncontrollably. Her body was shaking and she started to gag, as if she might vomit. Jayne put her hand on Carol's shoulder. "Do you want me to help you to the bathroom?"

Alan's phone rang. The techies sprang into action and by the second ring, had their headsets on and gave the indication to answer the call.

Alan's voice was weak; as if he'd been hit in the gut by a heavyweight's punch.

"Hello?"

The maniacal voice filled the room. "Now you see what you made me do? It was all your fault Alan. You told me to go fuck myself, so instead, ...I fucked your daughter."

Carol screamed, "No Billy. Don't hurt her. You don't know what you're doing. Please don't hurt her."

But Billy pressed on. "I know exactly what I'm doing. And at 9:05 tomorrow morning, if that money hasn't been wired, I'm going to fuck her again."

Click. Billy ended the call on his side and would never know what happened next.

Carol screamed. She was coughing and sobbing but her screams were those of a mother trying to save her child. "Billy, don't hurt her. Don't do this. You can't do this, Billy. Billy, you don't understand. She's yours, Billy. She's your daughter!"

⟫⟪

The room and the cell phone were silent for several moments. Carol, who had fallen to her knees, began to sob again and whispered, "Oh, my poor baby. My poor Mary Jane. My beautiful baby. Oh, Alan, please forgive me. This is all my fault."

At first, Frank thought Carol had played some sort of mind game with the caller. But Jayne understood this is what Carol had been trying to tell her. This was the secret Carol meant to share with Jayne before the first call came. This is what Carol wanted to tell Jayne but couldn't tell her husband; that fourteen years ago, just weeks before they were married, she became pregnant with Billy's baby. Months later, when she could no longer hide her pregnancy, rather than jeopardizing the life of privilege she was about to enjoy, she told Alan they were going to have a "honeymoon" baby.

Alan looked at his wife incredulously. "What are you saying?"

"I'm so sorry, Alan. There were so many times I wanted to tell you."

343

The communication guys pulled off their headsets. The senior agent turned to Frank and said, "He's gone. Not enough time to trace." And shook his head.

Alan asked again, "What are you saying, Carol?"

Carol lifted her head from the carpet. She was still on her knees. "I wanted to tell you so many times. I was pregnant with Mary Jane when we got married. I'm so sorry I lied to you."

Alan was frustrated by what he thought was an indirect answer. "So you were pregnant when we got married. But what did you mean when you said she was his daughter? Why would you say that?"

The room was suddenly a very uncomfortable place for the agents. This was a delicate family discussion. It was not a matter for the FBI, no matter how much they wanted to become flies on the wall. It was Frank who suggested, "Why don't we step out for a few minutes and give you some time alone?"

Alan paid him no attention but kept his focus on Carol. "Are you telling me you were sleeping with this guy right up to the time we got married? Is that what you're saying?"

"It wasn't that way." She offered between sobs.

"Well, what the hell was it then?

"We'll wait outside for a bit." Frank said as he motioned for the other agents to follow him toward the door.

"Is that why this guy is so hell-bent on hurting you; because you took his daughter away from him? Is that it, Carol?"

"No, no. He didn't know about Mary Jane. I never told him. I wanted her to be ours; yours and mine. I wanted it so badly." She reached out her hand for his but he stepped away.

"But she's not mine." He snapped.

"You're the only father she knows, Alan. You're the person she calls daddy. She is yours. She's just not yours..." She searched for the right word. "She's just not yours genetically. It doesn't change anything between you and me and Mary Jane. We're still a family. Please forgive me for one stupid thing I did fourteen years ago."

The agents shuffled out the apartment door and closed it behind them.

"Well there's a bombshell." One of the junior communications people said to no one in particular.

"That's a conversation you never want to have to have." Frank said with half a grin on his face.

They were leaning against the hallway walls, not knowing how long a wait they'd have.

"So, now what?" Jayne asked.

"What do you mean?" Frank said.

"I mean about the ransom. Now that he knows the kid's not his, is he still going to fork over six million bucks?"

"Worse yet," The junior agent added, "He's got to fork it over to the kid's real father! That's gotta sting."

"Man, that's a tough position to be in. For fourteen years you think she's your daughter, then you find out she's the bastard child of our wife's former lover and he wants six mil to give her back. That sucks."

Frank gave his subordinate a stern look and responded, "Thanks for the summary, Carter. But let's try to show a bit more professionalism in there. These poor people have been through some real shit the last few weeks. Now they have to deal with this."

"I say he pays." Jayne offered.

"This animal raped his own daughter. What makes any of you think he's not going to kill her, even if he gets the money?" Frank said.

"He didn't know who she was." Jayne observed, but wasn't convinced Frank wasn't right.

"Maybe. But I still wouldn't want to be on the other side of that door having that conversation."

CHAPTER 61

L T hadn't slept more than twenty minutes the entire night. Between the discomfort of the shackles and being on the floor, she was able to stay awake almost the entire evening. That had been her plan. If an assault on the house was coming, she wanted to be ready to do whatever she could to help and to protect Mary Jane.

But the clock on the cable box read 6:55 A.M. and there had been no assault. She couldn't understand it. By putting herself in the theoretical place of Ken, she tried to imagine what she would do if her partner had gone missing. They had to know what street she was on; her car was just a block away. They knew exactly what houses and what streets she'd been assigned and the order she was to canvas them, so finding the first place she 'didn't get to' shouldn't have been difficult. And once they knew the house, an assault should have been routine; a few percussion bombs, night-vision, a small tactical SWAT team and it could be done in less than three minutes. Surely, Suffolk County PD had such tools at their disposal.

No, it made no sense that Ken hadn't come for her. Something else must have happened. He would never leave her in the field.

Since a full assault in daylight was unlikely, she concluded none was coming and began working on plan B. The first thing she needed to do was wake up Mary Jane, who'd slept soundly through the night, and prep her for what was likely to happen. Actually, LT had no intentions of telling the young girl what was likely to really happen because the picture was grim. She understood that she and Mary Jane would be killed as soon as they'd outlived their usefulness. The trick was to sustain their usefulness.

The way she figured it, Mary Jane would become useless to Billy as soon as he got the ransom payment. There would no longer be a reason to keep her alive. LT, on the other hand, could remain useful as long as Billy needed her to aid in his escape. So LT needed to prolong the escape plan and make sure Mary Jane was a necessary part of it.

"Mary Jane! Wake up, kid." She tried to whisper loud enough to be heard but the child did not stir.

"Pssst. Hey kid, time to get up." She said a little louder. This time, the young girl rolled over and faced LT. But she still wasn't completely awake.

"Look, I need you to listen to me. We have to go over our plan for today." LT said.

Suddenly, as Mary Jane realized where she was, she snapped to life. "Oh, wait. I have to pee." And she hurried toward the bathroom door; something LT wished she could do.

Listening to the sounds of the toilet flush and running water made LT glad she'd only had a few mouthfuls of the Gatorade the night before. She knew her captors were unlikely to untie her hands just so she could pee.

When Mary Jane returned to the room, LT asked her to turn on the television. If there was anything on the news about their operation here in Commack, LT wanted to know about it. The morning news shows were just coming on but none of the three networks mentioned the TBD investigation. She tried the local Long Island station but, after watching thirty minutes and realizing they were beginning to repeat the same loop of news, she gave up. Instead, she focused on her plan.

"Mary Jane, I want you to understand something. This is very important."

The teen crossed her legs on the floor next to LT and listened attentively.

"I don't know exactly how this will go but I believe they are going to use us to try to escape this area. They know the police are looking for them around here so they'll need to get far away. They'll use us to do that. Both of us. If Billy's been thinking about the idea I planted in his tiny little brain last night, he'll probably want me to drive my car out of here with the three of you in the trunk. He knows I won't run away because he said he'd hurt you if I did. And I'm not going to let him hurt you."

Mary Jane nodded her understanding.

"I don't know where he'll have me drive. We have to assume it will be at least a few miles from here but it might also be a few hours from here. I just don't know. What I do know is that at some point we'll stop. He'll tell me to get out of the car and open the trunk so the three of you can get out. Here's what I need you to do." LT leaned in closer to her student.

"At some time while we're driving, I need you to position yourself in the trunk so that when I open the trunk hood, you'll be on top of them and you will have to get out first. I don't want them to have a way to get out first. You need to block them. Understand?

"Yes, but why?"

"Well, for one thing, there' a chance, if I can get you out first, I may be able to slam the hood down on them and contain them in the trunk. But, even if I can't do that, if you can climb out first, I want you to run, as fast as you can, away from the car. And don't stop running. The best thing to do would be to run in the direction the car will be facing."

LT knew that the moment Mary Jane climbs out of the trunk, would be her best chance at life. If they were both standing there when Billy climbed out of the trunk, he'd likely shoot them both. He and Nina would take the car leaving LT and Mary Jane to die on the side of the road. There was no reason to think he'd do anything other than that. Billy had already shown he had no regard for human life. He certainly wasn't going to risk leaving the two of them behind as he tried to disappear.

And although she thought her own chances of survival were slim, LT was determined to save the kid. By getting between Billy and Mary Jane, even for just a few seconds, she might be able to keep Billy distracted long enough to save one them; the younger one. Unfortunately, LT realized that distraction might mean taking a bullet so Mary Jane could get a head start.

She reviewed every aspect of her plan with Mary Jane two more times until Nina came down the stairs carrying a single bagel; this time without peanut butter.

"Sorry girls, this is all we have left." She said sarcastically. "Make it last. We have some traveling to do today."

"Where we going?" LT took a low-percentage shot, not expecting an answer.

"Don't you worry, honey." And just as abruptly as she came down the stairs, she was on her way back up.

Mary Jane offered the bagel to LT and said, "You have it. I'm not hungry at all. I'm going to get cleaned up." Then she realized LT had no way of eating it without her hands and that she'd have to feed her, so she knelt down beside her and ripped the bagel into smaller pieces. But LT only ate a little and told Mary Jane to have some herself. "It may be a long day, kid. You should have something in your stomach before we start."

At 8:45 A.M. Billy came down the creaky wooden stairs. He was wearing a white tee shirt with the words "Sonny's BBQ- Best in the South". LT noticed the Glock Billy had taken from her was tucked in his belt. Nina followed close behind with another pistol tucked in the front of her pants.

"Okay, girls. Here's our plan for the day. Please listen carefully." He paused to make sure he had their attention. In a few minutes,

Nina and I are going upstairs to get very rich. Assuming your parents," he looked at Mary Jane, "assuming your parents do as they've been instructed, at 9:05 my account at the Bank of Quebec should go from $206.00 to $6,000,206.00. If that's the case, congratulations, you get to live. So you better hope they do the right thing."

Billy walked closer to LT. "Then, agent Hadman, you are going to drive us out of this shithole you call Commack. Nina and I and the girl will be nice and cozy in your trunk. I've already gotten your car. By the way, you government people have got to step it up with your transportation. What a piece of shit."

Billy seemed to be enjoying himself. "I made a nice slice in the back seat so I can see you and hear you from the trunk. If you fuck up, in any way, know that the pain you feel in the back of your head will be a bullet from your own gun. And know that the next shot will be in the girl's mouth. Understood?"

"Understood." LT said with authority. "Now you need to understand one thing. The girl and I are a package. If you hurt her, you might as well kill me too because I'm not driving you anywhere." She used the word "hurt" rather than "kill" for Mary Jane's sake. "Understand this. If you hurt her, I figure there's a 100% chance you're going to hurt me too no matter what I do, so I might as well fuck up your plans. I'm quite prepared to die. Are we clear?"

"That's some tough talk from a lady. But I told you, after you get us out of here, I have no reason to hurt either of you. We'll drop you off about ten miles from here. You'll be fine. And we have another car, far nicer than yours, waiting for us for the rest of our trip. Nobody's going to get hurt, as long as you do as I say."

With those words, LT knew she'd be executed as soon as they stopped driving. There was no way Billy would leave them by the side of the road, alive, and able to summon help. She wouldn't if the roles were reversed. And so, her resolve to try to save Mary Jane became even stronger. Somehow, she had to buy the kid a little time to run.

CHAPTER 62

The screen on Billy's laptop was filled with icy blue. The Bank of Quebec site only had four lines of information under the majestic logo. It was the third line Billy was focused on, the one that said "Confirmed transfers". So far, it read "00,000,000.00". It was 9:06 A.M.

"Son of a bitch!" He screamed at the screen. "What's wrong with these people? Don't they think I'll do it? Don't they think I'll kill her?"

Nina came around behind him and rubbed his shoulders. "Give it a little more time, sweaty. Maybe the bank's computers are slow." She tried to sound supportive.

9:07 A.M.; Still nothing.

"I can't fucking believe these people. Don't they give a shit about their kid?"

He picked up his cell phone and began to dial Alan Wallace's number. He was about to push the number's last digit when the computer screen seemed to refresh. It took two seconds for the data to display one line at a time but when the digital readout got down to "Confirmed transfers", it now read USD=6,000,000.00.

"Yes!" Billy put the phone down and refocused on the computer screen. Nina threw her arms around him from behind.

"You did it, Billy. You did it." She screamed.

Billy's steely stare never left the screen. "Now watch this. We're going to make all that money disappear."

He brought up the Bank of Quebec's screen for external transfers. The data for account number 444-746-003-002 at Credit Suisse had been entered days before. All he had to do was confirm the amount, enter an eight digit password, and check the box that read *"Immediate transfer?"* He looked the information over for just a few seconds, and hit "ENTER".

The six million U.S. dollars were immediately transferred to an account in Switzerland and denominated in Euros; at the spot exchange, that came to 4,545,877 Euros.

He went back to the balance line on the Bank of Quebec site. It now read $206.00.

"Boy, we didn't have that money very long, did we Nina?" It was his maniacal voice again.

Then he brought up the website for Credit Suisse, clicked on "Private Banking", and entered the twelve digit account number and password he'd been given weeks earlier. The 652 Euros he deposited to open the account, a thousand U.S. dollars, showed as the current balance. But the next line indicated a pending transfer of 4,545,877 Euros.

There were two reasons for the transfer. First, the Swiss account was completely anonymous. Despite the United States' best efforts, numbered accounts at Swiss banks were still not subject to sovereign liens, or inspection. Only Billy Simon and the Swiss gentleman in the Armani suit, who opened the account for him, would ever know the money belonged to Billy.

The second reason for the transfer was to make sure the money had really arrived at the Bank of Quebec in the first place. Because he'd given Alan Wallace the wire instructions in advance, Billy wanted to make sure the FBI hadn't gotten involved and requested the Canadian bank to manipulate its website to show a false balance. Had that been the case, the transfer to Credit Suisse would have failed.

Billy made one more entry which transferred the money yet again. He sat back on his chair and said, "Okay, now we've done it. Let's get moving."

CHAPTER 63

Billy came down the basement stairs with a new bounce in his step. LT assumed he'd gotten his money and it was difficult not to let Mary Jane see her disappointment. LT understood the ransom payment meant the young girl was no longer of value to Billy. The teenager was now a serious liability that had to be dealt with. Her only remaining value was as a hostage in the trunk to ensure LT's compliance in their escape. And that value, as well as LT's, would diminish the further they got from the house.

"Looks like your parents really want you back." Billy smiled at Mary Jane. "And I was just getting to know you." The smile was wicked.

Mary Jane recoiled toward LT. The very sight of Billy now terrified her. She couldn't imagine having to climb into a car trunk with him; his hot breath on her neck, or maybe worse. She prayed that LT was wrong; that maybe the monster who raped her would come down the stairs and set her free as he'd promised. After all, he said he would if her parents paid the ransom.

"So we're all going for a ride." Billy was now looking directly at LT. "You're the driver."

"Not with my hands tied behind my back, I'm not. And not until I can pee." LT was hoping Billy would allow her a few minutes, unshackled in the bathroom. She could surely find something in there to use as a weapon; a broken piece of mirror, a toothbrush, something. Or better yet; maybe Billy would send Nina into the bathroom with her. LT was sure she could overtake and disarm Nina if given the chance.

"I've told you before, go ahead and piss yourself. I don't care."

LT decided this was her first and best chance to use the little leverage she had. "I'm not leaving this house until you give me two minutes in the bathroom. I told you before; I'm not afraid to die."

"Well, maybe it's time you start thinking about the kid. Your only chance to save her and yourself is to do exactly as I say." Billy was firm.

"And I told you; you touch one hair on her head and you'll die in this house because I won't drive you anywhere. And the way I see it, I'm the only way you'll ever get to see your six million. So, if we're going somewhere today, you'd better let me get to that bathroom."

Billy didn't like being out maneuvered, especially by a woman. But he realized she was right. Without her cooperation, he and Nina had little chance of leaving the house. He knew he'd been out flanked on this one. But he wasn't about to drop his guard.

"Okay, go piss your heart out." He reached into his pocket for his jack knife then walked behind LT. He cut the cable tie holding her to the cast iron pipe but left LT's hands secured to each other by the other tie. "Go ahead; you've got your two minutes."

"I need my hands, asshole." LT decided she would not back down just yet.

Billy thought for a moment. His military training told him to look for options and to try to put himself in his prisoner's place. What would he do if he were in her shoes? What would he do with two minutes alone in the bathroom? He didn't like the answer.

"Okay, the kid can go with you and give you a hand."

That wasn't what LT had expected, but it was better than nothing. Still, with her hands secured behind her back, there would be little she could do. She glanced at Mary Jane and said, "Sorry kid. I really have to go. Just give me a hand with my pants."

But when LT tried to stand, she found that after sitting so long in the same position, her legs were wobbly. The thought also occurred to her that maybe the blow to the back of her head may still be playing games with her balance. Either way, she stumbled to an upright position and, with Mary Jane's assistance, found her way to the bathroom.

"Two minutes." Billy shouted as Mary Jane pulled the door closed behind them. Once inside the cramped room, Mary Jane helped LT slide her pants down and back up. The task didn't seem to bother the teen and LT realized no one had ever done that for her before. It was more uncomfortable for the forty-something cop than it was for the high school freshman.

"Don't forget; you have to run like hell as soon as you're out of the trunk. Don't look back, no matter what you hear. Just keep running." LT was all too aware the child might hear a gun shot.

"You can do this kid. And before you know it, you'll be back home again. Just run until you find someone."

Mary Jane nodded her head.

"Time's up!" Came the call from just outside the door.

The three women and Billy Simon ascended the cellar stairs. LT could see that it was raining lightly outside the kitchen window. She tried to think of ways rain might factor into the next few minutes. Nothing sprang to mind.

"Okay, outside everybody." Billy had now pulled LT's gun from his belt and was pointing it menacingly at Mary Jane to ensure compliance. Mary Jane was only a few feet from Billy and when she saw the gun, realized finally, that her captor had no thought of releasing her. They were being taken to their execution. She began to cry.

They descended the three steps from the kitchen door. LT's Crown Victoria was in the drive way next to the kitchen door. LT glanced into the car to see if Billy had removed anything from the front seat. He had not. LT's jacket was folded on the passenger's seat. She tried to remember what she'd left in the pockets. Was there anything she could use as a weapon? She remembered putting her note pad in the top inside pocket; not much of a weapon against a loaded Glock.

It was unlikely she'd find anything useful in the glove compartment or center console either. These cars were used by whatever agent had the need and they generally didn't leave any personal items behind after a shift. LT tried to think quickly. Was there anything at all she could use as a weapon?

Billy noticed LT scanning the car's interior. "Take a good look at the back seat." He used his hand without the gun to point out the slit he'd made in the cloth upholstery. "From inside the trunk I'll be able to see and hear everything you do. You fuck up, and you're both dead."

"Yeah, you said that before. I get it. Now how do you plan on me driving with my hands tied behind my back?" LT hoped she'd have an instant of freedom. If Billy had Nina cut he clasps, LT assumed he'd have the business end of his gun pointed at her. But LT felt sure she'd be able to use Nina as a momentary shield and get her gun away from her. Billy may be able to get a shot off but LT thought she'd be able to respond. They were standing just a few feet apart. It would be a matter of who got lucky first. But LT was looking for any chance she could get.

But Billy had a plan of his own. "Let's all walk around to the back of this piece of shit car."

When they were all behind the car, Billy opened the trunk with the key fob. It sprang up a few inches and required manual intervention to raise it all the way. Nina pushed the huge hood to its fully opened position then said, "Okay kid. You get in first."

Mary Jane took a step toward the trunk but turned and gave LT a questioning look; a look that pleaded, "How am I supposed to be the first one out if I'm shoved in the back?"

LT responded with a calm look of reassurance, an emotion she had to fake for the girl's sake. Then, suddenly and without provocation,

Billy delivered a backhanded blow to Mary Jane's face using the hand in which he held the gun. Blood flew from her nose as the girl's knees buckled and she collapsed into the cavernous trunk.

LT cursed herself for not using that moment as her opportunity to leap toward Billy. But she'd been so surprised by the blow, it took her a second to realize the opportunity was there. And by the time she had, it was gone. Billy had the gun pointed directly at LT's face. "Don't get any ideas, honey."

"Why? Why'd you have to clock the kid? Are you that much of a coward?" LT was screaming at Billy.

"Quiet down bitch!" Billy shot back. Then he calmly said, "A quiet prisoner is a happy prisoner."

LT had to suppress a powerful urge to leap at Billy and tear at his smug face with her teeth. She wasn't sure she'd have another opportunity to be so close to him again and she was rapidly running out of options. But she didn't. Instinct told her to wait. Maybe there'd be a better chance. Still, her blood was boiling.

Billy waved his gun in a manner that indicated he wanted LT to take a few step back. She complied, never taking her eyes off his.

"Now turn around and get on your knees."

Panic raced through LT. Was he going to execute her right here in the driveway? That made no sense. He needed her to drive. Or did he have some other devious plan that she'd completely missed? She could feel her heart pounding against her chest.

"I said get on your knees. Do it now!" He barked.

She had only two options; comply and hope she hadn't miscalculated, or turn and charge at two maniacal killers with loaded guns.

She dropped to her knees. The graveled driveway pushed sharply against her skin. Then she felt the most terrifying thing she'd ever experienced as Billy pressed the barrel of his gun against the back of her head. It was cold and hard. She froze with fear, waiting for what was to come. An eternity was compressed into a few seconds.

Then suddenly, she felt a downward tug at her arms and she realized Billy had cut the plastic cable ties binding her wrists. The feeling of cold steel on the back of her head was also gone. Billy had taken a few steps back, away from her and toward the car.

"So here's what's going to happen. You're going to stay on your knees with your back to the car until you hear the trunk slam closed. Understand?"

LT nodded. She didn't want to speak. She didn't want him to hear the weakness in her voice at that moment.

"We'll be in the trunk. If you don't start the car within ten seconds, the kid's dead. Got it?"

Again, just a nod.

"You'll be able to hear me through the back seat and you'll do exactly as I tell you." Billy tossed the key ring in LT's direction. It landed on the gravel.

Then LT heard the sound of Nina and Billy positioning themselves around Mary Jane in the trunk.

Nina was nearly as small as Mary Jane so, even with the three people in the spacious trunk, there was still room to shift around. Billy had Mary Jane positioned between him and Nina so he had an unobstructed view through the slit in the rear seat. The teenager was still unconscious from the blow.

He called out to LT, "It's show time!" Then he pulled the trunk hood closed.

⟫⟪

LT steadied herself using one hand on the gravel and rose to her feet. Her legs were still wobbly. She picked up the keys and turned toward the black car. The trunk was closed.

She realized in an instant, this was her best chance to save herself. If she ran into the woods, she'd have a least a fifteen second head start on Billy and Nina, assuming they could extricate themselves from the trunk that quickly. It could even be as much as a minute before they were able to access the trunk release lever that's on the inside of all trunks. With that kind of head start, Billy wouldn't know in which direction to start looking for her. She estimated a ninety-nine percent chance of survival if she ran.

Like all living things, she wanted to keep living. The primordial urge to survive was strong; so strong, that she found herself turning in the direction of the woods and away from the car. But as soon as her back was to the car, she realized her escape meant certain death for the unconscious child in the trunk.

Was she willing to trade the child's life for her own? Would he kid do the same to her if the roles were reversed? Would anyone? She had but an instant to decide. Would she choose life or try to save another? It was an impossible decision to make with so little time to think.

She glared at the black car. Could she ever get that image from her mind if she ran? Would she wake up at night seeing the car and hearing the shots fired within the trunk?

But LT did what she'd been trained to do; protect and serve. She moved swiftly to the driver's door and sat. She quickly closed the door so she wouldn't be tempted to rethink her decision. Her pulse was pounding. She turned the ignition switch.

"Now drive us out of here and get on the Expressway heading east." The voice was a bit muffled but sounded like it was coming from someone just inches behind her ear.

LT turned and looked back at the small opening in the middle of the rear seat. She could see the tip of the Glock and one of Billy's eyes watching her from the dark abyss. As she twisted her body around to face the back, her right hand moved to the passenger's seat and brushed against her note pad. An idea sprang into focus. But she'd need time. She'd need to stall; just long enough.

"Are you sure you want me to go east?" She asked as she used her right hand, the one that was out of Billy's line of sight, to open the pad, remove the pen and begin writing.

"Just do as I say. I know where I want to go." The muffled voice came back.

She kept writing but she continued to look directly at Billy's evil eye. "And what do I do if they have the roads blocked? I told you there's only two ways out of here and they're likely to have men at both checking cars." She found it difficult to speak and write different words simultaneously.

"You'll tell them who you are. Your wallet's in the sun visor. Show them your badge, agent Hadman."

LT reached up and found her wallet above the visor. She used her right hand to remove it and dropped it on the seat next to the pad. Then she looked back at Billy.

"Are you ready?" She asked.

"Let's go."

She wasn't yet done writing but she needed to use her right hand to put the car into gear. Driving in reverse down the long driveway gave her a few more seconds to write. From Billy's vantage point, having her hand on the passenger seat wouldn't seem odd for someone traveling in reverse and looking back over their right shoulder.

Once on the road, she kept her left hand on the steering wheel while her right finished its message. She made a left and then a right. She spotted one of the junior agents dressed in LIPA attire walking from one house to another but the agent didn't see her and kept walking. She hoped she could continue to make unnecessary turns in search of a more astute agent without Billy or Nina realizing the circuitous trail, but there were no other agents on the street.

Finally, she turned onto the exit street and spotted what she'd hoped for; a Suffolk County patrol car was blocking their exit. She could see a police officer inside the car who seemed to be on his radio. Standing outside the car, right in the center of the street, was the most beautiful sight she'd ever seen; Agent Ken Stallings.

She was less than fifty yards from her partner and closing fast but she needed to tear the note from its pad without Billy hearing the tearing sound or seeing her doing it. So she disguised the sound with a question.

"Okay, we're approaching the east exit and there are two cops. One is my partner. What do you want me to do?" She said it a little louder than necessary to cover the paper tear. She palmed the small note in her right hand.

"Just be cool. Tell him you ran into an old friend last night and wound up sleeping on her couch." Billy seemed to have already thought this through.

LT only had about five seconds before she'd be in front of Ken and the road block. She had to think very fast. Forty yards, then thirty, then twenty and still no ideas. Now she could see that Ken had spotted her car and had his hands on his waist. It looked like a sarcastic "*Where the hell have you been?*" look. LT clasped the note tightly in her hand as she rolled up next to Ken. She lowered her window.

"Why haven't you returned my calls?" Was Ken's opening line. He sounded more worried than pissed.

"Hey partner." LT extended her right hand as if to shake Ken's. He immediately saw the folder paper in her hand and recognized the "Hey partner" as an unusual greeting. He extended his hand and took the paper discretely in his.

"Sorry, partner. I lost my phone. I ran into an old school buddy last night while making the rounds here on Jacobson Lane and we got to talking. Before I knew it, I was wasted, so I slept on her couch." LT hoped the use of the name Jacobson, their boss, would cause Ken's radar to go up. It did.

As LT went on about her school buddy, Ken dropped his right hand below the window level and opened the note. It read:

"TWO PERPS AND HOSTAGE IN TRUNK WITH GUN. THEY CAN HEAR AND SEE ME. FOLLOW AT A DISTANCE."

Ken shot LT a look that conveyed, "No shit?" And LT gave him the same look back but without the question mark. "So we had a great time but I've got to get going. I need a shower. I'll be back in a few hours." LT hoped the dialog would satisfy Billy.

"I got you partner. We'll see you later." Ken gave LT a wink, then called out, "You take care."

Satisfied that her partner understood her predicament, LT drove on. She checked her rearview mirror to be sure she had the tail she'd requested. She could see Ken running back to the patrol car. A few seconds later the patrol car began to follow. She was careful not to drive too fast. She assumed that Ken was calling in the cavalry; Suffolk PD Helicopter, unmarked cars along the Expressway and whatever else he could muster. There's an unwritten rule at the JTTF that says if an agent is taken hostage, Washington better start printing money. In other words, all resources will be used to safely retrieve an agent.

As she made the turn onto the eastbound Expressway, the voice from the rear seat was back. "Nicely done. Where are we?"

"Just getting on the Expressway."

"Good. Get off at the Sunken Meadow Parkway going north."

As LT drove in silence she regretted the mistakes she'd already made. She knew her note should have identified the perps so that if there was shooting, the good guys wouldn't be trying to take out the kid. And she regretted not asking Ken for a gun. Upon reflection, she felt certain he could have passed it to her without detection by Billy. After all, Billy couldn't see what was going on in front of her. Those were both life and death mistakes. She knew she couldn't afford any more.

"Where are we getting off the parkway?" LT asked.

"Get off at 25A going west."

LT realized they were only a few minutes away from that exit and was concerned there hadn't been enough time for Ken's cavalry to mobilize. Also, it was unlikely, Mary Jane would be conscious yet, and therefore unable to run from the car as instructed. LT tried to envision what would happen if Billy opened the trunk from within before Ken and the Suffolk PD arrived. She tried to come up with ways to delay but was coming up blank. The rain had turned to a light drizzle.

When she glanced in the rearview mirror LT didn't see the patrol car. She assumed it had fallen several cars behind to keep a safe distance but when she slowed down to allow cars to pass, there was still no sign of the police cruiser. She cursed herself for telling Ken to follow at a distance. There was no reason to keep a distance because Billy couldn't see what was behind them. How could she be so stupid?

The exit for route 25A was approaching and there was still no sign of the patrol car. But what LT didn't know was that Ken Stallings had allowed his car to fall well behind and out of sight so that an unmarked car could take a position just two cars behind LT. The black Dodge Charger had picked up the radio call just as LT turned onto the parkway and was in radio contact with both Ken's car and Suffolk County Incident Command. Its driver, a ten year veteran named Sergeant Maureen Peters, knew that it's possible to push out the taillights in a Crown Victoria and have a clear line of sight from inside the trunk. So she kept a comfortable distance but never lost sight of the lead car.

"Why you going so slow?" Came the question from the rear seat slit.

LT realized Billy could sense her stalling tactics. "I'm not. There's some traffic. You want to come up here and drive?"

"Don't wise off with me. Just get off at 25A then make your first right."

LT knew little about the area she was driving through. She knew there was a huge park at the end of the Parkway and that if she made her first right, she'd be very close to the edge of that park. But Billy had done his recon work. Weeks before, he'd scoured the area looking for the perfect place to leave a car. He'd found a small parking lot on the edge of Sunken Meadow State Park on Old Dock Road, that supported a boat launch. After boaters launched their boats into a creek leading to the Long Island Sound, they could leave their car and trailer in the parking lot. Because many boaters would spend several days on their boats, idle cars in the lot would not be viewed as unusual. Billy left a 2006 Jeep there two days before TBD.

LT switched off the wipers. The drizzle had stopped. She took the exit ramp a little sharper than necessary. Her hope was that any extra motion might help Mary Jane come to. If the kid was conscious, she might remember to maneuver herself to be first out of the trunk. If she was still unconscious when they stopped, it would probably cost her her life.

Route 25A curved away from the parkway and down a long steep hill. LT could feel the tires losing traction to the wet pavement. She quickly tried to determine the benefit of a head-on collision with a huge wooden lamp post she saw at the bottom of the hill. She assumed her seat belt and airbag would save her from serious injury but would there be enough impact to incapacitate her trunk guests? Perhaps not, since they were packed in there pretty tight. And if her airbag did deploy, how long would it then take her to extricate herself and deal with those in the trunk?

And what the hell happened to Ken? There was still no sign of him in her mirror. The Crown Vic was racing down the wet hill. She needed to make a decision quickly. She thought about putting the car into a tail spin, hoping to avoid a head-on in favor of a strong side-swipe on the rear panel. That might do sufficient damage to the trunk area. Maybe a rear end collision would trap the trunk occupants, or better yet, knock them unconscious.

But the kid was back there too. There just wasn't time to do all the analysis. She eased off the gas and began breaking for the turn at the bottom of the hill. Once on Old Dock Road, she was heading directly north, toward the Long Island Sound, which she estimated, couldn't be too far off. And she was right. After just a few moments, she saw that the road ended about a quarter mile ahead, at a boat ramp.

A voice came from the trunk. "You should see water ahead, right?"

"Yeah, it's about a quarter mile up."

"Good. Before you get there, you'll see a string of parking spots on the left. There should be a bunch of cars and boat trailers parked there."

"I see it."

"There should be a green Jeep without a trailer about half way up. Pull in next to that car, turn off the engine and stay in the driver's seat until I tell you to move."

LT envisioned Billy getting out of the trunk, walking up to the driver's window and executing her while she sat waiting for instructions. Then he'd go back to the trunk and kill the kid. So, as she rolled slowly into the parking area, she decided it wasn't going to end that way. She'd give herself a fighting chance, if only a small one. And she was still hopeful that Ken wasn't too far behind; although that was looking less likely by the second. She glanced in the mirror again. Nothing.

Time was running out.

Then she saw the boat ramp at the end of the road. It led directly into the harbor. If she sped up and drove the car down the ramp and into the water, she was confident she'd be able to get out before it sank. Maybe even jump from the car as it hit the water. The trunk occupants would have a lot more trouble getting out; if they got out at all.

But again, it was her need to save Mary Jane that caused her to abandon that plan. If she was going to give the kid up for dead, she should have done it back at the house when she had the chance to run. Now she was committed. She didn't want to face the nightmares or the kid's mother. What could she say?

There was no more time. She unclasped her seat belt. She'd need every possible second. She turned the car to the left and parked next to the Jeep. As she put the car in park, LT opened the door and leapt from the seat. Her feet hit loose gravel and slipped but she steadied herself with her left hand and never hit the ground. Instead, she sprinted toward the back of the car.

She was rounding the driver's side rear corner when she saw the trunk hood begin to rise. There was some sort of a thumping sound against the hood and she heard a man's voice yell, "Shit!"

The hood continued to rise and LT saw a leg extending from the rear. It was a woman's leg. It was Mary Jane's leg! The young girl had regained consciousness after just a few minutes in the trunk but either out of terror or calculated genius, she feigned unconsciousness until she felt the car stop and heard the motor shut down. Once Billy pulled the escape lever and light appeared through the opening, she rolled over onto Billy, drove her knee into his groin and used his belly to push herself out the ever widening opening.

LT thought she looked like a wild tiger being released from a cage. Mary Jane rolled over the trunk wall, fell onto the gravel and was on her feet running forward; all in one fluid motion. It was as if she'd rehearsed the move a thousand times. She ran directly into the heavily wooded area next to the parking lot.

LT saw Billy's left arm extend from the trunk, trying to grasp something for leverage. The trunk hood was open about three quarters of the way. LT could see Nina' face and the back of Billy's head but only Billy's arm extended beyond the trunk. Then she saw the muzzle of her Glock pointing directly at her from within the darkness. She readied herself for the pain of a bullet and reached up for the hood. She threw all her weight onto the hood and brought it crashing down on Billy's left forearm.

He let out a guttural scream. "God damn it!"

LT wasn't sure if she heard the shot first or felt the pain on her right side first. But a shot had been fired from within the trunk and the bullet tore through LT's flesh just under her arm pit. The bullet shattered one of her ribs then exited her body just above her back bra strap. The pain was excruciating. It caused LT to stumble backwards and fall to the ground The fall probably saved her life because the second shot that came from Nina's gun whizzed harmlessly just over her head and into a tree deep in the forest.

LT was now on her back on the ground, lying about ten feet from the rear of the car. The pain blurred her vision momentarily but she could make out the shape of Nina emerging from the trunk. LT tried to take a deep breath but the pain became worse. She was bleeding severely. The LIPA shirt was already drenched in thick red blood.

Then she heard the sound of Nina's footstep on the gravel. Suddenly, Nina was standing over her with the gun pointed at LT's face. "You fucking bitch!"

LT had nowhere to go. Nina was out of her reach even if she could have mustered the strength to react. All she could do was watch as Nina's grip tightened around the gun. LT heard the shot and felt blood splatter over her face. Time stood still as she waited for whatever death would feel like.

But all she felt was the pain on her side.

Then Nina fell directly onto LT. She'd been shot threw the upper chest and was dead before she hit the ground. Only her bulging eyes conveyed the shock of what had happened. LT rolled the lifeless body to her right and saw a uniformed police officer on one knee with her weapon aimed at the space Nina just surrendered. It was officer Maureen Peters and she was directly in front of her black Dodge Charger.

The officer cried out, "Are you okay, agent Hadman?"

The cavalry had come. Ken hadn't abandoned her. LT tried to respond but the words didn't come. Instead she heard another two shots. These came from the gun peering menacingly from the trunk opening. She saw the young policewoman fall backwards. She'd taken the first shot in her right thigh. The second was absorbed by her Kevlar vest but the force pushed her back and down. Her gun flew from her hand.

Adrenaline surged through LT. In a second she was on her feet and throwing her weight onto the hood again. This time it came down on Billy's hand, the one holding the gun, but he was able to withdraw it enough so that he didn't lose his grip on the weapon. LT realized she'd missed her chance. Billy still had a gun and would be forcing his way from the trunk in a moment.

LT spun around. Her eyes searched frantically for the gun Nina had been holding a moment before. It had to be somewhere near the woman's body. Or perhaps it had flown from Nina's hand and was now buried under the thick carpet of leaves. LT knew she had only a second or two to find it, then Billy would be out of the trunk. With an upper torso bullet wound she'd be no match for Billy.

The gun was gone and time was up. She needed to try to run.

CHAPTER 64

While her daughter was running for her life through a wood-ed area on eastern Long Island, Carol paced her kitchen floor. It had been nearly an hour since Alan wired the money. Carol, Alan and the two senior FBI agents waited for the call; the call that had been promised to come within five minutes of the ransom payment.

In the next room, the communication specialists sat watching CNN and waiting for the phone to ring. They knew there was little chance of getting a trace on the next call, if it came at all, but they had to try, at least for appearances.

But as each minute passed without a call, Carol's hope of ever seeing her daughter dimmed. She didn't know that Billy hadn't heard her confession. She'd hoped her words would soften his hate-filled heart and she couldn't believe a man would hurt his own flesh and blood. She told herself that once he knew Mary Jane was his daughter, Billy would keep his word; that he'd release her after he got the money.

Then a terrifying thought occurred to her. What if Billy decided to keep his daughter for himself? What if he decided the ultimate pain he could inflict on her and Alan would be to take the money and the child, leaving them with nothing? She pushed the horrible thought from her head.

Carol could hear her husband in his office. He was on a conference call with people from his office and clients in London. Although she hated to think about life without Mary Jane, what if they didn't get her back? She and Alan would never survive, not after he knew Mary Jane wasn't his and not after he'd wired over half their net worth to Carol's maniacal ex-lover. She knew their marriage would not survive now that she'd shared her secret with him. She felt it as she pleaded with Alan to pay the ransom. It had taken her two hours of pleading to get him to agree, and he did so with great reluctance.

No, things could never be the same again with her husband. With or without Mary Jane, she knew the marriage was over. The thin threads that had been holding it together weren't strong enough to withstand this.

Carol looked down at her hand, resting on the kitchen table. She squeezed it into a tight fist and pounded it on the wooden table top. She hoped the pain would wake her from this dreadful nightmare; that she'd wake up to find Mary Jane sleeping in her bedroom; that it had all been a horrible dream.

CHAPTER 65

LT

I don't remember most of what happened next. I don't remember running through the woods. I don't remember my shoes falling off and I don't remember hiding behind a large bolder near a steep cliff that fell off to the sea. It looked to be about a seventy foot drop. From my perch behind the rock I could see the crashing waves breaking onto the beach below.

What I do remember is the intense pain. Every time I exhaled I felt a sharp pain run through my chest. It felt as if someone was pushing a hot fire-poker through my back into my right lung. I was making a wheezing sound with each breath, which I knew meant my lung was filling with fluid; probably my blood.

I must have run some distance from the car, but I didn't know how far. I didn't want to look back over the rock to see. I just wanted to hide. I wanted to become part of the forest; silent and invisible. I wanted to hear the sound of Billy slamming a car door and driving away.

The rain had stopped and the sun began to shine through the thick pines sending its misty rays from the treetops onto the damp forest floor. It reminded me of the afternoons I would sit in a pew at St. Patrick's cathedral and the afternoon sun would come through the stained glass windows filling the dark dusty air with light.

I began to think. How long should I stay here? I'm bleeding; probably bleeding internally, but I was afraid to move. If I'm found, I'm dead. But if I stay here too long I may not have the strength to move and will bleed to death sitting next to this rock. I wasn't sure I had the strength to move anyway.

I looked at my watch. It was 10:54. I did some quick calculations and figured out that I couldn't have been running very long; probably just a minute or two. That meant I couldn't be very far from the car. I needed to stay put. I needed to let the forest swallow me; to become part of the landscape; to be invisible. I didn't want to be found. I wanted to live.

I sat there, leaning against that rock in silence. The only sound I heard was a bird chirping somewhere up in the canopy of leaves and my wheezing chest. I tried hard to breathe short shallow breaths. That seemed to make less noise and was less painful than deep breaths.

For the first time in my life, I thought about death. What would it feel like if I just got weaker and weaker sitting against this rock? Would that sort of death be dramatic or would I just fade away? Would the pain get worse as the end approached?

Breathing was becoming more difficult. With each inhalation my right lung made a sucking sound and with each exhalation, the wheezing became more pronounced. I didn't think I had the physical strength to do much more than walk very slowly, if at all. And so I began to think about my options. How long should I stay hidden? At some point, I needed to decide Billy wasn't coming after me or that he'd gone looking in another direction, and that it might be safe for me to walk out to the road again. There's a police officer lying in the street and Nina Morales not far from that. Someone would pass by and call the police. Soon there would be dozens of people working the crime scene; putting up yellow tape, taking prints off the town car, drawing diagrams. Surely, if I could make it back out to the road, I would be okay.

But what if I waited too long and, by the time I concluded Billy wasn't a threat, was too weak to walk? Would I die out here in the woods, so close to the road? On the other hand, what if I began to walk and thus exposed myself to Billy. A quick death was a certainty in that case.

The one thing I was sure of was that I hadn't yet lost so much blood that my judgment was impaired. I seemed to still be thinking logically and rationally.

It was at that point that I heard a sound. Someone had stepped on a fallen twig and made a distinctive sound of snapping wood. It came from the wooded area to my right. I froze. Seconds passed but there was no other sound. I dared not move from behind the rock.

Then I heard it again but this time it was closer. Then again; still moving closer with each slow step until it sounded like he was just on the other side of the rock; not five feet from me. Another twig snapped just to my right. In another second he'd be past the rock and able to see me. I thought about using the element of surprise to my advantage but decided I didn't have the strength to overtake him. I could barely move my right arm. So I stayed still and silent.

Then I saw him. A young male deer walked past the rock. Because I wasn't moving, my presence didn't seem to concern him. He looked at me for several seconds, then turned his attention back to the leafy bush he began munching to my right. His presence actually helped calm me down a bit. He was at ease in his peaceful world and moved with a graceful elegance. I envied him.

I watched the young deer eat as he continued his meandering stroll along the cliff's edge. He lingered in my area for three minutes. Then he abruptly turned his head back in my direction and froze. He'd seen or smelled something. A second later he sprang majestically into the ticket and was gone.

CHAPTER 66

Billy also saw the deer jump but its majesty was lost on him. He'd been searching for the kid and the cop in the thick woods and had nothing to show for it. He was sweating and his right wrist was beginning to swell from its collision with the trunk hood. He knew he needed to get back to the car before anyone came across the two bodies on the road.

He'd begun walking back to the car when the deer appeared. For Billy, it was a sign that time was running out. As much as he wanted to kill the bitch cop and kid, especially now that Nina was dead, he knew he needed to move on. It was a disappointment, but the only practical downside to their escape was that now he'd have to switch cars yet again. Surely the cop would remember the green jeep. They'd be looking for that as soon as the cop got out of the woods.

Other than that, their lives didn't matter to him any more. Nor did Nina's. He'd planned to kill her in a few days anyway. She was just too much of a liability. At some point before crossing the border, he would have shot her and left her body along the road. He had to. She never would have understood why he'd transferred the money to the VA Rehab center at Walter Reed. Those weren't her friends limping around in there. She isn't the one who watched the IED's rip apart so many fine young marines; turning their legs and arms into useless bloody stumps as they simply tried to drive back to camp after spending the day training other young Iraqi boys to be better soldiers.

No. Nina would not have understood. The life of wealthy privilege he promised would never happen. And eventually, without the money, she would have left him.

And so, other than not having the pleasure of fucking the kid again or killing the annoying bitch cop, his plan was still very much on track. He'd succeeded in reawakening his country's awareness about its enemies from the Middle East. There was no doubt about that. "Three Bombs Day", as it came to be called, was being dissected ad infinitum by the media. Everyone considered it an attack on America orchestrated by the five Yemeni men killed in the hotel explosion. There were pictures of all of them taken on surveillance cameras in every newspaper and weekly magazine. Sixty-Minutes had already done a story about the training facility in Yemen some of them attended. Their lives were open books by now. Even people who knew them in Yemen had begun posting messages on social media sites about their radical Islamic ideals.

Yes, TBD had been a huge success and at a relatively small cost; less than 500 American lives. Collateral damage of war. A minuscule price to pay for redirecting an entire nation's attention. Now America would focus on its real enemy. Now maybe all the political bickering over the distractions like gay marriage, gun control and a woman's right to choose, would give way to bipartisan loathing of all things Arab. Now maybe the country's liberals would stop whining about water-boarding and get on board with a single-minded agenda; one that would secure our boarders and strengthen our position as a world power.

Someday, when he was an old man, Billy planned to write about his role in TBD; how he'd recruited the five Yemeni boys, how he'd orchestrated the entire operation and directed his country's attention on the true enemy. Someday, he'd be a hero for all he'd done. He was sure of it.

And then there was Carol. He'd waited so many years to hurt her the way she'd hurt him. Revenge is indeed, a dish best served cold. He'd planned his diabolical mission while in Iraq; the pain from her rejection still a fresh wound in his side. He thought about the many nights he lay awake on his cot, looking up at the stars thinking that she might be looking up at the same stars at the same moment but safe and warm on her penthouse balcony. And in the arms of the pimp who bought her with his trinkets.

Billy was glad Alan would never know his money had gone to the VA Hospital. Better he think Billy was lighting Monte Cristo's with his hundred dollar bills. That would hurt more.

Suddenly Billy stopped walking. Something had moved in the distance. It was an image from the corner of his eye but it came from the same direction the deer had jumped a moment before. There was something else there. Something was near the ridge, near a large rock at the cliff's edge.

Then he saw her. The bitch was sitting on the side on the rock. She appeared to be supported by the rock; leaning against it for some reason. And her blouse was covered in blood. Her back was to him so he was able to take a few quiet steps towards LT without her knowing he was there. He raised the Glock in his right hand but steadied his wrist with his other hand. Billy was only sixty feet from his target. He fired.

The bullet tore through LT's right shoulder and ricocheted off the huge rock. In twenty years as a New York City cop she had never been shot. Now she'd been shot twice in one day; both slugs piercing her right upper torso. The pain was excruciating but she spun around to face her assailant, then slid down the side of the rock. She had no fight left in her.

Billy ran toward LT with the gun in his outstretched hand. He could tell she was wounded badly but, because his hand was so swollen, the shot had sailed too high and hadn't hit his target; the center of her bloody back. He did not intend to miss again. Now, just a few feet away, he steadied his weapon.

LT was lying on her back next to the rock. Blood was beginning to soak the leaves on the forest floor beneath her. She was conscious and resisting her body's urging to shut down. If the end was coming she wanted to see it coming. Still, she knew she could offer no resistance. She had nothing left. She'd lost too much blood from the first wound.

Billy could tell his prey was beaten and helpless. He walked around the large rock and faced her. He wanted to enjoy this.

"You've screwed up my schedule agent Hadman." He laughed.

LT was silent but held her defiant stare.

"But now I need to be on my way. It's too bad you won't be around to read the history books about all this." He sat on the edge of the rock.

"Someday, American children will be taught about the attacks in New York. They'll be taught that it took two attacks; 9-11 and my attacks, before their country woke up and did the right thing." He laughed. "In a way, it's kind of like the Japanese. They didn't get it after we dropped the bomb on Hiroshima. No, they didn't surrender until after we nuked another city. It took two events to wake them up."

LT was only catching every other word of Billy's monolog. She was drifting in and out of a semi-conscious state. Still, Billy continued, "And I'm proud to have played a part in it all; even though I won't get the credit. In just one day, I accomplished more for this country than I did in eleven years over in Sandland. And that cost us thousands of great men; a huge price to pay for so little accomplished. Shit, we lost more people in Iraq and Afghanistan than we did on 9-11 and my day combined."

LT rolled to her left side and pain shot through her like a hot spear. She looked up at Billy and whispered, "You're a fool."

"What did you say, bitch?" He growled.

She summoned all she had. "I said you're a fool." She stared back at him.

Billy raised the gun and pushed it against LT's forehead. "You've delayed me long enough."

LT felt the pressure of the gun's barrel. It was cold and hard. She drew what she expected to be her last earthly breath. Somehow, the acceptance of death gave her the strength to look him in the eye. Then there was a flash of light.

The light LT saw wasn't an actual light; it was Mary Jane's tee shirt reflecting what little sunlight filtered through the dense canopy. The young girl had been hiding behind a rotting log, just a few yards from LT and Billy. When she heard the shot Billy fired at LT, she froze, afraid that she'd been spotted and the shot was intended for her. But when she heard Billy talking to LT, she summoned the courage to peak out from her hiding spot and watched as Billy taunted LT.

Mary Jane was no more than twelve feet from where Billy stood. If he hadn't been so focused on LT, he would have spotted her as he approached the rock. She clutched a four-foot branch lying next to her. When she saw Billy press the gun to LT's head she leapt up with the heavy branch, ran five steps toward Billy's unsuspecting back, and brought the branch down on his head with all the might she could muster.

Billy's mouth gapped open as the concussive force echoed through his skull. He fell forward onto the huge rock. Mary Jane's momentum carried her over Billy's collapsing body and onto the rock. She hit it head-first and opened a deep gash in her forehead. Blood erupted and spilled onto the rock and LT's face. Then she fell to the ground.

For several seconds the forest was silent. Billy Simon was face down and unconscious. Mary Jane Wallace was stunned by the collision with the rock and lay bleeding quietly next to LT, who was just surprised to be alive. She gazed up at the tree tops.

⟞⟝

Ken Stallings and the young Suffolk County patrolman were only forty-five seconds behind the unmarked car of Officer Peters. But by the time they pulled up next to the black Charger, Officer Peters had exchanged fire with the perps and been shot twice. She lay bleeding on the street. Another woman was lying next to the Crown Vic. Ken was relieved to see the second woman wasn't his partner.

As he stepped from his car, Ken saw a man running into the wooded area next to the Crown Vic. He didn't see any sign of LT so he made the assumption that the man was running after his partner. As soon as they confirmed Officer Peters was alive, Ken told the patrolman to call for two ambulances and for back-up and to remain with the downed officer until help arrived. He checked the clip in his Smith and Wesson and knelt to check the pulse of the second victim. There was none. Then he headed into the woods in pursuit of LT and her pursuer.

As he ran through the woods he realized he'd forgotten his cell phone in the patrol car and cursed his carelessness. He could see the white shirt of the male perp in the distance and was careful not to get too close until he could be sure the perp was unarmed. At this point he didn't know he was chasing Billy Simon; nor did he know the dead woman was Nina Morales. And he had no idea the "hostage" LT referred to was Mary Jane Wallace; someone who was supposed to already be dead. In fact, as he slowed his pace to a cautious walk, it occurred to him that he actually had very few facts.

All he knew was his partner was in trouble, had no weapon, and was probably being pursued by the guy in the white shirt, whoever that was.

Ken Stallings was a big man. He wasn't someone who regularly jogged and the exertion was already wearing on him. He took off his suit jacket and dropped it on the path, hoping to retrieve it on his way out. He still had the white shirt in his sight but the image was growing weaker, camouflaged by the dense forest growth.

He walked further into the woods, remembering his days as a Boy Scout and earning his "tracking" merit badge. But that was fifty years ago and he was tracking another harmless twelve year old kid, not a potentially dangerous kidnapper. He began to question the wisdom of being there at all.

A thunderous shot pierced the silence. He crouched, froze and listened. It sounded like it came from the direction of the guy he was tailing, but it was difficult to tell in the forest. The white shirt was standing still in the distance. Ken wasn't about to move until he was sure the shot hadn't been fired at him.

Then he heard voices. It sounded like a man's voice. Ken cautiously advanced along the path, being careful to stay behind trees as much as possible. When he was about fifty yards from the man wearing the white shirt he could see that the man had a gun in an outstretched hand. He seemed to be pointing at something on the ground behind a large grey rock. It looked as though the man with the gun was talking to the rock.

Ken slowly inched closer. He secreted himself behind a thick maple tree trunk and strained to hear. He thought he heard the word "Japanese", then a few moments later, "Iraq and Afghanistan".

It made no sense. A moment later he distinctly heard a man say, "What did you say, bitch?"

LT? He had to be talking to LT. Ken left the safety of the tree trunk and began walking toward the white shirt with his gun leveled at the unknown man. He knew that at any moment the man would hear his footsteps on the forest floor and turn toward him. Ken was resolved to fire his weapon, something he hadn't done often, if the stranger raised his gun toward him.

He was about to announce his presence as a police officer when suddenly, someone was between he and the stranger and running at the man with a large branch. It was a young girl. The stranger didn't see her coming and took a violent blow to the head from the branch. The man and the girl seemed to tumble to the ground behind the rock. Ken froze.

"LT, can you hear me?" Ken was kneeling next to his partner. He'd already disarmed the man with the gun who was face-down in the leaves. He appeared to be unconscious but Ken used his plastic zip-ties to cuff the man's hands behind his back anyway. He could see the young girl's scalp was bleeding and that she was beginning to emerge from unconsciousness.

"LT, can you hear me?" He desperately wanted an answer. Her blouse was covered in so much blood Ken couldn't tell where it was coming from. He checked for a pulse. Just as he did, LT opened one eye.

"That you partner?" Her voice was soft and weak but beautiful music to Ken Stallings.

"It's me kid. I'm here. Where are you hit?"

LT used her left hand to motion toward her right side. "Shot two times in one day," She whispered. "How about that?"

Then she said, "Help me up", and she motioned for him to help her sit on the edge of the rock.

Ken took off his tie and used it to wipe the blood from her face. He didn't know it was a combination of Nina's and Mary Jane's blood. Then he ripped LT's shirt off her right side so he could see the wound. Her bra was completely stained red, but he saw the exit wounds; one in the front and one in the back.

Although he didn't believe it, he said, "You're going to okay, kid."

LT steadied herself on the rock. For some reason, sitting up made her feel a little better; a little less light-headed.

"Where's the rest of the cavalry?" Again, it was just a whisper.

Ken silently cursed himself again for not having his cell phone.

"They're on the street; only two minutes away. Hang in there, kid. Please, hang in there. For me."

Then he glanced over at the young girl with the head wound. She was waking up and seemed to be crying. Ken took the bloody tie and did the best he could to make a head bandage for her. He hoped to slow the bleeding but even with the tie circling her scalp, the blood continued to ooze. He applied pressure to the wound with his hand and the bleeding slowed.

He looked back at LT, "Any chance you're up to walking?"

LT shook her head slowly.

"I don't have a phone or radio. I need to run back to get help. We'll get stretchers in here for both of you. It'll only take me a few minutes." Then, to lighten the moment, he added, "I left a trail of breadcrumbs on my way here."

But the mood wasn't light. Ken knew his partner had lost a lot of blood and wasn't sure she could wait the ten to twelve minutes he estimated it would take for him to run back, then direct a team of EMT's back to their location. Time was working against LT and he knew it.

Then there was the shooter who was still lying face down and showing no signs of life. Ken knew he couldn't leave two injured women in the woods for ten or twelve minutes if this guy was alive, so he checked Billy's wrist for a pulse. As he did, Billy moved a bit. A groggy voice asked, "What the fuck happened?"

Ken rolled his prisoner over and was about to tell him to keep his mouth shut. But when he saw Billy's face, the face that had been the source of their manhunt, he recognized him immediately. There were a thousand things Ken wanted to say; a hundred questions he wanted to ask. Mostly, he wanted to read Simon his Miranda rights, but he didn't have the luxury of time. LT needed medical attention.

He pointed an angry finger at Billy Simon and said, "Don't move!" Then he pulled Billy's belt off his pants and secured it around his ankles. Ken looped the leather twice then pulled it tight.

Then he turned back to LT. "Look kid, I can't carry you out and leave him here. And it will take me too long to walk him back to the patrol car. I need to get you a doctor so I'm going to leave you my weapon and I'm going to high-tail it back to the cavalry. You up to keeping him in line?"

Ken thought about giving Billy a solid right on the jaw to send him back to lala land for a while. He'd feel better about leaving if the perp was unconscious. But before he could make a decision on that, LT said, "I got it. Give me your gun and take the kid with you. She's bleeding faster than I am. Even an old fart like you should be able to carry her a few hundred yards. She's tiny."

"You sure you got this?" Ken looked deep into his partner's eyes.

LT was sitting on the rock, only a few feet from where Billy was now lying on the ground. Blood was pooling at the base of the rock.

"Gimme the gun and hurry back." She said with conviction and a bit of desperation.

Ken put his Smith and Wesson into LT's left hand, the only one she could control, and said, "If he moves an inch, kill him." He said it loud enough for Billy to hear. Then he reached down and scooped up Mary Jane. She pulled back, but LT said, "It's okay kid. He's good people. He's the guy I told you was coming for us."

Mary Jane was still dazed from the head trauma but she could tell something was very wrong with her forehead. It burned terribly and blood was pouring down her face into her eyes. LT was certainly the only person she could trust and if LT said Ken was okay, that would have to do. She went limp and allowed Ken to pick her up.

Ken turned and looked back at his partner. "You sure about this?"

"Go, you're wasting time." Her voice was weak. Then she added, "See if you can keep some pressure on her head."

As Ken Stallings and Mary Jane Wallace disappeared into the forest, LT felt the pull of sleep. She wasn't sure she'd be able to fend off unconsciousness until he got back. She was light-headed and a little nauseous; both sure signs her body was retreating into shock.

But she desperately needed to stay awake. Six feet from her was a maniacal killer who would pounce on her the second he thought she couldn't defend herself. And so, she resisted the overwhelming urge to close her eyes by biting her upper lip until it hurt. Maybe a little more pain would help.

Billy stared at her. He understood there was nothing he could do with his hands and feet bound tightly. Even if LT passed out, from his position on the ground, and his feet secured together, he couldn't even stand. He knew it was over.

"Hey. You know what's funny?" He taunted LT.

She shook her head but held the gun firmly in her hand.

"This doesn't matter. I mean, so what? I get caught. I accomplished one hundred percent of my mission. That's what really matters." He smiled a devilish grin.

"Shut up."

"No..., really. Think about it. I got everyone focused again. Everyone understands how vulnerable we still are. Shit, if a bunch of third rate morons from Yemen can blow up tunnels, trains and bridges with so little effort and so little training, imagine what the guys who are serious can do? People needed to think about this; don't you see?"

"You're a fool."

"No. I'm going to be on the cover of Time magazine; the guy who got America thinking again. Don't you see? Our country was asleep. Now it's awake again; hopefully for a while longer than after 9-11. Maybe being awake will save us from the third-world mutts who want us dead. I dealt with these people for eleven years. They hate our guts. We send them billions in aid and they hate our guts because we have everything they really want; freedom, Starbucks, educated women and Disneyworld. They say it's about oppression but they're full of shit. They hate us because we steal their oil to put in our F-150's. That's the truth."

Billy glanced into the forest to see if anyone was coming yet.

"Yeah. Now that I think about it, this will be even better. Hey, pretty girl. If you live through this, you'll be a hero. You'll be the one who got Billy Simon. And I'll get to tell my story to everyone. And they'll listen. They'll listen because they have to listen.

Getting caught is going to work out. Everyone will want my story. They'll all want to hear..."

"Shut the fuck up!" LT used most of her remaining energy to make the words sound strong, but there was nothing behind them. "You're still a rapist, a pedophile, and a third rate kidnapper. That's how people will see it."

"No, no....., you're wrong. You don't know what happened. "Billy shook his head."

"I watched you rape a fourteen year old girl."

"Light collateral damage, honey. In the scheme of things, a lot of good will come from taking that kid. A lot of guys who deserve it will get better treatment because of what I did. Shit, they should name a wing of Walter Reed after me."

"You're delusional."

"You're wrong because you don't understand. But when I get to have my day in court, when all the media is listening and the world is watching, I'll tell them everything. That's why getting caught will be better. I get to stand up with everyone listening, and tell them all how foolish they've been. Next time, when we go into a zone to eliminate our enemy, we'll know who the enemy really is. And, next time, the rich can't just pay for it with cash. Next time, they'll have to send they sons not just their money. Money doesn't get it done." He was screaming at her.

"So when you see me in court, if you live that long, you'll listen to my story. Everyone will listen. I'll finally have a voice. And, like it or not, you gave me that voice. That's right. You will be responsible for my capture which gave me the platform. Standing in a courtroom will be magnificent. It's the perfect way to have my message taken seriously. And it's all thanks to you, agent Hadman." He spat the words.

"It's all thanks to you because you're the one who sent me to court."

LT's bloody eyes met his hateful stare. "But I'm not sending you to court." She whispered. "I'm sending you to hell."

CHAPTER 67

LT

The bartender at Vinny's was another new kid; one I hadn't seen before. Then again, I hadn't been around much lately. I ordered a Stella and waited for Ken to show. He promised to meet me right after work and said he was bringing me a surprise. He said it was something I've needed for a long time.

The bar nuts and pretzels were stale, which was about par for Vinny's, so I guess nothing much has changed while I was in the hospital. I pushed the bar stool next to me towards the bar rail so no one would take it before Ken arrived. Being the Friday before Christmas, a lot of people were already gathering for holiday parties and the obligatory drinks with the co-workers before the long holiday break began in earnest on Tuesday. The place was pretty crowded and it was only 6:30 P.M.

The first Stella tasted great; a taste I hadn't enjoyed in over ten weeks. So I ordered a second and reflected on the blur that occurred since Ken and I were put on the TBD case.

I must have passed out after sending Billy Simon to meet his creator, who I'll assume wasn't pleased with his creation, because all I remember is waking up in the hospital. I'm told I was there six days before I said a word. Stoneybrook University Medical Center must know what they're doing because my mom, who I'm told was at my bedside for five of the six days, told me the doctors said I'd lost half my blood by the time I got there. Apparently when you lose that much blood something called hypovolemic shock happens and your body starts allocating the blood to the most vital organs and away from the extremities. That, it seems, is what saved my ass.

After I regained consciousness, I was in intensive care for another four weeks. The first bullet that hit me must have torn the lining of my right lung because as a breathing device, it was pretty much useless for a long time and required three operations to fix. The second shot shattered my scapula and screwed up a bunch of nerves that control movement on my right side. It also caused most of the deep bleeding.

Ken filled me in on the details a couple of weeks after I came to. He said when he got back to the street carrying Mary Jane Wallace, two ambulances had already arrived. He handed the kid off to the first EMT he spotted and told the second one (luckily for me he was a full blown paramedic) to follow him back into the woods. He says he heard the shot just as he and the medic started running back, so he had some idea of what might have happened. As they approached the large rock, Ken saw Billy Simon and the small red hole to the left of his nose. Fortunately, my partner is a good cop and knew what to do.

He directed the medic's attention to me and shouted at him to, "Focus on her." So while the medic was assessing my sorry state and trying to figure out where all the red stuff was coming from, Ken used his pocketknife to cut the plastic ties on Simon's hands, shove them in his pocket, and removed the belt from his legs. The medic never noticed. Later, Ken would tell the two Suffolk P.D. who arrived a few moments later and were both pretty junior, that Simon must have rushed his wounded partner who fired once in self-defense. No one seemed interested in pressing the issue. I mean, I was shot twice and unconscious at that point, so they weren't getting anything out of me.

Ken never asked me what really happened or why. He probably never will.

For a short while, I was something of a celebrity in the law enforcement circles. After all, I was the woman who found and killed Billy Simon. And although the JTTF tried to downplay Billy's roll in the TBD, in order to keep the focus on the five guys from Yemen, the media ran a few days of stories about how they'd been recruited by this former marine and how he was the lone survivor of the hotel explosion. So the world saw Billy Simon as the last of the six terrorists that needed to be brought to justice and I was the one who did it. But by Thanksgiving, there were other things in the news that took the country's attention. Ironically, just as Billy feared, the country didn't stay focused very long.

Mary Jane Wallace and her mother actually visited me in the hospital about a week after my last surgery. The kid must have had a great plastic surgeon because I didn't see a scar where there had once been a deep head wound. Good for her. She had enough shit to deal with. She told me she was already back at school, although her mom was driving her every day. Understandably, she didn't feel good about school buses yet. She invited me to come to her winter concert. I guess, considering she saved my life by hitting Billy Simon with that branch, I should go. I probably will.

I hear a familiar voice and feel Ken's hand on the back of my neck. "There's my partner." Ken has arrived and he's got someone with him.

"LT Hadman, this is Hank Waldron. Hank's my buddy from the FBI that I called that day in the car. He's been doing all the follow up with Mrs. Wallace and the kid." Ken introduced Hank, a tall version of Kenny Rogers, silver beard and all.

Hank offered, "It's a pleasure to finally meet you LT. I can't tell you how much Ken's told me about you."

"Not too much, I hope." And I gave Ken a wink. He didn't think that was funny.

Hank turned out to be good people. He was a career bureau guy and thinking about retirement next year. I'm a pretty good judge of men's ages and I would guess he was about fifty; definitely no more than fifty-two. Like I said, he was a young, tall Kenny Rogers. I expected him to break into a chorus of "Lady" any minute. Hank, I assume, was the surprise Ken had promised. The hint about being "something I've needed for a long time" now made sense. Ken was right; it's been a long time since I was in a relationship.

Vinny's was getting pretty loud with all the office workers starting to drift down from their skyscrapers, so we moved to a booth and ordered dinner. I switched from beer to red wine and it was after my third that I mentioned that Mary Jane and her mom had visited me in the hospital. I told them, "The mother was really sweet and cried every time she thanked me for saving her daughter's life. I kept reminding her it was her daughter who saved mine."

"Did she tell you her husband left?" Hank said.

"What do you mean, left?" I asked.

"I mean just left. Apparently after Mrs. Wallace dropped the bombshell about she and Billy Simon, Mr. Wallace decided he had enough."

At this point, I didn't get it; so I asked, "What bombshell?"

I think Hank realized he was about to share information that went beyond protocol for a criminal case, so he leaned in over the wooden table and whispered, "Turns out, Billy was the kid's father."

"What kid?" I asked. "You mean Mary Jane Wallace?"

"Are you shitting me?" Ken said.

"Nope. The mom blurted it out when she found out he'd raped the girl. What a sick fuck; how could anyone do that to their daughter?"

I thought back to the night I was tied to the sewer pipe and watched Billy rap Mary Jane. It was hard enough watching that animal climb on top of the poor naked kid; if I had known she was his daughter I probably would have vomited out of disgust or found some super-human strength, fueled by rage and torn my arms free of the shackles so that I could rip him apart. Even now, the thought of it makes me sick.

If I had any doubts about taking out Billy Simon up to now, they disappeared in an instant.

"Does the kid know?" I asked.

"I don't know. I doubt it. But Mr. Wallace seemed like a prick, so I wouldn't be surprised if he tells her at some point." Hank said. "Anyway, he left right after the kid was released from the hospital. Carol Wallace told one of our agents that was working the case, that the six million was about half of everything they had. Apparently, the prick felt like he'd been set up. I mean he paid all that money to his wife's ex-lover for the return of a child that wasn't his. It's pretty bizarre."

Hank was right about that. This whole thing was bizarre. And yet, I was reminded of what Billy said to me in the woods just before he tried to kill me. He was boasting about how his plan had been completely successful. I guess, it some twisted way it was.

He certainly got the country's attention focused on the threat of more terrorism from the Middle East; at least for a while. And if part of his plan was to destroy his ex-lover's life, well; he accomplished that too. And put her through a lot of pain along the way. Yeah, I can see how in his warped mind, he was successful.

"How about another glass of wine and we forget about the Wallace's for the rest of the night?" Ken suggested.

⟝⟞

I sometimes wake up at night and wonder if I did the right thing. In my entire police career, I only had to discharge my weapon twice. On both occasions, I was dealing with animals who had raped young girls. Given the chance, they would probably have done it again. The two crack-heads in the ally had done it more than once and I saw the photos of their victims. I saw Mary Jane Wallace bound and gagged and savagely raped. I was less than ten feet away. I saw it and heard it and even smelled it as it happened. I think about it a lot. I have nightmares about it.

So I'm okay with what I've done.

I go back to sleep.

Made in the USA
Middletown, DE
19 January 2018